Astor Hill

Sydney Madison

Dedicated to the staff at our favorite restaurant, and our favorite booth, where we have spent countless hours drinking Diet Cokes and talking about every detail of our lives.

1

Olivia

Two years ago

I force a smile as I look across the crowd of people clasping their red cups, and watch Lily. The air is warm and the music is slightly too loud, but there's a buzz of excitement, particularly from the incoming freshmen. I can't lie—I feel it too— and so do the other underclassmen trying to get my best friend's attention. I've always admired her patience when crowded by people wanting to absorb her magnitude, the way she radiates goodness and light, all golden curls and soft smiles. In our sixteen years of friendship, I've never seen Lillian Newhouse want for anything, whether it be boys or friends. Things always seem to work out for her. She's poised like a first lady, if the first lady looked like a starlet with great taste. Her aura in general makes it easy for her to fit into the crowd at Astor Hill, the private liberal arts college known to the masses for its Division 1 basketball team *and* the elite, moneyed families who ship their adult children there every fall.

I feel a pang of jealousy as I observe Lily shifting her Chanel double flap over her jean jacket covered in patches of her favorite things, from a random song lyric to the number thirty-two, which she declared was lucky this past summer. The feeling quickly dissolves when my friend finally seems to notice me. We have a way of communicating that's so unspoken it feels like we're reading each other's minds. She slides her hand up the strap of her bag, tucking her hair behind her ear signaling that she needs an out.

I start to make my way over, immediately noticing William Chapman standing directly behind Lily, as if he's protecting her from the mob of desperation. Again, a surge of jealousy rises in my stomach. *They had to have met in the last fifteen minutes*, I think in an attempt to satiate my need to be the prettiest, the smartest, the best. I don't really know Will apart from the eavesdropping Lily and I did on a few upperclassmen girls in our dorm's bathroom the night before.

"Did you hear about the younger brother joining us this year, ladies?"

"You're kidding, there's a brother? How God has blessed us with another man from that family is beyond me."

"I am forever and always team Ben."

"You must not have seen Will yet."

The jealousy dissolves as I remember Lily letting out a loud huff after the snickering girls departed. Lily is beautiful and fragile, the perfect girl for an alpha male to set his sights on, yet she claims she's no longer interested in "popular jocks."

"I want a man of substance," she had said sprawled on the floor of my parent's beach house, frustrated with the lack of summer conquests the year prior, "not just a boy who can throw a ball and open a beer."

As I approach the inner circle of the crowd, I immediately feel self-conscious of my height. Even in flats, my 5'8" body towers over Lily's petite 5'4" frame, her delicate features and porcelain skin even prettier up close.

"Oh… hey," Will clears his throat, and I can't tell if he's nervous about meeting his new conquest's best friend or upset by my interruption.

I choose to ignore him, as is my way when I feel nervous. My father, a big-shot lawyer, told me at age six, "If anyone ever intimidates you- make them feel small." I like to think of that as my origin story.

"Look what the cat dragged in," Genevieve, Lily's new friend and the current bane of my existence, mutters. Lily apparently met the interloper at her orientation, which was scheduled the day before mine. Clearly, they got rather close because over the past week I've walked into countless hushed conversations that came to an abrupt stop the moment I was spotted, Gen fleeing the scene like I'm scum she can't bear to talk to. The only way I can even think to describe Genevieve is pointy, from her personality to her lanky frame. She's all bones and no feelings.

I send her my signature smirk— the one that says without saying, I'm sorry but, do I know you?

"Jessica, right?" I say, allowing my face to take on a friendly demeanor, wanting her to buy how unimportant I think she is.

"It's Gen. We've met multiple times," she says with a sneer, a blush spreading across her face. To be forgotten in front of Will Chapman must really have hurt her pride. I have never seen someone's cheeks turn that particular shade of crimson.

I finally give myself a moment to take in the towering male to my right. He's tall, probably 6'2", which I guess is necessary considering he is a basketball player. His dirty blonde pushed-back waves look effortless, but too perfect to be accidental. With blistering green eyes, he smells like only a boy could: Tide, salt, and some drugstore deodorant I can't quite remember the name of. He looks over my shoulder and I realize he's making eye contact with some-one. I turn around to check but whoever it was must've been on their way out.

"Livy, your cup is completely empty. Now that just won't do." Lily gives a tsk tsk, indicating this is apparently her escape plan.

"You'll have to excuse us, we plan on enjoying our last night before classes begin," I say, pointedly glaring at Gen.

"Mind if I tag along?" Will asks as he slides his long arms over Lily and I's shoulders.

"Thanks, but I think we can handle this. Why don't we catch up later?" Lily is nothing if not always polite, even though I can tell this Will guy is making her skin crawl. It's hard to imagine why.

Simply put, Will is one of the most attractive men I have ever seen, much less spoken to. It dawns on me that Lily might be avoiding his advances for my benefit, thinking back to my college vision board, plastered with pictures of attractive men and homecoming crowns. Lily refused to partake, claiming it was childish to plan out your year via magazine cutouts.

"It's cute— your quest to be the most popular girl in college. I

thought college was the time to stop caring about that," Lily had chided, picking at her cuticles that day.

"That's easy for you to say. Weren't you prom queen, homecoming queen, class president— shall I go on?" I'd teased.

"I'm excited to escape those titles Liv, not continue them." She seemed to zone out after this, almost like she was lost in the memory of her high school self. I'd rolled my eyes and continued cutting out the abs of the Calvin Klein model.

Looping her arm through mine, she uses her entire tiny body to steer me around toward the makeshift frat house bar. If she wasn't so graceful, it would look comical. I allow her to lead the way, which isn't hard since the crowd parts like the Red Sea as soon as Lily makes her destination clear. She attempts to parade us to the back of the line, but I decide it's time to use my obvious physical advantage to pull her to the front.

"Lily, please. We have never been and never will be line people."

It was meant as a joke, but it's true. As we approach the bar I recognize Grant Fielder, my guide during orientation. He's easy to spot as he's quite literally ginormous. His shoulders are so broad they almost cast a shadow on Lily and I as we approach.

"Olivia god damn Beckett," Grant beams, as if we are old friends rather than two strangers who met days earlier on a guided tour. Something about Grant makes me feel cozy and new like clean sheets during a rainstorm. Lily likes to refer to it as old money kindness: a person who never has to worry therefore has no reason not to be anything but warm.

"Grant!" I shout, feeling the ice wall I put up for Gen immediately melt in the presence of his megawatt smile.

"I'm still shocked the girl in the Harvard hoodie decided on a small school like Astor Hill," Grant chuckles.

"Oh this smart ass got into Harvard, but we are way too codependent for her to leave me at little old Astor Hill alone." Lily flips her loose curls over her shoulder, color rising to her cheeks. "I'm Lily, by the way." I instantly recognize the look in Lily's eyes, the one that mesmerized every boy at our high school for the past four years.

"Well hey there Lily, what would you like to drink?" Grant seems instantly enamored, taking in Lily's thickly lashed blue eyes. His cheeks flush as he glances down at his Converse caked in the mud of the backyard. I feel that familiar pang of annoyance as another boy I've come to know falls for my best friend.

"I'll take that," Will's long outstretched hand plucks the red solo cup out of Grant's. Turning toward Will, Grant's face goes from charmed to annoyed almost immediately.

"I actually have strict orders to keep you away from the bar. In fact, I was specifically told not to let you serve these two in particular." Grant tilts his head in my direction and Will steps a foot closer to him.

"You always take orders from your captain?"

While it's apparent that they're relatively the same height, Grant's muscle mass somehow doubles that of Will's, making him seem almost scrawny in comparison. I lightly place my hand on the bar in a gesture that I hope shows I have something to say. I don't think I'll get a response, but both boys instantly turn toward me.

"While this little display is flattering, we actually would like a drink." My eyes flit to Grant as I give him what I hope is a friendly and not flirty smile. I can practically feel Lily perspiring just staring at the guy. *Not into athletes* my ass.

Grant finally hands us two cold beers from the keg behind him.

"Maybe I'll catch you guys later?" It doesn't take a scientist to know that Grant's not asking me.

"I hope so," Lily winks, squeezing my hand as she turns her back on a sulking Will and wistful Grant. "So a captain has his sights on you," she whispers, surprised, pulling me to her ear.

"I'm pretty sure Grant said, and I quote, 'these two', meaning a captain likely has his sights set on *you*," I say with a hint of annoyance.

The night sits on my skin as we sip our drinks, the humidity making me feel cold and dewy. I watch a blue buzz-cut bob against the lit-up backyard, the owner of said buzz-cut chatting with a girl who looks older, maybe even too old to be in college.

"Lily, I hate to abandon you but—," I point towards Ian Rivers, his gold watch falling down his slender arm, his boyfriend, Jean, who I recognize from my hours of internet stalking, smoking a cigarette beside him.

"No, please do not leave me for those gross hipsters. Seriously. I can't do this without you." She gestures at the crowd behind us, a few of whom are clearly waiting for a window to approach her.

"Lily, you will be fine. These people are, quite literally, in love with you. Besides, you know I have to stick to the plan," I say, referencing the carefully mapped-out future that I laid out via mood boards covering the walls of our dorm. Step 1 of the plan is to make Ian Rivers my bitch.

"Fine, good luck with that, I guess," she says, rolling her eyes and mumbling something to herself. I make out the word pathetic but choose to ignore her.

I feel bad leaving Lily in the waiting hands of Gen and

Will, but I know she isn't edgy enough to introduce to Ian's crowd right out the gate. They glower as I approach, Jean cocking his eyebrow at me, clearly impressed with my outfit as his eyes openly assess my single-breasted Saint Laurent leather blazer. Ian is simply the person to know if you want to be connected to the most elite circles at Astor Hill. Despite only being a sophomore, he quickly climbed the ranks of both the paper and Astor society. Editor of the newspaper, apparent journalistic wizkid, and notorious party boy, his parents are new money, and he has no problem spending it.

The Astor Hill newspaper is a league of its own, run more like an underground magazine. Ian makes sure his reporters are free to write about the most slanderous of gossip. This means they need open access from events, to school board meetings; they're somehow invited to everything. Being that Astor Hill is home to some of the most elite families on the East Coast, every person here knows that no press is bad press.

Ian plays with the gold chain above the neckline of his crushed velvet button-down. His eyes almost dare me to speak.

"You've approached?" he mutters. It's obvious he was going for disdain, but I sense the curiosity in his tone. I ignore him. With a roll of my eyes, I give Jean a bone-chilling glance that makes its way down to his shoes.

"Can't go wrong with a vintage loafer," I say, confidently holding out my fingers for his cigarette. He hands it over, in awe that I've made Ian feel somewhat invisible.

"You're Olivia Beckett, right?" the older girl asks as she peeks out from under her sunglasses. I take the bait, even though people who wear sunglasses at night are almost always tacky.

"None other," I say with a tight smirk, trying to keep my cool under Ian's scrutiny.

"Ah, Olivia… your name has been on everyone's lips this evening," Ian finally gives in, his curiosity getting the best of him.

"Whose lips specifically?" I wink at him, giving a mischievous grin that I hope I can pull off. This seems to work as his face breaks into a smile.

"I can see why you're the talk of this extremely small town. What do I owe the pleasure?" I hand Jean back the cigarette, coolly fixing my stare on Ian.

"I want to work on the paper."

Ian cackles. "Aren't you a freshman?"

"Yes, but believe it or not, even freshmen gossip. Plus, you knew who I was before I even approached you. That kind of notoriety will have a way of getting me into some of the more exclusive events this school has seen. Not to mention… you were a freshman not too long ago." I try to make my voice sound nonchalant, even though I am aware that I am begging him for this position *and* comparing myself to him. He appraises me, taking a step back and hitting me with a judgmental smirk.

"You're interesting, I'll give you that. Plus, I love your jacket," he continues to ponder, glancing at his phone. "Look, I have to be somewhere. Why don't you send me over some of your work? I'm assuming you have written something before…?" he raises his eyebrows and I can't suppress the smile I've been trying to hold in.

"Of course."

"Cool—Jean will give you my details." He nods toward Jean before walking off.

I get the credentials from Jean shortly before I break from the group, ready to reunite with Lily.

Footsteps crunch behind me as I make my way across the lawn.

"Hey, wait up," a smooth deep voice calls out to me. I turn and meet Will's dimpled grin.

"Hi," I chirp. *Did I really just say hi in that octave?* I try to regain my composure, forcing the blush that formed on my cheeks to disperse. "Looking for Lily?"

Will's eyebrows knit above his pine green eyes, the kind of eyes that are dark and light at the same time.

"Lily? Why would I be looking for Lily…?" Will seems genuinely confused. "Olivia, I'm clearly looking for you."

Never in my life have I allowed myself to melt in front of a total stranger, but with the way Will is looking at me, I have no control over the grin that flourishes on my face, my blush rising from whatever deep pit I forced it into less than two minutes ago. Sensing my shock, he takes charge of the conversation.

"I've been wanting to talk to you all night. I gotta admit, it hurt my feelings when you ignored me back there."

His smirk is obliterating all my defenses and I feel discombobulated and sweaty under his gaze. He pushes his golden hair out of his emerald eyes and it suddenly becomes apparent that he's nervous too.

Nervous? To be talking to me? I quickly push down my inhibitions and force forward the carefully cultivated Olivia Beckett I know and love.

"I didn't know I was capable of hurting the feelings of someone like you," I spar.

"Someone like me?" He smiles playfully, like he knows exactly what I mean. My stomach flips as I bite my lip, trying to figure out how I can regain control of this conversation.

I move closer to him, lowering my voice as if I don't want others to hear.

"I mean, this may come as a shock to you, but I've overheard probably twelve girls at this party claim to be your soulmate."

He smiles this heart melting smile, the kind you'd tape up on your bedroom wall.

"I don't know if I believe in soulmates."

I feel my cheeks heat.

"Did someone go and break your heart Will Chapman?" I quirk a smile and poke him playfully in the shoulder. He looks down at our shoes, making it hard to read his face.

"You could say that." He lightly bumps his shoe into mine, a blush creeping up his neck, surprising me. There's a vulnerability to him that I get the feeling he doesn't let most people see.

"And you do? Believe in soulmates?" he clarifies, that mossy green gaze on mine. I consider whether I do or not and decide that in that moment, under the market lights at my first Astor kegger, with this perfect boy, that maybe I do.

"I think—"

"OLIVIA!" I hear Lily shout my name across the lawn. I squint, my eyes trying to spot her and when I finally do, I see clear frustration in her eyes. I sigh and look back at Will, an indistinguishable expression on his face, like a mix of angry and sad. A twisted sense of excitement fills me at the prospect that he could be this upset that our conversation was interrupted.

"I'm guessing you have to go." His voice is quiet, but I can hear a pang of something like disappointment.

I smile and bite my lip shyly. "It appears that way."

We stare at each other for a minute and I feel like my

stomach is a tidal wave inside me. He seems to be contemplating something.

"Give me your phone."

I look at him with suspicion, but ultimately hand it over.

He types something in and hands it back. "Now you can call me later… if you want," he says, giving me that shy smile again.

"Sure– I mean, maybe," I say entirely too fast, feeling my face on fire.

He chuckles. "Nice to meet you Olivia." I watch him walk away into the crowd.

I utilize the length of my legs to speed walk over to my friend, feeling like I'm floating on air. *I can't believe how well tonight is going,* I think to myself as I hurry over to Lily. It's like everything I set out to do has somehow fallen into place without me having to really exert any effort. As I approach Lily, I notice our attitudes are in complete contradiction to each other and feel myself dim a little.

"Why were you talking to him?" Lily spits, taking me by surprise.

"What? Who— Will?" I feel the confusion written all over my face.

"Clearly, Olivia…" she says in the voice she uses to make me feel like an idiot.

"I—" she cuts me off, sighing dramatically.

"Look, I know he's like the exact type of guy you'd have a crush on, but I just don't think you guys would be a good fit. Not to be a bitch, but I just don't want to see you get hurt or embarrassed. I get the feeling you're not his type."

She twirls her hair like this is something she's nervous to say to me, but it isn't something I hadn't heard from her before. I feel my throat thicken thinking about the boys I've liked over the years, all too popular, or too into her, for me. Tears prick in my eyes and I do everything in my power to keep them from falling.

"Oh… I—"

She quickly cuts me off again, staring off into the party, not even noticing the effect her words have on me.

"Liv, I'm just over this party and my head is killing me." She smiles tightly. "Let's go home."

2

Ben

Two years later, the start of Ben's senior year

Everything is the same here at Astor Hill, but thankfully I'm not.

Panting, I lean against the edge of the bridge I've stopped on. Beechwood Park is emptier than I thought it would've been at 6:30 in the morning. The cool weather alone was enough to convince me the park might be teeming with students, but the sunrise this morning is other-worldly. It feels criminal that I'm the only one here, on this bridge, witnessing it. I'm not complaining, though. After two years away from this place, I want to enjoy the beauty of this campus, not be thrown head first into shallow Ivy small talk while I try to finish my run.

I check my watch. 6:45 a.m. I don't have a class till this afternoon, but I want to be out of the way before the hordes of tittering Astor Heads shuffle their way to classes. If I start now, I can get two more laps in.

I pick up my pace, unzipping my hoodie as I feel the morning sun begin to warm the air around me. I let out a small huff, surprised and amused at myself. I'd worked up this day for months in therapy with Morgan, my therapist, helping me develop action steps for when I get over-whelmed, affirming my decision to come back here every time I had doubts. But running along the tree covered path of Beechwood, the same path I used to take with my former teammates, I feel none of the anxiety or angst I used to feel. I guess a year of intensive therapy will do that to you.

When I left Astor, I was burnt out. It wasn't until I was in the calm quiet of Pop's townhouse that I felt the perma-nent angst in my chest start to unfurl, felt the weight of everyone's expectations lift off my shoulders. In isolation, I don't think that night would have messed with me the way it did. It was just a party; Will, my brother, was just being a stereotypical dickish freshman; I was just being ogled in the same way I'd been for years. I don't even know when it all started to grate on me.

Coming to Astor was always the goal. Playing ball was always the goal, being captain was most definitely always the goal… and suddenly it all felt suffocating. Like I couldn't catch a breath, couldn't even get close to the surface. I'd been having panic attacks for months by the time it happened at that party, but I was so sure there was a tea I could drink, a walk I could go on, a meditation I could listen to that would quell the anxiety roaring in my chest. Anything to make the feeling disappear. When I tried to talk to mom about it, Dan just wormed his way into the conversation. Told me to grow the fuck up and be a man. Told me that it's normal to feel overwhelmed sometimes, but a real man wouldn't complain about it to his mother.

Told me I better get my shit together, because the Chapman's have an impeccable reputation at Astor, and he'd be damned if his *step*son sullied it for him. He always emphasizes the step part.

So I tried what he said. I stopped complaining, to my mom and to myself. I got my shit together, putting in two hundred percent at every summer training drill, organizing separate practice drills for the incoming freshman. I accepted my friends' offers to go out, picking up girls and taking them home like we'd always done. But it all felt like a hollow attempt to perform a version of myself I no longer identified with. That felt the most suffocating of all.

That night it felt like the universe, out of everyone, was listening to me. For the first time in months, I felt like I could move on from the anxiety, just turn a new leaf and be someone new. But nothing comes that easy, I've learned.

The path toward healing ended up involving a lot of uncomfortable self-reflection, hard work, and cognitive behavioral therapy.

Thankfully, my grandfather— my *Pop*, when he's in earshot— let me hide away and figure my shit out. By the end of what would've been my senior year, had I stayed, Pops gave me an ultimatum: go back home to Dan and my mother, or go to said therapy. I chose the latter. With Morgan's help, we worked through the dad issues, the stepdad issues, the brother issues, the validation issues— all of it. But just like practicing your three pointer for hours only matters if you get a chance to implement your technique mid game, talking about why you're fucked up and reframing years of deeply engrained beliefs about yourself is only effective if you're out in the world applying your newfound self-knowledge.

And I knew this, deep down. That at some point, I'd

have to come back and live my life again. I'm ready; I know that whole heartedly. I just don't know what living my life is going to look like now, especially with Will here.

I finish my last lap and move into a slow jog as I make my way to the locker rooms off the practice pool, rather than the lockers in the practice gym. Coach will know I'm here eventually, but that can wait for another day.

Students are meandering about campus, trailing each other through the cloisters, stopping to catch up on benches. The freshmen are the easiest to spot because, unlike the returning students, they walk alone, staring at the tops of the buildings looking for names. The west side of campus feels buoyant, and it's contagious.

My shower is peaceful, the scalding hot water cleansing the thin layer of sweat from my skin, sluicing down my chest, the sound of it putting me in a meditative trance. I lose track of time until I hear a group of guys filtering into the showers, the nostalgic sound of towels cracking.

I quickly shut the water off, toweling myself off in a hurry and snatching up my duffel bag. In the stall furthest from the men's swim team, I slip on my sweatpants and slide my shirt on, unceremoniously trading my running shoes for my Killshots, cringing at the way the collar scrunches. I escape from the lockers unnoticed, but my previously meditative trance is gone.

Deep breaths, Ben, I remind myself.

Slowing my pace, I stroll through the campus center.

My real concern isn't that some guy on the swim team will stop and ask me about the weather— though that would be annoying. It's that I might see Will, who I haven't spoken to in any meaningful capacity since I left. Which is fucked up, I know. He needed me more than he's probably ever needed anyone, and I chose myself. Thinking back to the space I was in, though, I'd probably choose myself again. And I don't need to be reminded of that, just like I don't need to be reminded of *her*. Don't need to be reminded of everything that happened.

I haven't been able to shake Olivia Beckett from my thoughts since that night. The pull I felt toward her was so new to me; the urge to go to her, listen to her, admire her, be near her, protect her was confusing. I hadn't even met the girl. But looking at her under the glow of those market lights, I felt a spark of hope. Even now it sounds like the most nonsensical thing, but I can recall how relieved I felt when I found her.

I was going to go to her, try to get her attention. I would've asked her everything there was to know about her before seeing her stifle a yawn and offering to drive her home. I wouldn't have tried to kiss her, wouldn't have made even the slightest move, mostly because it's exactly the type of thing I would have done to most girls. And I knew, just by the way she stood there, Olivia wouldn't be like most girls to me. She probably still isn't, but I wouldn't know.

Will's been dating her ever since, but he hasn't brought her home. Hasn't been welcome to, really. But then, I guess I haven't been welcome there either. It was a mess; it still is. It's been two years, and I know whatever connection I *think* I had to Olivia has been snuffed out by Will's claim to her, that and the fact she has no idea who I am. That doesn't stop me from dreaming of her on a regular basis.

Morgan thinks my fixation on Olivia is because I've tied her to this emotionally draining night, and that I've "romanticized this idea of her" in contrast with the women of my past because I'm "eager to shed the playboy act" I adopted when I came to Astor. Her words, not mine. She's probably right, though. Maybe I *was* on the precipice of a breakdown anyway, and that night just set me over the edge. Maybe I saw Olivia and felt like I could go be someone different with her, and that's the end of it. Regardless, I don't want to see him, I don't want to see her, and most importantly, I don't want to see them together.

I haven't even told Will I'm back. Neither Pops nor Morgan could convince me on that one. I'd rather just let that bomb explode at a later date.

Blinking back into the present, I witness a wisp of chestnut hair whip around a column as a girl gracefully strides out of Cliveden. *Of course. Like I summoned her with my thoughts.*

Not two seconds later do I see my brother speeding after her.

3

Olivia

The start of Olivia's junior year

I pick at the hole in my tights with the tip of my pen. If they were going to have a run in them I had to at least make it look intentional. Wrapping the thread around the point, I hear a satisfying rip. Gen's dark tendrils bounce as she turns, looking away from our astronomy professor to raise an eyebrow in my direction.

I toss her a look that I hope expresses how nauseous she makes me feel.

"Can I help you?"

A blush runs straight to her cheeks and I roll my eyes. This is the start of my third year at Astor Hill and honestly, the atmosphere here still feels as gray as it did when I was a freshman.

I begin writing the date in my notes and get the familiar ache as I write September 8th. Two years ago today I woke up beside my best friend after the final kegger of the summer, a basketball team tradition before the start of their season. My stomach knots at the memory of her back to me, blonde curls spilling over onto my pillow, tickling my face.

"Lily, your hair is so frustrating, chop it off," I muttered, yanking my pillow away. I was expecting her typical "I'll do the big cut if you do," but instead I was met with silence. She was so quiet on our way back to the dorm from the kegger the night before.

"I feel like shit," she'd mumbled.

"I bet you'll start your period tomorrow," I'd remarked optimistically. She'd just shrugged.

"Can I sleep with you?" Lily knew I was big on personal space but she looked so pathetic, I threw open my comforter and let her in.

"You better not get me sick bitch."

I force myself to look up from my laptop and focus on my astronomy professor's syllabus being projected on the large screen in front of me. Even now I can feel the cold slipperiness of Lily's forehead from when I reached over to check her temperature that morning. I press my fingers together to warm them up, a familiar action as I've done it about fifty times a day for the past couple of years. I feel the burn in my throat, the one that never left from that morning where the paramedics had to drag me out of the room, my fingers gripping the door jam unable to accept that my best friend was dead. An unexplainable brain aneurysm. Lily's mom fell to her knees upon receiving the news. I fell too and somehow still feel like I'm falling.

"Miss Beckett, so glad to have you back in my class," Professor Daniels says cheerfully, handing me my syllabus and bringing me back to reality. "It'll be great to have your perspective again this year, and that TA spot still stands," he says, pushing his glasses up his nose. Even with the semester I took off freshman year, I still had one of the highest GPAs at Astor Hill. My teachers were gracious during that time of course, sending me work via email so I could keep up with my peers.

"Thank you, but I—"

Before I have time to make up an excuse the door swings open with a loud creak and there stands William Chapman in all his glory. I can practically see Gen drool even three rows in front of me, her posture perking up ever so slightly.

I grab my bag from the seat beside me, smirking at Will sarcastically to signal him over. Professor Daniel's takes this as his cue and moves to the row below, continuing to pass out the papers in his hands. Will plops down with a huff. Normally I would associate Will's arrogant demeanor with sloppiness but his handsome face has the ability to over-power his most egregious actions. I would know.

"You're late," I hiss as he throws his arm over my shoul-der, crossing one leg over the other. Will was there the night before Lily died. We exchanged numbers before Lily and I left the kegger and I saw him again at Lily's funeral. Somehow he became a constant for me in what was the most tumultuous year of my life and I fell for him, hard. His shoulders are more broad than when we were fresh-man, his arm muscles accentuated in his navy Astor Hill polo, the sleeves stretched taut over his bicep.

Gen has completely turned in her seat now, fully facing Will and I, the desperation coming off her in waves. Will winks and I instantly seethe pulling away from him in my seat.

"C'mon I'm just humoring her," Will whispers, pulling my arms in his lap.

"Why don't you *humor* me by not flirting with any breathing specimen in a four foot radius, especially today," I look down at my hands, my statement which started as sarcasm ending with sincerity.

"Do you always have to do this?" Will whispers. I can see the frustration in his eyes.

"Do what?" I ask, letting how pissed off I am ring through in my tone.

"Make today a whole thing."

"Alright everyone make sure to sign your syllabus by 8 A.M. Wednesday and submit it to our online portal. If I don't have it by then I'll assume you want to be dropped," Professor Daniels calls out over the first day of the semester hubbub. I stand up, turning toward Will and toss my MacBook in my Louis.

"You're a bastard." I start to push by him but he grabs my hips and pulls me in, my back still turned.

"I'm sorry, you're just a lot every year on this day and you know I'm not good at handling these kinds of things. Look, let's not fight today. It already sucks," he says with his lips to my ear.

I glance around the room as I turn to face Will. I can feel the eyes on us; everyone knows Will's name and by proxy everyone knows mine. I'm the youngest homecoming queen in Astor Hill's history, the senior editor of the paper (under Ian of course), and I toyed with the idea of running for class president until Will shot that idea down.

"The whole school's already in our business, I really don't need more drama," he'd said.

I look into Will's thickly lashed eyes. He truly is beautiful, his skin bronze, his jaw hard and sharp.

"I will do my best to not let today get to me if you promise to at least be sensitive to how I'm feeling."

He brings his forehead down to mine and smiles mischievously. "Deal."

I expect him to kiss me but instead he proceeds to walk by me, smacking my ass on the way out. I'm slightly humiliated, but still feeling eyes on me, I force a smile and an eye roll as I grab my bag and leave the room. If anything, I know this argument is far from over.

* * *

We're halfway across the courtyard when I hear Will huff out, "Fucking slow down, Olivia."

I'm walking at breakneck speed, trying to put some much needed distance between us. I know why I'm on edge today, but the awareness does nothing to quell the irritation erupting in my chest.

I stop abruptly and spin around to face him.

"Slapping my ass? Right after I ask you to be sensitive to how I'm feeling? That's fucking disgusting."

"Jesus, Olivia. You take yourself too seriously."

"You don't take yourself seriously enough." His face shifts, and I see his jaw tense. He grabs my arm and pulls me into the notoriously empty exterior hallway of Churchill Hall, perfect for getting into domestic disputes, apparently.

"What the fuck does that mean, Olivia?" His face is close enough to kiss, but I'm not sure that would stop the anger mounting in his glare. Knowing there's no calming him, I double down.

"It means that your incessant galavanting around school with these simple whores is not just embarrassing for me, but for you. Do you think I haven't seen you talking to the girls from the dance team? Or look at your relationship with Gen? You basically parade her in front of me at this point. Slapping my ass like I'm another trophy on your shelf—

don't you think the white, male misogynist is a little overplayed?"

I can't tell if Will is angrier at my words or my bored tone. Sometimes I get the feeling he would prefer a girl who would immediately sob, apologizing profusely over a wrong she never committed. Unfortunately for Will, it takes a little more to get me to bend over.

"You think you're just so fucking smart, Liv," his tone is disgusted, as if the fact that I won't play good little girlfriend for him revolts him. "Unfortunately, no one wants to fuck the know it all."

I meet his eyes and give him a venomous grin.

"Interesting. You do."

He snorts, rolling his eyes, then looks into mine, the anger simmering down.

"I apologize for slapping your ass..." he says with one hand on his heart.

I roll my eyes. This is typical for Will and I. We get into these explosive arguments and then quickly move on from them, like an endless cycle.

Will's eyes catch on something behind me and he lets out a low whistle. I turn just as three seemingly freshman girls walk toward us escorted by Andrew, the basketball team's self proclaimed player. Andy is handsome; he's from California and looks every bit like he grew up on the West Coast with his sandy blonde hair and deep tan, but his bad boy attitude is overplayed and honestly a bit obnoxious.

"Are you fucking kidding me?" I violently whisper, looking back at Will.

He looks down as if remembering that I'm still standing directly in front of him and gives me a cocky smirk and winks at me. I narrow my eyes at him now simmering with rage.

"Fuck you, Will." I move to leave.

"Come on, Liv," he gently grabs my wrist in an attempt to keep me there.

"Let go," I whisper shout and yank my wrist away causing me to fall backward into what feels like a brick wall. A brick wall that also has arms, that are now steadying me.

I turn to see who just caught me from completely embarrassing myself and my mind goes blank. I imagine this is the reaction I would have had as a girl meeting my celebrity crush. I feel… starstruck. I scan his face. He's definitely not famous. In fact, I've never seen him before.

He's tall— like *towers* over me. Taller than Will, which is saying something. His dark wavy hair is tousled in a way that shows he has good personal hygiene, but isn't staring at himself for too long. Dark lashes frame his eyes which are so brown they feel like a bottomless pit, and maybe they are, because I'm having trouble looking away. I feel warmth rising up my neck.

What the fuck is going on with me?

He raises his eyebrows seemingly wondering the same thing.

"Are you okay?" His voice is deep and masculine in a way that makes my stomach drop.

His voice sounds alarm bells in my mind, and I literally feel my defenses fly up. Before I even think about what I'm saying, "Fuck off" is already out of my mouth.

4

Ben

Given the scowl painted across Olivia's face, one could correctly guess she is appalled by my intrusion. Not thankful for saving her from the dusty floor of Churchill Hall— she's appalled.

I can't seem to look away when I hear a silky, honeyed, "Fuck off."

The eye contact stills me. Her eyes are a rich, deep brown, speckled with amber, disguising the curiosity that only momentarily peaked through when she first turned around. It is quickly shuttered away as a red flush creeps up her neck.

"I'm sorry?" I murmur, trying to reassemble the fortitude necessary to deal with the situation at hand.

"I'm sure there are better places for you to practice your subpar vigilante skills than Astor. Fuck off and find them," she says, eyes wide, as she grabs Will's hand and begins to drag him out of the archway and across the courtyard. It isn't until I see Will tug her to a halt and catch his mouth angle toward her ear that she stills, making eye contact with me once again.

Her gaze is soft but impenetrable as she looks at me and I can't bring myself to look away. As much as I'm irritated by her proximity to Will, my unwillingness to disengage alarms me. I force myself to turn away, hoisting my bag over my shoulder.

* * *

Walking into the locker room throws me; the musty blend of male perspiration, Bath and Body Works Ocean Mist tinged with Tommy cologne, and stringent multi-purpose cleaner assaults my passageways and travels to that part of your brain that connects smell to memory. I'm lost in thought when I feel a massive block of man slam me into the nearest locker.

"Jesus, Grant. Nice to see you too." I can't help the slight smile that forms, even as I rub my most definitely bruised shoulder.

"Nice to fucking see you? You disappear for two years, refuse to come to a game, come for a coffee, refuse anything, and all you've got is nice to see you. You mysterious fuck." He's grinning as he berates me, unable to be serious for even a second, and I'm glad to see he hasn't changed.

When I quit the team and left Astor Hill two years ago, one of my hesitations was Grant. But when Grant asked me what was going on, and when I found myself unable to even vaguely explain my head to him, I just balked. I think I felt embarrassed by my inability to get a handle on my anxiety. Grant wouldn't have judged me, I know that now. I was so in my head though, I didn't believe it then. I packed my side of our apartment, threw two months rent on the counter, and left. I've answered the obligatory "Happy Birthday" texts he's sent my way, but largely ignored any attempt to pry deeper.

Despite my obvious avoidance, Grant sent:

see u there

only ten seconds after I sent:

the center gym in 15?

No questions asked. That's Grant for you— avoid him for two years but he'll still be down for a gym session if you need him.

I quickly change back into the clothes I used for my run, opting to keep my current shirt on but switching my pants, eager to blow off the unfinished steam from my encounter with Will. And Olivia.

Grant, forever the intuitive friend, senses this. "I'm assuming you saw your brother."

"Yup."

"And that went… poorly?"

"You could say that." I know he wants me to elaborate, but I'm not sure where to begin. Instead, I sit down on the first rowing machine in sight and begin securing the foot straps.

"Okay, let's try this a different way. Hey, Ben. How's your day so far? Do anything interesting?"

Sensing the end of his good will, I relent, shaking my head.

"Pretty sure I interrupted Will and his girlfriend in a fight. Probably wasn't the best moment to let him know I'm back." I pick up the pace on the rowing machine as I feel my adrenaline kick back in. Grant's attempting to match my speed, but something about his size makes it difficult for him to keep up.

"Shit. He didn't know? I'm guessing he was pissed." He's slightly huffing at this point, and it's definitely a boost to my ego. Two years off the court, competitively, and I've still got the endurance. I feel my adrenaline rising further and decide to keep my version of today's incident brief.

"You'd think that," I say, recalling Olivia's scathing reaction to me.

Grant turns his head toward me, his right eyebrow slightly raised. He picks up the pace a tad more, despite his clunking form. He's asking for more context and I know we're not leaving these rowers until he's content.

"What do you mean?"

"He didn't really do anything. His girlfriend though… I'm assuming it was his girlfriend." I add, feigning disinterest. "She was livid."

I knew exactly who Olivia was before I approached. Seeing them argue across the hall was part of why I decided to go over there in the first place. "I was just about to interrupt when she slammed into me and then… I don't know I just kind of froze up and she told me to fuck off."

"Damn," Grant chuckles, "so you met Olivia." He's beaming as if he's in on some joke that I have no clue about.

"Is she always like that? Kind of… rude?" I ask, thinking back to that moment in the corridor where I felt like I was seeing into her soul, only for her to sharply bring me out of my trance by basically calling me a great value super hero.

Grant's wearing a sheepish grin. "Not at all. Maybe

you're just not used to girls not falling all over you." I roll my eyes.

"I don't think she knew who I was." I smirk, sweat beading on my forehead as I pick up my pace.

"Will didn't mention you?" Grant asks, sounding out of breath.

"Apparently not. How's Will been? Do they fight often?" I direct the conversation back to what I should actually be worrying about. Grant's face goes solemn as he sighs.

"I don't know what Will's been up to lately, honestly. He hasn't really been hanging out as much. He's either at practice, or he's with Olivia. She spends a lot of time at the newspaper, so she hasn't been around much. I mean, I definitely have seen them argue— hell, the whole team has. Olivia's definitely not the type to let a guy walk all over her though. She can hold her own with him, if that's what you're asking." Relief washes over me at the thought that they're not good together and everyone knows it, but guilt follows quickly there after. I take a deep breath as I stretch my arms upward, preparing for the damage I know Grant is going to inflict on me when this workout gets started.

"Yeah, I believe it." Her reaction definitely set me on edge, but I can't stop remembering how it felt to exist under her gaze. How it felt to have her attention.

"He will get over you being back, don't worry," Grant cuts into my thoughts. "But Ben?"

I turn my head towards him, my brows arching in question.

"You haven't been around, and I know he's your brother and all but just … tread lightly. He's always been a hot head, but if you were hoping that girl would chill him out, you're in for a surprise." He shoots me a look, one that says he remembers more than he's letting on.

I think again about the incident this morning and what Grant's saying doesn't surprise me. Remembering the feeling of Olivia's delicate frame against my chest, I feel my face flush and I silently curse myself, hoping he doesn't notice. Grant's been a lot of things, but I wouldn't have said observant until today.

For a brief moment I have the urge to confide in him, confirm that his assumptions are more than likely true, but my common sense wins out. This thing with Olivia needs to stay where it is— in my head.

"Noted." I slow my rower, wiping the machine down with the towel on my shoulder. "Now show me the circuit you were bragging about."

5

Olivia

Conceptually, I knew Will had a brother. Practically, I had completely forgotten that Will *has* a brother. A living, breathing, talking, walking, *legendary* brother. The mysterious ex-captain of the basketball team. How am I the last person on this campus to realize that Will's brother is *Ben fucking Cabot?*

Will was almost embarrassed as he muttered the mystery man's identity to me in the courtyard earlier, confirming the truth of the matter: the objectively gorgeous man with tousled dark locks and fiery brown eyes was definitely his older brother.

Naturally, Will would have an attractive brother— I wouldn't expect anything less. Ben, though, is devastating. Objectively speaking. It's quite simply true; Will would agree, if it wasn't weird to tell your boyfriend that the brother he's failed to mention is genetically blessed beyond measure.

I think about how I told him off this morning and grimace at the memory. Under normal circumstances if someone caught me from stumbling backwards I probably wouldn't have told them to fuck off, but I panicked because I couldn't tear my gaze away from the stranger, and my boyfriend was literally standing right behind me watching me openly gawk at Ben.

I make a conscious effort to relax the jaw I've been tensing as I march down to the newspaper office. When Ian texted me this morning about an urgent assignment, right as Will decided to pick a fight, I was already brainstorming my counter offer. I don't get stories. I spot them, hunt them, chase them myself. Today, though, I've never been so glad for a straight forward story assignment in my life.

The door handle on the heavy Georgian revival door is slick with condensation, and I wipe my freshly manicured hand on the back of my tweed skirt. I see the blue fade of Ian's hair just above the Mac at the top desk.

"Olivia," he quips, clearly peeved that I've rushed over. The only thing Ian hates more than overeagerness is a bustling newsroom; both are the antithesis to the culture he's strived to create at the paper. I quickly mask my fluster with a calm smile, and I'm met with a small grin that says he's got some shit to spill. Ian and I are the same in this way; we love some good gossip. Part of what's made the paper so distinctly different from the Harvard Gazette or the Yale Daily News is our willingness to lean into dirt and scandal. Gossip is soothing to the soul; the best people engage in it. Obama's weekly basketball game with his security detail was not simply a physical release for a rapidly graying Barack. It was obviously his weekly gossip sesh. How else was one supposed to handle that one senator's incessant crying?

"Before you tell me to go fuck myself, listen to the pitch."

Little does he know, I need a distraction. I'll take almost anything he gives me after the traumatic morning I just had.

"Spill." I slide into the chair next to him and purse my lips in faint irritation, if only to give the illusion that this is painful for me.

"Okay. Hot jock disappears without a word two years ago, reappears all of a sudden to finish his senior year. Everyone's asking what will happen to the program now that he's back, if or how it'll upset the basketball team's perfectly laid plans— you know, sporty shit. Alice is covering that, don't worry. You come in with the—"

"I can't," I cut Ian off, my brain finally catching up with the gravity of Ian's request. I feel the panic in the form of sweat as my face flushes.

"Why not? Olivia. Not to pull this card, but I'm your editor, *so* you will." Ian walks toward the window overlooking the campus courtyard. "We need the why. *Why* Ben Cabot fled Astor Hill is the story anyone and everyone cares about." Ian turns back looking me directly in the eyes, his tone grave. "People like Ben don't just abandon their plans like that. Not only did he up and leave but he did so with no explanation. Not covering this would be a huge misstep. You *refusing* to cover this would be a massive misstep, for you." He looks down his nose at me, emphasizing the word you.

"You can't expect me to—"

"Not to mention, I already had Lauren reach out via email and Raya tried to get a quote from *your* boyfriend. Both massive fails, until I realized we literally have you," he adds, a smug smile settling on his face as he sits at the large plush armchair at his desk. His logic here is sound, but in true Ian fashion he fails to comprehend that I might not want to report on my boyfriend's brother. The word "ethics" is foreign to him, but I attempt to reason with him anyway.

"This is such a conflict of interest. I cannot ethically cover this story. You are correct, he *is* Will's older brother, as of this morning. I mean, as of always. You know what I mean." My words are becoming jumbled, my thoughts feel fragmented and I need an out. I've only just *met* the man and our first interaction was anything but perfect. I practically spat venom at him after he basically saved me from the embarrassment of falling on my face.

It hits me that Ian, who may be my only real friend here, has no idea of any of this. He must think I've known Ben for years. That I can just ask him to go out for coffee or, better yet, drill him with a quick line of questioning at their next family gathering. He probably assumes I already know why he left, and that I'm the easiest person to task this story with because it won't even require that much investigation.

I cut Ian off mid sentence, realizing I haven't even been listening.

"I'm too close to this," I explain, deciding against sharing the dismal truth about my relationship with Will's family. This is going to be a problem for Will, and beyond that I can see this becoming a problem for me. Ian crosses his legs, examining me closely.

"What's really going on here, Liv?" his tone changes from editor to concerned friend, which only happens on occasion.

"Will's just been having a really hard time lately and—" Ian rolls his eyes, cutting me off.

"Olivia, there has not been a time since I've known you that Will isn't going through some shit. At this point, I can't tell if he's got issues or if you do." I feel my face redden as I narrow my eyes. "Liv, you know I'm right. First it's that you can't run for class president, then he has an issue with you doing that study abroad program. Does he want you to fail or are you just scared to?"

I shift in my seat, regaining my confidence as anger blossoms inside me. "I know you think you know everything going on at this school, but your ignorance is really shining through right now."

He chuckles, giving me the bitchy smirk he only saves for when he knows he's won. "Exactly Olivia, I am ignorant. That is why I am not writing this story— you are." And I know I can't say no.

Ian's right, of course, I consider while walking down the strip of buildings housing the several coffee shops, book stores, and restaurants on campus. A gossip piece is best when messy; ideally, the mess wouldn't involve me. I thought this assignment would be a decent, albeit temporary, distraction from my issues with Will and the existence of his extremely attractive brother. Instead, the universe is telling me to deal with this head on. Fine. Head on was not my preferred manner of handling this, but it is certainly a manner I'm familiar with.

I'm about to pop my right AirPod into my ear when I hear "Beckett!" from behind me. A comforting warmth blooms in my chest.

"Hey," I offer with a sigh as I reach up to reciprocate Grant's signature bear hug.

"Where are you headed? I'll walk with you."

"I was just gonna grab a coffee from Nero. But you're

not a coffee guy, if I remember correctly." Grant pointedly avoided the cardboard carafe of Dunkin breakfast roast during the organic chemistry finals study session last semester.

"You remember! Do you always catalog details about your study mates?"

"Just the ones that bring the best notes and freshly baked *sponges*." I elbow what is essentially his hip. I'm a tall girl, but Grant is a literal tower next to me.

"I told you about my British Bake Off binge in confidence, Beckett. Don't make me regret it," Grant says with a chuckle. Grant might be teammates with Will, but this is the extent of our friendship. Quick exchanges between classes, brief chats at parties, and every now and again, random details about our lives in disparate study sessions. He's one of the few men on campus I can do this with. In another world, Grant and I might be real friends. In this one, the one with Will, I settle for his warm acquaintance.

"I seal these lips for no one… but I'm not beneath a coffee bribe," I offer with a friendly wink. Grant reaches ahead of me and opens the door, and I inhale the aroma of freshly roasted coffee beans. "Thanks."

Grant's frown reaches his brows as he lowers his voice.

"How're you holding up today?"

It's sweet of him to remember. He barely even knew Lily. I bite the inside of my lower lip as I shoot him a tense smile.

My purse audibly buzzes twice as we wait in line, and I'm grateful for the distraction most likely coming from Ian. Except when I check my messages, it's not; it's a text from Will.

I need to see you. Nero in ten?

I don't necessarily want to talk about earlier or tell Will about my meeting with Ian, but I can't bring myself to refuse. He wants to see me, *needs* to see me, and I hate the guilt that creeps up when I even consider telling him I'm busy. It's also the perfect opportunity to avoid a heart to heart with Grant.

I sigh as I turn toward him. "I'm gonna have to cut our impromptu coffee short. Rain check?" I offer with a raised brow. "I totally forgot I was meeting Will. But maybe we can all get food after?"

I'm lying about my forgetfulness, and by the questioning gleam in his eyes, he knows it.

"Sure, Beckett. Remind Will not to suck at practice, will you?"

I laugh, relieved and amused. "If only my words held that power."

He looks at me over his shoulder as he strolls away, a sad smile settling across his face. *Close call.* I'm not ready for the flood gates that might buckle under the strain of a conversation about Lily, especially not with someone as sensitive as Grant.

I find a secluded table in the corner by the French doors that lead to the garden and pull out my notebook, willing myself to switch gears. This morning feels long, especially after the hour I spent reading old papers about Ben in the newsroom. I'm in desperate need of a shower after my speed walk to the newsroom in the thick August fog, but if I have to wait for Will here I might as well get a head start on my questions.

Ian's directive was to dig into the "why" of Ben's depar-ture. That seems straightforward enough, but it could prove insufficient for a story. I'll need to generate more context, fill in the gaps of his life right before he left and over the past two years. More importantly, I'll need to pinpoint why he came back. As much as I'd like this to be a one and done assignment, my journalistic brain is eager to unfold something complex and layered. Maybe he had some sort of injury that led to a mental breakdown? Maybe he spent the past two years meditating in a monastery in Bhutan. Maybe the strain of athletic leadership pushed him to explore life without the pressure of the competitive sports world… I don't know. Maybe he just left, wanting a gap year. But Ian's made it my sole purpose to find out.

I'm slipping my notebook back into my bag when I look up and catch Will making small talk with a dancer; I'm pretty sure she's a freshman, because she's in a uniform and I haven't seen her before. She's tiny, probably reaching just below five feet and her blonde hair reaches her waist. Her eyes glitter with ambition as she flutters her eyelashes at him, a hollow laugh ringing out a little too forcefully. I watch him shift his weight, his hand reaching out to pick an eyelash off her face, and I feel my cheeks burn in frustration.

As if he feels my eyes on him, Will shoots me a subtle smile followed by a conspiratorial eye roll, like that move he just pulled was out of pity, or for my benefit, or something justifiable, and I unwittingly cool off.

I don't know how he does it— make me doubt him one second and make me feel like the only worthy person in the building the next. Will's far from perfect, but when I consider the kind of guy I need next to me, he kind of is. Yes, he can pull shit like this, but there are moments where he makes me feel powerful and wanted; it's what drew me to him in the first place. He's my most vocal fan and my loudest critic. And I love that about him, for the most part. No one else has ever made me feel the strange twinge of happiness and sadness that creeps into my chest like Will. I believe life is about balance, and I need someone who does that for me. Someone who elevates me and has no qualms about bringing me down a peg when I need it. Even if it feels like shit, sometimes.

Feeling like shit is still better than feeling nothing. I felt nothing for so long after Lily left but Will… he brought me back from that. That has to count for something.

He barely concludes whatever conversation he was having and waltzes to the front of the order line. The mousy girl with the thick wired glasses who'd been about to order says nothing, just giggles when he motions toward the counter and says, "Do you mind?"

A minute later, he places two iced coffees on my table and rotates the chair across from me so the back is to the table's edge. He sits with his arms crossed on the back of the chair and leans forward, his dark blonde waves falling slightly in his eyes. I suck in the side of my cheeks, the corners of my mouth turning upward into an unwilling smile.

"You're quite the celebrity today. First the dancer, then the librarian-in-waiting."

"Hmm. I didn't notice. I might've been too distracted by the smoke show sulking in the corner." A slight blush creeps up my neck, but I roll my eyes.

"I'm not sure what I dislike the most— that you accused me of sulking or that you used the term 'smoke show' to describe me."

"Who said I was talking about you?" I kick his right leg from under the table.

"Watch it, Chapman," I say, shaking my head with a grin so deep, I can feel my usually reluctant dimples emerge. He grabs my hand from across the table and runs his thumb along the back of it.

"You know you're beautiful." He peers through his lashes at me as if to give the impression that he's feeling shy, which we both know he isn't. I raise an appraising eyebrow at him as if to agree. "Does this mean you forgive me?" I'd already forgiven his flirtatiousness, but the groveling is a boon to my freshly injured ego.

"You're on thin ice… but yes. I forgive you." He pulls my hand to his lips and presses a soft kiss into my palm, smiling. It always went like this; Will being an asshat, me getting pissed off at his behavior, us having a heated argument, and ultimately, me forgiving him. "This could've waited until later, though."

His brows furrow in confusion, so I clarify. "You said you *needed* to see me. Seemed urgent," I add, now also confused.

"Oh. Yeah I, uh, wanted to talk to you about my brother." He says this with a grimace, like bad news is on the horizon, and I brace myself while fighting the urge to pick a fight. I fail.

"The brother I just met this morning? After two years of dating, you *now* need to urgently talk to me about your brother?"

His eyes burn with irritation, his tongue sliding against his teeth as I watch him bite back a reply. "Liv I already told you, we're not close. I'm assuming you're smart enough to realize that it's for a good reason."

I bite the inside of my cheek trying to temper my own anger. "What does that even mean?" I ask, frustrated by his obtuseness.

"He's just… I wouldn't say he's the best guy. He kind of

abandoned his team. I mean, if he thinks he's going to waltz back in there and pick up where he left off—"

"Will," I interrupt him, refocusing our conversation. "That seems rash. If you're not close, like you claim, then he's probably different than you remember." He scoffs, crossing his arm.

"Nah, Liv. We might not be close, but I know who Ben is. He doesn't give a fuck about the people around him, whether it's his family, his friends— especially not women. I just…" he shakes his head, not finishing his thought. I raise my brows, urging him to continue. "I just need you to keep your distance from him. I don't know why he's back, but I don't need him worming his way into my life. Into *our* life." He emphasizes 'our,' like Ben poses some existential threat.

A laugh escapes me, slightly more intense than I intend. "Worming his way into our life? You make him sound parasitic."

"I'm serious, babe. He's a shameless flirt and—"

"Oh! Must be a family trait," I cut him off, irritated by this sudden bravado and possessiveness.

"Olivia," he says, his jaw grinding in frustration. "Just… tell me you won't go out of your way to know him. If I wanted you to know my family, believe me, you would've met them by now." He says this like it perfectly explains his response to all of this, but I feel his words like a knife to the gut.

"No can do, Will," I answer, my voice seething, feeling burned by his reminder. "Ian just gave me a new story. Ben's the subject."

His nostril's flare and he tilts his head back, running his hands through his hair. He sighs visibly, his head leveling back so that he's looking me right in the eye. "Un-fucking-believable."

"I didn't *choose* this story. Believe me, I'm the last person who wants to get to know your brother."

His gaze narrows on me for a long second, like he's deciphering something.

"Just be careful, Liv," he says gently, sincerely, his earlier frustration replaced now by obvious worry. And as much as I'd like to say I have no idea what he's even worrying about, I know that would be a lie.

"If it makes you feel better, I'll be extra super careful," I tell him, saccharine sweet, as we both move to leave the table, reaching for each other's hand. I spin to face him once we're outside the cafe. "I need to go home and shower before dinner tonight. This humidity is ruining me."

Will grabs my wrist and pulls me in, wrapping his arms low around my waist. He gives me a quick kiss on the lips, then leaves a trail of brief, wet kisses down both sides of my neck. He returns his soft lips to mine and gives me one last kiss, this one deep and full of apology and promise.

"Wear something pretty for me," he says. Warmth creeps from my neck to my cheeks and while I'm sure desire is painted on my face, guilt settles in my chest as I walk away from campus and toward my apartment.

I don't want to do this story, but I'm also not going to sabotage my own work and as Ian very blatantly pointed out that's been a habit of mine when it comes to Will. I'm committed to producing this piece for Ian, and moving on as quickly as possible. If what Will said is true, then some well deployed charm on my part might be all I need to get this story done and dusted. Besides, what's a little bit of innocent flirting if it means I get the answers I'm looking for? It's not like Will has any room to judge. He's constantly deploying his charm to get what he wants.

What Will doesn't know won't hurt him. And besides, I think he'd rather I move on from this story quickly than get mired by it. Regardless of my methods, I think to myself, realizing my bottom lip is beginning to feel swollen from my unconscious biting.

Something continues to eat at me, and I see Will's worried face in my mind's eye. He can't know what I've been thinking, but his vocalized insecurities make me feel like I've done something wrong anyway.

Ben is already starting to feel like the bane of my existence.

6

Ben

If there's one thing the elite group of students at Astor Hill College hold a flame for it's the state championship winning basketball team, the Astor Lions. Even now, two years later, I'm stalked in the hallway by classmates that could easily be confused for adoring fans. When I was at the height of my game, I hated the attention I got for being the team's captain. There was always a spotlight shining on me and being 6'4" it was hard to duck out of. Even now, I pass by a group of snickering freshman girls whispering amongst each other.

"Oh my god look, it's Will's brother." They try and fail to sneakily look at me.

"Okay you were right, he's definitely hotter. How is that even possible?"

I glance at them as I turn toward the massive brick building flanked with the school's flags, causing them to burst into embarrassed laughter. When I first arrived at Astor, I found the Mark Maxwell Arena comical. How could what was essentially a basketball court look so regal?

Gifted in the 1960's by the Maxwell family the arena was built in a more turn of the century style. It was once the school's playhouse but when they realized that sports could easily outsell plays they renovated the inside into the court it is today. The path to the building's entrance is lined with cherry blossom trees, begging to bloom toward the end of the season, as if to celebrate the team's inevitable win.

I feel a breeze prickle the back of my neck, as a feeling of uneasiness washes over me. Is attending tonight's game a mistake? Am I instigating what will inevitably be a full out brawl between Will and I sometime in the near future? I curl my fingers into fists, a frown tugging at the corners of my mouth.

When we were little I remember teaching Will the basics of the game, sneaking out of our room into the massive family room, stealthily skipping over the creaky floorboards that made up the Tudor style house we stayed in every summer. We'd mute the TV and I'd set up NBA Street on my PS2 while Will snuck into the walk-in pantry stocking up on snacks. I'd whisper to him my thought process making the players move through the plays. The next morning at the crack of dawn Will would shake me awake, his tiny hands clawing into my arm. *"Can we practice free-throws?"* We both were obsessed, addicted even. We'd play every day from the crack of dawn until the sun started going down in the evening. It was thrilling, a game that was only ours. That was until Daniel Chapman, Will's dad and my step father, got a hold of how good we were a few summers later. How hard we were willing to work for the game we loved.

When Dan started joining us, coaching us, I noticed the small shifts in Will. One misstep and he'd punish himself, throwing the ball with all his force and Dan would punish him too, laughing at every misstep and always coming in fast with a snide comment. *"Ben would've made that shot."* He celebrated Will not for working with the team, but instead for moving to always make himself the most valuable player.

God forbid someone stepped on Will's toes. An innocent game could turn into a death match at the blink of an eye, an accidental foul turning into a fist fight.

"He's just emotional, he cares," Dan would say. *"You could use some of that passion."* Anytime Will would lash out, whether he was losing or his team mate wasn't performing each play to perfection, Dan found a way to turn it into a positive.

"Will, your competitive streak has a mind of its own. This fire will always make you the better player," Dan said, staring at my eight year old brother whose face was caked in dirt and tears after getting kicked out of his third basketball camp of the summer for blowing up on a ref for making a bad call.

Will peered at me. "Even better than Ben?" His smile was mischievous as usual but there was something else in it too, determination.

I take a deep breath as the smell of rubber fills my lungs. I feel my heart jump the way it does when I'm beginning to panic. I start the exercise I learned in therapy, silently naming the different objects around me in my head, trying to remain in the moment. Stepping in through the lobby's massive wooden doorway, a comfortable warmth wraps around me. I feel at home as I hear the squeak of sneakers in the distance. Feeling my lips flicker with a smile, I push my hands into my jean pockets and step inside.

The arena's lobby is teeming with impatient fans draped in Astor Hill's signature crisp white, the navy Lion insignia peppered throughout the crowd. And even if she hadn't been running through my mind since our encounter, she wouldn't have been difficult to spot. Using her black sunglasses she pushes back her dark tendrils, readjusting them to the top of her head. She looks lost. The only indicator that she is at a basketball game are the socks that hit above her ankle and the chunky white sneakers that give her an air of sportiness, enhancing her already mile long legs. Even I, the guy who picked this shirt up off the floor, can tell that her style is unparalleled. Her chest shimmers with perspiration as a tiny L dangles beneath her collarbone.

She quickly assesses the crowd, pursing her rose pink lips. She's obviously looking for someone and I realize that someone is me as her amber flecked eyes zero in. Even though I see her coming, I feel my heart speed up and sweat grip the back of my neck. I avert my gaze, briefly glancing at my classmates who seem to be doing the same. The effect Olivia has is overwhelming, and not just to me. She moves through the crowd fluidly, softly putting her hand on the backs of those in her way. With barely a tap it seems like she could move mountains.

The black strap of her rectangular leather bag hangs off her smooth shoulder, framing her left arm that she digs into the pouch of her purse. When she pulls her hand out, she's holding a black, glittery spiral notebook. On the other side of the strap her slender neck balances a head draped in thick, chestnut locks that fall in layers around her face as she puts her glasses in the bag.

I take a quiet breath to bring myself back to reality and am immediately met by a sultry, masculine scent. Her scent isn't the typical floral essence I'm familiar with from my escapades as captain all those years ago. Instead she smells mysterious, like a bonfire that had gone out in a rainstorm.

It reels me in, so much so that I don't even realize how close I've let myself stand in front of her.

"I knew I'd find you here," she says with an assessing smile. Her eyes leave mine and quickly roam the length of my body. I realize my face hasn't shifted, so I allow myself to meet her gaze.

"Bold of you to assume I'd be here," I respond, annoyed but excited about the incoming public confrontation.

She extends her right hand, and I notice that while her hands are strong, her fingers are dainty and delicately manicured.

"Olivia Beckett," she says with a slight eyebrow raise. "My sincerest apologies for telling you to fuck off the other day." She smiles tightly, obviously straining to make amends for her behavior. "You see, I have an aversion to strange, random men interrupting intimate conversations with my boyfriend. As it turns out, you are neither strange nor random to Will. So. Again, I apologize."

Wearily, I finally accept her outstretched hand and am not the least bit shocked by the firm handshake she initiates.

"Ben Cabot. I have an aversion to women telling me to 'fuck off' when they ran into me in the first place, but for you I'll make an exception." I wink and give her a smile that used to work wonders for me during my first years at Astor but as to be expected, Olivia seems wholly unaffected.

"The women I know don't usually enjoy being manhandled by total strangers." A cynical smile dances at the corners of her mouth and echoes at the edges of her eyes. "It seems your time away from civilization may have left you worse off when it comes to introductions."

"I'd hardly say Boston is uncivilized." She scribbles

down what I assume is "Boston" in her notebook. "I wasn't aware I was on the record."

I hear her sneakers squeak on the floor behind me as I move toward the arena to find my seat.

"Does Will know you're talking to me?" I ask abruptly. As much as I'm enjoying the banter, I shouldn't be.

I spin around, only to be met with a flash of irritation in her eyes, her lashes narrowing her stare into careful slits. Despite her cheeks that rise into high points and a jaw that reveals a strength evident in more than her physicality, there's a softness. Softness in her spiced brown eyes and the suppleness of her gently curved lips. Freckles scatter across the bridge of her sloped nose that arrives at a perfectly formed point. Her lashes are lush, and her brows are dense above her playful eyes.

"Do I have to ask Will's permission to get to know his aloof older brother?"

"I don't know, do you?" Her eyes relax into their natural almond shape and I see her bite the inside of her cheek. Her slender fingers clinch her pen. The only indication that she's feeling anything is the slight tap against her notepad, but even that only hints at boredom. I notice a slight blush creeping up the side of her neck, suggesting she might be enjoying this introduction as much as I am.

I find my seat in the wooden bleachers only to feel her slide into the spot next to me.

"So Ben, tell me, why come back to Astor Hill if you were living it up in Boston?"

"I wanted to finish school."

"There are more schools in Boston, no?"

"Yes there are more schools in Boston, Olivia."

My eyes are fixated on the court, even though the game hasn't started. Still, I can feel Olivia roll her eyes at my side, frustrated with my lack of clarity. I clench my jaw, which I'm hoping will indicate that I do not want to be questioned. To her benefit, I'm sure that Ian guy put her up to it, thinking there was some sort of juicy story happening in the background. I guess star player not being able to control his anxiety could be that, but Dan and my mother went to extremes trying to hide my 'issues' from the school and furthermore their peers, so giving Olivia the inside scoop could cause even more of a rift with my parents than the one that already exists. Sensing that she won't give up I toss out a question of my own.

"So, Will huh?"

"Is that a question or a statement?"

"A question, I guess. Based on what I walked into this morning it seems you don't actually mind being manhandled, or is it just when he does it?"

"Correct. Will can manhandle me whenever he likes." She tosses me a mischievous grin, but it doesn't meet her eyes. While it's obvious she's being sardonic her tone seems deflated, like if I keep tapping on this sore spot she won't be able to pretend it doesn't hurt. I fully break my eyes away from the court, glancing at her. She's tucking her hair behind her ear, looking down at her notebook. Her blush is more apparent now than it was before. *Did I just embarrass her?* Regret fills my stomach as I take in the only glimpse of vulnerability I'm sure to see from her tonight.

The players begin filing out of the locker rooms as loud music fills the stands. Olivia stands alongside the rest of the gymnasium cheering as each player is announced. She waves at Will when he finally comes out, the captain always being announced last. His gaze is impenetrable, I'd know that focus anywhere. It's the one thing we have in common when playing. Nothing could distract us during a game.

The players gather around the coach as he explains the play and the mass of fans fall back into their seats. I notice Grant who goofily shoots Olivia and I the middle finger. Olivia pretends to catch it and hold it to her heart, which cracks Grant up. Her smile is so genuine, I feel jealousy erupt within me. Boy, what I would give for her to smile at me like that? I shake the unwanted feeling away.

"So you know Grant?" I say, nudging her shoulder with mine. Her smile fades as her eyes go from Grant to Will who hasn't even glanced our way.

"We're in the same study group," Olivia states flatly, her tone guarded.

"Grant's one of the best people I know," I say, shifting toward her. "He's my best friend. I feel silly saying that, but it's true."

Olivia meets my gaze and seems to relax slightly, unhinging her shoulders as she turns toward me, and I see a small smile play at her lips. "Grant's one of the best people I know too, believe it or not."

Olivia's bare thigh grazes my jeans and I feel clammy and ill. I shouldn't be doing this, feeling these things.

"So are you going to help me out here at all Cabot, or am I being forced to revisit this at a later date?"

Her charm makes my entire body vibrate. I swallow hard. Ian made a few attempts to get me to answer the ever present question of why I left school last year. The reporters he sent me were ditzy blondes who seemed to want to sleep with me more than write a story, but it seems he's actually taking this story seriously now since he sent the one person I can't say no to, whether he knows it or not.

"Well we can't do that, now can we?" I say, my gaze shifting to my brother out on the court, trying to find a way to get her to back off this story. Her eyes follow mine until she lands on Will. She looks down at her pad, tapping her pen again.

"He doesn't own me," she says, defiance etched in the sudden slant of her eyes.

"I didn't say that he did," I retort, unable to contain my amusement.

"He doesn't have to know," she says, cracking a half smile, her eyes piercing into me.

I raise an eyebrow. "Olivia Beckett, I am shocked," I say in a fake mocking tone.

"If there's one thing to know about me, it's that I'm full of surprises." Her eyes flutter, an air of mischief in her tone.

"Oh, that I can tell," I give her a smile.

She licks her lips and looks at the court in an attempt to hide the flush that was getting rosier by the minute.

"So… Boston…?" She says in a playful impatient tone.

"My grandfather lives in Boston. He's getting old. I wanted to see him."

She scribbles into her notebook. I reach over into her lap and shut the notepad abruptly. Her face is hard to read, the blush appearing underneath the freckles I am now becoming familiar with. It's funny, for a girl that seemed to intimidate the entire school she's easy to rile up.

"Can we at least get to know each other before you give me the fifth degree?" I ask with mock innocence, pushing my thigh further into hers and letting the warmth of my body press against her, our arms now fully brushing.

She blows out a breath, attempting to regain control of the conversation but seemingly flustered by our closeness.

"We go to McKinley's on Saturday nights, if you want to pick this up then, " she says in almost a whisper, clearing her throat as she bounces up onto her feet before I have time to respond. Scribbling into her notebook she rips out the page and hands it to me. "Call me when you're ready to talk, Cabot. "

And like that she's gone, heads turning as she pushes her way through the double doors, light streaming into the arena around her.

Olivia wasn't wrong; I was surprised. Surprised by the way she presented herself and the way just her smile seemed to knock the wind out of me. She's breathtaking, and the thought of her tight dress hitting well above her knee makes my throat feel hoarse and my hands clammy— all the symptoms of attraction that I have only read about and haven't experienced myself.

I can't feel this way, I think to myself, the weight of the paper becoming heavy in my hand. Yet here I am, staring after my brother's girlfriend with the realization that I will never get over her and I haven't even had her yet.

The post game locker room vibe is infectious, especially hot off a win. The game was just a friendly, but a win is a win, and if the trap music blaring so loud that the floors vibrate is any indication, my ex-teammates feel the same way. I hear Grant before I see him, his boisterous laughter coming only seconds before I see him whip Andrew's back with a towel.

"You're *whipped*, bro." Andrew's eyes roll at Grant's accusation, but I see him bite back a grin.

"Yeah, well, you haven't seen her. She's got these—"

"We're talking about your imaginary girlfriend, again?"

Will cuts in, settling on the bench near Grant's locker, a towel draped over his shoulders and his back to me.

"Fuck off," Andrew says, exaggerating each vowel, before he notices me. "Ben the fucking Bogart! In the flesh! Shit, come here." His grin is the best welcome I could've asked for, but as I back out his quick, sweaty hug, I get the sense that not everyone's glad to see me.

Will's eyes seer into me, his irritation obvious.

"This is a closed locker room, or has it been so long that you forgot?" He's fuming, his jaw flickering with more than annoyance as he slams his locker shut.

"Chill, Chapman. I invited him," Grant says, like that should calm him down. Will just nods his head, his locked gaze unwavering.

"It's cool, Grant, I'll uh…" I back up, putting both hands up in mock surrender, because what the fuck have I done to him? It was naive of me to think I could come back and we'd turn a new leaf. That the hot and cold, ill will between us would just disappear. I didn't want it to be like this between us, not anymore, but his tone grates against me and I find it too easy to dip into that all too familiar well of antagonism. "I'll see you tomorrow at McKinley's. Olivia invited me." I shoot him a snarky smirk and give Grant a quick nod before exiting the locker room.

No part of me feels guilty for poking the bear like this, and that's concerning. A year of therapy, nowhere to be found the moment I *probably* needed it most.

This is exactly why Morgan wanted me to talk to him before I came back, I realize, making my way to my car. A hand grabs my arm just as I'm about to swing open my car door and I defensively whirl around, relieved to see my brother.

"Jesus Christ, you can't just—"

"What are you doing, Ben?" Worry creases between his brows as he shakes his head at me in disbelief. He's still in his game jersey, his duffel slung over his shoulder.

"I was attempting to go home, actually." I'm being evasive, but I also don't entirely know what he means.

"I'm serious, bro. Why are you even here?" It's eerie how much he reminds me of the boy I grew up with.

"I—" I pause, considering my answer. I came back to finish school, sure, but I could've done that anywhere. I considered it, but Astor was pulling me, calling me, like I had unfinished business here. Maybe it seems like I had a change of heart or just shifted gears when I left Astor, but to me it felt like I hit pause. Like a timeout where I just needed a minute to get my shit together. I came back here because I'm ready to hit play. I took a break and healed what needed to be healed. But I'm ready to get back to my life.

"You *left*, remember?" He's accusing me of more than just leaving my responsibilities. It feels like he's reminding me that I left him, and the flicker of hurt in his gaze would've been undetectable if I hadn't seen it so often in my own.

"Yeah, I did. And I want to talk to you about that, about Lily. Maybe we can—"

"Bro," he drawls out, exasperated. "That's not what this is about. You *left*, and the rest of us moved on with our lives. You're still stuck in the past, and I don't need you pulling the rest of us back into it."

I'm taken aback, in part because he's so flippant about Lily, which I haven't seen before— I'm used to his soul being crushed by the mere utterance of her name— but also because he's not wrong.

"I'm just here to finish school. Just want to get back to my life." I feel defeated. This is not how I wanted this to go.

"Cool. Do that, then. But stay the fuck out of mine." I shake my head in disbelief. I thought it could be different than this. "And while you're at it, stay away from Liv."

So this is about her. A shit eating grin takes over my face, that well of antagonism boiling to a point that it can't be ignored. "Sorry, brother. She really won't leave me alone for this story she's writing— she told you about that, didn't she?" I watch irritation flicker behind that gaze, but he quickly recovers, disgust replacing it.

"So what, you just come back? Try to get on *my* team? Try to mess with *my* girl?"

"Technically, I was here first." I can't help it, at this point, but I decide to reel it back when I catch his hand flex. I know my comments go against everything I learned in therapy but it's hard when I've been hearing around school all the ways in which Will mistreats Olivia. Regardless, I take a breath trying to regain control of the situation. "Hey, I'm kidding. I was serious when I said I just want to get my life back… but not at your expense." I let that settle with him, watch him take a breath. "It's been a while since we coexisted like this, Will."

"Yeah, no kidding." His jaw relaxes, but his posture is still guarded as he combs his hand through his hair.

"I'm not here to fuck up your life. I wouldn't do that to you." The words feel so perfect, and I mean them, but I regret them the moment they're out of my mouth.

I spent months in therapy working hard to not be the version of myself I was when I left here. It took just a few words from Will, one seething glare, for me to dip back into the person I was. One conversation with Olivia and, once again, she's consuming my thoughts, my conscience struggling to have any regard for my brother. I thought being a better brother to Will was going to be easy, but it might be the hardest part of this journey I'm on.

He gives me one last assessing look before nodding his head and walking off.

7

Olivia

I make my way from the parking lot to the wooden structure that barely passes for a bar. While McKinley's attempt at having a collegiate air was valiant, the over-whelming sense of debauchery couldn't be masked. The silhouette of a lion, the Astor Mascot, plagues the establish-ment— from the signage outside to the pint glasses my fellow students are holding to their lips. I reach for the door handle, the stickiness hugging each crevice of my palm. I grimace, ducking into the dimly lit bar while rubbing my hand on the side of my mini dress.

Almost immediately, I'm flanked with massive biceps and a chest that engulfs me. I let myself be swallowed by Grant's hug, the safety oozing through my body. I wasn't lying when I told Ben that Grant was one of my favorite people. He has a way of making me feel like everything will be okay.

"Olivia, how are you doing?" I feel him murmuring into my hair.

"I'm fine. This week's been hard but it always is this

time of year," I say, giving Grant a sad smile. It's odd how I never feel uncomfortable being vulnerable around him. He gives me a solemn nod, knowing he's one of the few people who still remember the anniversary of Lily's death.

"So I did something and I really hope it's not crossing a line. The last thing I want to do is upset you." His tone is serious and kind. I can't imagine a single thing Grant could do that would make me feel upset.

"I'm sure whatever you did will make me anything but sad." I look up at him, my eyes feeling glassy and tired.

He spins me around, softly gripping my shoulders. He pushes me toward the bar where I'm met with the most beautiful sign. Surprising, considering the atmosphere.

The Lily:
One part gin
Two parts tonic
Garnished with a Lily

I chuckle with the realization that the bar essentially is just making gin and tonics but even with my laughter I feel the tears that have been missing all week fall onto my cheeks. I wipe my face with my palms and playfully push Grant.

"You're amazing, you know that?"

"Now what are you doing calling another man amazing when your handsome boyfriend is right here?"

I feel Will's long arms wrap around my waist, his lips pressing into my neck.

"Don't be slutty at my party, Liv," he whispers, his breath reeking of alcohol.

Grant's eyes go cold in front of me, his lips forming a

straight line as he puts his hands in his pockets to hide the fact that his fists are clenched. Behind me, the door creaks open and in walks Ben, his 6 '4" frame towering over every-one, and his gaze immediately finds mine. I feel my stomach turn and suddenly feel hot, the way I did when his thigh pressed against mine at the game.

"Well, look who it is! My older brother," Will slurs, his tone friendly but his eyes something else entirely.

"You're drunk, Will," Ben retorts, without emotion. Annoyingly, his unaffected demeanor when it comes to Will's childish behavior turns me on even more than his perfect physique.

"I just don't want Big Foot over here killing everyone's vibe. The anniversary of Lily's death is *over*— why do we need to keep dwelling on this?" Will's voice has the familiar lilt it gets when he's trying to piss me off and it works. I feel my face falter at the public humiliation that comes along with your boyfriend disrespecting your best friend's death in the middle of a crowded college bar.

I see Gen approach Will and lightly grab his arm as if to pull him away.

"Let's get a drink." *Fucking Genevieve.* I pluck her hand off of him and she drops it to her side, her expression a mixture of disgusted and confused.

"Thank you, but that won't be necessary," I say, giving her a steely glance. "If you're going to be *drinking* anything, let it be water. You're not an attractive drunk, Will." I can see the visible rage in his eyes, the embarrassment when he notices how many people are watching, his fists tight balls at his sides.

Surprisingly Ben reaches for him, pulling him by the shoulder. "Let's get some air." Even more shocking, Will lets Ben drag him out. Something about Ben's commanding demeanor makes my spine tingle in a probably not so appropriate way.

"Hmm, saved by the older brother, huh, Livy?" Gen's slithering tone fills the silence of their absence immediately. Grant's gaze slides to the interloper. "Hello, Grant," she offers with a tight smile before quickly dismissing him.

"Gen," Grant begrudgingly acknowledges her. Not even Grant can extend his good graces to a girl like her.

"Genevieve, I'm shocked to see you here." I muster as much sincerity in my voice as I can, given how embarrassed I am by the scene that just unfolded.

Gen looks at me suspiciously, flashing a saccharine smile. "I've been everywhere, Livy. I know my way around."

"Particularly places you're not wanted, it seems," I retort.

"Wanted…. unwanted… guess it depends on who you ask," Gen taunts, batting her eyelashes. If I didn't have two unfortunate years of experience with her, I'd assume her audacious comments were an act. But I knew better.

I rub my fingertips together to warm them up, hearing Lily's voice in my head, *"Don't be mean to her Liv, she's sad, like your dad says— sad people tend to prey on the happy."*

I push her out of my mind. "If you're trying to imply that my boyfriend wants you here— I don't know if you noticed, but he completely ignored your offer to get a drink and went outside with his brother. I know you may just be immune to his constant rejection to your advances by now, but watching it in real time is truly mortifying for everyone involved." We square off, both shooting each other venomous looks before she shakes her head at me, raising her eyebrows slightly, as if I know nothing, as if I'm missing some sort of key piece of information, and when it comes to their relationship I probably am.

I try to ignore the women clamoring for their chance to be a part of Will's life, but when it comes to him and Gen, how close they are, how she seems to know everything before I do when it comes to Will, it becomes difficult to fight off all of my insecurities. Especially when the alarm bells are ringing in my head that the rumors swirling about the two of them just might be true.

Grant gingerly puts his hand on my shoulder. "C'mon Liv, she's not worth it." He stares bullets at Gen and something in her face shifts. It's almost indistinguishable, but I can tell those words from Grant meant something to her as he pulls me away.

* * *

"I'll take a Lily." I'm thankful for the heavy pour the bartenders here seem prone to. Grant stepped outside saying there was something he needed to take care of, and I assume it was related to a girl considering the complete lack of context he gave me. Alone at the bar, I take the drink, picking the lily out of the glass and rolling it between my fingertips in an attempt to warm them up.

"Can I just get an IPA?" A deep voice behind me finally inspires me to look up. I'm met with Ben's heated brown eyes, the darkness of them mysterious in all the right ways. I feel the pulse in my throat quicken.

To be frank, Ben is handsome in a way Will can't measure up to. Although Will's boyishness is charming, flutter inducing even, Ben has a darkness to him that draws something deep inside of me. His devilish, molten gaze is so intense you might not be able to find your way out of it. His coolness starkly contrasts the warmth that rolls off him, enveloping me like a wave in the middle of July.

I sense his broad chest crowd the space behind me as he reaches over me to grab his beer, feeling his breath blow in steady streams against the back of head. My shoulders brush against his hard chest as he moves to sit next to me, and a breath hitches in my throat. The coolness that emerges behind my back is quickly replaced by his persistent warmth at my side as he takes the seat next to me. His eyes flicker with worry as I stare back, too lost in all that he is to speak.

I swallow the lump that's been lodged in my throat from the moment he sat down.

"Do you think anyone realized that drink is basically just a gin and tonic," he asks, taking a long sip from his beer. I smile into my drink feeling his dark eyes assessing me.

"How's Will doing?" I ask, staring straight ahead at the liquor lined shelves of the bar, knowing if I meet his eyes the warmth of the liquor and his molten gaze will make it impossible to hide the heat from my face. He sighs and I feel him shift in the seat beside me.

"Well, he's definitely drunk," he glances over in Will's direction and we both spot him making small talk with a blonde girl in a shirt barely covering her chest. I roll my eyes and shake my head, not even surprised, feeling my face burn with shame, a knot forming in my throat.

Ben rests one arm on the bar, his muscled forearm making me feel lightheaded. I shouldn't be looking at him like this, but there is something about the alcohol flowing through my system, and knowing my boyfriend is talking up a girl across the bar, that makes me feel less guilty about checking Ben out. The short sleeves of his heathered, forest green t-shirt cut right beneath the slight swell of his bicep, his muscles subtly twining down the length of his arm. I instantly feel his closeness, his scent perfectly capturing the humidity right before it rains. Leaves, dirt, air— a smell that only the earth could concoct. His hand lightly laying beside his glass, begging to be held, causes me to shift a bit in my seat.

"So is the bar remembrance thing a yearly thing— or?" We both know he's trying to change the subject and I'm glad he's picked up on the fact that I don't want to acknowledge Will's whereabouts.

"No," I sigh, a frown stealing its way on my face and I bite my lip. "Grant put this together. Silly that I hadn't thought of it before… it's exactly the kind of thing she would've liked." My mind drifts to the night Lily and I stumbled into a happy hour in the Hamptons. We were high school juniors, but Lily was able to twist her tiny frame and bat her eyes enough to earn us a few drinks on the house. Before rounding the block to make the wobbly walk back to the house, she spotted a bunch of wildflowers, ripped them out of the ground, and ran back to shove them at our gracious bartender.

"When did you guys meet?" His voice has softened, the only hint of any shyness on his behalf. I try to ignore the fact that Will tends to avoid conversations about my best friend and her sudden death. I justify it by the thought that Will was there when everything happened— he went to Lily's funeral with me, he held my hand. Ben's kindness in this moment is disarming, and I have never been disarmed.

"Aren't I supposed to be the one interviewing you?" I say, cracking a smile that I hope conceals my sadness, and suddenly I feel the tears brimming in my eyes. I quickly blink them away while fixing my eyes back toward the liquor bottles.

What is going on with me? Since when am I emotionally

disarmed by a complete stranger. Sure— a handsome stranger, a stranger who happens to be the brother of my boyfriend of two years, the boyfriend who is currently flirting with some random girl at my best friend's pseudo memorial— but still, this isn't like me.

"I assume you were friends for a long time." He says again hesitantly, as if he realizes his questions may have overstepped my boundaries.

A few tears fall from my eyes, I wipe them off before Ben can get a good look at a girl who's apparently crumbling before him. "You could say that."

I suddenly have the intrusive thought to lay my head on his shoulder, burying my face into his neck. He seems like he would feel soft yet firm. I straighten in my seat trying to shake off all the emotions flowing through me about Lily and apparently now Ben.

"I'm sorry Will is…" he trails off, adeptly changing the subject.

"A dick?" I laugh, and he reaches out, wiping a tear off my right cheek as if we've known each other for years and didn't just meet a few days earlier. What's stranger is that I let him. My face flushes against his warmth and I feel a hum of electricity engulfing us as if there is some magnetic field pulling me toward him.

Our closeness registers as I take in the crowded bar with all of our peers and I sit myself firmly on my stool, careful to subtly correct the way I'd been leaning into Ben.

"Yeah, I guess you know him better than I do these days." I glimpse a hint of sadness, but he quickly ushers it away.

"Ha," I literally say as I scoff, "I know him so well that in the two years we've been together, this week was the first time I've met a single family member. The Chapmans are always too busy for me…" That's how it seemed. Almost like they went out of their way to avoid me.

His eyebrows pull together, then relax in resignation. "Well, lucky for you, I'm not a Chapman. You don't want to know them anyway." His soft smile buffers whatever sadness dwells just beneath the surface of those words and I can't help but offer a sympathetic one back.

"Don't look at me like that, Beckett," he distracts me with a flirtatious tone.

"Hmph," I hum, squinting at him in the dark corner of this bar. "Well, Chapman or not, I'm glad you came back."

His eyebrows shoot up in mock surprise. "Really? I've been upgraded from vigilante this quickly?"

My eyes roll without my express permission and I can't help but grin at him. "If you hold everything I say in the heat of the moment against me, you're going to have a hard time being my friend, Cabot."

"I think I'm going to have a hard time being your friend, regardless." He says more to himself than me as his gaze heats just enough for me to notice before it cools, as if he realizes that maybe he crossed a line by flirting with me so brazenly. He pushes back from his stool clearing his throat. "I should, uh, probably go find Will." I feel a weird sense of disappointment knowing this conversation is over. I glance around the bar realizing him and Grant are the only people here who I currently want to talk to and Grant seems to have disappeared.

"Yeah… Thank you. I don't have the capacity to deal with drunk Will right now," I say, pushing up from my own stool. "Can you let him know I walked home? I have an early day tomorrow."

He hesitates, concern flickering over his face. "Let me

walk with you," he says, shifting directions toward the front door rather than the back one Will walked out of.

"I'm starting to think you have a death wish, Cabot."

His smile reaches the corners of his eyes as they twinkle with mischief. "I can handle my *little* brother, Olivia."

"Who said anything about Will?" I wink, and as I do, I notice that my eyes are no longer damp.

I feel Ben's gaze on my back as I approach the front door, but when I turn around for a final wave goodbye, he's already gone. I wonder if I imagined the attention he paid me the last half hour, but I'm not delusional enough to imagine the way I felt. I shouldn't feel this way, right? Maybe it's not weird that I find Ben's company nice, or comforting, or oddly familiar, because I am dating his brother. Or I'm rationalizing because being near him makes me feel warm and safe, and the way he looks at me heats me in places I should definitely not be heated for anyone but Will. I take a deep, cleansing breath, deciding not to let the guilt bother me as I finally spot Will, the blonde girl leaning so far over the bar table you can now completely see down her shirt.

Barring our unfortunate meeting, my time with Ben has been an unexpected pocket of joy in the usually dark, never ending pit of grief this week brings. And I don't think I need to intellectualize that.

The thick coolness of the evening August breeze reminds me of my last night with Lily. Normally, this would have thrown me through my third spiral of the day, but it's about to rain, and the air is filled with more than fragments of the past.

8

Ben

Picking up the lily Olivia left on the bar, I tuck it into the pocket of my wallet, carefully flattening it in a way that it won't get crushed. I can't help but recognize the tattered stem, as if she had spun it between her fingertips a hundred times.

I can only imagine what it must be like to lose a friend, especially the way Olivia did. I looked it up after the fact: the odds of someone so young having a brain aneurysm are slim but… it happens. It feels almost surreal to me, that the night I was hoping to shoot my shot with her was the last night she spent with her best friend. That she went into that night imagining a very different tomorrow than the one that occurred. That after that night, things went so awry.

Dread trickles down my spine as I think back to our conversation about Lily. *She doesn't fucking know.* The thought haunts me, but I push it away, saving it for another time.

I suddenly feel Grant's mammoth sized bicep drunkenly wrap around my neck.

"Cabot, if you don't ask the coach to get back on the

team, I'll kick your ass myself." I chuckle knowing Grant wouldn't hurt a fly much less his best friend.

"So... Olivia Beckett..." he says with a smirk and a raise of his eyebrows, finally acknowledging his assumption out loud.

"Olivia is Will's, Grant," I sigh, feeling heat prickle up my neck.

"If there's one thing I know about that girl, it's that Olivia belongs to Olivia. She takes orders from no one," Grant's southern accent drawls.

"Granty-boy, are you talking about my girl again?" Will, also clearly intoxicated, stumbles over, half fighting, half laughing at Grant for thinking he has a shot.

"Relax Will, I brought her up," I say, rolling my eyes at my younger brother's unfounded confidence.

"She looked good tonight, didn't she big bro?" Will's eyes glimmer half jokingly, half seemingly wanting my approval. He is beyond his normal levels of hammered, that much is clear; his breath reeks of a scent reminiscent of rubbing alcohol. I spot Genevieve, her eyes clouded with emotion as she looks at Will across the bar.

"Looks like someone else wants your attention too," I nod to her, my seconds of eye contact making a deep flush overpower her entire body clearly embarrassed that I caught her gaping at Will, not for the first time in the past decade.

"Lately Gen seems more *your* type— thirsty, unless you've changed it up. Maybe Red over at the bar?" Will's eyes swim with mischief as he pours over the red head to our left. I can tell Gen overheard because she seems to have disappeared.

I stand to my full height, two inches above Will's frame. I dip my head just low enough for only Will to hear.

"I'm not the captain anymore, remember." His face twitches with irritation when he recognizes I won't take the bait. He's clearly attempting to formulate a coherent thought despite his drunken state when a thundering voice approaches from behind us.

"Will Chapman." Behind Will is a man who makes up in bulk what he lacks in height. Will turns to see who the voice belongs to.

With a drunken, arrogant laugh he says, "And who the fuck are you?"

I feel my shoulders tense, Will's reckless tone like oxygen feeding the impending fire.

"*Her* boyfriend," he points to the blonde girl Olivia and I saw talking to Will, currently cowering in the right corner of the bar, her pink crop top barely covering her breasts. Black mascara drips down her face as she cries, embarrassed by the scene brought on by her jealous boyfriend. Will laughs harder.

"It's always the short guys who get the most jealous." Still laughing, Will slaps my chest as if to ask if I agree. I grit my teeth, not wanting to get involved in Will's latest conquest. "Don't worry man, nothing was going to happen there. I always say hi to my fans," he winks at the girl whose expression is the picture of embarrassment. My jaw clenches further. Apparently, Will didn't come to fuck this girl, he came to fight her boyfriend.

The brick wall of a man in front of us clenches his fists so hard his knuckles have gone completely white. Struggling to quell his anger, we watch him attempt a calming breath. Trying to be the bigger person the guy says, "Whatever" and begins to turn.

"I was a little worried when you got back that I wouldn't be swimming in it. *Clearly,* I was wrong. That girl was dying to leave here with me. Who knows, she still might." Will directs this to me, but considering his volume it's clearly intended for the jealous boyfriend's ears.

His face turning from a strawberry blush to a deep beet red, the stout wall manages three quick steps back in our direction. Sensing his alcohol fueled fury, I step in front of Will.

"Listen, man," I say, shifting my face into the responsible, level-headed mask I've been known to wield. "He's just—"

One of those tightly clenched fists flies through the air, knocking into my cheek before skipping off my cheek bone. My assailant tumbles forward and catches himself on a stray bar stool. The pain instantly erupts through my cheekbone.

I feel Will before I see him as he steps toward me and the idiot who picked this fight. As if he recognizes his mistake, the dumbass puts his hands, now unclenched, palms out in the air. Will gives me a cocky smile, as if to say *'See? This guy is a moron,'* and I shake my head. At the same time, I feel what seems to be one of the stout man's friends grab my shoulders.

Will's smile is large now and if there's one thing to know about how we were raised, it's that we never back down from a fight. A small smile flits across my own features as my adrenaline spikes. This isn't the first bar fight my brother and I have gotten into. Nothing brings on a sense of camaraderie like a common enemy. Grant steps in as a few more of the smaller man's buddies move into what feels like a storm of fists. I feel blood trickle down my mouth and can sense that a black eye is forming as I grab a random man by his shoulders after he tackles Will. It feels like no time has passed when security finally breaks us up. But looking around, Grant and Will are almost as beat up as I am. Lucky for them, it seems their faces weren't affected.

The red and blue flashing lights coming in through the bar's windows snap me back to reality, enough to see Will on his knees doubled over as if this was the funniest thing he's ever seen. Grant can't keep himself from laughing, either, as we watch the smaller man get cuffed for starting the 'riot,' which is what the group of girls now flocking to Will told the police. I sigh as I extend my hand to Will, helping him up off the floor, the girls surrounding us like we're heroes, when in reality the fight was totally our fault to begin with.

Will rubs his hands on his jeans, his knuckles bloody.

"Thanks for stepping in, but don't make it a habit." His tone is weary as he shakes off the remnants of adrenaline the fight left behind, and I feel a pang of sadness. It's times like this where I miss my little brother, wish we had a closer relationship, or some semblance of a relationship in general.

"Yeah, sure. Won't happen again." I hear the defeat in my own voice as I watch Will leave the bar.

9

Olivia

Sitting in my early, Monday morning seminar, I'm hyper aware of rifling hands, rapidly clicking pens, and floppy notebooks hitting the tables. Topics in Women's Literature doesn't start until 8:45, but I'm here at 8:30 to suss out the most advantageous seat. Professor Delphi rarely teaches undergraduate seminars anymore, spending most of her time at Astor with her carefully selected circle of graduate students. While I was intrigued by the reading list, I was even more excited by the prospect of entering her orbit. A recommendation from Delphi, a woman publishing the kind of books that get you a meeting with the president, carries the weight of one library donation. At least.

The room is in the new English wing of Astor, funded in part by a hefty donation from the Newhouses. Three creamy ivory walls are interrupted by a series of four long paned windows conjoined to form the front of the seminar space, while the wall behind me is crowded with faculty publications and a heavy wooden door, engraved with the Astor Lion insignia. Above the door is a thinly framed clock with intricate hands. I check the time— 8:38. A few more students file in, and I see a red headed girl throw a sidelong glance at me and the seat I occupy. My eyes narrow and I shoot her a tight-lipped smile as I place my tote on the seat next to me. The early bird gets the worm, bitch.

I pull my legal pad out of my tote, placing it on the mahogany table in front of me. I'm dating the top right corner of the sheet when I hear a heavy door shut at the front of the room. A tall woman in chunky loafers strolls in, slamming her messenger bag onto the chair by the podium at the front of the room. Brushing her tawny bangs out of her face, she glances up from a freshly acquired notepad.

"Topics in Women's Literature?" she asks, scrunching her eyebrows at me.

I sense the girls around me freeze, and I answer "Yup" before the red head beats me to it. Delphi smirks at me, and I know I've already scored a point.

"Great," she continues. "It's 8:40, but we're going to get started. We've got a lot to cover, logistics to figure out, and I like to get out of here early. Driving around here is unbearable after 10:30." A few students chuckle nervously, obviously unsettled by Delphi's cavalier attitude. "Okay… who can tell me what they *think* is the first femin—"

The back door creaks open and heavy footsteps audibly mar the wooden floors. Determined to appear focused, I keep my eyes glued on Delphi. I start sifting through early feminist pieces of literature: *Wollstonecraft technically… but maybe Christine… the french one? The City of whatever? Shit.* I already know red-head is about to score a point. I'm managing the intense competitiveness surging through me when I hear a familiar voice.

"Sorry, my schedule said 8:45. It won't happen again," the faceless voice remarks softly, obviously self conscious about the masculine echo emanating from where he shuffles toward the front. I feel myself shiver recognizing immediately who that velvety deep voice belongs to.

"Oh, I started early. I just gave my 'Let's get out of here early spiel.' And now I'm doing my 'guess the earliest feminist work' bit, so you haven't missed much. Just grab a seat… if you can find one." Delphi flashes a crooked smile at the intruder, and I glance at the empty seat next to me. *Please let there be another seat. Please don't fill the air and space around me with all of your voice and scent and warmth and sarcasm and wit and—*

"Here's free! I think I recognize you from the other night?" the redhead squeakily offers. My jaw unwillingly tenses and I pointedly flip the pages of the syllabus that just landed in front of me.

I'm registering the absence of a response when I hear a low chuckle next to me.

"I think I'll sit here, but thanks." Ben responds as he slowly presses into the seat I'd so valiantly guarded just minutes before.

I take a deep breath and steel myself against the warmth that's already emerging from his body. There's really no reason for our chairs to be this close. Are they even that close? I refuse to glance anywhere but straight ahead.

"On time is late, Cabot," I mutter through closed teeth, slightly tilting my head to ensure he hears me. He chuckles in reply.

"Wollstonecraft," the cheeky red-haired girl remarks a bit pointedly, clearly frustrated by Ben choosing the seat beside me. I clear my throat, attempting to mask my glee at her obviously wrong answer. Even with the extra response time granted by Ben's late-but-on-time arrival, she still got it wrong.

"I am so glad you said so! But no. Anyone else?" Delphi's enthusiasm buffers the rejection apparent in her reaction and I can't help but smile. Knowing the coast is clear for even a partially correct answer, I readjust in my seat.

"*The Book of the City of Ladies,*" the voice next to me casually states. An unruly heat tingles from my neck to my breasts, swirling into my abdomen and threatens to travel further before I bite my lip and readjust in my seat. I'm too busy stifling how hot my body finds his knowledge of fifteenth century literature to be pissed that he basically cut me off.

I clear my throat attempting to regain my composure and add, "Christine de Pizan." Delphi confirms my answer with a warm smile.

"Yes," she commends, slightly nodding to me, then Ben. "Wollstonecraft was the first to explicitly outline a feminist manifesto of sorts, that is true, but Pizan's text is really our first recorded piece of literature whose purpose is feminist in nature."

Feeling Ben glance at me with a conspiratorial smile on his face, I shift my eyes down to my legal pad and begin writing notes, pressing the tip of my pen hard against the lined sheet, hoping the exertion will suppress the heat pulsing from my various erogenous zones. Delphi waxes poetic about the Brontë sisters, Woolf, Austen, Hurston, Morrison, and I struggle to keep up with her stream of consciousness lecture as the heady scent filling the seemingly shrinking gap between Ben and I overwhelms my senses. I still refuse to look, unwilling to break the focused persona I've crafted for Delphi.

"Now that I've given you the Spark notes history of women's literature, we can pivot to the content of our course." Delphi's smile is smug as her eyes survey the room. I gently place my pen on my legal pad, willing my gaze to remain steady. The scribbling of pens stops so quickly, I know I'm not the only one who feels like they've made a fool of themselves by frantically taking note of every syllable flying out of Delphi's mouth for the last thirty minutes. Ben leans forward in his seat, and I get a glimpse of his firm forearms as he places his elbows on our shared table. He is, naturally, unfazed by Delphi's pivot, seeing as he hasn't even taken out a sheet of paper.

"This year, I want to focus on the literature women are writing and reading *now*. If you want a class on the classics, feel free to visit the registrar and enroll in a different seminar. But if you're open to exploring how we might use feminist frameworks to decipher the allure and intention of contemporary women's fiction... then yeah. This is the class." One chair screeches against the floor, and the back door slams shut. I see the corner of Ben's determined jaw as he briefly rests his head on his hand and glances to the back of the room.

"Cool. Better than I thought," Delphi remarks, mostly to herself. "By the next seminar you'll need to have read Radway's 'Women Read the Romance,' and come prepared to discuss. Because I *despise* fluff discussions where you obviously haven't spent a minute considering the ideas I asked you to read about—" she pauses, taking a breath before continuing, "you're going to be going through all of our readings with a partner." I'm hoping the gulp that just traveled down my throat wasn't loud enough for Ben to hear. "I hate grouping students, so who you're next to is fine. Partner up, read the essay, come back next week ready to share your thoughts on popular women's fiction. Off you go!" And with that, Delphi gathers her notepad and pen, stuffs both into her faded cross body bag, and slides out the front door.

"So I guess we're gonna be—"

"Partners," I let out with a breath as I finally turn to face Ben. His warm eyes dance with amusement and he smiles at me. The smile draws my eye to his cheekbone, highlighted with bluish-purple hues. My fingers itch to reach out and brush it, but I brush them against each other instead. I feel a rush of worry accompanied by a wave of heat. The flush that had been confined to the clothed parts of my body spreads beyond my t-shirt and I feel it begin to creep up my neck. Eager to quell the biological reaction my body has to Ben's smile, I turn back to my notepad. "Perfect. Just another opportunity for me to get that story out of you."

"As if you needed an opportunity," he says, the slight lilt in his voice doing nothing to disguise his increasing amusement.

"Aren't you a quick study?" I arch my eyebrows, feigning surprise. "I guess you'll bring something to the table in this partnership, after all."

"You'll find I bring a lot more to the table than that." I catch his jaw tense briefly before he smiles sardonically, casually laying his arm across the back of my chair as if the tight space can't contain his tall frame.

"Ah, he's presumptuous too," I coolly drawl, attempting to put a lid on the heat his flirtation is stirring and the warmth of his arm now spreading across my back.

He lets out a soft huff, drawing his top teeth over his pillowy bottom lip. His eyes narrow and his warm gaze heats my face before it moves to the side, catching the time on the clock.

"If you have somewhere to be, please—" I blurt out, eager to end this exchange.

"I…" he hesitates, glancing at the clock again. "I actually registered for a morning lab so, yeah, I do. And if I'm going to walk and get there on time…" He pulls his arm away instantly leaving my body feeling empty with its absence as he moves to stand.

"Of course. Just text me so we can coordinate that partner reading."

"Partner reading?" That sardonic smile, again. I resent the blush I feel burn on the apples of my cheeks.

"Or not. She won't know we didn't read together." I force my right shoulder to shrug slightly. That chiseled jaw flicks again as he pauses, visibly considering my words.

The smile reemerges, the mocking partially replaced with what looks like delight.

"We can read together, Olivia. That's fine." He starts to push his chair back, but stops suddenly, pulling the legal pad from beneath my palm. The pen in my hand disappears as his fingers brush against mine, and he scribbles a series of numbers on the paper. "There. Now you won't have to ask Will."

Rolling my eyes, I forcefully push myself out of my seat. I'm embarrassed by his mention of Will, especially as I'm unable to douse the desire that has been lapping against me since he answered that stupid question.

Staring down at him I elongate my spine, shifting back into myself. I soften my features, allowing what I know is a luxuriously playful smile to grace my face. I float my hand to his shoulder, pushing past the hot sensitivity in my fingertips as they graze the soft cotton of his t-shirt.

"And he's thoughtful," I say, subtly tilting my head. "Don't worry. I can handle your brother," I almost whisper with a mischievous wink. I sweep my legal pad and pen into my tote before I meet Ben's gaze again. The amusement from moments ago is gone, now replaced by something I simply refuse to investigate.

"Bye, Benjamin," I cheekily throw over my shoulder as I make my way to the heavy wooden exit. I feel his eyes on me until I reach the bright September morning on the other side of the door. The late summer sun replaces Ben as the source of my full body flush as I survey the quickly crowding campus. *He's definitely going to be late.*

* * *

Sitting down on the cleanest patch of grass on Mawbry Lawn, I slip my legal pad out of my tote and type Ben's number into my phone. The bottom quarter of the sheet tears as I tug at the corner with the elegantly scribbled digits. Crumpling the sliver of paper in my hands, I stuff it to the bottom of my tote and make a mental note to find a trash can later.

"As if you needed an opportunity." I scoff quietly to myself as I rifle through my tote for my lip gloss.

"You'll find I bring a lot more to the table than that." The wand of my gloss slowly glides back and forth and back and forth over my chapped lip as I relive the bodily sensations that invaded me the moment Ben's words left his pretty mouth. I'm lost in thought when I feel two broad hands cup my shoulders from behind. Will's breath tickles the side of my neck.

"Hey you," he says before pressing a soft kiss to the spot

his breath caressed just moments before. Guilt inches up my throat and I swallow it down.

"Coffee?" I ask, tilting my head back with an innocent smile, focusing my brain's train of thought on the present. My hand reaches out to the side in anticipation of the cardboard cup Will is about to place in it. Not a moment later, an icy Americano in sheer plastic is in my grasp.

"I figured it was too warm for a hot one." It was.

Will was good at this, sometimes. Anticipating my thoughts and feelings when they weren't too complex, making decisions in my best interest when they weren't too high stakes. I slowly sip my midnight black iced coffee with one hand, passing my gloss to Will with the other. He slips it into my bag, and my heart skips a beat as I remember the wad of paper I'd shoved to the bottom of my tote just minutes ago.

It isn't that I'm hiding my association with Ben from Will; he knows I'm writing this story, so I'll obviously have to spend some time with him. And it isn't that I'm afraid of what Will might do or say, though I *would* rather avoid the fallout. I actually don't know why, exactly, I'm so hesitant to let Will into this tiny pocket of my life right now. The attraction is unsettling, yes, but I'm also not some shallow whore, powerless in the face of an extraordinarily beautiful man. Genevieve comes to mind.

It's that Ben both eases and unnerves me, and I don't know what to do with that. I think the unnerving has to do with his intense attention to my relationship with Will. Every time Will comes up, I feel like he's cracked open my head and taken a magnifying glass to it. His eyes get so earnest and thoughtful and I start to notice my chest aches.

Unnerving, to say the least. Anyone would say so. And

the fact that he, every now and again, puts me at ease, isn't so odd now that I think of it. *Grant puts me at ease, and I've never contemplated my friendship with him.* I'm being over analytical.

Will should have been more transparent with me about Ben. *Who dates someone for over a year and doesn't mention their literal brother? That's the source of all this weirdness.*

I smile, satisfied with my logic.

"Sip, babe. You're catatonic over there." Will's voice pierces my thought bubble and I feel my awareness click into place. Here, with Will, on Mawbry Lawn, on a beautiful, albeit warm, Monday morning. I turn my head so I'm taking in all of Will's boyish charm at once.

The sleeves of his Astor Hill Basketball crewneck are bunched up to his elbows, revealing bronzy, tanned forearms taught with the muscles he must've used while doing dribbling drills this morning. His hand reaches toward my face and his calloused thumb grazes an errant smudge of lip gloss beneath my lip.

"How were drills this morning?" I ask, snatching his hand with mine, pulling it into my lap. Rather than making contact with his usually smooth skin, I'm met by a rough gauzy surface. I look down, noticing slight bruising where the bandage fails to cover an obvious injury. It reminds me of the bruise I noticed on Ben's cheek earlier this morning; my mind is racing, considering all the explanations for what I'm realizing was a fight between Will and Ben.

"They were—"

"Did you hit him?" I demand, dropping his hand from my grasp in disgust.

"Wait, hit who?" Will's brows furrow in annoyance as the reality of who I'm talking about dawns on him. "Why the fuck do you care? It's not like you know him." I'm surprised by the irritation that overwhelms me.

He's not wrong. I don't know Ben, and I shouldn't care. I should be relieved that he's dropping his fixation on Ben even speaking to me, but part of me is disappointed that the person who is supposed to be consuming my thoughts doesn't know that someone else is.

In an attempt to shield my unfounded fury, I rise off the grass, brushing debris off the back of my thigh.

"Are you serious? Why are you making this into something? Olivia, you're being dramatic," Will huffs, his non-bandaged hand wrapping around my calf.

Looking down on him, I shake him off. "Oh, I'm sorry. Would you rather me assault you when I'm annoyed?" I see him roll his eyes right as I start to turn away.

"Fine. Genevieve just texted me that she got me some ice from Nero. Pretty thoughtful, huh?"

"I'm surprised she didn't get it from the food hall, considering her taste for sloppy seconds."

The sly glint in Will's eyes turns slightly feral. "Who says she's the one getting sloppy seconds?" My eyes widen. I know he's just trying to get a rise out of me but his blatant disrespect for me and our relationship seems to be the only consistency we have right now. Without a word I grab my bag and move to leave. "Wait—" Will says standing and dusting the grass off his jeans. "Chill— that was clearly a joke."

I refuse to speak to him blatantly, looking away as to not make eye contact with him. His arm circles around my waist and I roll my eyes, my aggravation subsiding only slightly at his gentle touch. He kisses me tenderly on the cheek.

"I really am running late, but I'm sorry. Call me when you calm down?" He grabs his basketball duffel off the ground leaving me standing there looking after him, wondering how many times I'm going to have the same argument until I can't anymore.

10

Ben

The gym door creaks open as my nostrils are assaulted by the familiar stench of sweat and rubber. The squeaking of sneakers fills the room as I hear the *thump, thump, thump* of basketballs hitting the vinyl flooring. The door slams shut behind me causing an abrupt stop to the series of drills being run by my former teammates. Slowly, every player on the court turns toward me, forming a line in front of the wall displaying a jersey with the number thirty-two and "Cabot" embroidered in white. Grant moves to the front of the line pushing the corner of the frame with his index finger until it gives. Catching it with ease he pulls the Jersey out and approaches.

"Finally, we've been waiting for you man," Grant says, so earnestly it makes my palms sweat with nerves, the men behind him beaming and clapping as if I had returned from war and not driven in from Boston.

"Cabot. Office— now," I hear Coach Arthur Wilson's voice boom from behind me. "The rest of you hit the showers." Coach Wilson is known for being tough on his players but had won March Madness the past several seasons, so his abrasiveness is well worth it.

I quickly pick up my pace to meet Coach Wilson in his office at the edge of the gymnasium. Jersey in hand, I wrap on the door with my fist, him having already beat me to the office.

"No need to knock son, I called you in, remember?" He's wearing a smirk on his grumpy withered face, one that he always had up his sleeve but only showed a few of his key players. *Don't need everyone thinking I'm soft*, plays through my head as I'm hit with instant nostalgia.

"Right, sorry." Grabbing the handle, I push the door shut softly and take a seat in front of him.

"What can I do for you today, Cabot?" Coach grumbles but under his tough as leather exterior his eyes betray him, filled with anticipation.

"I heard you gave Will my spot," I taunt, knowing confidence goes a long way with Arthur Wilson, and that beating around the bush gets you nowhere in this office.

"Your 'spot'? Ha!" He slaps his knee clearly trying to amplify how humorous he finds my claim. "Boy, that spot was gone the minute you stepped out of the building before your senior year. It wasn't my fault the best player we had was your little brother." Coach's eyes meet mine as if to say he wouldn't have picked Will if he didn't have to. I look away not wanting to admit that my own brother was my rival on the team or that the coach carried such harsh feelings about him.

"I want my team back," I gulp, meeting Coach Wilson's eyes. His brows furrow as if he is considering my statement.

"Your team?" Coach chides, this time laughing hard.

"I'll join even if I can't be captain again, hell I'll even try out." I can feel my pulse quicken as what was intended to be a demand to rejoin my basketball team turns to begging.

Coach looks out his office window at the court in contemplation. "You know… I haven't seen those men out there unify over something as quickly as they did when you walked into this building today. You're a good player Cabot, but you were an even better captain."

I feel my smile give away the cool exterior I was trying to put on in the face of my relentless coach. "Cool it, Cabot. You're a good captain, but you decided to leave. Here's the deal… I'm going to let you rejoin the team— I'll even let you be captain. With one condition…"

I tense my jaw having a pretty good idea what this "condition" would be.

"He has to be your co-captain," his eyes shift to the opening doors of the gym, the ones Will just walked through, "and you have to tell him."

As I leave the gym a gust of warm air hits my face. It's only September, but it's surprisingly hot for Massachusetts this time of year. I walk toward Mallard Hall where I'm meeting up with Grant outside the science lab, again thankful that I have a friend on the team. Even with the support of the guys, no one is brave enough to face the impending wrath Will is bound to release when I tell him the news. It was apparent Coach Wilson was afraid to tell Will himself, and thus gave me the job in doing it as some sort of sick punishment. Maybe he thinks Will won't implode on his own brother, but I know how wrong that assumption is.

I enter through the thick mahogany door of the building and am surprised when I'm met again with one of my framed jerseys. I wasn't here that long but apparently the several championship wins I brought the team were noted. I let the confidence filter through me, liking how important it makes me feel. Lord knows I haven't felt this way in a while.

That's when I see her.

My gaze goes from the white sneakers she's wearing all the way up her long tanned legs to the hem of her even starker white tennis skirt. My throat feels thick and hoarse as I try to blink, breaking my gaze only to be met by eyes like dictionaries, big and holding every truth I'd ever want to know. I try to remember the confidence I felt only moments ago but as soon as I feel her close in, it evaporates almost instantly.

"Come," she says, those big eyes filled with something like anger.

I follow, knowing I would follow her to the end of the earth if she asked me to, but trying to up the annoyance on my face to hide that fact. Finally, after following her halfway down the hall, I realize I have my size as an advantage. I slightly elevate the length of my stride, stepping in front of her like a wall. She's an inch away from my chest and blows out a stream of air before taking a step back.

"Do you need something from me? I'm meeting some-one," I say in an attempt to keep my voice even knowing my palms are sweating with anticipation.

Her face flushes and I feel bad for the coolness in my tone, but steel myself so my eyes don't betray me.

"When were you going to tell me that Will fucking hit you?"

I squint, trying to make sense of what she's talking about. I apparently look confused, as she reaches up and softly swipes her thumb over the bruise under my eye. I swallow hard, the touch rippling through me. I feel it in every single cell. She quickly pulls her arm away, biting her lip.

"Don't downplay your intelligence, Ben. It's hard to miss." I know the look she's giving me is meant to come across as cruel, but her pout draws my attention so intently that it's hard for me to think straight, much less answer her ridiculous question. "I guess you aren't 'downplaying' after all." She starts to push by me and I gently grab her arm. Again, electricity shoots up into my neck. I feel my pulse quicken as I let her go.

Her eyes go wide and narrow, but her face is too pretty to look as angry as she's hoping it will. I finally crack a smile which seemingly makes her more pissed.

"Are you going to talk?"

Laughing, I look down into her dark brown orbital eyes. "You think that Will… *Will* did this to me?" I shake my head, letting my laugh pick up when I see the pink beginning to fill out her complexion.

"He said he hit someone, and you look like someone who might deserve to be hit." Her teeth are gritted in anger and embarrassment, somehow making me more attracted to her. I push the thought away.

"Will didn't do this. Trust me, you would know if he did."

"And how's that?" she says crossing her arms over her ample chest.

"Well you saw him today, didn't you?" I look down at her, letting myself fully assess her body. I smile when she notices, her face flushing harder than before as she shifts uncomfortably.

"Obviously," she hisses. Her anger grips at my heart in an unhealthy way, her tense face consuming me.

"If he hit me, you wouldn't have." For a second I see her anger dissipate, biting her lip and looking up at me like she's assessing me for the first time. Luckily, before I start shifting uncomfortably under *her* entrancing gaze, I hear my name chanted across the hall.

"Cabot, Cabot, Cabot," three of my fellow teammates approach behind me. One of them, Andrew Spellman, throws his arm around my neck jostling me a bit. My eyes don't leave Olivia's.

"Ben the Bogart," Andrew croons, "I forgot to ask when you were in the locker room, but are you comin' to the bonfire tonight? The whole team will be there, and now that you're a Lion again you're obliged."

My eyes search Olivia's for any hint of excitement. Instead, I'm met with impenetrable darkness.

"You're back on the team?" Her eyebrows raise with interest.

"He's back baby," Andrew sings, patting me hard on the back. "Will better watch out because what Ben wants Ben gets. We don't call him Bogart for nothing." He gives a pointed wink to Olivia and I feel my jaw tense. I know Andy's good natured but I don't want Olivia to see the version of me he is referencing. The part left in the past.

I shake Andrew off, finally breaking my gaze from Olivia who seems to be studying me more intensely now. "Give me a minute, will you?" I grumble.

Andrew throws his hands up in defense. "Again, what

Ben wants Ben gets," he states, backing up and shooting yet another wink over my shoulder to the beautiful girl scouring me with her dark impenetrable gaze.

I turn to her, dropping my shoulders in an attempt to look relaxed… vulnerable. "Look, I haven't told Will yet. Could you keep this between us, at least until I talk to him tonight?" Her eyes continue to scour mine but I see a smile form at the upper right peak of her mouth.

She clasps her manicured hand onto my shoulder looking directly into my eyes. "I guess I'll give him my goodbyes." I look back quizzically, raising an eyebrow. Giving me a playful exaggerated pout and then turning it into a demure grin, she pushes past me. "Well he's definitely going to hit you now." Again the brush against my shoulder makes my entire body tingle with need.

I turn watching her hips wrapped in that tiny tennis skirt swing. She walks a couple feet tossing her dark chestnut locks, and looks over her shoulder, the glint in her eye letting me know that she's won the argument she set out for.

"Bye Ben, the *bogart*, was it?" she taunts, her voice electric.

The fire is huge by the time I arrive at the party and the air is filled with a thick smoke that fills my lungs. Instantly, I'm aware that the police will at some point arrive tonight as I make my way through the yard that is mostly dirt and sand, with small patches of grass scattered throughout.

I've been to a lot of parties but somehow these bonfires seem to get bigger every year. There have to be two hundred of my peers in attendance and again I'm shocked by how many recognize me. I was used to this when I was at Astor a few years ago but right now, it feels strange. Like I'm posing as someone I'm not. A school's basketball star without a care in the world, yet in reality I go to therapy twice a week and have to count my breathing anytime something gives me even a twinge of anxiety.

I approach the team who are grouped around the fire with their various girlfriends and groupies. In the center of the crowd is Will and Olivia. Seeing them from afar, it's clear why they would be together. Will, the classic golden boy, and Olivia… well Olivia would compliment anyone. It's hard to think straight when looking at her and I feel myself shift my gaze. Immediately I feel intimidated, as if the crowd didn't part for me like the red sea when I arrived. I used to run this school and even now I hear the giggling of a group of girls closely following.

I turn and meet the eyes of the redhead in my women's lit class with a blonde and brunette clamoring at her side. In a past life I would've seen the three of them as a total score, but tonight I just feel tired, already knowing I'm going to kindly pass. It's not that she isn't extremely attractive— she is; her freckles contrast with some of the fairest skin I've ever seen and her red hair is thick and long, glorious even. Her pink top is clinging to her tightly, exposing both her cleavage and her midriff. Some would consider her beautiful. Even so I feel my gaze go cold in their direction, although the three of them seem oblivious to what I hoped was clear rejection in my eyes.

The brunette shrieks, "Oh my god Sara, he's looking right at you!"

I turn forward letting my eyes privately roll. When I refocus I'm met with an amused smirk that ties me in knots and a face that Sara's doesn't stand a chance against. Olivia's.

As I approach, I hear Andrew call out to me.

"Hey Ben, don't look now but the ultimate threesome is behind you!"

I furrow my brows in frustration. Olivia's eyes cast an intense glower at the girls following, her interest piqued. I can almost hear Sara's audible gulp. She must notice Olivia's face too. The entire team turns toward me expectantly as I make my final stride into the inner circle. I can feel Olivia's gaze on my skin, assessing me carelessly considering Will is at her side.

"Interesting you decided to show up considering this event is for the basketball team." Will is seemingly trying to impress the girls surrounding him on both sides, and to his benefit Gen does seem impressed, her shoulders shaking in quiet laughter. Olivia on the other hand seems irritated.

"There's over a hundred people here— it seems word got out babe." She rolls her eyes. I feel my stomach twist, at the awareness that she's defending me. Her eyes again wander to the girls hovering about twenty paces behind me and I witness her delicate hands curl into small fists at her side. Instantly, her jealousy turns me on as I watch her glower in frustration.

My interest is interrupted by Grant's buoyant laughter.

"He knows it's an event for the team Will, that's why he's here." My stare snaps from Olivia to Will as her eyes move from Sara to me.

"And how the fuck does that make sense?" Will spits at Grant. His rage is clear as his entire frame tenses. I catch Grant realize his mistake as he looks between me and my brother. His voice goes small in a way that's almost comical for such a giant specimen.

"I… I thought you knew Ben was back on the team, man." Will huffs loudly as he realizes that the entire team is now staring at him due to his outburst. He takes a step toward me. His hot breath comes out in short spurts of anger as he tries to regain his composure.

"Is that it, you're just back on the team?" I feel his glare consume me as he tries to piece together my expression. It isn't until I meet his eyes that he knows the truth. The message passes through me wordlessly, both guilt and pride blazing from my frame as I look down on my younger brother. Grant must sense that Will understands the full picture now as he somehow is right behind my brother with his massive hand on his shoulder. "You took my captain spot?" Will's voice is riddled with betrayal. Even Olivia flinches at his tone. The entire group has gone silent all watching to see what will happen next.

"Calm down man, it's just a game," Grant's hushed tone meant to be calming but coming off afraid.

"Just a game?" Will's hands ball Grant's shirt pulling him tightly to him. "He stole my seat as captain and you're telling me to calm down. He fucking left. He gave that seat up."

"We're sharing it," I say firmly, my eyes laser focused on Will. "The spot— we are sharing it." I let out a breath.

I see Olivia shift uncomfortably, and she seems to have schooled her expression to appear bored, but the way she seems to almost rhythmically tap her fingers together indicates she's as worried as the rest of the audience. Finally, Grant, who seemingly has had enough, gently plucks Will's hands from his shirt. Will may be strong and large, but Grant is stronger and larger, and Will knows it.

"This is fucking unbelievable." Will growls.

"Let's get a drink, calm you down a bit." Grant now has

Will by the arm, forcibly moving him through the crowd. A couple paces in, Will shakes him off stomping forward to the bar. The crowd seems to watch for a moment longer before Andy breaks the silence.

"Now that *that* is over, is anyone up for a game of flip cup?" A few people get up to go to the long fold out table to our right while others pick up where they left off in their conversations. I quickly realize it's only Olivia and I who are still standing there looking at Will.

"That was some show. Do you always steal other's dreams and aspirations, Cabot?" Olivia looks at me slyly, seemingly unbothered by Will storming off. My adrenaline is still running high. A few years ago I would've brought Will to the ground in front of everyone if he had put his hands on Grant like that. I'd have purposefully shown him his place in front of everyone just to knock him down a peg.

"That depends, has Will been dreaming about you lately?" It comes out before I can stop it and instantly I regret what I said. I know it's wrong, I know that I'm just repeating the cycle that is my damaged relationship with my brother.

Olivia's eyes widen only slightly. I caught her off guard and the only proof is the heat that has now risen above her cleavage and up her neck. She takes a couple paces forward, closing the space between us. Her fingers flick to my shoulder brushing off an invisible piece of lint and then moving down to lightly press against my chest. The knot in my stomach has made its way into my throat. Tingles multiply up and down the trunk of my body. She stands taller, bringing herself up to her tiptoes, she whispers, "I should get back to my boyfriend."

My stomach drops as if I threw myself off a thirty story building. I feel cold sweat form at my temple. Not even twenty feet away, three beautiful women are giggling at the idea of taking me back to their dorms and yet here I am entranced and gutted by a girl who I can never have. She walks toward the bar turning at the last minute to peer back at me with a smile that disorients me.

"Don't forget we're studying at your place Friday."

With that she disappears into the crowd.

11

Ben

The sky is black as I walk toward the gym. It's 5:30 a.m. as I chug my protein pre-workout coffee, hoping the caffeine gives me a much needed boost at my first practice back. Lucky for me, Coach typically sits this one out, doing game scheduling and play making with the assistant coaches, while the captain, or I guess now *captains*, take the team through speed drills. I walk in and almost everyone's already there warming up. I spot Will, immediately making my way towards him. I've thought a lot over the course of the past few days about how I hope our partnership can go. We both take basketball more seriously than anything else in our lives and I doubt he wants me to get in the way of it just as much as I don't want him to.

His eyes acknowledge me as I reach him.

"Yo," he says, stretching his hamstring.

"Hey— so I was thinking we could lead the team through some basic drill conditioning. Maybe a few passing drills too?" I move to the mat beside him attempting to do some calf stretches.

"Sorry man, we're doing shooting drills." He says it dismissively as if I'm merely suggesting something. As if I'm a second string power forward and not the leading point guard and co-captain of this team. I bite the inside of my cheek trying to be cognizant of the fact that Will has been running the team the past few years I've been out and he hasn't done a bad job. Granted, they've only won one championship, but they've still been in the top 5 college teams every year.

"I think it may be more beneficial, since it's the start of the season, to get in touch with the basics." I try to hone my tone into one that will be more palatable, knowing how easy it is to set Will off when it comes to how to best play this game.

"*You* might need to get back 'in touch' with the basics, considering you haven't played on a team in years," Will says, his tone mocking, "but I think the rest of us are ready to drill half court shots."

I feel my eyes narrow and I try the breathing techniques as I move through my stretches. I know that I spent the entire time I stayed at Pop's training, but Will doesn't. I would constantly pick up games at the local gym, playing against anyone who was able. Lucky for me, Pop's gym was one of the best in the metro Boston area and numerous athletes trained there.

"Of all the shooting drills to do, you think half court is what we should be spending our time on?" My tone is incredulous and Will's frustration is coming off him in waves.

"Brothers, brothers," Andy chimes in trying to use humor to get us to calm down. "You're in luck, because I have the perfect idea for this conditioning practice." Will and I both roll our eyes, used to Andy's typically idiotic ideas. "A scrimmage."

Will's eyes light up as he glances at me, trying to gauge what I think of the idea. I shift on to my feet, frustrated that we aren't going to do the drills I think would be most valuable. But a scrimmage would be fun, and what better way to show Will how hard I've been training than to publicly kick his ass.

"I can't believe I'm saying this Andy but, good idea." I nod toward Will. "You want first pick of teams?" Wills eyes dance, loving the idea of getting to compete.

"Nah bro— why don't you pick first? You need that home field advantage." He winks, patting my chest before kicking up a nearby basketball, dribbling it once before shooting a perfectly arched 3 pointer. Grant lets out a low whistle.

"Line up boys— we're starting," I yell, getting the team's attention, instantly in game mode.

The scrimmage starts slow but I immediately recognize that Will's not playing for fun. He's playing to win. This meaningless friendly game isn't meaningless or friendly to either of us.

Grant whips the ball toward me as I go in to do a layup. The score board, though changing frequently, is neck and neck.

"Yo Will— I'm free," Andy yells, but Will moves forward, ever the MVP, and goes for a three-pointer that bounces off the frame into my waiting palm.

"Fuck," he growls, running full speed to successfully block the hook shot I'm about to throw. I square my jaw as the team around us starts to fade and all I see is Will. He moves to half court where I quickly disrupt. He's quick, sweeping the ball in a turnover. This goes on, both of us running back and forth across the court, not allowing the others to make a single shot until I'm brought back to reality with the coach's whistle.

I freeze the ball above my head getting ready to throw a 3-pointer and Will slams to a stop in front of me, his hands stretched high to block. We both turn, seeming to realize at the same time the rest of the team is now sitting on the bleachers in awe of what has unfolded in front of them. How many shots did we block from each other? How long did this play go on? Why didn't anyone stop us? Did they try?

"CABOT, CHAPMAN. YOU'RE DONE FOR THE DAY. LOCKER ROOMS NOW. THE REST OF YOU RUN DRILLS. COACH WALTERS WILL LEAD," our coach's voice booms and he's clearly pissed at us hijacking practice, but he can't hide how impressed he is by the game of 1:1 he just saw play out.

We get to the locker room and Will immediately slams his duffel bag on to a nearby bench.

"Fuck," he shouts out, banging a passing locker with his hand. He chugs his water, pouring it over his head, trying to get a hold of the adrenaline I feel pulsing through me too. He sits on the bench roughly, putting his head in his hands.

"You good man?" I ask taking a drink from my own water bottle.

"Who did you train with?" he asks, his tone accusatory.

"What?"

"Don't play dumb, Ben. Who did you train with when you were in Boston? Clearly, you weren't just sitting around doing nothing."

I feel flattered but I can tell it's not meant to be taken that way. Will's pissed; I'm sure he was hoping for my immediate demise. That I would show up out of shape and out of practice and be made second string.

"Some of us are just naturally gifted, I guess," I try to crack a joke, the way I used to years ago after winning a scrimmage. But things aren't the same and that's obvious as Will slams the locker he's standing beside with his fist. "Will —" My concern is immediately cut off.

"This isn't fucking funny, Ben. My life isn't some sort of joke you can just come in and fuck up." Rage seems to waft off him as he pushes his hand through his hair. "Why can't I have anything? Why do you take everything that's mine?"

I swallow, starting to hear Will for what feels like the first time.

"C'mon man, basketball has always been our sport." I move toward him.

"Stop— Ben, just stop. 'Our sport,'" he repeats the words to himself shaking his head. "Everyone has made it very fucking clear that basketball is your sport. YOUR. SPORT. One that I happen to also be good at. But never as good as the great Ben *fucking* Cabot."

I sigh leaning against my locker knowing there's more coming by the look on Will's face.

"And basketball isn't enough for you is it, Ben?" His eyes narrow as his tone turns steely.

"What are you talking about?" I ask even though I know exactly what he's talking about.

"Does Olivia ring a bell to you?" He inches toward me getting right up in my face. "You know, 5'8", brown eyes, drop dead gorgeous? Oh, and I almost forgot, my *fucking girlfriend*, who somehow keeps talking to you." I clench my jaw knowing that if he throws a punch I won't be able to stop myself from hitting him back. He steps back shaking his head in disbelief when he spots my clenched fist.

"You're unbelievable man, you know that?" My teeth grind together trying not to lash back out. "Do you have nothing to fucking say?"

I close my eyes and take a steadying breath.

"Why are you lying to her?" My voice is cool but calm as I narrow my eyes at my brother. His eyes shift from anger to confusion to pure rage.

"Fuck you, Ben. You don't know what you're talking about."

I move closer now, getting in his face but I keep my voice calm.

"Lily, Will. I'm talking about Lily."

He pushes me back not hard enough for me to fall but enough to send a message.

"Don't fucking say her name again." His tone is low and seething. His eyes have turned into an emotion I haven't seen. The piping anger is so hot that if I say one more word we both will probably get kicked off the team from the altercation that would inevitably happen.

"She doesn't know. How could you not tell her?" Faster than I can get the words out Will has me pushed hard up against a locker, his entire body trembling with anger.

"It's none of your fucking business. It's no one's fucking business. It never was." He pushes me hard and I let him, taking into account the flurry of emotions traveling across his face. His anger turned into sadness and back again. Two years worth of grief filtering through him in only a few moments.

"Hey." My tone is soft as I put a steadying hand on his shoulder, something I learned in therapy that Pop's used to do for me. I sense there is more going on here than me beating him at basketball or flirting with Olivia. This seems to help some of his anger subside as he releases his fists from my jersey, stepping away from me and running his hands over his face. "What's going on with you?" I ask, trying to not cause him to spiral into another anger induced rampage.

"I just don't want to talk about her. Not now, not ever. That part of my life is over and if Olivia ever found out… You don't get it man. When you left, she was all I had." He sits on the bench behind him staring at the ground.

I shake my head stunned. I try not to think about how I left Will hanging, left him to deal with everything alone. I refused to see that him jumping into a relationship with Olivia wasn't him being a shit stirrer, but instead was him refusing to deal with his own emotions. I sit beside him trying to think through what I should do.

"I know this is shitty Will, but there are other people's emotions at play here."

Will sneers. "You mean your emotions, right?"

I scoff, surprised. "What are you talking about?"

"Don't play dumb Ben, it's so fucking obvious. I see how you look at her and I get it. Why wouldn't you? Hell, the whole school looks at her that way. But at the end of the day Ben, it's me and Olivia." He stands throwing his duffel over his shoulder. "Do you understand what I'm saying? She's mine, Ben. I won. So stop fucking with my life and move on."

I feel my fists curl, unable to control the anger now a rising tide within me. To some degree I know he's right— it is him and Olivia but the fact that he treats her like a trophy on his mantle, that is what my temper can't seem to handle. I stand to my full height getting close to my brother and looking down into his eyes. He matches my glare but I sense his unease as he clenches his jaw.

"Understand this, Will. You may think you 'won' but as

you saw today you only 'win' when I'm not playing." I shove him a few inches backward. "If you don't tell her, I will." I spit the words out and he flinches.

"You wouldn't." He shakes his head incredulously.

"Wouldn't I?" I feel the sinister grin spread across my face before it falls. "You walk around here treating her like she's half the woman she is. You're right when you said I look at her the way everyone else at this school does. Everyone at this school except you." I shove him again, my anger building. "The only reason I'm not taking care of this for you is *because* you're my little brother. You need to handle your shit, Will. You want to beat your 'big bro'? You wanna be the 'big man' on campus?" I shake my head at him as if he's the most pathetic person I've ever seen. "Then fucking act like a man and handle it." I finally shove past him pushing out the double doors into the autumn sun.

The parking lot is basically empty as the first cool gusts of autumn waft through the leaves. I take a deep inhale trying to dwell the panic gurgling within me. My phone buzzes and I feel my breath hitch when I see the name on the screen.

OLIVIA

Still on to study Friday?

I take a long drag of the cool outside air, letting the breath coat my lungs.

Can't wait.

12

Olivia

Climbing up the brick staircase, I feel my phone buzz in my bag.

BEN

Door's open.

Definitely not a man of many words, at least not over text. I reach the third story of the brick building, relieved that the old world exterior does not extend to the interior furnishing. Not that I don't love old world charm— I *am* a Nor'easter. I just appreciate an updated take on the 18th century. As I glance around, I notice that the wall sconces, while authentic, have been polished, but the crown molding has been swapped out and freshly stained a deep walnut shade. My eyes dart between the unit numbers on either side of the hallway, finally spotting *314* at the far end. The largest suite. Of course.

Standing in front of the door, I check the text again. *Door's open.* Something about just waltzing into his apartment feels too familiar. I gently rap my knuckles against the door, the sound swallowed by what I now understand to be an original piece of infrastructure in this colonial brownstone.

Sighing, I turn the brass knob, pushing forward to reveal dark walnut floors that mimic the crown molding. The walls are a soft white, clean except for a few strategically placed art pieces. *I did not take Ben for an art guy*. I round the corner, escaping the narrow entryway, and notice that the spacious living room is equally as clean and bright as the foyer. Hearing a subtle whir, I whip around to see the kitchen. My eyes and ears track the whirring to a vacuum leaving its dock, clearly just beginning its scheduled task. I notice the tidiness of the kitchen and living room, the pristineness on full display over the kitchen's glossy bar top, when a deep inhale has me registering notes of cedar and musk. I trail the scent deeper into the apartment, taking a left rather than a right, pausing on the fact that there is a left *and* a right to take. *I did not take Ben for an old-money apartment kind of guy, either*. A sunny room takes shape to my right, lined on either side by two brilliant, beautiful built-in bookcases. The wall between the two is consumed by two nooks and two sets of french windows. The tiny slivers of wall not possessed by the nooks or the case are, like the rest of the apartment, a soft white. In the center of the room sits an oversized, deep green ottoman, creamy pillows scattered across the almost bed-sized expanse. The piece sits atop a simple ivory rug, waffled but seemingly plush. I'm scanning the books lining the walls when I remember why I'm here.

Annoyance pushes my curiosity far away when I realize I'm wandering around Ben's apartment, un-greeted. The books and burning candle fumes hint that he's near, so I release an audible huff and plop onto the ottoman that was, truly, beckoning me anyway. I slip off my flats, testing the plushness of the rug and hearing the creak of a door, I quickly slide them back on. Attempting to look as bored as possible, I gaze out the window. *About time.*

Summoning a tart smirk, I remark, "Don't worry, your vacuum did a perfect job of greeting me."

I pull my gaze up the solid, towering form that's appeared before me, clad in only a bath towel secured by the hand on his hip. The quirk of his lips, struggling to stifle an amused smile, does quick work of my annoyance. It's gone before I can reel it back, replaced instead by a flush of embarrassment and… something else. His chest is bare, revealing the hardened muscles I'd assumed were there. What stun me are the intricately tattooed lines, curves, and sketches that highlight the muscled terrain of his chest. They stop just above his bicep, which I'm guessing is why I'd never imagined him like *this.*

Which I definitely haven't. Not even after he made that comment about stealing me from Will's dreams.

His hair, freshly tousled by a towel, lays and doesn't lay every which way, quietly dripping water on the wooden floor.

"I'm greeting you now," he says with a playful grin. "I'm sure you'd rather be greeted like this than by me dripping in sweat after practicing in the outdoor gym." My mind briefly considers Ben like this: sweaty, exhausted, muscles tense from hours of strenuous dribbling up and down the long expanse of the court. I'm not sure I'd be any less affected.

"I don't think I could bring myself to care either way."

He's staring at me, his brows furrowed in what seems like a challenge or a question. I feel my pulse quicken, so I stand up and stride over to the bookcase on the left. Pretending to inspect what is obviously the post-modern section of the collection, I play with snarky remarks in my head.

"I assume you're going to get dressed now, unless you're developmentally stuck in that one phase… where you're preoccupied with your own nudity?"

I sneak a glance over my shoulder, catching his grin widen. I wait for the reply, only to hear what I assume is his bedroom door shut with speed.

I'm mulling over the wittiness of my remark when I hear him approach the bookcase, stopping to stand nearly shoulder to… temple with me. Standing like this, I'm struck by the height of this man. He's a pillar next to me, grounded and towering, immovable it seems. His hair is still a tousled mess, but it's damp rather than dripping, and the beautifully tattooed skin taut over his tight, muscled chest is now hidden by a light gray t-shirt.

"Assessing my development or thinking about me nude, Beckett?" he asks, dipping his head to the right.

I know he's being his facetious, flirtatious self but my face warms anyways. Feeling my phone vibrate again, I use it as an excuse to avoid answering the question and slip it out of my back pocket.

Will.

A red dress loads as the first message, two thin straps held up by two feminine hands.

Gen.

The dress is fine, a little slutty, and not my type.

> WILL
>
> For the gala. ;)

I would have preferred it in black, but who am I to have a prefer-ence. I shut my eyes and feel them roll. Forcing them open, I take a slow, deep breath, pushing my anger back into the vat of emotions I frequently access when I'm dealing with Will.

I click my phone screen off, feeling Ben's gaze on the screen. Clearing my throat, I roll my eyes upward, my brows rising in irritation.

"Do you have something to say?

His mouth opens then shuts, finally sighing and breathing through his nose.

"Just seems obvious you wouldn't wear a dress like that," he says, looking everywhere but at me. My skin prickles, my pulse fluttering high in my throat like it did whenever Lily would see right through me like this.

"Maybe I would," I say a little too defensively, pushing my hair behind my ear, willing my eyes to keep contact when he finally looks at me. I hold his gaze that has turned inquisitive, assessing. "Stop looking at me like that."

"Like what, Olivia?"

My arms cross on their own, my body suddenly feeling naked under his stare.

"Like you know something I don't. If you have something to say just say it, Ben."

He breaks his stare, but not before I see the fire in his eyes cool. "I'm sorry," he says, his tone shifting into slight annoyance. "It's *your* boyfriend buying you lingerie with another woman, not me. I'm just your study partner, Olivia."

And then he's down the hall. I'm instantly cold, the sensitivity of my skin now transformed into chilled goosebumps— the heat I've come to associate with Ben's nearness replaced by the coolness of his disdain.

I pull my Astor crewneck out of my bag, pulling it over my head and onto my chilled body. Cracking my neck, I focus on regaining my composure and trace the steps he made to what I assume is his bedroom. I find him at the desk adjacent to the bed in the middle of the room. It's slightly raised, covered in simple navy linens laid atop white sheets. Like the rest of the apartment, the walls are white and contrast with the walnut floors and crown molding. I awkwardly stand at the threshold, wondering if I should just leave. I refuse to be anywhere I'm not wanted but… against my better judgment, I cross into his room.

Searching my mind for the right thing to say, I land on, "I'm sorry if I was… a bitch."

Without looking at me, he says, "Don't call yourself that, Olivia."

Grabbing two stacks of papers, he leans out of his chair and hands me the article we're supposed to be reading. I'm half expecting the fiery, molten gaze I've grown used to when he meets my mine, but all I find are cool, dark pools of indifference. He smirks, but it fails to reach his eyes.

"I guessed you didn't bring your own copy, so I made you one."

"Thanks," I offer with a warm smile, accepting the article. He's right, I didn't. *Just like he was right that I wouldn't wear a dress like that.*

Glancing around the room, I notice there aren't any other chairs for me to sit on. "I can grab a chair from…" The dining room, I want to finish, but I didn't quite get to that wing of the apartment.

"I can grab you one, or you can use the bed."

He catches my hesitation and adds, "Don't worry, I won't be on it," that familiar mischievous glint slightly peaking through.

Stop being weird, Olivia. You made this weird. Make it unweird. Be normal. Reaching into my well of charm I respond, "What a gentleman. Don't mind if I do." I sling my bag on the bed, sliding my flats off before I propel myself onto the neat arrangement of sheets, landing in a thud.

Making a show of inhaling the sheets, truly enamored by the scent. "You know, I don't think I've ever been in a guy's bed that smells *this* good. What *is* your secret, Cabot?" Sitting up, arms slightly stretched behind me, I catch him watching me. Ignoring the surveillance, I move my brows in question.

He blinks twice, subtly shaking head before answering. "Money. And a daily cleaning service." The playful grin is back, his eyes pleasant. An improvement.

"Well. I have got to get one, because this—" I inhale one more time, deeply— "is unreal." I finally hear a chuckle escape, his shoulders releasing just a bit. "Okay. How do you want to do this? We could take turns or read alone and stop at intervals to discuss?"

He picks up the article, rifling through, counting how many pages we have to get through. "Let's read it alone, share thoughts at the end, compare notes?"

Slightly disappointed that he chose the isolated option, I mutter, "Cool."

"Okay. See you in thirty." Flashing a soft smile at me, he grabs the over-ear headphones on his desk and slides them on. He uses his phone to set a thirty minute timer and balances it against the back ledge of the desk so I can see. I watch him grab a pen and highlighter from a pen holder, the pen quickly becoming a spinning baton between his fingers.

I'm mesmerized by the adeptness with which he twirls the pen, swiftly stopping to jot a note, seamlessly resuming the twirl, when I notice there are only twenty minutes left on the timer. I start reading, only to realize that I didn't bring a pen. Inching myself off the bed, I quietly walk to the desk and reach across the article Ben is pouring over to grab one of his pens. I'm mid reach when I feel the fingers that were preoccupied with the pen wrap around my wrist. His other hand pulls his headphones down around his neck, and his head cocks to the side, a smirk of disbelief gracing his face. The skin around my wrist grows hotter the longer his fingers firmly grip me.

His eyes squint up at me, mocking me. "No article, no pen? I'm just admiring *how* unprepared you are." His grip brings my attention to the quickening pulse in my wrist. He suddenly releases it, the mockery in his eyes guarded with the kind of caution you use with a stranger. He nods, permitting me to grab a pen, and offers me a shallow grin.

I roll my eyes, grateful his mood has improved enough that teasing me is on the table, even if it was fleeting. Taking the pen, I hop back onto the bed and finish the article. My eyes are heavy, intent on falling shut, when I hear the alarm on Ben's phone go off.

Stretching my arms above my head and legs out across the bed, I stifle a yawn. "I think I need to sit with this, " I admit, certain I don't have any coherent thoughts after half-reading-half-sleeping through the article. It's not that it wasn't interesting, it was that half way through I was overcome with exhaustion. I'm not about to offer my half-baked ideas to Mr. Feminist Literature Aficionado over here.

Standing out of his chair, Ben mimics my upward stretch before agreeing. The hem of his shirt inches upward, and despite the fact that I just saw him shirtless an hour ago, my mind takes the bait. My hands tingle with the desire to fist the sides of his shirt, and I imagine him leaning over me on this bed, making it easy for me to pull the shirt off him. I picture my hands tracing the labyrinth of ink on his chest, his hard, smooth muscles possibly twitching in anticipation of where my hand might go next. "Let's regroup tomorrow. I can't say I totally grasped everything either," he says before grabbing my bag and placing my now slightly crumpled article into it.

"Well, thank you," I say with a breath, reaching for the bag in his hand. "The bed *was* insanely comfortable. Ten out of ten. Truly." I wink just as his fingers brush mine, and I feel him still just as I do. Our gazes are locked for a second too long, broken only when I watch his gaze settle on my mouth. The attention is unnerving, and I involuntarily bite my lip before pressing them together. If there were only an inch between my lips and his, I wouldn't be surprised. Despite the distance between our faces, my face heats anticipating him closing the distance with ease. My pulse is erratic, waiting for him to press those supple lips against mine. I lean in just enough for him to notice, and his gaze shifts back to mine. Ben's lips betray him by erupting in a smile. He looks away, scoffing, his hand running through his hair, and when he lands back on me his eyes glitter with amusement. I release a breath I didn't know I'd been holding, the anticipation fleeing my body, lust-filled regret moving in to replace it. A nervous laugh escapes me as I pull the bag over my shoulder and move toward the door.

"Okay well… I'll leave the way I came I guess." What I'm sure is an awkward smile graces my face. I couldn't pretend to be unaffected if I tried.

"Not a chance, Beckett. I'm opening your doors and everything." His hand rests on the top of the door frame, an easy feat given his height. I walk ahead of him, slightly ducking my head to hide the girlish grin I'm biting down. We approach the front door and I spin around to offer him my hand. He looks down, studying my manicured hand before firmly gripping it and tilting his head in question. His hand feels so good in mine, and I feel like I've won a prize just by holding a part of him like this.

"This is a partnership, remember, Cabot?" I remind him, shaking his hand. "Today you brought… pens. And paper. Tomorrow I'll send you earth-shattering revelations about popular romance and women's reading culture."

Returning the shake, he releases my hand and reaches behind me to grab the door handle. The angle results in him crowding me, the top of his chest just inches from my nose and I can't help but try to breathe him in. His scent brings me back to that night in the bar. I'm brought out of the thought when his hand gently grips my waist, adeptly rotating me just enough to pull the door open. I'm halfway through the threshold, my back to him, when I feel him murmur, "I wouldn't expect anything less."

* * *

Walking down the tree lined street, I tilt my face toward the sun and angle it into the breeze, eager to feel the incoming season wash over me. Unlike so many college campuses, Astor's immediate vicinity is carefully curated, the student housing mixed in with storied brownstones, interspersed with both mom and pop shops and restaurants attractive to both students and faculty. Our proximity to Boston means we don't need much else; a quick 30 minute drive and you're already in Beacon Hill. I almost drove to Ben's, but the moment I stepped outside today I knew it was walking weather.

Brownstones line the cobblestone streets, the stones differing shades of brown and terracotta. I'm rarely over on this side anymore; the cobblestones aren't necessarily compatible with some of the footwear I'm known to live in when I'm spending time at the newspaper office. This side of campus isn't practical for that, nor is it near the places I frequent for any of my stories. Ian doesn't keep me on the preppy, lifestyle beat— thank god— but that doesn't mean I would *mind* having to be here. *I guess I don't need a reason, but a reason always helps.* The thought appears the moment my eye snags on the bus stop that would drop Lily and I off on our little city quests.

Lily would drag me down here for any reason. The stop at Astor was definitely not the closest stop on the way to Boston's city center, but we took any chance we could to get close to our future school. The farmer's market, obscure metal concert, pop-up shop, dog adoptions, skateboarding competition, regional book fair— anything. She never needed a reason to do something that she thought would bring her, or me, joy. The vigor with which she lived had always left me in awe of her. She was so intentional. I could find a million excuses not to come down here, but every time we did, and we sauntered back to the bus station to head back to our prep school, we were filled to the brim with excitement. We'd arrive back to the dorms sated by our expedition, Lily *always* the commander who just knew what we needed.

Lily knew for the both of us. She knew that whatever compass existed in others, the compass that points true north or whatever, didn't point true north for me. That with my mother barely around, I needed her to guide me through this life. She was my touchstone. I felt rooted when I was with her. Her death detached me from that rootedness, but there are moments when I feel it again. Like that night at the bar. Like right now, walking through the autumn breeze after an afternoon with Ben.

An afternoon with Ben. Something flutters in my stomach at the thought of more afternoons with Ben, but I fight the urge to identify the something as butterflies. My best attempts to ignore my attraction to Ben are trampled by the way he simply *looks* at me. Ben's eyes search me, sear me, *explore* me— I've never been so looked at in my life. His gaze, so focused and restrained, makes my body hum with excitement. I can't keep away either, if I'm being honest with myself, and *that* is the problem. The extent to which I'm drawn to him unsettles me.

Of course I had to ask him to stop. I can't encourage whatever this thing is between us.

Rounding the corner toward the outskirts of campus, my contemplative bubble is burst by a shrill reminder of my current reality.

"Olivia, did you not die when you saw that dress? I died." Sleaze oozes from Genevieve's voice. You wouldn't know it looking at her. While she's not a demure girl, she's not an overtly sexual one either— that is, until she leans over the table and grabs your boyfriend's hand in playful banter. She's a snake, Gen is. She slithers in the grass, playing coy and harmless, until she rears her head and you see the vicious colors hiding on the underbelly. While she hasn't shown it to me yet, I know it's coming.

"Pity you were somehow resurrected," I jeer, unable to conceal the ire reemerging now that I'm faced with this bitch.

"You know, you really should be nice to me, Olivia. I'm *helping* you." The fake pity in Gen's eyes only fans my anger. Scraping my teeth over my upper lip, I glance away before settling my wrathful gaze on her.

Titling my head, I ask her, "In what universe do I need your help, Genevieve? Is it the one in which you're—" I gasp for effect "—desirable? Irresistible? The girl everyone here is undressing in their mind the moment she walks into a room?" I huff a disinterested laugh. "Gen, we *know* that's not you. But let me know if you find her. We can compare notes," I snap out, my patience for her delusion dissipating.

Expecting her to retreat, I'm surprised when I feel her close the distance between us, her face just inches from mine. An elusive smirk slides into place.

"You're right, Olivia. I'm *not* like you. Maybe that's what *he* likes." Brushing past me, her shoulder knocks against mine, her quiet cackle echoing as I feel my face grow hot with humiliation. I hear Lily's voice as soon as the heat overwhelms me.

You always lose when you get like this, but you do it anyway.

Teeth gritting against each other, I pick up my pace down through the network of housing strategically built near the athletics facility.

By the time I reach Will's apartment, only half the rage from my encounter with Gen has evaporated. The other half is still hot, boiling just under the surface of my outwardly cool composure. As I slip the key into the lock, I notice the differences between this apartment and the one I left just twenty minutes ago. Stepping into the apartment, I can't help but compare the modern trapping of Will's cold, steel space to Ben's refreshing, but comforting home.

Dropping the key on the counter, I let my bag drop to the floor.

"Will," I throw out, unwilling to give him an inch in the upcoming confrontation. He's coming to me.

He's slipping on a powder blue short sleeve button up, just beginning to do the buttons.

"Jesus, Olivia. Where were you? Everyone's going to be at Vida's at 8." By everyone, I'm assuming he means Grant,

Gen, Andrew, Scott, and whoever is dangling off Scott's arm this month. Sounds like a wonderful time.

It crosses my mind that I did not, in fact, tell Will about my study session with Ben. I'm considering hiding this when I remember the source of my seething anger, and instead decide that honesty is the best policy.

"I was at Ben's," I say very matter of factly, and I watch the fury consume the mild irritation that danced across Will's face when he walked out of the bedroom. He's waiting for me to elaborate, but I won't.

"Why the fuck were you at Ben's?" he barely gets out, his teeth so tense I can see his jaw flicker.

To lie, or not to lie. I look over at the clock and see we only have an hour until we're supposed to meet our friends. *A lie would draw this out. Another day.*

"Because we're partners in this women's lit class we're both in, and we had to do a partner reading. I could've sworn I told you." *Okay, maybe a little lie to get him going a little bit. It's the least I can do.* A small, sinister smile settles on my face, full of vengeance and the desire to make him feel the way I felt seeing Gen in his photo and having to listen to her insinuate horrible shit to me about her and Will over and over again.

Taking a few careful steps toward me, Will counters, " Well you didn't. I would've remembered."

"Well, apparently you don't." I step around him. "Now where's the dress your favorite fan-girl picked out for me?" The disgust in my voice is palpable.

"Olivia. Stop." His anger swirls with concern, and I feel him grab the same wrist his brother grabbed earlier. This time, the grip feels cool and suffocating.

"No, you stop. I ran into Gen on my walk here. She always has such glowing things to say about your company." He releases my wrist, crossing his arms as if I'm lying about Gen insinuating they are sleeping together. He always finds little ways like this to take her side and honestly, it hurts more than if I found out he was actually cheating.

"I went shopping for *you* with my childhood best friend because *you* were busy. You conveniently forgot to tell me why you were busy, probably because you knew that it would piss me off." The volume of his voice creeps higher and higher, until he looks me over once and glances away, shaking his head. "And I'm the fucking bad guy? I specifically told you to stay away from him, Liv," he adds, hurt coloring his expression.

"I'm not a dog, Will. You can't just tell me to sit and stay." My anger at his afternoon with Gen only intensifies at the notion that I should blindly follow his direction, like I'm his lackey and not his literal girlfriend. "I've told you numerous times how uncomfortable I am with Gen, but *still* you do shit like you did today."

"Unbelievable," he scoffs. "So, how was it then?" His eyes are back on me, part repulsion and part possession.

I feel my pulse quicken at the suggestion that there was anything more than studying going on between Ben and I. I roll my eyes at his question. "Why don't you ask him?"

I walk around him and into the bedroom, spotting the red dress in a garment bag in the open closet. Bringing it into the bathroom, I begin slipping it off the hanger. I see Will in the mirror, slipping his arms around my waist, his mouth by my ear.

"Just… tell me I'm being crazy, Liv," he says, the words landing like a sandbag in my gut, the guilt I feel so heavy. I push it away, telling myself it's fleeting— the guilt, the attraction, all of it— but Will isn't. I turn around and my hand cups his smooth, arrogant jaw, angling it so that my lips easily lock with his.

Like velvet against me, his kiss caresses my mouth, slightly ajar as I inhale the scent of him. He's lemon and fresh soap, mingled with crisp cedar and warm spice. He coaxes me open and I feel him glide against me once before he suddenly pulls back.

"Liv," he barely murmurs before diving back into me. My hand pushes up the back of his head, gripping his golden locks and I feel his palm descend just below the small of my back. Nudging me into him, he deepens our kiss, twirling around me with tortuous sleekness. His wet warmth evades my next pass, his teeth now softly biting my bottom lip. My head falls back, leaving bare the neck he quickly begins warming with those plush lips, his tongue tracing circles on my skin. I place my hands on his chest, gently pushing him away. Swiftly, he spins me around and I feel him press into me, firm, twitching with need. His lips return to the side of my neck, his hand brushing away the chestnut locks shielding that sensitive part of me Will is definitely seeking.

"I could do without a hickey, Will," I manage between shallow breaths, attempting to regain control over my traitorous body. "And I'd rather not be late."

His hands wrap around my waist from behind, his face buried in my hair. "We're resuming this later," he whispers in my ear, his hand now tracing circles on the sensitive plane beneath my hip bone and above where Will knows I'm already pulsing with need.

"If you say so." I push away from his body, oozing pleasure and sultry charm. "Let me just try this on." I watch him walk away in the mirror, clearly satisfied by what he thinks was the end of that argument.

I watch myself step into the slinky dress in the mirror. My neck is flushed from the attention he paid to it just moments earlier, and I lean closer to inspect whether or not concealer is necessary. I bring my hand to my neck, my palm feeling for the warmth radiating there.

This is how it goes with Will and I. We fight, usually because he finds something I've done or said unacceptable, and just as I gain ground, he nullifies every doubt or worry with his touch. And every time he wraps me in his arms, murmurs my name in my ear, worships me with his hands and lips, I truly forgot how fucking awful I felt *because* of him just seconds before. And when we're done I'm exhausted, wrapped in his sheets, dwelling on how perfectly we fit together— in bed, in a room full of people, on the cover of Boston Common, at galas like the one we're going to soon. And if my thoughts veer toward the ways in which we don't fit, the post-intimacy euphoria usually chases it away.

I can't chase it away right now.

You wouldn't wear a dress like that, Ben had said to me.

Dread and embarrassment coalesce in my chest as I imagine Will in a Neiman Marcus, Gen by his side, his hand at the small of her back like it is at mine when we stand together. I push the image out of my mind with a deep breath, but the feeling remains, so I think of Ben in some sort of secret, mental revenge and righteousness washes it away.

13

Olivia

Vida's calls itself upscale dining, but the $14 nacho platter being slid in front of Andrew suggests otherwise. Pendant lights hang over the secluded, plush booths that mostly encase the dark mahogany tables, and floor to ceiling sheer drapes attempt to shield restaurant goers from onlookers. But make no mistake, the food is pathetic. Nevertheless, it's the only place near campus that actually serves something other than watered down beer or sickly sweet wine, so it's usually the spot we end up at.

"Yes," Andy groans out, indecently, as he pulls a loaded nacho away from his plate. Gen looks on in disgust, sipping her vodka soda.

"We could do without the grotesque sound effects," she reprimands him with her judgmental glare, and I laugh despite myself because, for once, I agree with her.

"Awe come on, Gen. Don't take your sexual frustration out on poor ol' Andy," Scott drawls, already buzzed before the mains have been served. "If you're in need of hearing a man groan, I'm always—"

"Babe!" the busty blonde next to him squeals, slapping his arm. His eyes go wide at the rest of us, like the problem is that she clearly can't take a joke. Grant just shoots him a menacing glare.

"Gen knows I'm kidding, right?"

She clears her throat glancing away, obviously uncomfortable.

"Not cool, man," Will adds, and I can't help but roll my eyes. Neither can Grant, apparently, and we send each other knowing looks.

Scott disgusts me as much as he does the next person, but the last thing I want to do is hear Will stick up for Gen tonight.

"Anyway…" I quickly attempt to redirect the convo. "Did you guys hear about Rebecca Banks and her pantomime professor? First of all— pantomime? And second of all—"

"Ohmygod!" Gen squeaks, slapping Will's arm from where she sits across the table. "Do you remember Becky Banks? Honestly, I'm not totally shocked. She was always *such* a teacher's pet." Will's laughter stokes my irritation.

"Jesus, I didn't even realize she went here. Yeah, she really was. Fucking annoying, too."

Gen gasps again as she recalls yet another thing they both, undoubtedly, remember and I flag down our server.

"Can I get another gin and tonic as soon as you get a second?" She gives me an earnest nod before rushing back to the bar. I turn my attention to Grant, and witness the only scowl I've ever seen him produce.

Having missed the first part of their conversation I am lost at what's going on. All I see is Gen grabbing Will's hand playfully, her tone a little too flirty.

"Will, can we please go back there? Maybe in a few weeks?"

Will's grinning at her, unaware that I'm listening.

"Sure, let's make a day out of it."

My stomach drops and I feel nauseated. I rub my fingers together, warming them, trying to convince myself this must be some childhood place that would make sense for them to go together, alone.

"How's practice been since, well, you know?" I shift my attention to Grant, deciding his still very present scowl is not worth acknowledging at this moment, and instead opting to find a neutral subject to get us both out of our heads.

"Ha! He didn't tell you about our scrimmage?" Grant's voice comes out dry but his eyes seem to be dancing with amusement.

"A scrimmage? Now I'm glad I didn't ask," I laugh, relieved by Grant's company.

"Olivia, it was EPIC," Andy interjects, his voice comically exaggerated. "We were literally tied when—"

"Can we not talk about him?" Will cuts in, ever the commanding captain. Gen gives him a sympathetic smile and I roll my eyes for what feels like the tenth time this evening.

"You were tied when what?" I urge Andy to continue, ignoring Will.

"Ben steals the—" Andy tries to explain.

"Olivia, are you fucking deaf? I said drop it," he snaps at me, his voice dripping with contempt.

"Hey, you really can't just call people deaf anymore..." Scott speaks up as Grant abruptly slides out of the booth.

"I'm getting a drink. Gen— do you want to join me?"

The whole table gets quiet, clearly confused at Grant's invitation.

"I'm good?" She gives Will a pointed glance suggesting she's just as confused as the rest of us. Grant clenches his jaw, his posture faltering as he makes his way to the bar without another word.

I grab the fresh gin and tonic sitting in front of me, downing it in one gulp, while the rest of the table awkwardly resumes the conversation, Will and Gen laughing at Grant's expense quietly to my left. I grab my phone and scroll through my conversations until I find the one I'm looking for.

Fuck it.

Hi

I type, hitting send before my prefrontal cortex can chime in and click my screen off, placing it screen side down on the table. I know this is probably petty and definitely immature, but I'm doing it all the same. When I see the edges of my phone light up not ten seconds later, I quickly retrieve it.

BEN

Already have your thoughts together?

Lol no. Still baking.

BEN

Ah— so you miss me already?

A rush of adrenaline courses through me as I consider what to say, the gin definitely clouding my judgment. I take a steadying breath.

Gen's, unfortunately, melodic laughter floats past me as Will lets out a chuckle.

"Okay, but you *have* to tell Andy about that time we went crab hunting and you literally piss—" Will cuts her off with the drunken wave of his hand, completely unaware that I'm even still here.

"Enough, enough! It's bad enough you've seen me like that. I don't need everyone here to have a mental picture of it." His laugh is infectious and carefree, and I can't help but think about how I rarely hear it like that.

"Okay, but Ben was definitely worse." Her face speaks volumes. It says the time she's recalling was a good one; that it involved Ben, and Will, and her, and it was happy; that she is privy to a time and space I probably never will be.

"Yeah," Will says, distantly.

"It was good once. It could be like that again." Her shrug seems noncommittal, but I'd know that scheming glance anywhere. "Maybe give him a chance to prove you wrong."

"Not really looking to give him anything, Gen." His smile goes taut before relaxing for her benefit. "But thanks." He grabs my hand, kissing it gently in a way that isn't directed at me but instead as a jab to Gen, probably for bringing up a subject she knows he's uncomfortable with. Gen's expression immediately changes, her eyes pained and her smile flattening into a shell of what it was just moments before, and I realize I feel sympathy for her and anger blooming inside me toward Will.

I mostly believe Will when he tells me there's nothing

going on with Gen, that they've just been friends for as long as he can remember, but when I have a front row seat to this— the fruits of an obviously deep rooted friendship— I can't help but feel like I've been deprived of something special with Will. The more I sit in that feeling though, I realize that I'm not jealous of her… I'm jealous of them. Gen obviously wants something more, but I would kill to have a friendship like that again.

She sighs, shifting the conversation to Scott's date who, apparently, is from California. Riveting. Grant finally slides back into the booth, a proverbial rain cloud over his head.

I release the breath I was unwittingly holding, checking my phone.

BEN

Daydreaming about my bed, Beckett?

I battle the urge to smile against the rim of my glass, my third drink of the evening making me reflective, reckless, and apparently careless.

Maybe I just wanted to talk to you

BEN

You're at a table full of people.

I glance around the restaurant, the guys now talking basketball. I'm almost positive I'm going to find a smirking Ben at a booth if I just look hard enough.

Spying on me, are we?

BEN

Grant may have mentioned your dinner.

So you're saying Grant is your spy, and you are spying on me? You are dangerous…

BEN

What are you drinking?

Wouldn't you like to know

BEN

Remember when you texted me because you wanted to talk?

Uh yeah— you are infinitely better company than the guy to my left… hint— it's not Grant!!

BEN

Don't let Will catch you talking to me.

Will who? :)

"Liv." Will's irritated voice brings me back to our booth at Vida's. "Your food's gonna get cold," he says, nodding toward my salmon salad. I narrow my eyes at him, feeling light and buoyant in my seat.

"It's a salad?" My brows quirk, my alcohol fueled assessment of him clear.

"You've been on your phone this entire time," he mutters to me under his breath, clearly bothered.

"So glad you noticed between nostalgia sessions with Gen," I snipe, aware of my exaggerated expression. His jaw flickers with irritation, sand he silently swaps my cocktail for his water, turning away from me.

Good riddance, I think to myself, both pleased to have pissed him off and annoyed that he didn't take the bait. Remembering I'm in the middle of a conversation, I click my screen back on.

BEN

Goodnight, Olivia. Get home safely.

I click my phone shut and shove it into my bag, the text sobering me in an instant. I feel stupid, and I'm wracking through every possible impression Ben has of me when I feel Will nudge me to move out of the bench.

"You coming, babe?" The look on his face tells me he couldn't care less, and I realize I couldn't either. This day has been an emotional rollercoaster, and I'm desperate for the quiet solitude of my bedroom for a few hours.

"I'm just gonna head home." His gaze settles on me for more than a moment, irritation flickering behind it. It seems like he's about to say something, but he just gives me a tight smile instead.

"Don't worry— I'll make sure he doesn't get into any trouble," Gen mockingly reassures me, her gaze sliding up to Grant as he approaches.

"I'll give you a ride back. I can't imagine being out for another hour." Grant and I walk out of Vida's together, pausing in anticipation of the group, but they just keep going. We stare after Will, Gen, Scott, Andy, and the girl whose name I never asked as they cross the street.

"Not even a goodbye to you? Jesus Christ," Grant says mostly to himself, but I hear him.

"It's really okay, Grant. I'm used to it." I hear the apathy in my voice and hope he doesn't notice.

"You're not the only one." He swipes a hand across the top of his head before resettling his baseball cap and unlocking his car, opening the passenger door for me without a second thought.

"God, you are the epitome of southern charm, you know that?"

His eyes twinkle with amusement as he grins, settling into the driver's seat. "I know."

The drive from Vida's to my apartment is less than five minutes, but he refuses to even put the car in drive unless I have my seatbelt on. Once we're finally moving, I turn toward him, suddenly curious.

"So, what was bothering you tonight?" I'm nowhere near as tipsy as I was an hour ago, but it seems I'm still just as chatty.

"Who says anything was bothering me?" I make a mental note that he did not even spare a glance as he answered.

"Either something was bothering you, or you've been cloned and your jovial essence didn't make the trip."

"My jovial essence?" He smirks, finally sparing me a glance.

"Is jovial not a word in the Bible Belt?" He laughs at this, his tenseness starting to evaporate.

"You know, I did have to be a little smart to get here."

"Sure," I tease. I raise my eyebrows, nonverbally reiterating my earlier question. He takes a deep breath, sighing.

"Maybe one day it'll be worth telling you about. But for now, don't you worry your pretty little head over it." I make a face of disgust at his over exaggerated southern accent as he pats my head, surprised to find us both laughing in earnest.

"Thanks for the ride. I really didn't want to walk home in these shoes." I glance down at my heels, grateful I didn't have to trudge back here in pain or barefoot.

"Anything for a friend."

He waits in his car until I'm inside, the wheels of his car audibly spinning away only once I've turned on my lights. I swish my front curtains shut, doing a quick closing shift of my living area, before begrudgingly washing the day off my face.

I can't believe I texted him.

I rifle through my closet, in search of the comfiest pajamas within which to wallow in supreme embarrassment. I decide on my pink La Perla set, because if I'm going to feel like a fool it should at least be a beautiful one.

Collapsing into my bed, I relish the softness of the sheets against my skin but realize that my bed is nowhere as cozy as Ben's. I reach for the planner on my nightstand, hoping tomorrow I'll have enough time for a mind clearing manicure. Relief washes over me when I realize I have absolutely zero plans. I have all the time in the world to shop my worries away.

14

Olivia

Slapping for my phone, I blindly press the stop button on the alarm that's been going off repeatedly for the past hour. It's only nine a.m.; I haven't slept in too much. I just couldn't bring myself to spring out of bed, not when the crisp morning air was filtering through my cracked window so beautifully.

I love Saturdays. Especially when the sky is clear, the air is cool, and you've the whole day to spend traipsing around, just indulging yourself. Because that is what I plan to do today— indulge myself. That might be just what I need to clear my head.

When I got back home last night, I could barely keep my eyes open. It's only now that I remember Will probably spent the better part of his night out drinking, without me. I guess Gen was good enough company in my absence, because when I check my messages, there's only one. And it's not from Will.

BEN

You left the sparkly interrogation notebook
on my bed. Just fyi. I'll bring it to class.

His text to me feels mechanical, especially after the way he basically dismissed me last night. *I can ruminate over this another day.* I toss my phone on my bed as I finally leap from it. The original hardwood of my room is cool on the soles of my feet, and I hurry to slip on my Tasmans. My gaze lands on my to-do list, and I steal my phone back from the cloud that is my bed, tempted to just lay back in it with a steaming cup of tea.

I'm about to hit **buy now** on an old school harlequin paperback I need for class before I realize that shipping is a two week minimum. *Why does anything take two weeks to ship these days?*

A quick search of the title relieves me when it becomes apparent that the middle aged women of Boston are keeping bodice ripping paperbacks stocked in the independent book shops off Massachusetts Avenue. I can't think of a more indulgent morning than one spent strolling along the cobbled streets, searching for a book, and maybe stopping by Veronica Beard.

Assuming he didn't have the foresight to order this week's in advance, I shoot Ben a quick text, asking if he wants me to also grab him a copy when I find the book. He may have hurt my feelings, but he doesn't need to know that. I barely have time to put my phone down when a notification materializes on my home screen.

BEN

Or I could just go with you.

Not even a question; just a statement. This time, heat

flares inside me. There's no reason for him to come along, just like there's no reason for me to have such a bodily reaction to his text messages. Another one appears, and anticipation blooms where my heart should be.

BEN

I really don't have any other plans, if that's what you're thinking.

That would've been my response, actually. *How does he know what I'm thinking?* I'm unsure of his motives, especially after the way our conversation ended last night. But when I consider it, Ben tagging along for this, realistically, quick errand would be the perfect time to continue interviewing him. And he has my notebook. And he can just help me search for the book and be on his way when we're done.

Apprehension trickles down my spine, but anticipation wells up inside me when I realize I might see him today.

Sure.

I quickly press send, tossing my phone away like it's fire. I search my closet, settling on my black Sandro pleated mini skirt, a cream cable knit sweater, a sheer pair of hose because it *is* a bit chilly, and my favorite black Chloé boots. Running my hands through my hair, I work through a few tangles but decide to leave it down, the messiness of a good night's sleep making it look carelessly wavy.

I'm carefully assessing myself when I hear a knock on my door, my stomach briefly sinking. Will would show up, unannounced, with not even a "good morning" text. The sinking in my stomach quickly morphs into annoyance as I haphazardly fling my front door open.

"I figured I would swing by here, since you weren't

answering my texts… but I can go?" Ben greets me, confusion swirling in his eyes, the corners of his mouth upturned in a slight, mischievous grin. I take a steadying breath and breathe deeper when his scent envelops me— rain and cedar— and a startling familiar feeling sets into my bones.

"Sorry," I smile, shaking my thoughts away. "I thought you were Will."

"Oh," Ben hesitates, suddenly uncertain. "I can go. I didn't realize—"

"No! No, I mean, don't go. I'm not expecting him."

"You weren't expecting me either," he replies, a flirtatious smirk gracing his face. My lips press together in an attempt to stifle yet another smile.

I eye him carefully before looking away. "Let me just grab my bag and we can go." I whirl around to find my bag resting on the bench to my left and check to make sure I have my wallet.

Locking the door, I feel Ben's presence behind me, the warmth from his closeness a sharp contrast to the cool wind whispering about my pantyhose clad knees. It isn't until I'm standing at his car, the passenger door held open by him, that I register what we're doing.

This feels like a date.

But it's not a date; Ben's chivalrous door opening is, in fact, not chivalry at all but common decency. *I really need to stop reading so much fluff*, I chastise myself as the passenger door deftly falls shut. According to Will, Ben is like this with everyone; it's me who's reading into it.

"You can DJ," Ben offers, shooting a playful glance my way as we make our way into the city center, smiling knowingly. "Since you're already pairing your phone to my car."

"While I appreciate the permission, I would've anyway. Passenger princess, and all that," I brashly reply, surprised at myself. He hums in acknowledgement as I press play on one of my daily mixes. Fleetwood Mac's "Gypsy" weaves its way through the speakers. I catch Ben's eyebrows raise in my peripherals.

"Yes, Cabot?" I turn in my seat to face him, ready to defend my choice. "Don't tell me you're shocked."

"Okay— I'm not shocked," he laughs, shaking his head. "I just didn't take you for a girl into the oldies."

"First of all, I resent the idea that oldies can be used in reference to Stevie Nicks. She is timeless. Second of all, if you were a teen girl anytime in the past two decades and you *didn't* go through a Fleetwood Mac-record shop phase, you are an anomaly," I explain with rapidity. I shake my head in mock disbelief. "I'd love to know what kind of girls you've known who *don't* scream "Dreams" every time it comes on."

"Well maybe," Ben begins, the start of a sarcastic remark on his lips, "you're just *not like other girls*." He slyly glances at me out of the corner of his eye, grinning.

"Oh come off it, Cabot. I'm exactly like other girls," I roll my eyes, amused. "Well, maybe slightly better," I add, righting myself in my seat so that I'm looking ahead. Ben murmurs something to himself, but it's drowned out by the embarrassingly loud growl of stomach.

"Sorry. I'm also a breakfast girl, but I overslept. If you just stop at—" Ben's blinker cuts me off, indicating a sudden detour. His car slows, bumping along the cobble-stone side street he's turned into. He parallel parks in record time in front of a worn, but clean building.

When I look out the window, I'm met by a royal blue sign in cursive lettering, most certainly at least three decades old. Inside, stereotypical diner booths skirt the perimeter of the tiny spot, with a few tables clustered in the middle. A waitress wearing a checkered apron makes her rounds. As Ben opens the door for me, I'm met by the comforting aroma of diner coffee.

We're seated quickly, two dark blue mugs are slid towards us, and the steaming coffee pot pours.

"I'll give you guys a minute to look over the menu. Good to see you, Ben," the waitress offers with a smile before quickly winking at Ben. Something stirs in me… jealousy? Most definitely not that.

"One of your non-Fleetwood Mac girls?" I'm kicking myself before it's even out.

"Uh, no," Ben says hesitantly. "I used to come here." He pauses like he has more to say but isn't sure if he should say it. I squint, trying to read him, but not wanting to pry. *But you should pry— isn't that the whole reason you agreed to this highly suspicious, possibly inappropriate* non-date?

"Before you came back to Astor?" I ask, attempting to hide my journalistic tone with one of curiosity— because I *am* curious. What was he doing these past few years? Why have I *never* seen him? Those are pertinent to the story I'm meant to be investigating, but they also feel pertinent to… me.

Ben subtly scoffs, disappointment shading his gaze. "So this *is* an interview for your story?"

His disappointment wounds me, for whatever reason, but it's good. Ben shouldn't be disappointed by me to begin with.

"I never said I *wasn't* an opportunist, Ben," I quip with a slight tilt of my head, like he should know better.

His assessing gaze unsettles me, eyes squinting for a moment, searching my own, and I'm worried what he might find. I don't even *know* what he might find. Like he senses my unease, he unlocks from his target and finally answers my question.

"Yeah. Before I came back to Astor," is all he gives me. A beat goes by. Then another. "You want to know why I left."

"Yes, I—"

"Well, the paper wants to know why I left, right?" he interrupts, sardonically. My heart knocks about inside my chest cavity, his disdain destabilizing me further. Whatever resolve I had concocted just an hour ago when I framed this time with Ben as part of my assignment dissipates under his scrutiny.

"Yes," I admit. "I do need to know, for the paper. But *I* want to know… for me. It would help me make sense of things."

Ben sighs in playful resignation, but his face speaks to how vulnerable this conversation makes him feel. I have the sudden urge to rest my hand on his forearm as he brings his mug down from the sip of coffee he just took. Tell him that he's okay, and I can take and hold space for whatever he needs to say— but I know that's an intrusive thought because I barely know this man. I offer him a soft smile instead and wait for his answer.

"I left because…" he pauses, staring into the pocket of space just past me. "I just needed a break. Everything started feeling like too much and stepping away felt like the only option. When I left I found myself here, a lot." His smile is tight as he flags down our waitress for another refill of his coffee.

I get the sense that's all I'll be getting from Ben, so I leave it alone. What was I expecting to find anyway? Without knowing Ben's family, I can barely make sense of anything. To me, it makes sense that Ben would only abandon his captainship for some sort of family crisis, but I have no clue what that would even be. Will's completely shut me out of that part of his life. I know that's what Ian's hoping for though— some kind of tea on the elusive Chapman clan.

It's honestly odd, in hindsight, that anyone would care to read about the family woes and subsequent consequences of the Chapmans. We wealthy nor'easters really do feed on the miseries of others, via all and any gossip channels— even college newspapers.

Sipping my coffee, I consider that there are major swaths of Will's life that I knew nothing about until Ben showed up. It had never bothered me that Will kept pieces of himself private, but I was beginning to feel robbed. Ben was willing to share more with me in the few weeks that I've known him than Will has in the past two years. But it isn't sadness I feel as I consider this; it's longing. I offer my mug to the waitress for a refill and take another sip.

"I kind of have a place like this— in Nantucket," I say, surprising myself. "Shitty diner coffee is like a balm for the soul."

"Yeah," he agrees, a soft smile settling on his face. "It kind of is. What's in Nantucket?"

"My dad and I spend Thanksgiving there." I catch his expression shift, and I know what he's wondering. "My mom is alive, Ben," I laugh, watching his shoulders relax. "She's just never really around." Before he can press me on my mom, I switch gears.

"So what does Ben Cabot order at—" I peek down at the menu, "Winchester's Diner?"

"Is this still an interview, Beckett?" The lighthearted gleam in his eyes tells me he's letting his question go for now.

"No. This isn't an interview anymore," I offer, more slyly than I mean to, a blush creeping up my neck. He nods in agreement to whatever he thinks I've implied.

"The Home Run is usually what I go for, but something tells me you're not into savory breakfast."

"I very much enjoy eggs benedict, I'll have you know. But…" I begrudgingly admit, "you are correct. Recommend me something else. I don't trust our server."

"No? I think she's spoken like, twenty words in total," he laughs airily, the laugh cascading out and around us, winding through the handles of our coffee mugs, weaving its way through my hair, brushing across the bridge of my nose. Or so it feels.

"It's that eye. Something about it screams 'don't trust any of my food recommendations'," I flippantly reply.

"Definitely *don't* get a Boston waffle then. It's buttery, topped with caramelized apples, dusted with powdered sugar, even comes with a side of syrup if that's not sweet enough for you… but Bethany did tell me once that it's her favorite. So." Ben smirks, flagging down *Bethany* again.

When she finally arrives at our table, I find it hard not to look at her with derision. She's slightly older than us, the barely there wrinkles at the corner of her eyes when she smiles only slightly deeper than my own. She could just be happier than me, I guess. But no, she's definitely older. Her ashy blonde hair lays on one shoulder in a long braid that reaches just beneath her barely there chest. Maybe not barely there, but that is besides the point. She's pretty in the way so many girls are unremarkably pretty, and— there's a wedding band on her left hand.

"And what'll you have?" she asks, sweet as can be. "If you're looking for something sweet, I love the—"

"I'll just take the Boston waffle," I interject before she

has the chance to recommend it to me. Ben stifles a laugh behind his menu before handing it to Bethany.

"That'll be right out," she throws over her shoulder, hurrying off to a table of elderly men playing dominoes.

"Okay, there are seven book shops within a five mile radius of the city center that claim to have at least one copy of the book. Can you believe I couldn't get a single bookseller to tell me how many copies they had? Anyway, we can split up, you know, divide and conquer. That way we're not both trekking uphill and downhill just to find this book all day."

"While I appreciate your logic and your prior preparation, I *did* think we'd be trekking uphill and downhill together. Were your designer boots not designed for such strenuous exercise?" he teases, that mischievous glint in his eyes.

"Well, no I— I'm not sure actually. They feel industrial, but I guess we'll find out. Just remember that I offered you a way out, Cabot. I've built a couple pit stops in my route. If we won't divide and conquer, then you are along for the ride," I say, giving him one more opportunity to back track.

At every turn, he's choosing to spend this time with me, and I'm choosing to let him. I should make him stay away, but the words don't make their way out of my mouth. *I don't want to turn him away. I don't think I could if I tried.*

"Funny, I don't remember asking for a way out," he replies, smug with satisfaction.

* * *

By the time we've located two copies of the book *and* visited Veronica Beard— because I was not going to give that up for anybody— the sun is past its peak, its warming powers quickly diminishing. We're only a few blocks from where Ben parked, if I remember correctly, when he pauses to answer his phone.

"Hey, Mom," Ben softly mutters, sympathy padding each word. "I can't right now I'm— well no I'm—" My brows furrow in question, and I attempt to mime that I'm up for whatever, but instead I think I look like I'm sternly shaking my head. He checks the time on his phone before sighing, running a hand through his hair. "Yeah no, I understand that. I'll text you once I'm with him. Kay. You too." When he hangs up the phone, I catch the tension flickering in his jaw.

"Everything good?" I essentially chirp in my best attempt to be easygoing.

"Actually, no. There's something I need to do, but I understand if you need to go. I can call you an Uber or—"

"Don't be ridiculous, Ben. I do not Uber," I jokingly scoff, though I am dead serious. "I don't have anywhere I need to be. Honestly. Is everything okay?" I add when I clock the look of worry on his face.

"My mom can't get a hold of her dad— my grandfather. He lives here," he pauses, like he's revealed something he didn't mean to. "This happens sometimes, and he's probably fine but…"

"She wants you to check on him," I state, looping my arm through his. "Lead the way. I've already added "Wellness Check" to the itinerary. If we can stop at Veronica Beard's we can stop at…?"

"Theodore Cabot's," he finishes, a reserved smile disguising any worry that was just there.

"Good old Teddy. I'm sure he's just fine," I reassure him, gazing up into his eyes swirling with worry, curiosity, and something else that causes my stomach to flutter.

His smile morphs into a brilliant beam, transforms into an open mouthed chuckle.

"What?" If he's laughing at me, I'd like to know what about.

"I just had no clue that the girl who told me to fuck off could be this… sunny," he says, staring at me in bewilderment. I must look the same because I feel incredibly bewildered by such an assessment.

"In no universe would anyone, not even my father, call me a single ray of sunshine. Let's get going, Cabot. I think you're weary from our journey," I joke, patting his forearm in an attempt to downplay whatever he meant. It must work, because he doesn't bring it up again.

Suddenly, we're before a brownstone, the door painted red. Ben pulls out a set of keys and opens the door. Immediately, my nose is assaulted by the smell of Pine Sol, that one sickly sweet vanilla scented candle, and elderly man. Once the assault wears off, I realize the smell is pleasant, and I imagine it to be the smell I might associate with a loving grandparent, if I had any.

"Grandfather!" Ben shouts out, through the opulent townhouse.

Nothing. Silence. "Grandfather?"

Again, nothing. Ben shakes his head in disbelief. "Pop!" he shouts, exasperated.

A walker glides out from a doorway near the rear, followed by Pop whose hands desperately grasp the handles. "If I hear you call me *grandfather* one more damn time, I'll —" Ben clears his throat gruffly, censuring Theodore. "Who's this?" the old man grumbles, face scrunching up at the sight of me.

"Olivia, sir," I say, offering my hand, walking up to him.

The closer I get the clearer it is that amusement, not consternation, dances in his tired eyes.

"Olivia? And how do you know my Ben?" We both glance Ben's way as we see him slip his phone back into his pocket.

"Oh, well… we have—" I begin, but Ben takes over.

"Olivia is Will's girl, Pop," he says with such finality, I feel it like a fresh wound littered with salt. "But we're in a seminar together. We were just running an errand for it." *An errand to run, like a tedious task to check off as quickly as possible.* I shift my weight, eager to escape. "Mom said you weren't answering again," he swiftly switches subjects.

"Well it never rang! It—" Ben swipes his grandfather's phone off the counter, setting the ringer off silent and to an audible level. "I don't see why house phones fell out of fashion. This wouldn't be a problem," Theodore grumbles, shuffling towards Ben.

I watch Ben explain the mechanics of keeping your phone off silent to his grandfather, all too aware of how he patiently re-explains every confusion Theodore has. When he's done, he checks the dates on his perishables in the fridge, reviews the log for the caretaker who comes once a week, and enlists me to call in his favorite lasagna from a restaurant down the road. He radiates calm, reassurance, safety— love. Before we leave, Pop releases his walker to envelope me in a bony embrace. He backs away slightly, just enough to peer into my eyes for a moment.

He lets out a decisive "hmph," kisses my cheek, and retreats back to his walker before saying goodbye to Ben, quietly grumbling as he does. Ben's soft gaze hardens, Pop smiles sympathetically, and I feel like an intruder.

"And remember to charge your phone!" Ben throws

over his shoulder when we leave, just as Theodore shuts and locks his door.

"Thank you for coming with me. Pop— grandfather, can be a handful."

"Why don't you call him Pop? He obviously prefers it."

"A story for another day. Maybe if you meet my family one day, you'll understand," he answers.

"Ha! Unlikely," I scoff, feeling increasingly bitter after being referred to as a tedious errand. I may be exaggerating, but feelings are subjective.

"Olivia," Ben interrupts as my internal thoughts spiral, lightly grabbing my arm to stop me just before his car. "What's wrong?" he asks, concern floating in his gaze.

I contemplate saying that nothing is wrong, but that feels like waste of this moment, on this day that was meant to be an indulgence. Instead, I indulge myself by speaking my mind.

"Why did you even come with me?"

"Where is this coming from?" His confusion is palpable.

"Well, I can't say I appreciated the way you introduced me." He tilts his head, asking for clarity. "You said you were 'just running an errand.' You made it sound like I was…" I trail off, realizing I'm being dramatic.

"Like you were what?" he asks, steadily, like he's acutely listening to me.

Indulging myself, remember? I take a shallow breath, rolling my eyes at myself. "Like I was an inconvenience. Which I now recognize is silly when I say it aloud, considering you literally offered to—" I'm stopped by the warmth of his palms, pressing through my sweater and to my shoulders.

"No, don't logic your way out of your feelings. I'm sorry I made it sound like you were an inconvenience, Olivia. You are anything but that." His hands travel from my shoulders to my back, crossing each other until I'm surrounded by him. I press my cheek into the solid warmth in front of me, unconsciously breathing in cedar and rain and the questionably erotic scent of manly exertion that most certainly came from lugging my bags up and down the cobbled streets.

When he releases me his gaze is heated, and the moment feels like it sits on the edge of a mountain, just waiting to be pushed over or reeled back in.

"That was quite a hug, Cabot," I remark, smiling at him in gratitude.

He opens the passenger door, nodding in acknowledgment as he gazes just above my head, but I swear I can still see the warmth in his eyes. Then, he drives me home.

15

Ben

I almost kissed her. Again.

That thought intermittently interjects itself mid sentence, off and on, all day, just like it did yesterday. It invaded my thoughts every time I'd glance at Olivia, sitting beside me seemingly unaware of the calamity I want to cause when I'm near her, unfazed by the heat that rolls between us like the unbearable heat waves of summer. So unbothered, so cool, so… neutral, that I doubt that she even feels it.

The icy chill of the lab room, as well as the sterile stench of lab equipment, does a good enough job of dousing the fire I've come to associate with being around Olivia. It takes every ounce of my self control not to act on pure instinct around her. The drive to hug her, kiss her, *hold her hand*, is unsettling, and it needs to stop. If her indifference to me this morning was any indication, or the way she let Will squeeze her ass after seminar— in full view of everyone, that delicious flush creeping up her neck the way it does when she's flustered— she doesn't want me to act on pure instinct. I need to start showing some restraint. Thankfully, we don't need to spend any time together for our class this week, so putting some space between us should be easy enough. In theory.

"*Ben the Bogart!*" Andrew exclaims with childish glee. I can't help the chuckle that escapes me when I feel him and Grant sidle up beside me on our way to the practice gym. "*Please* tell me we have plans tonight. Please. When I tell you this one," he shoots a playful glare at Grant, "is too polite to pick up anyone at a bar anymore! Unbelievable. Thank god you're here."

And while the idea of going out and picking up anyone who *isn't* Olivia makes me slick with unease, it's exactly what I need to do to snuff out this fire I keep feeding.

"Yeah… we have plans. But you can't call me Bogart when we go out later. Actually, can you stop calling me that in general?" I say, eyebrows raised.

"Thank you," he says in mock exasperation, clasping his hands together. Andrew, while an invaluable member of the team, is also a bit of a theatrical person. He is literally involved in the theater department. Our own, slightly aged, Troy Bolton. "No can do on the Bogart thing, though. We can start at Pub 24 and make our way around the city center. I'm tired of Astor girls."

"Or they're tired of you," Grant taunts with a grin and the shake of his head.

"Either way, I think it's time to dabble in new waters," Andrew retorts, making a show of his declaration by spreading his arms wide, knocking into me and Grant.

I playfully knock his arm out of the way. "Couldn't have said it better myself, Andy."

* * *

Pub 24 is an Irish pub, and decidedly *not* a college hangout spot. Fresh graduates putting in ten hour days at whatever fancy firm they landed after leaving one of the many Ivies up here come to trade office tales, desperate to one up each other with subtle brags about the deals they closed or clients they landed. Almost like a college hangout spot, but replace the fresh faced optimism that comes with not having graduated yet with the exhaustion and disenchantment of actually joining the workforce. Why Andrew thinks he'll be able to flirt his way into going home with any of the women here is beyond me. He is persistent though, slyly making his way to every blonde he sees and quickly recovering when they turn their nose up at him.

"I think they smell the 'college' on him," I joke to Grant, who is obsessively checking his phone while cradling his Guinness in his other hand. His nose crinkles in disgust as he takes another sip. "They definitely smell something on him. I still don't get the Guinness hype," he says without looking up.

"And yet, you keep trying," I say, cheering his bottle with my Modelo to get his attention.

"We're at an Irish bar, I figure why not give it another go?" He finally puts his phone on the table face down with a little more force than if he had done it carelessly.

"Calling this an Irish bar is pretty generous." He gives a *hmph* in response flipping back over his phone only to see his home screen still only displaying the time.

"Grant… are you waiting for a girl to text you?" I ask feigning shock for comedic effect.

"I, uh—" his face flushes as he quickly moves his phone

into his pocket. "Sort of," he sighs, taking a long pull of his Guinness, grimacing as he sets back down his glass.

"And who is the lucky lady?" His face turns a deep shade of red as he picks up his beer and finishes it off.

"You wouldn't know her," he says in sort of a mumble, clearly wanting to change the subject which only spikes my curiosity more.

"C'mon man, talk to me." I flag the waitress down. "Two Modelo's please." I give Grant and his Guinness a pointed look and he finally cracks a smile.

He sighs rubbing a hand over his face.

"I don't know man, it's complicated." He pauses for a second, seeming to contemplate what he's going to say. "Have you ever really liked a girl and I mean *really* liked her, like you can't get her out of your head for even a second. Every thought ultimately leads to her and you know there's something real there. When you're near her it's like the rest of the world doesn't exist and you just really see her and she really sees you. Nothing else matters." His words hit me hard and I immediately think about Olivia. I nod without realizing as he continues. "Except it does matter at the end of the day," he sighs as the waitress brings us our new beers and he mumbles, "all of it matters." We sit for a second in comfortable silence, both staring into our beers.

I clear my throat. "Yeah man, I know exactly how that feels."

We stare at each other and he gives me a firm nod. "I figured," Grant says, giving me a sad smile. He squints past me, surprise lighting his eyes and bringing us both out of the moment. "I think I see Sloane?"

"Isn't she in San Francisco?" I peer around my shoulder and immediately spot her. Similarly to Grant, his sister towers over the group she's with. She's hard to miss, her strawberry blonde hair pushed back from her face, carelessly falling down to her waist. Her face is friendly and open just like Grant's but from what I remember she's not nearly as happy go lucky. They're polar opposites, Grant and his fraternal twin. Where he's athletic, she's artsy; where he radiates predictability and sturdiness, Sloane is carefree, whimsical, and a little flakey. Even so, they have that twin telepathy, built-in best friend thing going that makes you feel left out in their presence. Last he told me, she'd just secured an insane offer curating for a major museum in San Francisco, with the possibility of hosting her own show at some point. From the look on Grant's face, I can tell he's shocked to see her and unsettled that she wouldn't have told him she was in town.

"She's supposed to be. She just started her new gig there." He pushes back from the bar as Sloane, having spotted us, awkwardly approaches.

"Hi," she says in the voice you use with your parents when you just got caught doing something you're not supposed to.

"What are you doing back here?" With eyebrows raised and arms crossed, it's clear that Grant is no longer concerned with the girl he was mulling about just moments before.

"I— uh. I'm not technically back," she says, her face turning more red by the second.

I squint at her. "What do you mean 'technically'?" I speak on behalf of Grant who is currently taking another long pull of his beer.

"Meaning—" she huffs, "I am 'technically' not supposed to be here, nor does anyone know that I am." She gives me a tilt of her head, that Sloane attitude I've come to know shining through. It instantly reminds me of Olivia and I think about how much they would probably get along.

"What the fuck is that supposed to mean Sloane?" Grant's eyes are wide with panic, familiar with Sloane's history. I'm sure he thinks she's bailing on one of the biggest opportunities of her career right now — and maybe she is.

She flinches slightly. "I had to get out of there, Grant." She gives him this look that I've come to realize is some sort of twin telepathy thing because he quickly understands he needs to drop it. He moves forward with open arms trapping her into a giant bear hug. Her arms stay limp at her sides but she rolls her eyes and smiles until she finally wraps her arms around him, too. "Speaking of being back—" she says eyebrows raised, "I'm pretty sure the last time I was here you were in some sort of witness protection program or something?" I roll my eyes and Grant gives an exaggerated "HA!"

"Close— I was mostly just avoiding you."

She laughs and flips me the bird. "Asshole." I grin as Andrew approaches.

"Nice find," he says under his breath, swinging his arm over my shoulder.

"Goddammit, Andy," I groan.

"That's my sister, you sick fuck," Grant says, playfully shoving Andrew.

"Whoa whoa.." he says, hands raised. "Forgive me," he picks up Sloane's hand as if he's going to give it a peck. "You look nothing like syour brother." He winks and Sloane promptly pulls her hand away and slaps Andrew upside the head with it.

"I need a drink," she says, rolling her eyes for probably the twentieth time in the past thirty minutes.

"I'll join you," Grant and Andy say in unison. Grant

shoves him again, but nonetheless they both trail Sloane, Grant like the protective brother he is and Andrew like a lovesick puppy.

Alone, I realize I should probably do what I set out to do. I scan the bar and notice plenty of girls who peer back at me, eyes widening as my gaze meets theirs, but anytime I give it a second thought it's like there's a lead brick in my stomach as my mind immediately turns to Olivia. Just as I'm about to give up, an auburn haired girl slides into the spot Grant was previously taking up. She shoots me an easy smile.

"Come here often?" she says, a drunken giggle in her voice, amused at her own joke.

"No," I offer, laughing softly. "My friends wanted to do something different tonight."

"Pick up women somewhere other than your college bar?" she asks, smirking.

"So we *are* that transparent," I admit, chuckling, and I decide I can talk to this girl. She's funny, not overly eager, and seems self assured.

"I won't hold it against you," she winks, resting her hand on my bicep. I can tell she's feeling for their size by the way her hand wanders, and I have the urge to pick her off me. *But this is the point of tonight*, I remind myself.

"So," I begin, "what do you do?"

"I'm a third year at Harvard Law, actually." Pride beams from her, any modicum of modesty nowhere to be found.

"Wow. So, almost done?"

"Yeah, almost. And you go to Astor, right? Is it true that everyone who goes there is loaded?"

There's a mischievous glint in her eyes as she attempts to appear unsure of herself. "Sorry, my friend spotted you and told me who you were. I'm sure they're glad to have you back."

Annoyance tries to peak its way through, but I bat it away, committed to my plan.

"Yeah. So I'm Ben," I force a laugh. "And you are …? "

"Melanie," she offers me her hand, shaking mine over aggressively.

"Melanie," I turn her name over out loud. "What are you doing picking up college men? I mean you're practically out of the nest, and I'm still in it." I attempt to tap into my prior flirtatious persona, but end up feeling like I'm watching myself from across the bar.

"I…" she starts, fluttering her eyelashes, her hand traveling back up my arm. "I've heard incredible things about … well you, your family, and I thought I'd come see if they're true."

Shame washes over me when I think about who I was just a couple of years ago. I should be reveling in this attention, the way I would have before, but apparently the twice weekly therapy *has* made a dent in whatever validation void I was supposedly filling. Morgan coined that phrase for me.

Immediately, I hear her asking me that same question: *what do you think you should want, and what do you actually want?*

"I'm sorry, Melanie," I apologize, genuinely sorry for leading her on for even a second. "I'm… not really looking for anything right now." Partially a lie, but partially true. I'm not looking for anything, because I stumbled into the only thing I've really wanted since that night.

An embarrassed flush spreads across her face, her hand quickly wrapping itself around her drink. "No, of course, I—"

"I promise, it's really not you. My friend Andrew over there—" I point to Andrew, busy throwing darts like a showman as Sloane looks on annoyed but seemingly amused— "is who you should be looking for. Never known a woman to complain." I shrug in nonchalance, hoping she takes the bait. Sure enough, she gives me a quick nod before striding away, but I catch the look she sends her friends. I don't care if she saves face at my expense.

In fact I don't care about anything going on in this bar, and I realize I should just head home. When I search for Grant, I catch him at a high top rapidly typing something in his phone, Sloane to his right cheering Andy on as he hits the bullseye. Andrew's clearly soaking it up as that Melanie girl is also looking on. They won't miss me if I slip out.

My thoughts wander back to Olivia as I wait for my Uber to pull up. I open my phone finding her in my contact list.

What are you doing?

Backspace.

Where are you?

Backspace.

Can I see you?

Backspace.

I miss you.

She's probably with Will. I immediately hit the backspace, deleting the words as the thought lands like a pit in my stomach. Tonight may not have worked like I intended it to, but I have to keep trying. I have to keep trying to get her off my mind.

I'm going to hurt someone if I keep this going, but I just can't seem to stop. I think back to Grant's words. Everything I'm doing *does* matter. I can explain it away as innocent but I am well aware that my thoughts are anything but. I need to get over this. Not just for Will's sake, but for hers.

16

Olivia

My Neverfull ungracefully slides off my arm and onto Ian's couch, weighed down by my laptop *and* the multiple copies of this week's newspaper he demanded I transport for him.

"I thought we had people for this," I whine, tossing the copies his way.

"We do. You're just one of the people I rarely choose." His tart smile causes the corners of his eyes to crinkle, and I can't stay annoyed for long. If anything, I should be glad he's being this chill with me. I've been severely slacking on the column I cowrite, have only been to one meeting in the past two weeks, and still have nothing to show for Ben's story.

The thought of Ben's story makes my teeth grind against each other, and I hope that Ian won't bring it up.

"So where's my story?" he asks, resting his chin on his hands. *Dammit.* The expectant look on his face isn't necessarily aggressive, but it does tell me he's ready to lay the pressure on me. "A little birdie told me you two were awfully cozy in the city the other day." His eyes glitter with mischief, and while I don't want him to pry, I'm grateful Ian "the hard hitting editor-in-chief" isn't going to be hard hitting me. He wants gossip. *But how much can I tell him without ending up in the gossip column myself?*

"First of all, I resent the fact that you have little birdies spying on me— a staff member."

"You may be on staff here, Liv, but you're also one of *them*." He says "them" like the word itself is greasy, and I'm reminded that Ian harbors some resentment for the distinction between old money and new. It usually never comes to bear when he's with me, but I guess today he's feeling feisty.

I sigh, wishing I would've come up with an excuse when he texted me. Instead, I'm in his apartment getting the third degree.

"Second of all, we were on a class errand. There was nothing cozy about it," I add, shrugging nonchalantly. My day with Ben *had* felt cozy, but his radio silence, other than when we're in class, has felt anything but. I push the thought away, unwilling to let him consume even more of my thoughts.

"He was carrying your bags," he prods, his brows raising slightly.

My eyes narrow, intent on ending his speculation. "Because they were heavy?" I say this like it's obvious, which it kind of is. His eyes search mine, seeking the truth of the matter.

He purses his lips, like he's considering his next words wisely. "What are you doing, Liv?

"I mean, I've been busy, but I've already outlined my angle and—"

"No, what are you doing with *Ben*?"

I run my tongue across the top row of my teeth, wondering the same thing.

"Nothing," I tell him, because that *is* true. Nothing is happening between us.

"Listen," he leans in closer from across the counter, his expression uncharacteristically genuine. "I'm the first one to call Will out for the douchebag he is." I roll my eyes. "But things look messy from where I stand. And the Olivia Beckett I know doesn't do mess." He stands back from the counter, picking up the papers I tossed there earlier. He glances at the door, apparently dismissing me already. "So clean it up. And get me my story."

"I don't know if you're confused, Ian," I start, irritation prickling my neck, "but the value I add to the paper isn't in cheap sports gossip. I'll entertain your shallow assignments," I pause, watching him flush. "But I won't be treated like a junior contributor who can't point to a deadline on a whiteboard."

His flush dissipates, my words only unsettling him for a moment. "I see I've poked the bear," he says, a smug, playful grin on his lips. "So there is something there."

A sigh, over this conversation. "And even if there were, *you* would be the last person I would tell about it." I grab my bag and make my way to the door.

"Wiser words were never spoken!" he calls out as the door shuts, the mirth in his voice evidence that he won't hold my wit against me.

* * *

"Babe, I'm sure you look fine. Can we please get going?" Will complains from my kitchen, hurrying me along.

I take one last glance in the mirror, liking what I see. I've paired my blue knit dress with black Stuart Weitzman thigh highs and thrown the black cashmere cardigan I bought while out with Ben the other day over the dress. Half of my hair is swept up with a banana clip, the front pieces continuously escaping no matter what I try. This is what's taking so long. Shaking my hair out so it's all down again, I grab my clutch and head toward the kitchen.

"See. Totally fine!" Will exclaims after a cursory glance at my ensemble.

"Thanks," I grumble, snatching my keys off the counter and heading toward my car.

We're on our way to a team dinner, sanctioned by their coach and caused by "the recent discord amongst the players," or so Will said. Apparently dining at an upscale restaurant is meant to solve whatever problems the guys are having. Plus ones were invited, maybe as a buffer, so here I am. Most of the team is there when we finally show up, and Will is bristling with irritation at our tardiness.

"Andy's not even here yet, Will," I say, smoothing my hand down his arm. "I think we're okay."

He glances around the table to verify and I feel the tension dissipate almost immediately.

"Sorry babe," he apologizes, setting his green eyes on me, that boyish grin reappearing. "It's been a long week." He grabs my hand, pressing a hard kiss to it, and leads me to our seat.

It isn't until we're about to be seated across from him that I realize this dinner will involve being in the same room as Will *and* Ben. Not that it should matter, but he's been missing in action since our seminar on Monday. He's answered my texts about class, but nothing else. *There shouldn't be anything else*, I remind myself, but the disappointment remains.

My gaze lands on a gorgeous copper tinted blonde, laughing far too intensely at something Ben just said. She seems overly familiar with him, her posture not nearly nervous enough to be on a first, second, or even third date. Annoyance rolls over me before I swat it away. *Who am I to judge Ben for his choice in women? Why do I even care?*

I clutch Will's hand tightly under the table, and move it to my thigh, flirtatiously glancing his way as he caresses it. I sneak a glance at Ben who, oblivious to us, rolls his eyes, smirking at mystery girl's amusement, before recognizing the couple who just sat before him, something like alarm flashing in his eyes. He quickly recovers, giving us a friendly wave.

"Hey, Will," he says, a tepid smile on his lips. "Olivia," he nods, like we're barely acquaintances. I can't help but feel offended, even though I shouldn't. I haven't even *told* Will about my day with Ben, yet. He almost flipped when I told him we studied together. What would he do if I told him we spent the day in the city? *This is for the best*, I convince myself. *For all intents and purposes we aren't anything more than acquaintances, anyway.*

"Hi," the blonde squeaks with a hint of southern drawl, snatching my hand and clutching it tightly. "I'm Sloane. Where did you get that sweater? I absolutely love," she exaggerates the word love, reaching across the table to run her hand over the cashmere.

Rarely taken aback, I stutter. "Uh… Veronica Beard, over on Newbury." I peek at Ben to find his gaze coolly resting on me.

The girl abruptly turns to Grant, seated to her left, and grabs his arm. "Remind me to stop at Veronica Beard when we go to Newbury tomorrow. I *have* to have that sweater. Do they have it in anything less… dreary?" she asks, squinting one eye as if that somehow makes her characterization of my favorite color better.

"I see you've met my sister," a tight, but loving expression on his face. Understanding dawns on me, and I realize this girl is most likely *not* Ben's date at all.

"Sorry, I was just so distracted by how soft your sweater looks," she all but giggles.

"I'm glad someone likes it," I reply, deciding I find Sloane incredibly endearing. I tilt my head toward Will as I say, "This one thought it was just 'fine'."

Sloane gasps in mock disbelief.

"I said you look *totally* fine, to be clear. And yeah, I mean it's nothing to write home about. Not worth being late over," he adds, mumbling audibly. Sloane squints at Will, disdain seeping from her gaze.

"You look great, Olivia," Ben contradicts his brother, apparently deciding I'm worth speaking to. "You were right when you saw it on the rack— that color suits you," he says, reaching across Sloan to grab a piece of bread. His gaze isn't on me though, it's on Will, an antagonistic smirk settled on his face.

"What does he mean 'you were right'?" Will mutters to me under his breath, sharply pulling his hand off my thigh. *Fuck.*

"We had to run an errand for that class we're in and I wanted to stop by a couple stores. I could have sworn I told you," I casually remark, wanting to kick Ben under the table for even mentioning it, but when I nudge my foot forward I most certainly come into contact with Sloane's calf.

"Hmph," Will scoffs. "You keep swearing you told me things, and I keep swearing you didn't." I hum in agreement, brushing him off, and thank the heavens when the waiter finally makes his way to our section.

The rest of the dinner continues without another disturbance; Sloane and Grant switch spots so that he can more easily converse with Ben and Will, and Sloane and I discuss the democratization of art which I admittedly know little about, but Sloane gives me quite the education. By the time we're debating whether to grab dessert here or at the ice cream parlor down the street, I've completely forgotten about Ben's subtle admission.

"The lavender bacon ice cream sounds like an odd pairing, but I swear—" I'm extolling the virtues of Little Boo's ice cream flavors when Will cuts me off.

"I think we're gonna get going though, right babe?" he demands more than asks, irritation lurking in his eyes.

I give in, choosing to have this out in the comfort of my home rather than Little Boo's tiny store font.

"Oh my gosh, you're right. We were…" I hesitate to generate a quick lie, and Ben's calculating stare clocks it. "We were going to watch that new A24 movie together. And we already have ice cream in my freezer. But get the lavender bacon, Sloane— I promise you'll love it."

"Yeah, sure," Sloane reassures me, suspiciously glancing at Will before pushing up from the table. "Hopefully, I'll see you around. I'm here *indefinitely*." She says indefinitely like the word itself is haunted and laughs.

"Yes," I smile, eager to have a friend. "Will you be at the gala?"

"No, I'm seeing a show that night, but I'll text you!"

I feel Will pulling my chair out, signaling that it's time to go. "Yes— get my number from Grant," I say, not wanting to make Will wait any longer.

Once we're in the car, an uncomfortable silence sets in. His mouth is set in a determined line, and he hasn't so much as glanced at me since we got in the car. He's fuming, and for once he's not totally wrong for it. I didn't tell him about my day with Ben because I *knew*, regardless of when he found out, this would happen. Maybe I was hoping to staunch the fallout, but on some level I knew this was inevitable. My heart races as I consider how this could go, a pit forming in my stomach.

"Sloane was nice," I blandly state.

"Yup," Will says, dedicated to the silent treatment I'm now sure he's giving me. *I guess I'll be the one to rip off the bandaid.*

"Will," I start, glancing at him in my passenger seat. "I didn't think it was crucial you know I did a thing for class. Since when do we tell each other every single thing we did each day? 'Today, I chose my checkered mug over my floral one.' I just—"

"Cut the shit, Liv. I'm not an idiot, and neither are you," he cuts in, looking out the window. I pause, guilt jacketing me in my seat.

"You're right. I'm sorry I didn't tell you I was with Ben. I knew you would get weird and I… just wanted to avoid it, because there is nothing to be weird or worry about." I feel the lie the moment it comes out of my mouth. I catch the fire erupt in Will's eyes, and something in me begins to unfurl itself. Like that lie was the last one in a long line of them, the lie that broke the camel's back. It feels… not as horrible as I thought it would, and the dread in my stomach transforms into a fire of my own.

"Really? There is *nothing* to worry about? I told you to stay away from him," he presses, looking directly at me now.

"You know, Will, for the first time in a long time, I wasn't even thinking about what you would think when I chose to go into the city," I reply, defiance settling in my bones. "I just did it. Because he offered to come with me and it made sense. There was no special calculus, no agenda. But this reaction is *why* I didn't tell you."

"I can't *trust* you, Liv." His hands tangle with his blonde waves, his eyes pressing shut.

"I have done nothing but be everything you want me to be, for years, Will. For years. But the minute I don't let you control me, because that *is* what this is, you can't trust me?" I scoff, unable to meet his gaze as I feel him look at me.

"I control you, now?" His laughter is laced with venom as he shakes his head at me. "Seemed like we were on the same page until Ben showed up."

"A page you chose! When, in the past two years, have we made choices that center me? It's always about you, Will."

"So this is about control?" He gives me a withering look, full of disdain. "That's fucking pathetic." I feel anger climb up my throat, incensed by his commitment to this narrative he's crafting about me.

"You know what is pathetic? The number of times I've watched you hit on women, *in front of me*, and done nothing. What's pathetic is how you let Gen cosplay as your girlfriend when I'm not around, and I blame *her*. What's pathetic is how I let you speak to me, the way you did tonight, and turn the other cheek." I feel tears prick at my eyes, frustration welling there instead of sadness. "I don't even know how we ended up here." I think back to the night of that kegger, the way he told me he'd been looking for me. The way he took charge of our conversation and how charming I found it, found him. "You know, that night we met I could've sworn you were looking for Lily." I finally turn toward him, contempt settling in my chest.

"I told you—"

"I know what you told me, Will, and it isn't even about

that. It's about how from the start, it has never felt like I'm a priority."

"Of course you're my priority, Liv—"

"If this is what being your priority feels like, then I don't want it anymore," I say exasperated, but with clarity. I think I'd been feeling this way for a while, but was just in denial.

"Where is this coming from?" His eyes search mine intensely, like he'll find something he can hook into and reclaim, when suddenly, he scoffs. "Something happened, didn't it?"

I narrow my eyes at him, the suggestion making my heart race. "How dare you, of all people, ask me that."

"That isn't an answer, Liv."

"Of course nothing happened! Are you—" I take a deep breath, willing the chaos of this conversation to end. "I need a break, Will. I need a break from this. From you," I decide, relief washing over me the moment the words are out in the ether.

"I don't," he says, his voice tinged with confusion and laced with panic. "We don't need a break. What we need is—"

"You don't *trust* me, Will! You just accused me of *cheating* on you." I'm shaking my head in disbelief, his denial of the shit-show we've become astounding to me. I know I've been crossing lines with Ben, lines that I never should have approached, and I feel guilty for that. But I have not, and I would not, cheat.

"I..." his voice drifts off, his lips pressing firmly together. "I can't lose you."

I watch his jaw twitch, his teeth undoubtedly grinding against each other in irritation.

"Why not, Will?" I give him the chance to explain, to tell me why this fight should be like all our other ones. He opens and closes his mouth once, twice, before his shoulders barely shrug.

"I just… can't, Liv."

I roll my lips, unsurprised.

"The right answer would've been because you love me."

His eyes roll, annoyance and frustration rolling off him in waves.

"Of course, I love you! I wouldn't be over here losing my mind if I didn't."

"But is that love, or is that possession?" He's shaking his head, denial etched in every line of his face. "I'm serious, Will. I can't do this anymore."

"You said a break, Liv. Please just… let's take a break," he pleads, those beautiful green eyes shining with desperation. I just want this to be over, but some small part of me can't bear to do it. To end it right now and deal with the fall out. I never imagined what it would be like to break up with Will, but if I had, it wouldn't have been like this.

I imagined us invincible, forever. I imagined there would be scandal and joy and heartbreak and shock and worry and hope, but that regardless we would find a way through. I imagined that our partnership, our alignment, our relationship, would be able to weather any storm because we were bound by something so much more stable than love. Will and I were bonded by this common vision we held for our futures. Those early months were dark for me, in so many ways, but Will built the concept of us with me, brick by brick, while I waded out of that darkness, and he gave me hope. It felt so immovable then, and I just don't understand why it doesn't feel so now. Instead, it feels suffocating.

"A break, Will," I sigh. "And I don't think we should go

to the gala together. I think if this is going to work, I need you to actually give me space."

His gears spin, his eyes tracking something on my expression, before he sighs in resignation.

"Yeah, okay, Liv." He looks at me from under his lashes, his eyes weary. "I guess I'll see you later." He opens the car door and steps out before ducking back in. "I do love you, Olivia."

"Okay," I nod, his reassurance doing nothing for me. He stays there for a moment, waiting for something more from me, before shutting the door and walking away.

I believe that Will thinks he loves me. I'm just not sure he knows what love is.

My phone lights up in my center console and I check, half expecting a monologue from Will.

BEN

Hope everything's ok?

I smile, despite myself. This entire argument happened because of Ben, but I can't find it in me to blame him for the way it went. This fight felt inevitable, but it also feels unfinished. If anything, Ben was just blowing oxygen into the fire, which would've happened anyway.

It will be.

BEN

Sorry I said anything. I wasn't thinking.

Don't be.

Only one us had to get ice cream with Gen.

BEN

Ha. Goodnight, Beckett.

Night.

Clicking my phone shut, I pull out of Will's complex, feeling lighter than I've felt in months. Maybe years. I don't know what I'll do next with Will, but I know that I have time to figure that out. For the first time in a long time, I feel untethered, free to question myself without contradicting all my plans. I'm accepting that, maybe, just maybe, my best laid plans aren't everything I've made them out to be.

17

Ben

The Annual Charity Celebration Gala, which pointedly takes place before anyone has actually donated to any charitable organizations for the academic year, is a legacy event at Astor Hill. While membership in a prestigious society or campus organization might get you in the room, what matters more is family and money. Get a room full of the wealthiest people in Boston together and you're guaranteed to attract donors for everything from the Boys and Girls Club of Boston to the for-profit organization masquerading as a 501c. It's the night when the "who's who" of Boston and Astor Hill elite get to bump shoulders and validate the existence of said elite.

An event like this should, in theory, veer on the side of cost-efficient, modest decor and accommodations, but one look around this room makes it clear money was no object. The State Room sits at the top of 60 State Street, overlooking the harbor. Walking in, I'm drawn to the glass paned walls that offer crystal clear views of the water, shimmering with the echoes of Boston lights at night. A black and white checkered dance floor consumes a quarter of the space, the heavy, wooden full bars and velvety green cocktail tables assuming the rest of it. Light refracts and glimmers from up above, and I notice that disco balls are hung from the insanely high ceilings between the elaborate, suspended clusters of white flowers. Beyond the line of disco balls exists a balcony that I now realize is connected to the level I am on by a wide, grand staircase.

"Ben Cabot! Well, if it isn't the man himself, in the *flesh*," a gravely, feminine voice coos from behind me. I turn to see a woman, tightly wrapped in black velvety fabric, a champagne glass delicately resting between her middle and ring fingers, her elbow resting in the small nook of her hip. She's leering at me, her crooked smile calculating as her eyes travel across my face. My mind struggles to produce a name for the face before me.

"I'm sorry, it's been a while. Do I...," I offer with a neutral chuckle, unsure if I know this woman or not.

"Know me? I'm afraid not. See this——" she purrs as she steps closer to me "—— is me amending that. Elizabeth Phillips." Her free hand juts forward, and I take it, not at all surprised that it's slightly clammy and uncomfortable in mine.

Shaking her hand, I recall, "And I'm Ben... as you know." My eyes search above her head for an escape. I'm not necessarily looking for what I think she's seeking. Lucky for me, I see Grant ascend the grand staircase. "I'm sure we'll meet again, Ms. Phillips," I say politely, nodding my head in the most 'you are definitely my elder' fashion, trying my best to stifle the laughter forming at her audacity.

She clings to my hand a moment longer before releasing it. Behind me, I hear, "Call me Lizzie!"

Grant sees me before I reach the top of the staircase, his

welcoming smile resuming its usual spot on his face. "Wanna tell me why your phone went to voicemail and the ride I thought I had to this shit ghosted me?" As I get closer, I see that smile floats on a sea of concern.

Stuffing my hands in my pockets, I stand next to Grant at the balcony overlooking the bustling gala below. I'd completely forgotten I was supposed to take Grant until just now, and I feel like a shit friend for it.

"I'm sorry, man. Time got away from me this afternoon, and then I forgot about tonight until maybe an hour ago."

The concern on his face slightly abates, but I know he still has questions for me. I spent the afternoon at a rescheduled therapy appointment with Morgan, but Grant doesn't need to know that. Most of my session was spent unraveling my complicated feelings for Olivia. Turns out your therapist can't solve the unethical attraction you have for your brother's girlfriend. All she had to offer was: "Try to give it some space." I'd given it nothing but space, but here I am, scouring the clusters of attendees for the delicate slope of her shoulder and listening for the lilt of her laugh.

"Apology accepted," he insists, elbowing me in the side. "I ended up driving with Will anyway."

"... and Olivia?" I assume, confused at his non-mention of her.

"No, she wasn't with him. He said she was meeting him here." I feel Grant quickly glance over at me, but my expression remains cool and unfazed. Beneath it, I'm mulling over every reason Olivia might have to show up separate from Will.

"Hmph." In my pockets, my hands itch at the inside fabric of the tuxedo pants, eager to fidget with something other than the flimsy thoughts in my mind.

"My sentiments exactly," Grants says, suppressing a huff. "It's so hot and cold with those two."

My teeth grind against each other without my permission. "Yeah, I've noticed," I grimace. "Where is he, anyway?"

Grant's eyes slant toward me and he winces.

"Never mind," I decide, already reminded of Will's text to Olivia the other week. I hadn't been able to keep it to myself, the anger I feel every time she lets him make her feel like she comes second and the suffocating feeling that overwhelms me when I witness her doubting herself. The surety that radiates when she's fucking decimated with a verbal jab, a picture, a sneer; and yet, she stays. God knows why. She's so conditioned to accept it. She did it with me at the end of our day in the city. How she could ever think she was *inconvenient* to me is… unbelievable. But I have Will to blame for that.

"I better head down there and do some schmoozing. You're not gonna catch me running laps tomorrow morning," Grant says, pretending to be exasperated. The schmoozing is, of course, a necessity on nights like this, especially when you're on the basketball team. Securing community sponsors, while beneficial for the handful of scholarships we dole out every year, is also crucial for our image in the greater Boston area. Coach takes it very seriously; so much so, that our gala attendance comes with a quota— secure at least one community sponsor.

Grant steps his way down the stairs, his hulking form restricted in the shoulders by his curtly tailored tux jacket. I'm standing on the balcony alone, hands braced on the railing when I spot a head of thick, chestnut waves settled over bare shoulders. I'd know that luscious head of hair from a mile away.

Noticing I haven't breathed since I spotted her, I pull in a breath only to feel it collect shallowly in my chest. My pulse quickens as I watch her move through the room. Rolling her lips together, she searches the room for, I'm assuming, Will.

Dress swishing around her legs, the glistening coffee-colored fabric shifting to hide and then reveal the most distracting swath of skin up to her thigh, she almost floats. I have the sudden urge to go to her, the feeling almost identical to the pull I felt that night I first saw her, when I see her join Gen at the bar. I've been staring, I recognize in alarm, so I run my hand down the back of my head in an attempt to reorient myself. I can't be ogling my brother's girlfriend at a public event. I can't be ogling my brother's girlfriend, period.

"Benjamin Cabot, welcome back!" a vaguely familiar man says, patting my back, voice booming. After a moment I realize he's been one of our biggest donors, an alumni who started a tech company that eventually sold itself to Facebook. The man's loaded *and* influential.

I glance over his shoulder toward the bar, my stomach somersaulting at the sight of Olivia's beauty even from across the room. *Guess I better get started on that quota*, I think to myself, welcoming the distraction.

"Thank you, sir," I say, cringing at myself. The man is middle aged, but something about the solid gray shirt he decided to wear to a black tie function tells me he doesn't appreciate "sir."

"What took you so long? Me and the rest of the alumni folk kept pestering Wilson about your return. Told him he should drag you back, if that's what it takes!" His laugh is boisterous, so far from the laugh I'd expect from him.

"My gap year took a little longer than expected," I awkwardly chuckle, looking past him for a way out.

"Gap years aren't really the kind of thing *we* do, though, are they?" he asks, the glint in his eye suggesting his agenda here isn't to offer the team money, but to pry information out of me. There is no part of me that cares to protect Dan from what is, objectively, not even that scandalous— that I left because I was in a mental health crisis. But every part of me wants to avoid the possibly negative attention that my brother, myself, and my team would get if that information were to circulate amongst these circles.

I give him a simple shrug, hoping he'll let it go. "I think I see someone I need to grab," I say, feeling only a little bad that I'm dismissing him without securing any funding.

These nights are always tedious, but the focus on my departure and return is kind of unexpected to me. *It's going to be a long night*, I think to myself, when I see that flash of metallic brown again. *But I'm not leaving until I see her.*

18

Olivia

I knew this night was a disaster waiting to happen. I chose to wear a metallic, deep espresso gown as opposed to the slinky ensemble Will so thoughtfully (read: lazily) picked out for me, knowing that wearing the red dress he purchased would send him some sort of signal that things were going to be fine between us. That this so-called 'break' was really just temporary, but the feelings that rushed through me the moment I stepped out of his car implied anything but.

For the first time since Lily's death, I feel like I finally have the space to take a step back and really look at my life — my feelings— without the burden of how those feelings are going to make *Will* feel. It felt like the first step to getting back to the person I'm meant to be, instead of orbiting a man who I *thought* was protecting me from the grief that's built up inside me since my best friend's death, but was maybe just hindering me from moving past it.

I allow myself to move through the lobby of the state room, a bar and lounge area to the left and a coat check to the right. I decided to forgo a coat for this event, not wanting to hide my gown, but I feel a chill climb up my spine like an omen. I instantly regret it. I'm met with the cutting stare of Gen's deep hazel eyes at the bar. If she wasn't such a bitch I would admit that they were striking, maybe even beautiful, but she is, so I'll equate her eyes to that of the walking dead— intense, but utterly soulless. She's standing at the bar alone in the gown she's sporting, pitch black as if any light within her doesn't exist, the skirt flowing across the floor in a pool around her feet. It's not completely hideous; it was clearly meant to one-up what she chose for me. I shudder at the thought of her and Will holding what was essentially lingerie, laughing at me.

"Will won't be pleased seeing you in that. He spent *countless* hours with me, trying to find a dress that would really suit you," she says down her nose, the insult not reaching her eyes. Her tone seems… sad actually. I feel a pang deep down in the bottom of my stomach as I see her eyes move back to the olive at the end of her toothpick. She pulls it out, picking up the martini and downing it.

"Speaking of, I assume you know where my estranged boyfriend is?" I say, rolling my eyes and ignoring whatever bizarre sympathetic reaction my body is having toward Gen. I scan the bar, my plan tonight one of avoidance. I'm hoping to avoid any sort of public confrontation, if at all possible. I don't need Will to incessantly bring up that we are on a break in every conversation, and I definitely don't need him insinuating that it's temporary until I've fully made up my mind. The only reason I'm even mentioning it to Gen is because I know she is likely well aware of all things Will, as per usual.

"I don't know how you did it," she says sloppily, wiping her hand over her upper lip. She looks up at me, her eyes even more severe as tears bloom at the corners, making the hazel almost kaleidoscopic with the gold and brown tones melting into green. Her dark pinned up tendrils fall loose around her face. "How you didn't have more self respect all these years." Her sad tone turns into a drunken giggle, as if my lack of 'self respect' is the funniest thing in the world to her.

I feel my face turn pink as I squint my eyes, confused as to what is going on here.

"Bartender, please cut her off. This woman has had enough to drink," I fake yell to the bartender a good 20 feet away, but Gen's the only one who hears me and the comment makes her laugh harder. A few of the older patrons surrounding us turn toward the gorgeous ballerina, seemingly completely off her rocker. Her laughs begin to settle and she puts her hand into her face, her shoulders shaking and it's hard to tell if she's still laughing or beginning to cry.

"Gen… are you alright?" I say quietly, real concern taking over my face.

Gen pushes up abruptly, causing her to wobble slightly before sitting back down. Her face has transformed in mere seconds to the venomous one I've grown accustomed to. She pulls out a hundred dollar bill slamming it on the counter with dramatic effect, making her drunken state even more obvious as the martini was likely only thirteen dollars.

"Olivia, let's be honest," she slurs as she slowly angles her body toward mine. "If I needed someone's pity it certainly wouldn't be yours. Do you want to know where your "boyfriend" is?" Her hushed voice is filled with rage as she uses air quotes with the word boyfriend. "Maybe ask the slut who went into the coat check with him," she says, tears running down her face.

She uses the back of her hand again, smearing her black charcoal mascara across her cheek. Just as she turns to leave, we both see Will duck out of the coat check, straightening his tie and mussing his hair. A few seconds later a petite busty girl with jet black hair walks out behind him, her white mini dress barely covering her.

With her back turned to me Gen whispers under her breath, "I feel sorry for you." Her posture seems to wilt as she gazes at the scene before us and I quickly realize that mine doesn't change at all.

My eyes trail Will and the small raven-haired girl speed walking to keep up with him.

Gen's body sinks back down on the barstool closest to me and I ask the bartender for two shots of tequila. He eyes me suspiciously.

"We don't really do shots at this sort of thing..." his voice trails.

I set down two one hundred dollar bills, finally understanding the level of Gen's desperation for a drink. "Two shots, coming up!"

I suck in my cheeks observing Gen, her head hung low as she uses a tissue and compact to try and salvage her makeup, even though tears are still streaming down her face. *That should be me*, I think to myself. I observe the crease of her brow, how the hand holding the tissue is shaking as her breathing remains unsteady, clearly trying to hold back the emotions building up inside her. I look down at my legs sheathed in the reflective fabric of my gown. Biting my lip, I realize how numb I feel. Sure, I'm surprised that Will would so publicly disrespect me, but mostly because it will affect his reputation, something Will is very cognizant of.

"You must be in shock," Gen sniffs beside me, handing

me a tissue only to see that I'm not crying when she meets my eyes.

"I actually think I'm fine, weirdly enough," I sigh. "Are you okay though, Gen?" she squints at me as if she can't comprehend my emotionless response.

"Am *I* okay?" she emphasizes the I as if to say 'you're the one who has a cheating boyfriend'.

I sigh, offering her a sad laugh. "I'm sure this wasn't your desired outcome, if Will and I were to end things…"

She bites her lip considering what I'm saying. "Why did you stay with him?" she asks, staring into the bar, trying to school her own emotions. I roll my lips together thinking about this. Will was a lot of things but a *consistently* good boyfriend wasn't one of them. Memories of the past few years filter through my memory, especially the months after Lily's death and how Will somehow brought me back to life. Though now, I'm realizing, there are cracks, pieces of myself I haven't completely mended or dealt with because he shielded me from them. So, maybe that's why I stayed with him for so long; I wasn't ready to thoroughly heal. I didn't think I deserved to.

I look at Gen for what feels like the first time and I really see her. She's undoubtedly beautiful. Tall and lean from hours upon hours spent at her dance studio, her arms are slender and muscular. Her skin is a creamy brown without a single imperfection and her dark tendrils frame her face that radiantly glows. I never noticed before. She's probably one of the most stunning people I've ever seen and she is in love with Will, so devoted to him in a way I never have been.

It begs the question: why did he *never* want to be with *her*, this nearly perfect girl sitting before me? It reminds me of my dad anytime I'd bring up all the ways I was jealous of Lily.

"You won't be happy until you're happy with yourself," he'd say.

I think that sentiment holds true for Will. It's almost like he was using me too, a shield from all the small cracks he didn't want to face and I realize I don't blame him for it.

I look at Gen again and she meets my eyes, that question dancing between both of us unanswered. *Why did you stay with him?*

"We both stayed with him, Gen."

Her eyes go sad again but she motions to the bartender, taking out two more hundreds. "Another round?"

Now sufficiently buzzed, my drunken brain has convinced myself that I can continue evading Will as long as I spend the rest of my night getting hammered at this gala. Gen left shortly after the second shot, claiming she had to "meet someone." I was glad for her departure.

Despite the chaotic heart to heart we just had, there's still this resentful tension between us, but it's something to work out at a later date.

I stand and the world fuzzes around me. After gulping down four tequila shots I'm more drunk than I originally intended, and my four-inch stilettos seem like maybe not the best choice. The bartender eyes me and hands me a glass of water, my flirtatious smile lighting him up as he watches me chug the contents of the cup. Thankfully the water steadies me, but I know those shots are going to get me in trouble tonight.

As I move away from the bar I hear someone behind

me rather loudly say, "Well look at this intergalactic princess." I turn and am met with a blue buzzed head and a blindingly handsome smile. Ian.

"Thank god!" I yelp and pull him into a hug.

He pulls back immediately suspicious. "My, my, Olivia. You're drunk."

"Not drunk… a little drunk." I swat his arm.

"I'm assuming you saw Will and the gnat that's been following him around all evening." With his arm around me he guides me into the ballroom. Grand chandeliers glitter across the vast ceiling, an ornate balcony houses a second bar that looks down on the checkerboard dance floor, and on the grand staircase a harpist plays a melody that can't be heard over the DJ. What a waste.

"I wasn't the only one who saw. Gen was… upset to say the least."

Ian smiled at this. "Oh yeah, we saw old raccoon eyes when we arrived."

That foreign feeling of guilt toward Gen pangs inside my stomach.

"So, my little protege, what will you do with this knowl-edge?" I swallow, the question sobering me up slightly. It was times like this I yearned for Lily or just female compan-ionship in general. Ian was great but everything with him was plotting or scheming. He had a zero tolerance policy when it came to conversations about feelings.

"Well— we are on a break—"

"Excuse me? When were you going to tell me this?" he asks, eyebrows raised.

"When I was ready for the entire world to know, meaning when I knew the 'break' wouldn't be a temporary thing." I give him a pointed stare.

"Right, yeah, running a gossip paper tends to make one a bit of a 'blabber mouth.'" He rolls his eyes. "I'm assuming then, since you're now telling me, that you've made that decision."

"No comment," I say drunkenly, batting my lashes at him as he playfully shoves me.

Ian kisses my cheek as he says his goodbyes, saying he has a lead on a story he has to run down. I watch him trot up the stairs past the harpist and just as my gaze shifts, I feel *him* watching me.

My entire body heats as my eyes move up his torso, his perfectly tailored suit making my drunkenness hit me like a wave as my stomach does a complete one eighty. *Ben would have that effect on any girl who's four shots deep*, I tell myself. I pivot my eyes to the dance floor and pretend I'm looking for someone, trying to get a handle on my face burning with heat. I swallow as my gaze shifts back to him, a shy smile plastered across his handsome face. Either he caught me looking or he's genuinely happy to see me. My breath catches and comes out in a rough gasp. Realizing more than likely too late that I'm utterly giving my attraction away, I begin moving toward him.

I round the final stair on the grand staircase and take him in. His hair is mussed the way it was when we studied, like he just dried it with a towel out of the bath. His suit is expertly tailored, highlighting his broad frame in a way that makes it apparent he commands not only the basketball team but any space he walks into. I suck in a breath, mustering up my confidence.

"Well, don't you look nice," I say, making a point to run my eyes down his body.

He smiles, a blush blooming across his face. "You look

nice too, Olivia." He looks down at his shoes, trying to avoid my gaze.

I sigh, annoyed he's not giving me the reaction I'm craving. "Let's try this again, Ben," I say with false, booze filled bravado. "Well, don't you look handsome."

He lifts his eyes, meeting mine, his so dark I feel like they're sucking me into them. I have no choice but to lower my own and am met again with his immaculate body, my tequila infused brain having no problem allowing my eyes to make their way down it a second time. I catch the corner of his mouth twitching, attempting to reign in his smile as he observes me.

He ducks his head, his minty breath against my ear sending an involuntary shiver down my back.

"I like your dress."

I feel the red creeping up my chest, his hand lightly grazing my hip. All of the lights seem to twinkle a little brighter, the music a little more finely tuned. I glance around, trying to bring myself back to reality. While I am not planning for this break to be a temporary thing with Will, I'm also not looking to completely embarrass him. Besides, Ben isn't flirting with me, is he? I'm drunk and he's just being polite. *But that feeling of his hand grazing my hip.* I shake my head, trying to snap myself out of this trance.

The harpist I saw earlier begins playing a soft melody that I instantly recognize. It takes me back to my etiquette school days, the balls Lily and I attended, and the boys who seemed to flock to her as I navigated my awkward middle school body.

"Livy, you have to dance with us," Lily shouts as Colin Hemmes, the most sought after boy in the grade above us begins pulling Lily toward the dance floor. "I hear Jeffrey really likes you— ask him! You two would be so cute together!" she yelps as she finally lets Colin pull

her in for a slow dance. My eyes drift to Jeffrey, a shy boy with pretty terrible acne who hasn't quite grown out of his baby fat. I would look cute with him? He's at least two feet shorter than me. I look down at my gangly long legs and my feet that seem clownish compared to the petite feet of my friends.

My heart sinks as I watch Colin's golden blonde hair fall into his eyes as he looks longingly at my best friend, her silken hair almost glowing in the lights around her. My vision blurs at the realization that they look cute together, perfect even.

I begin to feel hot with embarrassment at the memory and feel exposed underneath Ben's handsome gaze. I subconsciously wrap my arms around myself now embarrassed that I so openly flirted with Ben. I just sort of blew up my life and not necessarily *for* Ben but still, this nagging feeling inside me knows that he was definitely a factor. I never considered the possibility that he could reject me, but those old insecurities that Lily would bring out still plague me. When they come up mid conversation, it's hard to shake the feeling that I'm still that awkward teenager with the beautiful best friend.

"Hey… you okay?" Ben asks, pulling back to look down at me, concern flashing across his gaze as he notices my body language has changed. I clear my voice, trying to shake the drunken memory I somehow landed in.

"Should we dance?" I say motioning toward the dance floor at the bottom of the stairs. His eyes track the ballroom and I know he's basing his decision on the whereabouts of his brother. "It's worth noting that Will and I broke up." I try to keep my tone neutral although there is a twinge of desperation in my voice that even I'm not used to.

Ben instantly freezes. "What?" It's barely audible and I can't help but feel a twinge of disappointment that he isn't jumping for joy, but of course he isn't. Will is his brother.

What did I think, that we'd end things and Ben would want to just pick up in his place? Clearly his loyalty lies with Will. I feel nervous beads of sweat forming along my hairline. "When?" His voice is a whisper his face a picture of shock.

"Well, technically we are on a 'break' but— I don't know there's a lot going on." I blurt out, wishing I hadn't said anything in the first place.

"Oliv—" he starts but I cut him off.

"Look I know this situation is complicated and I completely get it if you don't want to be seen with me but —" He stops me short, wrapping his long arms around me in an embrace. His face nuzzles into my hair inhaling my scent. The hug is comfort incarnate, all warmth and safety as if no one can see me outside the walls of his arms.

He slowly releases me and I feel completely and utterly vulnerable. "You okay?" he asks softly.

"I just want to not think about all of it. I just want to have one good night before I have to deal with it. Can we just dance?" Drunkenness fuels my desperation as I grasp Ben's hand. For a moment he stares into my eyes and I can no longer tell if I feel unsteady because of the alcohol or his gaze.

"Of course I'll dance with you, Liv." It comes out quietly, gingerly, almost a whisper but not quite. His face is innocent and shy and perfect. I instantly forget the optics of what this looks like, or maybe I just don't care.

I pull Ben toward the dance floor just as they start to play a slow song. He raises an eyebrow at me as if to say *he's game if I am.* I softly put my hand on his shoulder to reassure him as he draws me in at the waist. I rest my head on his chest and we sway and listen to the sound of each other breathing. He somehow smells like all of my favorite things, his body warm and firm, allowing me to melt into him. The song ends and another begins but we lose the rhythm.

He feels like my childhood home, a lit candle in a freshly clean kitchen, a hot cup of tea with just a little milk and sugar. The world fades and I realize I never felt like this with Will, like the entire world was moved off its axis when we were together, like us being together happened by some miracle and now all the pieces of myself seem to fit together more perfectly. I don't feel the need to tuck parts of myself away, hide them from his view. I close my eyes and let the smell of him, the closeness of him, seep into me.

A song with a quicker tempo comes on and pulls us out of our trance.

"We should get a drink," I suggest.

Realistically, I shouldn't get plastered at the biggest event of the academic year but something about Ben makes me feel safe, like I can let loose and everything will be fine. A smile pulls on the corner of his lips.

"What?" I blurt a blush rising to my cheeks. Maybe he thinks I've gone insane. Maybe he doesn't want to waste his whole night with me.

"I like you like this."

My blush deepens. *Is he making fun of me?* "Like what?" I say a bit defiantly.

"A bit unraveled. Uncensored." Ben's eyes twinkle with mischief as he looks down at me.

"So is that a yes to the drink?" I say, rolling my lips together to hide my own smile. He makes a face like he's considering and then grabs my hand, leading me to the bar. I laugh, a real laugh, not a snarky one or a flirtatious one—a real, full laugh.

Ben is grinning when we get to the bar, his gaze mulling over me like a warm blanket. "I love that sound."

I smile, and he orders us a round of shots. I realize the bartenders don't give him nearly the hard time they gave me. He hands me my shot and holds his up in a toast.

"To one good night," he says, his face like a child with a secret.

"To one good night."

19

Ben

"So, here's the plan—" I say as Olivia looks up at me, hands on her hips and her game face on, like she's one of my teammates ready for the next drill. "You're going to go up to those women and start singing my praises." She crosses her arms, shooting one eyebrow up, which makes me laugh. "Trust me!" I say, chuckling.

"You really think they are going to donate just because of your charm and good looks?" she says, eyebrows still raised.

"So you're saying I look good?" I wink and she bursts out laughing. Her laughter radiates through me, not for the first time tonight. I somehow feel whole with her, complete. Like she is the cure to every ailment I've ever known.

We've been playing this game since we left the dance floor. Anytime one of us gets a donation from one of the alumni for over ten grand, we take a shot. So far we have taken two, both awarded by her.

"Isn't there another group you could try and get money

from?" Her back is now turned to me as she stares daggers at the aging divorcees.

"Are you jealous?" I say as I move closer, my chest against her back and my mouth mere centimeters from her ear. I feel her shiver in front of me, instantly making me hard. I laugh to shake it off as she whips around lightly slapping my chest.

"You're a real narcissist, you know that?" She's grinning like she has been all night and I'll never get used to that real unbridled smile. I catch her hand as she hits me and feel engulfed by her wide eyes.

"I have never been more jealous than I was watching you rob these men blind the past two rounds." I see her throat bob as she nervously licks her lips and I can't look away as I stare at them. It takes everything in my power not to kiss her right here in front of the entire student body. We've definitely gotten a few glances tonight, but Olivia seems to not give it a second thought, and after hearing the rumor circulating about Will and the coat check girl, my conscience hasn't taken a single hit. She moves closer to me, now standing on her tiptoes.

"Fine," she whispers, then gently pushes me away before striding to the divorcees. I signal the bartender for another beer as I watch her approach them, unable to tear my eyes away from her, even for a second.

She really is a natural. I've never seen someone more charming or who could so easily get the eyes and ears of everyone in a crowd. It took almost everything in my power to not tear off the limbs of each man she got a donation from in the past hour. To their benefit, they were both in their early seventies, but the way she let their eyes glide up her body— my fist clenches around my beer at the thought and I take a long drink.

Her schmoozing seems to be working as the divorcees scan the room for who I assume is me. Olivia gives me the 'signal' we've been using all night when it's time to move into the next phase of our plan. I feel myself smirk, watching her pull at her ear, her eyes wide as if to say *"Can you hurry the hell up?"* I push off the bar standing to my full height and begin making my way toward the group. It's obvious a few of the women notice me, their faces flushed and eyes wide, sizing me up as if I'm their prey. I move my eyes back to Olivia's though, and her smile beams. Her eyes, the dress she's wearing, hugging her in all the right places, make it impossible to acknowledge anyone else as I finally get to the group.

"Hey." My eyes are trained directly on her, not even glancing toward any of the other women. Her gaze shifts uncomfortably, glancing at the other women who want my attention, a flush creeping up her neck.

"You must be Benjamin. Olivia here has been telling us so much about you," a fifty something blonde woman says to my right. Her voice is low, the seductive tone forced.

"In the flesh," I respond. My eyes don't leave Olivia's which causes her to turn a brighter shade of red, the blonde woman letting out a low *hmph* at my snub.

"We'd love to hear more about the basketball team's endeavors this year. We hear you are quite the star," a dark haired woman with a slight European accent says somewhere on my far left. I barely hear her as I lick my lips absorbing the way Olivia's hair is glistening in the light of the chandelier, her earrings grazing the nape of her neck. I meet her eyes and Olivia silently urges me with her gaze to follow through with our plan.

I sigh, finally giving the group the most charming grin I can muster. "Sorry ladies, I'm just not myself today." I give them a sort of manly version of pouting, causing Olivia to cover her smile with her hand. "I think I might be in a sort of unrequited love situation…" I put a hand on my heart and hear a few of the women sigh, one audibly *awww*-ing, while the blonde from before squeezes my bicep.

"Oh sweetie, tell us all about it." I glance at Olivia, giving her a conspiratorial look as she rolls her eyes trying to suppress a grin, her face completely pink.

"You see, my dream girl— she's with another man." The blonde gasps, squeezing my bicep tighter which causes me to inwardly cringe.

The European woman moves closer, her hand cupping my face. "But who could be more handsome than you?" Her slight accent adds to the dramatics of the interaction which causes Olivia to give a low giggle and the snarkier women of the group give her a dirty look in return.

"Alright ladies, I think his ego has had enough for one day," Olivia says, squeezing between myself and the blonde woman, causing her arm which was previously squeezing my bicep to fall to her side. They all look very frustrated by Olivia's interruption and I can't help but be amused by the bombshell beside me, seemingly jealous of a few divorcees. "Please make your checks out to the Astor Hill Alumni Foundation," she calls over her shoulder while pushing me forward, back toward the bar. I grab her hand, leading her to one of the outdoor terraces.

It's October, and the northeastern air has cooled significantly since the sun set a few hours ago. The breeze caresses her bare shoulders and, before she can even shiver, I shrug off my jacket and drape it over her. She looks up at me in a way that makes my stomach somersault, like I could have her, like should could be all mine. I can't help but stare back, mesmerized by her, feeling the same pang I did the night of that kegger all those years ago.

"You look the way you looked the night I first saw you."

Her brows furrow in confusion. "You mean that *morning* in the courtyard?"

"I—" I sigh and I know I need to tell her. I know that this truth is the only thing standing in the way of what I really want. I want her to know. She deserves to know exactly how I know Lily.

"I saw you at that party. I saw you with Lily and—"

"You saw me and Lily?" she cuts me off, her body going rigid against my touch.

"Yeah. I mean mostly, I saw you. You were on a mission. You looked so determined, like you knew exactly how you would get everyone in this school to fall for you. You were breath taking, Liv. You still are." I huff a nervous laugh, my face burning. I'm scared if I meet her eyes she'll push me away.

"Yeah well, that's 'best-friend confidence' for you," she says, smiling sadly now.

"Best-friend confidence?" I feel my face scrunch up. There's something about the way she talks about Lily, the way she seems to always put herself down in the process, and I want to wash that away.

"Yeah, like… everyone has someone who's like their touchstone. And if they don't, that's a tragedy." Tears brim at the corners of her eyes and I reach my hand out to swipe them away. "Lily was like… a siren, minus all the negative stuff. She just lured you in, lured me in, but kept you there with all her goodness. Like, obviously, Lily was gorgeous. Perfectly petite, hair out of a freakin fairytale." She's smiling now, but it's just a different version of that same sad smile, the one I've seen her wear when Will belittles her, the one that says *I'm not enough.* "She was the ideal everything. And when I was with her I was so close to that. She bolstered me. Every horrible thought I had, every awkward moment, every disgustingly mismatched outfit, she had an antidote."

I can't help but lift my eyebrows because the way she perceived Lily and the way she continues to perceive herself don't line up at all with the Olivia I know.

"What?" she says, her breath hitching, my sleeve brushing her bare skin as I duck my body over hers, shielding her from the gala guests around us.

"It's nothing, I just..."

Our eyes meet and a blush creeps up my cheeks. I stand there rubbing my lips together trying to figure out how I can tell her I love her without telling her I love her. How can I kiss her in front of all these people knowing she's still somewhat with Will.

"You describe Lily the way I see you," I say, pausing. I rub my hand over my face willing myself to say the words I've been thinking since I met her, to put caution to the wind and just say what everyone should have told her all along.

I take her hands, peering back down into her eyes. "You're magnificent, Olivia. Breathtaking. Every time I see you... every day I get to *speak* to you, is my best day. You don't *need* a touchstone, you *are* the touchstone. You are the ideal, the antidote, the siren— all the goodness in the world that you're so quick to see in others. *You* are Olivia. Not Lily. Not anyone else. Just you."

Her eyes brim with tears. I can't tell right away if I said something wrong, but the way she seems to be absorbing my words tells me she needed to hear that. I wipe the tears away from her cheek, brushing a kiss over her forehead so slightly that it barely resonates and let my body do what it needs to by embracing her.

"I'm sorry if that was the wrong thing to say," my voice comes out, almost a whisper my head sitting on top of hers.

"That was the perfect thing to say," she says into my chest.

I pull back peering into the dark orbs that haunt my dreams and give her the faintest hint of a smile. There's a gleam in her eyes, as if she's daring me to make the next move. I move ever the slightest bit closer, the alcohol fueling my bravery. She tilts her head up slightly, almost an invitation. I'm just about to move in when I feel a massive hand on my back. I close my eyes, taking my hands off the girl of my dreams, the girl I was so close to finally kissing, and catch Grant's head tilt and brows furrow as if to say *"Are you insane?"*

"Where have you two been?" Grant's deep voice has some levity but in a way that says he's not going to ask any questions and continue looking the blind eye.

I take a step backward realizing I'm still way too close to Olivia for Grant to even attempt to pretend he doesn't know what's going on. My mind is reeling, with what that could have turned into, what that would've meant for my relationship with Will and the truth I ultimately failed to expose. Olivia quickly tries to recover, rubbing at her flushed neck but I catch the look she gives me with a ghost of a smile.

"The real question is where have you been, Grant? I definitely would have seen you towering over this crowd," Olivia says, cocking her head to the patrons scattered around the balcony. There are very few, none even looking our way, most being our more elderly donors.

"It's a secret," Grant says, almost giddy, smiling from ear to ear.

"A secret, huh…?" Olivia grins at Grant, poking his abs playfully. I've noticed she acts differently around him, more open, the way she's been acting with me all night. I wish she let more people see her like this.

"Does someone have a secret girlfriend?" Olivia asks in a sing-song voice, one eyebrow raised.

Grant turns beet red for a minute. "A man can dream," he says, his expression almost wistful. I clap my palm over his shoulder.

"Alright loverboy, who is it?" I scan the crowd.

"Like I said, it's a secret," Grant says again, a sly smile on his face now. "Besides, what are you two doing over here all alone?" He raises a knowing brow.

I pointedly look at Olivia, signifying the ball is in her court with this line of questioning and I notice her expression has changed, her lips in a tight line. Her eyes seem almost panicked but it's apparent she's trying to reign it in. I'm just about to ask if she's alright when I feel a presence approaching behind me.

"I should've known I'd find you over here with *him*. Is this why you wanted a break?" I hear my brother slur, grabbing Olivia around her waist as he pushes past Grant and I, giving me a look of disgust. I instantly feel the guilt crash into my stomach. Olivia does too, apparently, as she won't meet my gaze, but it's mixed with something like fury, her jaw clenched and her posture rigid.

The environment shifts and I watch as Olivia's walls slide back up, completely closing herself off to all of us and becoming that impenetrable fortress I was first met with. Her dainty hand grabs his fingers, pulling them off her waist and dropping them with disgust.

"*This* is not why I wanted a break," she gestures to Grant and I in a hushed tone. "*This* however," her hands gesture at him and he pushes them away. "You are full of shit."

His voice is all venom and I take a step forward, the blood flooding my ears.

"You thought you could end things with me and I wouldn't move on?" he says through gritted teeth.

"Take it easy man. Don't make a scene," Grant puts a hand on Will's shoulder trying to pull him back from Olivia and Will shoves him off. His eyes are dark as he shoots Grant a glare.

"Touch me again and the scene I will make will ruin both of our careers." My brother is serious and Grant and I both know it.

Olivia's eyes meet mine full of emotion. My ears are ringing now and I feel my hands form fists, every muscle in my arms tensing.

"And you," Will sneers, his drunk face morphing into someone I barely know and yet am all too familiar with, as his glare redirects to me.

"If you want to fuck her so bad, do it." He nudges Olivia forward into my chest. "Take my sloppy seconds bro, please I'm begging you. Heads up though man, she's a lousy liar *and* a lousy lay. That's why I have to fuck cocktail waitresses in coat closets whenever I get the chance."

Without thinking I move, my fist meeting Will's face with such force it causes him to fall backward into a cocktail table, knocking it and himself over onto the floor. I move to hit him again when Olivia stops me. I feel her hands on my chest and she's yelling something, but I can barely hear her, just see her eyes so full of tears waiting to fall. My stomach bottoms out and all I hear is the blood rushing through my veins until finally I hear her.

"BEN, STOP."

20

Olivia

Will's face is gushing blood as I push Ben away from him. I've seen Will angry before, but the fury that is Benjamin Cabot in this moment is not even comparable. All eyes are on us as other donors have filtered onto our balcony to see what is going on. My voice has gone hoarse with each shout. It's like he can't hear me, that or he doesn't want to.

"BEN, STOP," I scream, right into his face this time, and finally he sees me. His eyes meet mine and his gaze moves through emotions so quickly it's hard to keep track of how he's feeling. I feel the whispers of my peers like hail on my back.

"How could she cheat on Will?"

"What a whore?"

"I don't blame her. Ben's hot, but his brother? That's cold."

I feel outside of myself as I move through the next motions. I try to help Will up as he spits blood, his eyebrow completely split and needing a stitch or two. He shrugs me off, tears in his eyes either from the pain, the embarrassment, or what he considers my betrayal. I keep my voice low in order to avoid the numerous onlookers.

"Let's go." I see Ben flinch, clearly hearing me, but I need to do this before I lose my momentum, before the thoughts of my peers and their impressions of me sway me. I meet Ben's eyes, but there's something broken in them, and I feel my throat bob. He shakes his head and turns, Grant clapping his. I feel like I ruined something, but I have to keep moving.

I pull Will through the crowd, grabbing a towel off a waiter's arm and dumping some ice out of the water on a nearby table. I hold it to his face. Once we get to the valet and I pull Will's wallet out of his coat pocket, his posture relaxes.

"Liv—" his voice is the one he's always used. Every fight, every time we've bickered, when it's time for me to forgive him he pulls out this voice.

"No— Will. Don't." For a second he looks like he's going to argue, but then he nods once and lets me speak, which is a first in our relationship. "I wanted a break so I could think about things. I didn't realize this going to be all the time I needed to really know what decision to make." His posture is rigid again as if he knows what's coming. It would be surprising if he didn't after the shit he just pulled.

I take a deep breath, steadying myself.

"This relationship is over Will, and I mean that. It has nothing to do with your brother or the coat check girl, or hell, even Gen. We don't work Will, we've never worked. I am not myself when I'm with you and *you* are hiding from yourself when you're with me."

His feet shift as he looks up, tears streaking his face. "I fucked up, Olivia. I'm fucked up." His voice is filled with desperation as if me giving him a second chance will fix him, fix this. For a second I pause and take in the boy I was head over heels for when first coming to Astor. He's older now, taller and wider somehow, more handsome, but something changed. We worked against each other; we made each other smaller and smaller until we both disappeared.

"I can't fix you Will and you can't fix me." He meets my gaze, his lips a thinly formed line as if he's coming to terms with the fact that this is really over just as his car arrives.

"Just come home with me, please. Just tonight." His eyes brim with tears as he softly grabs my hand and I feel my own tears fall down my cheeks.

"I can't." We stand there for a second longer. He finally nods, getting in the car and shutting the door.

* * *

It's Tuesday morning and I just got a text from Ian that there is a *"911 Newspaper emergency."* I stuffed my feet in an old pair of Uggs I had tucked away in my closet and threw on one of my Dad's old flannels that I sometimes sleep in because they smell like home.

I haven't heard from Ben in a few days and I'm wondering if I was too forward. Maybe he regrets the things he said, the things he almost did. I clench my jaw trying to quell my embarrassment. I felt so seen when he said all the things I've yearned to hear for so long after I confided in him about Lily. About how ordinary she made me feel. After that fight though, with all those eyes on us, it's like I completely reverted to the girl I described myself as. The pressure I felt from having an audience, to be *pretty, to be perfect, to be better.* I just wanted their eyes off me. I needed to make the spectacle end. So I left, but not before officially ending things with Will.

I think when we age, we assume the behaviors of our younger years were due to a lack of maturity, and when we no longer behave that way, we attribute it to "changing" or "personal growth" or whatever. That is not the case, at least for me anyway. So much of my adolescence was spent feeling embarrassed, whether it was warranted or not, and lately that feeling has come up more and more. Having a friend who is so enigmatic, like Lily, means that you will at some point feel a flush of shame wash over you when they point out the weird or subpar thing you did. That's youth, though, I think and yet, that feeling haunts me. We're all automatically, subconsciously, assessing each other for faults and virtues, usually keeping a quiet score in our head. Lily didn't have to keep a quiet score because somehow I always came up short and every time she highlighted my faults, I froze, recovered, and brushed it under my rug of resentment.

It feels gross, resenting a dead person, your dead best friend. But last night, when I was tossed back into my eighth grade form in a room of bodies in black tie, the feeling I felt after stupidity was resentment. And maybe that, mixed with the realization that I've brushed so much under the rug with Will, too, is why I'm letting the ginger tea I put in my thermos this morning scald my esophagus.

The weather matches my mood, the gray clouds hanging low in the sky seeming to sag with rain begging to be let out. The humidity hits my nose and I'm teleported again to the summer I spent with Lily in the Hamptons. I have a tendency to always think of the beginning of that summer and not the end. I was so excited to be spending a summer with Lily, that she just wanted *me* to go with her, ignoring the pleas to join her from the rest of our friend group.

I pull the heavy door of the journalism building and find Ian in 'The Stacks,' otherwise known as the Astor Hills archives. The mothball scent of old newspapers hits my nose as I observe Ian frantically skimming the papers in row E. If there's one thing I've never seen Ian be, it's frantic. I'm instantly on edge as I approach.

"Hey…" I say, wearily.

"Hey," he says without glancing my way, completely focused on whatever task is at hand.

"What, no you look like you got hit by a bus, Olivia?" I attempt a joke and Ian finally glances my way.

He rolls his eyes. "You do look like a bus hit you but that is the least of my worries right now." He picks up a large bin filled with papers and all but shoves them into my hands. "Look through this and then start rows F and G and tell me if you see any papers from September 2022."

Holding the large box I look up at him incredulously. He's basically just asked me to look through hundreds of newspapers for only five or six that have gone missing.

"Why are we doing this?" I ask. My head is pounding from a hangover and lack of sleep. The last thing I want is to sift through old newspapers. He rolls his eyes, clearly frustrated with my questioning. He stands up straighter, assessing me.

"So I take it you made the 'break' official?" he asks, sitting on the corner of his desk.

I clench my jaw not really wanting to deal with Ian's journalistic line of questioning. I used to think it was his convoluted way of friendship, the only way he knew how to communicate. Lately, I've started wondering if maybe he's just always seen me as a ticking time bomb, the next big story to plaster on the front page of the school paper. After what happened at the gala, I wouldn't put it past him. I set down the bin he basically assaulted me with and begin sifting, averting his gaze.

"I'll take that as a yes," he says, his tone incredulous, frustrated I'm evading his questions.

"I don't see how that is relevant to the task at hand," I say through gritted teeth. It's not like I expected sympathy from Ian, but maybe a *'How are you holding up?'* The realization that he'll ultimately give me the third degree and move on without considering how I feel is grating on my nerves.

"How is this *relevant*?" He twists his features in mockery. "Wow, Olivia. One break up and you really have let your journalistic instincts fall to the wayside." I grimace into the box. He might be right— it's not like I took the time to stop and think about the significance of the misplaced papers. But on a day like today, it would be nice for him to just spell it out for me. I give him a look that says 'not today' and he sighs, giving me what I feel is his version of a break. "Liv, what happened in September 2022?" He raises his eyebrows at me gesturing with his hand for me to give him the response he's looking for. My anger comes to a boil, knowing exactly what *event* he's referencing— Ben leaving Astor.

"Is this really about my story, Ian?"

He rolls his eyes. "You mean the biggest story to come this year? A story that we can't just not report on because you've become entangled in what appears to be a pretty big mess of your own?"

I cross my arms staring at him. I know he's right— that this is the exact story we should be focusing on. And because he's already done me a favor by not sending out a breaking news notification to all our online subscribers about the disaster that was the gala, I decide to humor him.

"Okay, so the papers from the month Ben disappeared

are missing—" I make a hand gesture as if to imply this is all so spooky. "What's your point— that his parents tried to hide something? That's pretty obvious."

"I thought so too, which is why I told you to find out *what* they were hiding, and yet you fell short," he says, hands clasped together. "I took it upon myself to begin threading the needle for you, so to speak. Maybe inspire you to, I don't know, do your job?"

I scowl at him even though I know he's right. To any journalist this would be a significant finding, but still I fail to see this as groundbreaking.

"Okay, so you found some missing papers. How do you know Ben was the reason they went missing? It could have been anything," I say, doing my best to play along, but still feeling like Ian is shooting blanks.

"Interesting you say that. I asked myself the same thing and I found a rather intriguing through line for you to chew on, maybe *explore* a little bit, as *any* journalist probably would," he says pointedly and I roll my eyes.

"Let's hear it." My voice comes out defeated and pissed off, which I can tell irritates Ian, but he lets it go.

"Well Olivia, what else happened in September of 2022? The second biggest story on campus that year?" His eyebrows are raised and I quickly pick up what he's putting down. My body physically recoils. I'm offended he would even insinuate this, much less ask me to explore it.

"You're fucking kidding me, right?" I seethe. "You're not actually telling me to look into this? You seriously think Lily's death is at all related to Ben's absence?" I knew Ian was insensitive but didn't peg him as completely and utterly tone deaf.

"Listen Liv, I'll give you some time to decide and poten-tially find a relation here— if this is out of your depth I'll give it to someone else, but regardless this story is going to be written." His tone is straight forward, rather matter of fact, for what is essentially a threat.

I grab my bag and turn to leave.

"Think about it as a journalist, *not* as Olivia," Ian calls to my turned back as I march out the doors. Ian's journalist instincts are good, great even but he typically spirals until he finds an actual *"thread,"* as he put it. I've worked on stories with him where we grasped at straws just like this, spinning it in several ill-informed and unrealistic directions until it finally landed. I know this process, I've done this process, but I will not entertain this. This idea is too outside the realm of reality and a total waste of time.

I chew on my lip thinking about my night with Ben, how every piece of my life seemed to come into focus in a way it hadn't before. I smile at the memory, my stomach fluttering with the anticipation of seeing him again. But my brain continues to buzz with Ian's words about Ben leaving and the realization that I have this well of grief deep inside me that I've refused to deal with for the past two years.

I remember Ben's face the moment I left with Will, defeat so etched in his gaze that it sealed my decision to end things with Will. I push the theories Ian strung out of my mind. There's only one thing I want to focus on and that's figuring out where Ben and I stand.

21

Ben

The sun is sitting low as I walk out of the practice gym tonight. Tuesdays are usually spent in the weight room, but Coach had us running laps to "release the goddamned tension between you sons of bitches." His exact words. Turns out pretending the douchebag dating the woman you can't stop thinking about, who happens to be your brother, isn't possible when he's two teammates down from you, jabbering about said woman. My only relief is the black eye he's not so proudly sporting. When Scott brought up the scene between him and Olivia, Will was all too pleased to relive the details of their night together. Grinding my teeth did nothing to staunch the disgust I felt as he replayed what I hoped hadn't happened after they left last night. When I came back into the room after abruptly dropping my weights and taking a quick lap as a distraction, Coach was in the middle of a rant, chastising the use of vulgar language about sex acts while in the locker room.

I'm glad I left, because even though I have no standing with Olivia, no right to be upset if she *did* leave the gala and consummate their supposed reunion, I know I wouldn't have been able to stop from making Will's eyes match.

By the time I get to my apartment, it's half past six. I told Olivia I'd be at hers by seven to work on this project, but that was last week, before the gala. The most I'd spoken to her since was a brief text from her this morning.

OLIVIA

See you at 7?

Yeah. See you then.

I was half hoping she'd have some explanation for the other night. Now, as I jump out of the shower and into my team hoodie and sweats, I realize I'd better stop hoping. Will basically confirmed what I'd been wondering for days.

I ruminate over her and Will and me, and this whole fucking mess, the entire way over to her apartment. I go to knock on her door but my hand is met with air, the door quickly pulled open to reveal a fresh faced Olivia, smiling softly on the other side.

"You're late," she says, and I can tell she's relieved. The frustration that was simmering inside me on my walk over begins to burn on the surface.

"I'm here," I reply, the tight smile on my face unable to reach my eyes. When I look into hers, I can tell she's wounded. She rolls her eyes, waving me inside. We're standing in her kitchen, silent as she fills a kettle with water, places it on a burner, and grabs two mugs.

"How are you?" she finally breaks the minutes long silence, turning around to face me, her hands behind her on the counter.

"Uh…" I stutter, shocked by how easily she can act like nothing's wrong. "Fine," I tell her, shoving my hands in my pocket. The words 'what's going on with you and Will?' bubble at the top of my throat but I push them down. "How are you?" The conversation feels stale, so different from the way it usually feels.

She searches my eyes for a moment before giving a noncommittal shrug and nods. "Yeah, I'm… okay." Pressing her lips together, she spins around to the mugs, dropping a tea bag in each seemingly out of nowhere. I watch the hot steam rise and diffuse into the air, the space around us quickly smelling of clove and warm spices.

"Sorry, did you want tea?" she asks over her shoulder. She sounds annoyed and exhausted. Before I can answer, she's extending the steaming cup of autumn to me.

"Thanks, Liv." I accept the mug, taking note of the way her mouth curves into a gentler version of her usual smile when I say her name. I jump on the shred of courage her smile gives me, deciding to satisfy my morbid curiosity now or never. "So. You and Will are back together then?"

As soon as the words are out my mouth, I regret them. She spins around, confusion and irritation swirling on her face.

"What did you just ask me?" Her tone is one of disbelief, and as incensed as I am that she's offended by my curiosity, I know she's right.

"No, you're right, I— it's none of my business." My lips press together as if to keep my actual feeling under wraps.

"It's none of your business?" Her eyes are pools of hurt and fury and I feel my pushed down frustration rise to the top. "You ignore me for *days* and then show up here like we didn't—"

My brows furrow in disbelief as I feel myself erupt. "Ignoring you, Olivia? I didn't realize you were expecting a follow up conversation after you *left with Will*. Because that is what you're referring to, right? That I've been *ignoring* you since the gala?" She flinches at the mention, but I feel vindicated by the opportunity to show how I've been feeling.

"Yes Ben, I was," her chin raising slightly in defiance. "I expected… *something* after we…" She blushes, turning away.

"What were you expecting, Olivia?" I ask, the anger I feel turning into a palpable heat. "You left with him." My heart sinks at my own words, reminded of the way she walked out those doors with him. I watch her think carefully, her eyes searching my face before she answers.

"I just," she pauses, considering her next words. "I thought we were friends," she tells me, sounding painfully unsure, and my heart sinks even more.

"We've never been friends, Olivia," I tell her, and her eyes shutter. And I know what she thinks I mean in that moment, but it isn't what I mean at all. "And I know about what happened after you left — pretty sure the entire team knows now." I shake my head and turn toward her door, expecting her dismissal anyway. If I stay any longer, I'll only handle her decision to get back together with Will with more immaturity than I already have.

"What the *fuck* does that mean?" she all but shouts at me, inviting me and my heart back to be ripped to shreds in the middle of her kitchen. And I do it because when will I have the right to feel anything for her again?

"I know you're with him, Olivia! For god knows what reason. It means I know you went home with him, that you slept with him after he—"

"That I slept with him after he fucked the coat check girl?" she interrupts me, crossing her arms. She tilts her head, her hair falling to one side, as she eyes me with derision. "I guess we never were friends if you believe I could be that pathetic." She dismisses me with a quick glance at the door, turning to collect a mixing bowl off her counter.

Guilt crashes into me as I watch her listlessly clean up a nonexistent mess in her kitchen. I wallow in my anger at this situation for all of ten seconds before I walk up behind her, stilling her hands. I came here hoping for some resolution, or some closure, for me; I didn't come here to upset her.

"Olivia," I say, willing her to turn around and face me. When she does, my eyes immediately land on her mouth before taking her in. Rich, brown waves frame her face, the remnants of summer freckles dust the bridge of her nose, trailing off into the slight blush of her cheeks, and her long, delicate lashes frame amber speckled eyes that glisten with wetness. The slow pace of her chest rising and falling makes this moment feel like it's happening in slow motion. And it's the slowness of this moment that reminds me that I still can't kiss this girl.

So I say, instead, "We were never *just* friends. You've always been more. Since the moment I saw you at the party, you have consumed my thoughts," I admit, feeling more vulnerable than I've felt in years. "I didn't text you, because I can't tell if this... thing I'm feeling with you is all in my head or if it's real. If I imagined our night together or if you felt it, too." I pause, feeling like I'm revealing too much but deciding that I have nothing left to loose. "You are always on my mind, even and *especially* when you shouldn't be."

She tilts her head up at me in silent defiance, and I can tell she's biting the inside of her cheek. Her gaze lingers on my mouth before sliding up to mine, telling me that she feels this too.

"And I know I shouldn't be telling you any of this if

you're still with him, if you're still—" I stop, knowing I have to give this up if she is. I swallow, feeling the question I want to ask like a lump in my throat, knowing her answer has the power to decimate me. "Are you still with him?"

My stomach sinks when I see her bite her lip, something like embarrassment flashing momentarily. She looks down at the ground in contemplation and she might as well rip out my anatomical heart because this is tortuous and I think I should've left when I had the chance.

I think all of this in the five seconds that it happens and then she looks up at me earnestly through those thick lashes.

"No," she says, clear and quiet. "I'm not with him."

22

Olivia

I hadn't spoken to Ben since the gala because I didn't want Will to be right about me. At the end of the day, Will and I didn't work because of issues that predate Ben's entrance in our lives. Ben just... pulled the curtain back. And even though I feel this is true in my bones, a tiny voice in my head— that sounds an awful lot like Will— tells me I am as selfish as he says I am.

Looking up at Ben, I recognize the darkness swirling in his eyes for pain. *He's waiting for me to tell him I left Will, and I'm contemplating not saying I did because I shouldn't be selfish?* I ended things with Will, in part, so that I wouldn't feel like this. Like there are parts of me I should suppress or ignore because it doesn't serve someone else's purposes. I left him so I could be true to myself. I don't know if Ben wants me the way I want him, but I'm willing to feel stupid if there's any chance he does.

I focus my gaze on Ben, and tell him.

"No. I'm not with him."

His shoulders relax as he tries to suppress a giddy grin

and I feel it too. The way the air around us vibrates with possibility, the way the tension between us is pulled so taut but relief finally feels on the horizon. *Please kiss me*, I think to myself, desperate for my read on him to be right.

"Okay," is all he says, but his assessing gaze says so much more. He takes his time looking me over, like he's committing my body to memory, his gaze heated but so painfully casual. Like he actually has all the time in the world. My body hums with an incessant urgency, willing him to do something, *anything*. Because I am paralyzed, afraid to move for fear that I might miss the exact moment that I burst into flames or erupt into light. He glances away, clearing his throat. "Now that's cleared up," he says, smirking, "we should probably get to studying."

I quickly recover from the disappointment, brazenly asking him, "So to be clear, you apologize?"

"I apologize," he says, his smile growing.

I spin around, making my way to my printer and pulling out two copies of the reading we're meant to be doing.

"Now we're even," I say with a subtle arch of my brow, handing him his copy. "Wait! Actually—" I grab his hand without thinking, realizing I did so when I feel the warm embrace of his hand in mine. I don't let go.

I lead him to my room, recognizing what this seems like and deciding that I don't care. I playfully shove him toward my bed, surprised when he lets himself fall into it.

"*Now* we're even." I'm smiling, incapable of stopping, because when I look at him embedded in my sheets, he is too.

"You getting in here, Beckett?"

Heart racing, I will my nervous system to chill out. *I will not be over eager*, I decide from one moment to the next, aware of how this man's presence is making it difficult to be consistent. I sprawl myself opposite him and hand him a pen, shaking my article for emphasis.

"We have work to do," I remind him, smiling down at my reading. I hear him hum in acknowledgement and force myself to concentrate on something other than Ben Cabot for even a minute.

The sun is nowhere to be found by the time our study session nears its end, and the flutter in my stomach has yet to abate. Not that reading about romance novels has done anything to ease the sexual tension so thick, I could cut it with a knife. When I look across to Ben, his large frame exaggerated by the way he's so casually laid himself opposite me, he's squinting at the paper as if that will help him understand what he's read any better.

"I think what she's trying to say," I start to explain, "is that even though these novels are often expressing real problems or realistic relationship dynamics, they're ultimately unrealistic. That in an ideal world, these issues would no longer persist, we would have achieved real equality, and we would be free to choose relationship dynamics that seem unstable or unhealthy, or whatever." He's squinting again when I meet his eyes, more questions now than before I bothered trying to explain this stupid paper.

"So you're saying women want a world where they can be submissive, or stay with the toxic guy, without judgment?" I ponder this for a moment, unsure.

"No I think… I think women like to read about worlds where women get to choose what it is they want. They want to experience vicariously through these texts, what it is like to realize what you want and actually, for once, choose it." I feel my cheeks heat at my interpretation. "Like, these books aren't some project in humanity, but they do allow women to imagine what it would be like to go after what they want and get that happily ever after, peanut gallery be damned."

He's contemplating me, studying me like he could discover whatever he wanted to know if he just looked hard enough. "Paper get boring?" I quip, suddenly feeling vulnerable and wishing it would stop.

"What do *you* want, Olivia?" He says this contemplatively, but his gaze intensifies.

"What do I want?" I laugh, knowing full well what he's referring to.

"Yeah. It's a simple question," he shoots back, a playful grin failing to hide the seriousness in his gaze.

My stomach flutters, my mind reformulating what I should say over and over again, deciding it's too risky. Yes, I want him to kiss me. Yes, I want him to close this distance and touch me. But verbalizing that feels like a quick ride to vocalizing other things, and that scares the shit out of me. I just got out of a relationship with his *brother*, for god's sake. The thought train I'm on has me stalling, engaging in old strategies to get myself out of this corner I'm starting to feel backed into. I give him a look that says the answer is obvious, subtly rolling my eyes.

"I want what every girl wants— a happily ever after. I told you, I'm just like the rest of them," I shrug, pleased with my response.

"Don't do that Olivia," he says, his gaze steady and heated as he tilts his head to the side, deciphering me. The move unsettles me and I feel hot under his scrutiny.

"Do what?" I play dumb, but heat creeps up my neck.

"Deflect," he says with nonchalance, like he *isn't* aware of his question's significance. Something at my core heats and twirls around itself simply because of the way he's regarding me.

"I told you. It's not my fault you don't like my answer," I tell him, quickly opening a random book. Before I can even pretend to be deep in intellectual thought, Ben's oversized hand— really it's unsurprising he plays basketball— juts out and steals the book away.

"Ben!" I leap across my bed ready to steal back my book and wind up unceremoniously straddling the book snatcher. I'm acutely aware of the way my body is resting on his, the hardness of his quads and the warmth of his skin radiating beneath me. He looks up at me through thick lashes, a sheepish grin painted on his stupidly perfect face. He holds the book up, as if inspecting it.

"Well, this isn't on our reading list."

"I was—" I reach out to grab *Social Principles and the Democratic State* only to find my wrist clutched in Ben's *other* oversized, wonderfully warm, rough but not too rough hand.

"What do you want, Olivia?" he cuts me off, his grin wavering, his jaw set in determination and restraint.

And I've seen this look before. Not in real life, and not directed at me, but I've read it in books and I've seen it in movies. This is the moment where the dam breaks. Where their carefully charted plans fail, and everything goes to shit in the most spectacular of ways. It's the moment they say "fuck it" and disregard the world around them. And I feel myself at the precipice of this moment with Ben, and I am terrified and electrified at the same time. I've never been on the other side of this kind of disaster.

What do I want?

I want to talk about books and disagree over how to interpret an article and steal heated glances while we do so. I want to sit in comfortable silence and feel valued just for existing in the same space as them. I want to be *more* to someone, not because I play a perfect role in the life they've created, but because I'm simply enough for them just the way I am. I want to feel like the person I'm with is more interested in the thoughts swirling inside my head than thoughts swirling around in the ether about me, about us.

This all-consuming look leaves little room for interpretation. I know that if I leaned forward just an inch and angled my head slightly down and to the right; if I placed my free hand on his chest and pressed my lips against his, it'd take all his strength not to kiss me back.

What do I want?

I want Ben to kiss me, now.

Logic evaporates from any part of my being as I lean forward, angling my head toward him. I watch his sharp intake of breath as he registers the move, but that's all he does. Like the ball is in my court. And I guess it is because this is about *what I want*. He is asking me what I want because it matters to him.

"What do you want, Olivia?" he almost whispers, his lips barely moving, his body frozen besides the way his chest rises and falls.

"I think you know what I want," I say, secretly hoping I'm right.

I catch the mischievous glint in his eyes just before he closes the distance between us.

When his lips touch mine it's feather soft, like he's memorizing every line on my mouth with his. My eyes fall shut the moment his hand slides through my hair from the nape of my neck, and I feel the reverberations of it everywhere. He's barely touched me and I'm buzzing with anticipation, internally begging him for more.

Like he senses this, he kisses me deeply, his tongue sliding and twirling with mine, his other hand slowly descending from my collar bone to my breast. His hand cups me, lightly caressing me there, coiling whatever was heating in my core earlier tighter.

"Is this okay, Liv?" he asks against my mouth, pausing only long enough to register my vigorous nodding.

"Yes," I manage to express between kisses, his lips and tongue moving with mine in perfect harmony. It almost feels unreal— like I'm dreaming this, his touch so intoxicating in this moment that it must be a figment of my overactive imagination. I can taste the hints of cinnamon in the tea I gave him earlier, the mintiness of his toothpaste, and *him*. It invades my senses as I kiss him, this almost feral need to be as close as I can to his very essence. I restraddle him, subtly rubbing against him, satisfaction coursing through me when I feel how affected he is. I reach for his belt buckle at the exact moment that his hands grasp my hips, rolling me against him before adeptly laying me back. He's above me now, grinning down at me with those kiss swollen lips.

"This still okay, Olivia?" he asks, with a seriousness in his tone despite the ravenous look in his eye.

"Please stop talking, Ben," I beg him before pulling him to me. Strong arms rest on either side of me, the beautifully corded muscles of his forearm barely twitching as he holds himself above me. His lips traverse the expanse that is me, with kisses that feel like the softest kindling, leaving warm, stirring fire in their wake. When he gets to the part of me that needs him most, sliding my pants off and tossing them on the floor, it's all I can do not to levitate off my bed. His hand splays against my lower stomach, keeping me in place while he pulls me apart, his fingers moving in perfect tandem with his tongue. Just when that coil couldn't be spun any tighter, stars erupt in my vision, sparks skitter across my skin, I pulse with the most infatuating sense of pleasure and I come apart.

I sit slightly up on my forearms, catching Ben's gaze just as he licks his lips, and I'm already pulsing again with insatiable need. Never did I ever think I'd be on the receiving end of this kind of pleasure; again— books, movies, but not me. He presses sensuous kisses back up my body, his hands gripping and caressing me, my hands gripping and caressing him, until his lips are whispering in my ear.

"Tell me to stop, Liv." And while something in my brain holds up a warning sign, waves it in the air, screams at me to pause, I simply don't want to.

"Don't stop." I feel his smile against my ear before he sits up and pulls off his crewneck. We peel off our clothing, his fingers caressing my ribcage as he pulls my sweater up my torso and over my head. Those same fingers make quick work of my balconette bra, tugging my underwear off, his eyes on mine, before suddenly pausing.

I breathe in sharply, literally naked under his gaze. His teeth worry his bottom lip, and I watch him swallow.

"You can't be real, Olivia." A slow smile spreads over my face as his mouth comes back down to me, claiming my mouth, his hand gently gripping my waist, the other settling between us.

"Ben, it really won't happen again," I insist, despite feeling myself spun tighter and tighter with every touch.

"Is that a challenge?" he growls against my ear, and I feel his mouth upturn in a knowing smile.

"No, I—" I gasp, his fingers reaching that spot deep inside me, before retreating. "Again," I demand, but I know I'm not in control here.

"Patience, Liv." He coaxes me open, his kiss consuming me and driving me even further toward the edge. My hands slide against his skin, now slick with a thin layer of sweat, exploring each dip and hard line of his chest the way I wanted to that day in his apartment. His hands roam, tracing circles and rubbing gently against every sensitive spot I know and *don't* know on my body. I hear a rip and he reaches between us again, and I silently, irrationally wish he wouldn't put anything between us. He captures my mouth again, bracing his hand on my left hip, his other on the bed as he lines himself up against me. I feel him already, and the anticipation itself is enough to send me over the edge.

And then he's inside me, and I'm so full of him, so completely connected to him, and I know I will never not want this. Never not need this. It's intoxicating, euphoric, *perfect*. His forehead rests against mine as we breathe in tandem, everything about us so perfectly in sync in this moment. His lips move to my neck the moment my body wishes they were there, and his hand reaches behind me, sliding down my back before aggressively claiming me the second my mind asks for it.

"Ben, I'm—"

"I know," he says, and of course he does.

This time, I don't just come apart— I shatter. I dig into his shoulders, the feeling almost unbearable, when I feel him go rigid beneath me, the euphoric strain of his climax painted on his face. My release intensifies and I kiss him, desperate to be connected in every way, until I feel him relax above. He rolls to his back, taking me with him, my head resting on his chest, and I hear his heart beating.

Nothing has ever been this perfect, I think to myself as I feel a smile tug at the corners of my mouth.

* * *

"I guess I can see why you have a reputation," is the first thing I think to say out loud when it seems both of our heart rates have stabilized as we lay side by side in my bed. I feel Ben freeze in an instant and I turn to look at him. "It was a joke, Ben," I add, slightly annoyed that he can't just indulge my humor.

"Would it be just as funny if I said it to you?"

"Well no… but I don't *actually* have a reputation. I mean I've only been with—" I stop, because we can both assume who I'm going to say. "What I meant to say, what I was trying to relay to you was how… amazing that was. Because it was incredible. It's never been that way for me, but it probably has been for you, which I guess makes me feel a little unsure of myself? So I made a joke, which was obviously a bad joke, and—"

"Olivia," he stops me, his brows furrowed. "It has never been like that for me."

His admission sits heavy between us, the enormity of what he's confirming causing my heart to skip a beat. He sits up and I follow him, wrapping myself in my throw blanket. "I'm not going to sit here and tell you that I don't have a past, because I do. I did a lot of things I'm not proud of, treated a lot of people in ways that are… shitty. I was a different person when I left Astor, Liv. I need you to know that." He pauses, his hand caressing the side of my face, and I internally whimper. "But the way it just was between us… that's just as new to me as it is to you."

Vulnerability in his gaze, I wrap my arms around his neck, my throw falling away as I tilt my neck up to look at him.

"Then I guess we can figure this out together." His arms settle low around my hips, his fingers lightly trailing my lower back.

"Together?" he asks, subtly surprised. I take a breath, feeling self conscious. I'm jumping to conclusions, assuming Ben sees the same "us" I do.

"I mean," I start, feeling his surprise turn into amusement. "We can just… see where this goes," I tell him, my tone oozing nonchalance, like I didn't just have the most intense orgasm of my life. Something unclear flashes in his eyes before they turn heated, that sly grin quickly taking up residence on his face, and I assume he's glad I'm not asking for anything more than this. *Maybe he doesn't want more than this*, I tell myself, disappointment landing like a pit in my stomach.

"And what does that look like to you, Olivia?" he asks, his voice intense but hushed, his gaze intently on me.

"We can keep doing what we've been doing… plus what we just did," I add, blushing, "but I don't expect you to exclusively be with me." The words feel foreign to me, so far from anything I would ever want, but I can acknowledge how chaotic it is for me to want to be with Ben so soon after ending things with Will. His *brother*.

"Do you want me to be with other people?" he asks, even more intensely than before, and his face is suddenly so close to mine. His eyes search mine as he waits for me to reply.

"No," I admit, my lips barely moving, I feel so paralyzed by his attention.

"Good," he tells me. "There is no one else, Olivia. Not for me, not for you. Not after this." My heart beats so loudly in my ears, I swear he can hear it, too. Those words, full of possession and control, should alarm me considering the dynamic I just left. But instead, his words settle deep in my core, warming me, embracing me, full of belonging.

"No one else," I repeat, watching his lips curve into the most delicious smirk, and kiss him.

"I love that I can just do this now," I say, smiling against his mouth. He's still grinning but he puts some space between us, his face telling me there's a caveat.

"We should talk about what this looks like out there." He nods toward my door, referencing the world beyond the haven that is just us. "We should probably be mindful of—"

"Oh my god, of course," I cut in, guilt washing over me when I remember Will. The guilt isn't even about my relationship with Ben. It's the fact that I was ready to loudly, proudly claim Ben as mine without any thought to how Will might feel about it. *What is wrong with me?* "Let's keep this between us, for now."

He gives me a weary look. "Are you sure, Liv?"

"Yes. I just wasn't thinking. How is he?" I ask, more timid than I'd like to be. I don't know what this will be like now, talking about Will with him. He takes a deep breath, sighing, the heaviness of his relationship with Will evident.

"He's been better." His smile is tight, but he doesn't elaborate.

"Yeah, of course. I guess I was hoping he would take this better than he probably is," I add, feeling shitty.

"It's not you, Liv." He shakes his head, his gaze not meeting mine. "Will has a lot of shit to figure out, and… this breakup is just bringing a lot up for him." He finally raises his gaze to mine, and I'm startled by the regret I find there. "You were really important to him, I know that. And if he reaches out to you, I want you to talk to him. For me, okay?"

His question feels dire, like I can't say no, so I just nod. "And when things settle, I plan to do this," he leans into me, his hand finding its way back to the nape of my neck, "whenever I can, just because." He closes the distance, his mouth crashing into mine with unexpected fervor, and I welcome it, eager to move on from this conversation.

Wrapped in my sheets, tangled with this man, I can't help but feel like the stars have conspired *for* me. Like every moment before this, meeting Will and being with Will, were for this greater good. And as I kiss Ben back, I thank those stars for their scheming.

23

Ben

A breeze rustles the leaves and notes of cinnamon waft out of the cardboard cup in Grant's hand.

"Dude, what the hell is that?" A black, hot coffee warms my hand, the weather just now cool enough to warrant a light sweater and hot beverages.

"It's a chai tea?" he replies, like it would be weirder if it wasn't. I can't help but laugh to myself as we walk away from Nero, which apparently, serves tea now.

Campus is littered with orange and red hues, the trees already beginning to shed the fruits of summer. Blankets not only lay on the lawn but across the shoulders of their owners. Animal ears spring from the heads of a few freshmen still unsure of their status as young adults, reminding me that today is Halloween.

"You're going to the party tonight, right?" I ask him, remembering that, too. I haven't been to the Halloween party hosted by the hockey team since before I left Astor, but unless the invitation rules have changed, the entire team will be there.

"Of course. You think I'm missing a party that doesn't require a suit?"

Grant was just as used to a black tie affair as the rest of us, but he's the only one who seems bothered by them. The hockey team, a group of literal bruisers, usually hosts their party at one of the player's frat houses. Those frat houses, all brick and colonial architecture, aren't any less stuffy than the venues Grant's shading, but the vibes are. Top shelf liquor is banned and unless the beer is in a can, don't even bother. It's always a costume party, but with a twist. One year, I remember, the twist was that your costume could only come from 1980's pop culture. Another year, the costumes had to be espionage themed. I remember looking forward to it every year, like Grant is, but this year apprehension settles in my chest when I think about it.

"You are, too…?" Grant picks up on my hesitation.

"Yeah, totally, man. I just haven't come up with a costume yet." This is true, but definitely not the whole of it.

What I can't tell him is that I don't know how I'm going to keep my hands off Olivia, because keeping things platonic on campus has been hard enough. Every shred of free time I have is hers, like I'm compensating for all the moments I can't simply rest my hand on the small of her back or whisper how I can't wait to be alone with her. We decided we would do this, keep our relationship to ourselves, to spare Will but maybe also ourselves. After years of being relentlessly perceived, I'm seriously relishing being with Olivia without the opinion of others. It's not that I'm worried what people will say; honestly, I couldn't care less. I just know that once anyone knows about us, reality will start to creep in and taint the euphoric cloud we seem to be nestled in. I just want that space to ourselves a little while longer.

"I'm just going in my letterman, saying I'm a jock, and calling it a day. It's masquerade themed, anyway," Grant cuts into my thoughts.

"Smart," is all I reply, already tortured by the thought of Olivia in a less than subtle, probably insanely sexy disguise. Olivia has to be there, per Ian's orders, but I know she's just as excited for a non-stuffy party as Grant, especially after the gala. Doesn't stop me from secretly wishing we could just have the night to ourselves.

* * *

After five minutes of deliberation, I copied Grant's costume idea, throwing on my letterman, feeling the stiffness of the embroidered thirty-two on my back. Andy has, unsurprisingly, four masks to choose from, rambling on about an experimental stage adaptation he did of "The Masque of the Red Death" when I stop by his apartment before we head to the party. He's still rambling when I check my phone and see that Olivia texted me she's already there.

"I was just an extra when I was cast, but I really think my commitment to the role is what helped me—"

"You ready?" I interrupt him, watching his face falter. "I just don't want to get caught in the rain if we're walking," I smoothly lie, omitting that the thought of Olivia at this party, where the news of her newly single status is more than likely circulating, is making me antsy.

The walk to the frat house is a short one, Andy living in the housing just off the residential street that's become known as fraternity row. As we approach, the yard is already littered with PBRs and it's only 10:00 pm. *Just like I remember*, I think to myself. The familiarity of the sight brings me back to the time my mental health started to deteriorate. Andy swings the doors open and music reverberates through the walls, disco balls causing the hallway to glitter. Every inch of the house is lined by couples and clusters, all masked, clutching red cups and silvery cans in their hands, trying to talk over the music.

I wait for my mind to wander, for my thoughts to spiral and my chest to feel tight, like it did the last time I was at a party like this, and I take a deep, calculated breath, hoping to keep the feelings at bay. I wait another second, sure it's about to rear its head, ready to use my grounding techniques, but nothing. Instead of feeling overwhelmed, I feel… excited. At this realization, I feel myself smile, making a mental note to bring this up in therapy, because this feels like a win.

Andy insists we find the beer fridge, cracking our cans open and cheering before he spots Sloane and makes off like a lovesick puppy dog. Even over the din of the music, I think I hear her call him a "skirt chaser," but his grin only widens.

I glance around the party, the bar by the kitchen a sort of central vantage point from which to see everything happening. Well, everything downstairs, anyway. I spot Will reclined in the corner of a plush sectional, a blonde angel perched on his lap. He kicks his head back, a booze filled laugh escaping him, and when his head levels his eyes lock with mine. I give him an acknowledging nod, noticing the devil horns he's matched with his cherry red mask, and decide that tonight is not the night to talk to him, especially considering we've only exchanged the bare minimum during practices and games.

Taking one last look and not finding her, I casually make my way to the back deck hoping to see Olivia. I know I can't be with her the way I want to be tonight, but I can look. We can talk. *Maybe* we can touch. I walk through the double doors and spot her hair cascading over her shoulder immediately. She sits on the circular, built-in bench that surrounds the fire blazing at the center, a vaguely familiar girl to her right and one of the hockey guys. His slightly shaggy hair falls across his mask as he turns his head to talk to Olivia, his body language giving away every single one of his intentions. I feel my jaw clench, possession flooding me. The smile she gives him tells me she's uninterested, and the way he scoots closer tells me he's either an idiot or an asshole and doesn't care.

My feet move before my brain has time to catch up, and by the time it has I've rationalized that being seen *talking* to Olivia can't be any worse than being seen together the night of the gala. I arrive behind them, clearing my throat before interrupting whatever inane thing this guy is telling her.

"Mind if I sit here?" I feign politeness in my voice, but I know my expression leaves little room for interpretation. He looks pissed, his eyes squinting behind his mask at me as if to say 'what the hell,' but he renews the distance between him and Olivia anyway.

"I was wondering when you'd finally come over here," she says, not looking at me and totally unsurprised. She's smirking into the fire, a can in her hand. "I knew you couldn't keep away," she whispers.

I laugh, but I mimic her nonchalance and gaze into the fire when I hear my name in a voice dramatically different from Olivia's.

"Oh my god, I was hoping I'd see you here!" the redhead next to Olivia squeaks, leaning across her and lightly smacking my arm.

"Were you?" I hear Olivia mutter under her breath, clearing her throat.

I realize the girl is from our literature seminar, and politely smile at her, giving her a brief wave. I expect to see her expression fall, but instead she just turns inward, creating the impression that the three of us are in conversation which, I guess, we now are.

"I was just telling Olivia how much I *loathe* these parties. It's like everyone is just coupled up and in their own worlds, or they're trying to couple up," she crones. "Which one are you?" she asks flirtatiously, fluttering her lashes.

"There's not a third option?" Olivia interjects, her tone mocking, but it goes over the girl's head. She grins and I stifle a laugh.

"I'm coupled up, actually." Now her face falters, her expression confused as she readjusts her green velvet mask. It would seem she's Fiona from *Shrek*. Interesting.

"Are you?" Olivia's gaze snaps to mine, finally giving me a clear view of her. Her eyes spark with warmth, the fire reflecting in them, amber hues twining with shades of brown that accentuate the way her hair gleams chocolatey brown in the moonlight. A mask of black, intricate lace leaves half her face hidden, drawing attention to the suppleness of her lips, painted red for the occasion. I catch her lips quirk in a seductive smile, acknowledging the attention I'm paying them. My eyes scan down further, finding her shoulders bare but her arms covered in see-through black fabric, and my mind begs me to find a way to peel it off her. My eyes make their way back to hers and I try to cool my eager grin. I roll my lips together, aware this other girl is waiting for an answer, too.

I look at her, trying to appear apologetic. "I am. Actually, I'm supposed to meet them upstairs, so if you'll excuse me." I feel more than see Olivia's eyes widen and now it's her turn to suppress her grin as I stand up and begin making my way back toward the house, hoping she'll follow my cue.

"*Upstairs?*" The girl all but whines, a listless sigh escaping her. "Have fun with your rendezvous," she calls after me, her buzz now apparent in her over exaggerated gestures as I glance back to see if Olivia's following me. "One day our princes will come, Olivia. Don't worry," she says, patting Olivia's back before getting entranced in the fire.

By the time I get to the staircase, I see Olivia attempting to dodge conversation with a member of the baseball team, her eyes locking with mine as she nods in agreement to whatever he said before walking toward me. I glance around, making sure no one's paying attention to us, and find that everyone is blissfully in their own worlds.

After knocking on a few doors, and avoiding another few altogether, I finally find one that's empty. I pull out my phone, texting her to open the third door to her right, and hear it creak open a few moments later.

I feel my pulse beat erratically, still pinching myself that this is real. That we are a we, that she is looking at me like I mean something to her, that I get to sneak away with her. She makes her way to me, her mile long legs bare despite the chill outside, pushing her mask up and back so that I can clearly make out the way her eyes squint at me mischievously. She twines her arms around my neck, tilting her head up to look at me, and I kiss her, relief washing over me as my mouth collides with hers.

"You know I'm not having sex with you at a frat party," she says against my mouth, but I feel her smile against my lips.

"I wouldn't dream of asking you to," I smirk, shaking my head as I only slightly pull away. "I just couldn't see you tonight and not do this." My hands cradle the delicate sides of her face as my lips descend, kissing her softly, backing her against the wall. I feel her arms tighten around my neck, the space between us becoming nonexistent, the two of us getting lost in the give and take of our kiss. And I lose track of time, the way I have every time I've kissed this girl, when she pulls away with a resigned moan.

"If only I had lower standards." She looks up at me through her lashes, her mouth lush and pouty as she juts out her lower lip, a smile in her eyes.

"If only we weren't at this party," I counter, smoothing her hair back from her face, admiring the way her eyes glitter with playful condescension. She hums in response, a wistful smile on her face, and I raise my brows, silently asking her to leave with me.

"It's not even midnight, Ben! Nothing worth reporting will happen until at *least* 1 am."

"No, you're right." I run a hand through my hair, considering my next words wisely. "I guess I could be your second set of eyes and ears until 3 am the latest…"

"You don't have to wait for me if you don't want to," she says, furrowing her brow.

"There isn't a world where I wouldn't want to wait for you, Liv. Least of all this one." I hold her gaze, waiting for her to decide that what I've said is too much, too soon, but she presses her lips together, stifling a smile.

"I guess we should begin our nightly watch then, Cabot." She takes my hand and leads me out, and it isn't until I see Grant walk out of a room that either of us notice. We drop our contact, the loss of her warmth making me question everything about our secrecy in a split second, but not before Grant's brows raise in suspicion.

"And what the fuck are you two doing up here?" He doesn't seem shocked, only somewhat antsy. There's only one reason why anyone comes up here, and Grant knows that. But so do I.

"I could ask you the same question," I reply, realizing his tone has less to do about Olivia and I and more about whatever he's up to. I hear a small gasp from Olivia and follow her gaze, only seeing a head of dark waves disappear behind the curve of the staircase. Grant's gaze narrows on Olivia, unspoken words passing between them. Her eyes go wide just as he grinds his jaw. "If someone could clue me in, that would be great."

"Not a word, Beckett. She doesn't want anyone to know." The defeat in Grant's face is heartbreaking, even with the little context I have, but I make a mental note to ask Olivia about it later. "I think we're all entitled to our *secrets*." He emphasizes 'secrets,' the special attention he's paying me making me believe he's not just referring to Olivia and I, and I wonder how much he knows.

Olivia gives him a sympathetic nod before pushing past us and making her way downstairs, disappearing into the crowd, and I linger behind so as not to draw attention.

"Well, that was quick," he throws at me, and I swear I hear judgment in his tone.

"I don't know what your problem is, bro." I can understand him feeling hurt that maybe I didn't tell him about this, but he knew how unhappy Will and Olivia were.

He shakes his head as if to shake off his disdain, his expression softening. "There's no problem. I'm happy for you, man. Just a little jealous how quickly shit worked out for you."

"I don't know if I'd call two years quick," I huff out a laugh, reminded of how long I've wanted this. Wanted her.

"Two years?" he repeats in wonder staring in the direction Olivia and his mystery woman escaped toward. "Nothing worth having comes easy, I guess."

"No, Grant. Not even close." I didn't know Olivia when I started to fall in love with her, but I didn't need to. I saw her and something in me identified with something in her and I just knew. But *knowing* Olivia, and being allowed behind the fortress she lets so few behind, is an entirely different experience all together. I would do the past two years over again, exactly as they happened, if it meant I would still get this chance with her.

I pat his back as I make my way down the stairs, committed to serving Olivia all the salacious gossip she needs once we discreetly leave in a few hours, and anything else she asks for.

24

Olivia

"I can't believe you've never been," Ben repeats himself, unable to comprehend that I haven't been to a particular *museum*. Of all the things I've learned about Ben over the past few weeks, his appreciation for fine art has been the most enlightening.

"I *have* been… but on like a class trip in the sixth grade. Pretty sure Lily and I snuck away as soon as we could to try the menthol slims she stole from her grandma." I smile to myself at the memory, in awe that we were so bold at twelve years old. I feel his eyes go wide, his shock real.

"Okay, Beckett," he laughs, shaking his head as he turns into the parking lot.

"I know. We were quite the delinquents," I shrug, mocking the rebellious intentions of my younger self. "Our fixation only lasted a few weeks. The aftertaste was nauseating. When did you have your first cigarette?" I turn in my seat as Ben makes another loop around the lot.

"I've never had one." He says this like it's obvious, like

in no universe would he have ever been tempted to try a cigarette, and I think I must have misunderstood him.

"No, not like a menthol, but any cigarette." He's shaking his head, confirming my initial conclusion. "Wow, okay. Did you not have friends…?" His laugh is light-hearted, my sarcastic jab at his social life not at all misunderstood, and I think about how nice it is to be able to do this.

"Plenty," he replies with a wink that spurs a whirl of jealousy in me. "But more importantly, I had a Daniel Chapman. Cigarette smoke would never have gotten past him. Someone probably offered it at a party in high school — not when I was *twelve*—" he glances at me out of the corner of his eye, smirking, "but it didn't seem worth it to me. Dan was intense, but I'm also an athlete so it was pretty easy to say no."

Will never talked about his dad, so hearing Ben bring him up so casually is completely new to me. The way we rarely spoke about his family seemed so commonplace to me at the time, but I realize now that beyond feeling offended that it seemed they didn't want to know me, I didn't actually care to know how Will felt about them.

The urge to know everything about Ben rests in my bones like the urge to breathe, the need I have to under-stand him almost overwhelming. It feels like there will never be enough time to memorize him completely, and that feeling didn't exist with Will.

I recall the only thing Will did tell me about his father. "He played for Astor, didn't he?"

Ben sighs, like the topic is cumbersome, and I wait for him to evade my question.

"Yeah," he replies instead, and contentment unfurls in my chest. "He got injured in his senior year and couldn't participate in the draft like he planned. Lucky for him, he got me when he married my mom, and then along came Will." Bitterness laces his voice.

"I take it you're not a fan?" I ask, gingerly.

"Of Dan? No," he scoffs. "I've had a long time to unpack the shit he put me through, make my peace with it, but I'm his step son so I can kind of rationalize how easy it was for him to be who he was with me. But Will… that's his son. I can't really forgive him for that."

I tilt my head, silently urging him to tell me more, my heart already breaking for the both of them.

"Just a lot of emotional abuse…" he ponders for a moment, I assume to consider how much he should share. "I'm sure you can tell Will and I don't have the best relationship. Dan kind of used rivalry as his chief parenting tactic. He really pitted us against each other, to the point that he wouldn't step in when things escalated into violence."

"Your mom didn't do anything?"

He sighs again, his demeanor shifting slightly.

"She couldn't, really. It's complicated… my mom loves us but she, like the rest of us, has her shit too," he shrugs like it isn't a big deal, obviously trying to bring some levity back to the conversation, and I let him, humming in agreement.

"I guess we all do, don't we?" I throw him an understanding smile, but the looks he gives me back I can't interpret. "What?"

He shakes his head, unbuckling his seatbelt. "Nothing, Beckett." It doesn't feel like nothing, but I let it go, shutting the car door before walking around to the driver's side to join him. He grabs my hand, claiming it, his grip slightly tighter than usual, so I rub my thumb over his in reassurance. And I know it registers, because I catch him smiling to himself out of the corner of my eye as we walk toward the museum.

This— anticipating what he might need and feeling like I can comfort or reassure him— is new to me. It's not the way I operate, not usually. But there's something about the way he is with me, the way he parses together what I might want to ask for but for whatever reason won't, that makes me feel like I can be that for him. Like when he stayed well past the time he would've liked to stay at that Halloween party, just to keep me company from a distance. It's foreign and refreshing and feels so *good*. I take him in, admiring the way his tousled hair is blown by the breeze. He notices me doing so, pressing a soft kiss against my cheek. This time, it's my turn to smile.

As we walk through the lobby and out to the courtyard, I internally admit that Ben might be onto something with these museums. The Venetian architecture is so incredible, I forget we're even in Boston.

We've only been to one other museum, and this already feels more my speed. We walk through the rooms, pausing without speaking at every other piece. And we can do this — just exist with each other, melting into our collective silence, not feeling the need to fill it with anything but us. I've lost count of how many dates we've been on now, but each one has only reinforced how right this feels.

I'm older than I was when I met Will, and that counts for something, but I've never been pursued the way Ben is pursuing me. When he told me there would be no one else, for him or for me, that was it. I was sold, convinced, ready to dive into this with him, but there is something so vali-dating about how intentional he is being. Like he wants me to know that he doesn't take me for granted. I could lie and say I don't need that kind of validation, but I guess I do. There's a part of me that feels like the other shoe is going to drop here, that there's something coming I need to brace for.

I guess I have our status as a "secret relationship" to blame for that. Of course I agreed to keeping this private until we feel that Will can handle it, but the resentment is still there. It feels like I'm finally happy, finally secure about something, and the universe is telling me to hold my horses. And that would be the wiser way to approach my relationship with Ben, but instead, I'm swept away. Our on-campus abstinence only makes me want him more, only makes every private moment I have with him feel like an oxygen tank that I can't inhale fast enough. The most alarming feeling is realizing that until now, I hadn't really been feeling at all.

I pause in front of a painting, entranced by the way the statue seems to come to life as a man kisses her. "So this is why you love it so much," I say to Ben, tilting my head toward him but still studying the painting, but I feel his brows rise in question. "Museums," I clarify.

"Mm," he hums in acknowledgement. "Feeling something, are we?" His voice caresses my neck, and I realize he's standing so close behind me it's almost indecent.

I bite my lip to stifle my grin, looking over my shoulder to meet his gaze. "Maybe."

"If you like this, you have to come look at something else," he says, a suggestive twinkle in his eye. He takes my hand in his and leads me down a winding staircase; when we reach the bottom, I'm met by a janitorial closet to my left, but a sprawling library to my right. The stacks are close together, interrupted only by a few tables with bankers lamps. To my surprise though, it's not dark, and when I look up the most intricate stained glass mosaic filters the sunlight into shades of pink, yellow, and orange.

"How?" I ask, in awe. "We went down the stairs…?"

"I'll show you when we leave, but this doesn't sit directly beneath the rest of the museum." His smile is adoring, like it's cute that I didn't figure that out, and I nod like I would have come to that conclusion anyway. "The woman who started the original collection here had this imported from Italy. She imagined it as a cafe, but eventually it became the room that collects books."

I make my way through the stacks, appreciating the warm hues that seem to bleed across the aging book spines. I find an early edition of one of my favorites, *Wuthering Heights,* and make a note to call about purchasing it later. Turning around to investigate the stack behind me, I find Ben leaning against said stack, his warm gaze on me.

"Hi," I sigh, contentment washing over me as I return the attention. It feels like we're the only people in this hidden library, like a single soul couldn't exist outside of ours. "Thank you for taking me here."

"I had a feeling it would make you happy." He worries his bottom lip as he gives me a once over, his eyes heating in that way I've become so familiar with.

"Mm," I hum, smirking at him, feeling bold. "I could think of a few ways you could make me even happier." He pretends to look around the corner before pushing off the stack and closing the distance between us, his hand threading its way up the nape of my neck and through my hair.

"Does the museum library meet your standards?" He's grinning at me, his lips mere inches from mine, and I relish in the anticipation.

"The museum library meets my standards," I confirm, biting my lip as a sly smile forms on my lips.

His mouth comes down on mine with an urgency that reminds me we're in public, not in my bedroom, and the thought heightens everything about his touch. His grip on my hair tightens ever so slightly and I welcome it, digging my fingers into his shoulder. His arm winds around my back, pulling us closer, and I take advantage of our proximity, pressing my chest against his. Breaking our kiss, his lips trail my neck first, then continue lower before my logic intercepts my arousal.

"We don't have time," I remind him, remembering we're in the back of this underground library at a very public museum. "Anyone could walk by."

He looks up at me, his eyes molten chocolate, swirling with unbridled desire that almost makes me take it back. "Or you could let me do this now… and we can finish the rest later." He licks his lips before rolling them together, but it does nothing to suppress the eagerness rolling off him. I know he sees the moment I let myself have this, have him, because he stops stifling his smile, holding my gaze as his hand slips up my dress.

* * *

I try to calm the flush that is still on my cheeks, sipping my ice water with a vengeance. The heat still radiates there, just like I still feel the intensity of the orgasm Ben just gave me in a library. A *library*. I suppress the giggle that almost escapes as I remember the "Sh!" I heard just after I finished, and now I'm blushing. Again. I glance up at Ben as he reaches for a fry, popping it into his mouth with amusement.

"Remind me to shock you more often, Beckett." He smiles smugly, his cockiness surprisingly charming to me at this moment. *Not surprisingly*, I think to myself. *Not surprising at all. I love him.*

The thought comes but doesn't go, and I know worry must be etched in my expression because concern is etched in his.

"What happened, Liv?"

I shake my head vigorously, unwilling to open that can of worms. That thought was intrusive and orgasm induced. I know better than to pay it any mind.

"Just remembered I need to call my mom," I offer, and it's not a complete lie. I do need to call her, even if she can't make the time to call me. He nods, understanding crossing his face, and I feel bad for not being honest. There's a part of me that feels like he deserves every unbridled truth I have. It's the same part that thinks I love him.

"The mom who's never really around?" he recalls our conversation at his favorite diner, and I give him a curt smile.

"The one and only," I sigh. "It's not as sad as you think it is. I don't miss having a present mom because I never had one." I shrug, hoping my explanation suffices. My mother takes up so little of my mental energy, just as I'm sure I take up very little of hers.

"You don't think you might have… missed out on something?" His question is cautious, like he still can't place my attitude toward her.

"I mean, I probably did. It isn't a love thing… I know she loves me. But I think she felt like she had to have me? And then she did and it was kind of a disappointment. Not me— I could disappoint no one." I sarcastically roll my eyes, hoping to lighten what I've just shared. "Just the whole motherhood thing. She's there when she needs to be, but otherwise it's just me and my dad." He hums in acknowledgement, and I know he's done pressing.

"Our mom was kind of like that but… the opposite. Like motherhood happened to her and it overwhelmed her. Instead of getting ahead of it or out of it, she kind of just drowned." He's looking just past me, a haunted look taking root in his eyes.

"Will never really talked about your parents. I kind of assumed it was because they were perfect." I scoff at my misguided notions about their family, wondering how different my life would be if I had considered they were anything but.

"Yeah well, he really got the short end of the stick." He leans back in his chair, running a hand through his hair. "I was so young when she had Will, but I remember how dark it was. How she barely held him, how the nanny would pace up and down trying to calm him down and she would be sitting on our balcony, just staring into the forest. I see it for what it was— depression. But I also wasn't the kid who got that version of her, for whatever reason. It had nothing to do with Will, it was just chance."

I think about a young Will, trying to connect with a mother battling her own demons, a mother still learning how to be this new person and effectively being ignored. It breaks my heart all over again.

"I'm so sorry. I never knew."

"You can't know something no one ever shared," he tells me. "Besides, as soon as she was medicated, she tried her best to make it up to him. He can't always see it; he thinks she's being overdramatic or overbearing but… she's just trying to show him she cares."

"She sounds like a good mother," I say, because she

does, and because I can hear in his voice his need to defend her.

"I mean, like I said, we all have our shit, but she is. We summer in the Hamptons, which Will thinks is just some family tradition, but we only started doing it when I was seven, so he can't remember a time we didn't when we were kids," he's smiling to himself, a memory playing in his mind. "She would take us crab hunting at night. We'd be scared shitless until we finally caught one. We'd get ice cream sundaes on the boardwalk for breakfast and she'd make us promise not to mention a word to Dan." He laughs, the fondness of those summers evident in the way his shoulders relax the more he talks. "As we got older, the mother-son outings kind of petered out, except for Albert's. It's her favorite place on the boardwalk and Will's too, so I guess it just kind of stuck." His eyes gleam with a distant, childlike happiness, and I think he's right that I missed out on something.

"Having one magical summer is a gift, but having a whole childhood full of them? It's really beautiful that she gave you guys that." At my insight his shoulders sag.

"I haven't been since before I left. Haven't really seen her, either. Just on the occasional holiday."

I place my hand over his on our table, tilting my head to the side. "That's the great thing about a tradition. It doesn't just disappear when you stop honoring it; it sits there, just waiting for you to come back to it."

His eyes squint at me, his mouth turning up at the corners. "Where'd you get this wisdom from, Beckett?"

"Definitely not *my* mother." The laugh that escapes me surprises even myself, the realization that we're sharing such heavy parts of ourselves with each other filling my heart with joy.

"So do you guys have a lot of traditions?"

"Not really. Thanksgiving with me and my dad is the big one, but even Christmas is inconsistent. Sometimes my mom's side wants to see us, sometimes my dad's does. But the *idea* of a tradition makes me feel cozy inside, so I just started making some for myself."

"Like?" Curiosity and amusement sparkle in eyes as he regards me, his hand resting on his chin.

"Like… on the first day of fall I sit outside with a cup of tea and start *Dracula*," I inform him, raising my eyebrows for dramatic effect.

"*Dracula*?"

"Ben. I'm obviously a vampire girl, please don't pretend to be shocked."

"I guess your first words to me were pretty venomous," he smirks, his eyes pools of laughter, and I roll my eyes with a smirk of my own.

"In December, I usually pick one Saturday where I'm not obligated to be anywhere, and I go to the holiday market by myself. I always get a countdown calendar, and I almost always have to open the first ten boxes and eat them as soon as I get home because the month's already started."

"Is the 'by yourself' part of the tradition, or is that flexible?"

I sigh, pretending his question is inconvenient and not heartwarming. "I *guess* I can make room for you. But you have to get your own countdown calendar," I warn him.

"Noted. In return, I'll let you summer with me in the Hamptons until we're gray and old."

The thought of summering in the Hamptons reminds me of Lily, and it feels like a rain cloud attempts to settle above me, but it's cleared away by the thought of Ben and I, old and happy, strolling along the shoreline.

"Who says I can't just summer there on my own?" I ask him, a silent challenge in my eyes. He's saying more than I could hope for, and still, I demand this validation from him, but I can't help myself.

"Do you want to be alone, Olivia?" His gaze rests on me intently as he throws the ball back in my court. Instead of blind validation, he's giving me space to choose, and I don't know why I'm surprised.

Contentment floods me once more as I answer him. "No, I don't think I do."

"Good. Because I was already adding museum sex to our growing list of traditions." Leaning back to avoid the playful smack I'm attempting to plant on his arm, he throws me a subtle wink.

"What am I going to do with you, Ben Cabot?" I shake my head, my nose wrinkling as I try to hide my flustered smile.

"I keep asking myself the same question."

I bite my lip at his answer and say nothing else; I just look at him and wonder if this is what it feels like when you've met your soulmate.

Is it this easy? Do you feel like you've known them your whole life but there still won't ever be enough time to know them completely? Does it feel like your entire self is being pulled under, and instead of suffocating angst you feel relief? Like you're coming back to a place you've been before, the feeling so familiar but you can't put your finger on why?

It must be what this feels like, because every instinct in my body is telling me yes: I've never felt this way before for a reason.

25

Olivia

It feels like an eternity since Ben dropped me off at home. I roll over and look at the clock, for what feels like the hundredth time, and see it's nearly 1:30 a.m. I feel hyper and giddy, my mind full of excitement, the way I used to after an amazing date. Like this burst of adrenaline is streaming through me and I just want to talk to someone who will examine the evening I had with Ben in thirty different ways without batting an eye. In the past, on nights like tonight I'd talk to Lily, force her to wake up and let me rant about every thought swirling in my brain.

I scroll through my contacts, quickly remembering I have no one.

Over the years I've learned these are the moments you take for granted after losing your best friend. The times she'd help scrutinize a reply I was sending a boy for over an hour. How she would watch me try on twelve different outfits before my college interviews to find one that was stylish yet professional. All the coffee runs in our pajamas or dinners in our favorite booth at our favorite restaurant, drinking Diet Cokes and talking about every detail of our lives. The silence used to be deafening in my room on nights like this, but tonight it's something softer and for the first time since Lily's death I don't pull away.

I roll out of bed, my socks sinking into the plush, thickly padded rug on the floor. I've decided I'm giving up on sleep. Putting my kettle on the stove, I sit at the counter looking at the one photo of Lily and I that I have framed in my home. The one I've kept out just in case the day arrived that I wanted to remember, that I wanted to see my best friend. I stare at it for a long second, allowing myself to start to feel the precipice of things I have been actively avoiding for the past few years. My grief is like a storm, quiet but strong, begging to be let out, and for once I decide to feel a grain of what she meant to me— nothing more, nothing less. It's so small, the emotion I allow to seep into myself, and yet I see how the longer I've kept this sadness inside me the more it's grown.

In some ways, I've always known this. I've felt it in the shadows of everything I do. Even now with Ben, it's here: that unbearable want for everything to go back to how it was before. I close my eyes breathing in through my nose, trying to will myself not to find a distraction but to allow this brief intermission of Lily into my thoughts.

My kettle begins to whistle so I take it off the burner and go toward the pantry, looking for the right herbal remedy to calm the inner plight inside me, when a box crashes to the ground as I open the closet sliding door. I freeze, my hand still clenching the door. I know exactly what it is before I even look down. My Lily box. I haven't looked at the contents in years and yet here it is, crashing down in front of me like she's here egging me on. I gravitate toward it. I quickly pick it up and dump the contents on the kitchen table.

Tears prick my eyes as the memories flood my table's surface. Photos of two smiling girls getting ready for their debutante ball; another of us as toddlers with giant rollers in our hair and makeup that we clearly did with no supervision; pages of old journals we passed between ourselves with lists of crushes and gossip about the girls we didn't like. Lily's whimsical handwriting in the margins that are filled with quotes, lyrics, and all sorts of her favorite symbols from her favorite number thirty-two to her horoscope, Gemini.

I touch my fingertips together as everything starts rushing back, all the emotions I tend to clamp down with an iron like grip bubbling up. I push back against the wave swelling inside me. *This is too much, too fast,* I hear that inner voice, begging me to forget. I push it down and begin moving through the different items. It's interesting what you deem worthy to save in those moments right after someone you love dies. These inanimate objects that make up who they were, all of them a reflection of how you interpreted their life to be.

My fingers trail a light pink measuring tape as I think back to the summer that Lily and I measured our bodies, comparing the inches to those of Victoria Secret models.

"It's okay Liv, not all of us have the genes to walk the runway, some of us have to be the brains behind the operation," Lily winks.

My gut roils as I push the tape off the table. I find the deck of cards Lily used to teach me to shuffle during one spring break and the yearbook from seventh grade that I used a Sharpie to color my face out of instead of signing my name at our end of year celebration.

To my left is the beaded pouch she got at the beach

our last summer together. I run my hands against it considering how it felt like everything changed that summer, how distant she was. She was sneaking out, not inviting me to any of the parties she was going to. Like she wanted to separate herself from me completely. My mind reels thinking about one of the nights I tried to go with her.

"Let me come with you." I place my book down, moving to grab a dress out of my closet to go to one of the beach bonfires Lily has been sneaking out to over the past month

"It's not really your scene, Liv." She doesn't glance at me applying lipstick in the vanity mirror.

"Cmon. We've barely hung out this whole summer… Why don't you want me there?" I feel the flush spread against my face as I whine. I've really grown into myself this past year, I realize as I look over her shoulder into the vanity mirror. My hair is shoulder length but growing, my teeth newly straight from years in braces. I'm still tall, but my face and body have slimmed out considerably. I squint my eyes really trying to see what flaws Lily might be seeing.

"Olivia, chill." She's looking at me over her shoulder like I've just had some sort of outburst and not just asked her a simple question. Seeing what I'm sure is insecurity flickering over me she gives me a faux pout then quickly stands straightening her mini dress.

"Look— this has nothing to do with you. I told you I am on an independence journey this summer! Besides, I'm dumping someone tonight so the vibe will be off." She saunters over and grabs my shoul-ders. "Liv, I love you, you know that." I look down at my socked feet, embarrassment rolling off me. She nudges me, her voice softening. "Sometimes, I just need to be able to do my own thing. I'm always here if you need me, but I just need to know you're going to be okay when I'm not around."

I feel my stomach turn the same way I did that night, but this time it's different. She needed to know I'd be okay without her and I never gave that to her. Guilt instantly washes over me.

Lily is gone— *my* Lily.

I glance over again at the photo of us as girls, rollers haphazardly in our hair, our makeup glittery and over dramatic, and I stare at it for a while. She was just a girl and so was I.

I decide to keep some of the photos out and open the beaded pouch to store them. Inside is a neatly folded piece of paper and a woven bracelet I recognize from one of the boardwalk vendors from that final summer with her. I throw the bracelet back in the box and am about to trash the paper but decide to open it, curiosity taking over. It's a receipt.

You're perfect, I love you.

The script is clean and neat, definitely not Lily's, but I recognize her random doodling on the edges. I squint, re-reading the restaurant's name: *Albert's on the Boardwalk*. My eyes widen realizing this is the exact restaurant Ben was talking about earlier. I feel the corners of my mouth lifting in a smile as my eyes well with tears. In a weird way, I feel like this is some sort of sign from my friend. Like she wanted me to find this and know that all those details I needed to share about my date with Ben were heard. That she's always been here when I've needed her. That she knows I'm going to be okay.

26

Ben

Wednesday mornings, and by extension Wednesdays themselves, are unreasonable. We're expected to be in the weight room by 5:30 in the morning, only to condition on the, thankfully, indoor track an hour later. This is in addition to the normal practice we have in the afternoon. So the fact that Grant and I barely speak a word to each other until we're halfway through our fourth set of the morning isn't wild. What is wild is the haggard look on Grant's face. He's not a morning person, but the tortured expression I see every time I sneak a glimpse at him is haunting considering he's usually so… okay.

I can't say I look much better. I was happy walking into the gym this morning after leaving Olivia's, walking on air even, but one look at Will and my mood immediately deteriorated. The past few weeks with Olivia have been some of the best of my life, but seeing Will across the weight room is like a sucker punch to the gut. I feel like my entire life is tangled in this web of lies, from hiding the truth about how I know Lily, to keeping my relationship with Olivia from

Will. Seeing my brother is an ugly reminder of the mess we've both created. I feel that familiar sensation in my chest, the one that's been missing the past few weeks with Olivia. My heart rate feels jumpy as I keep pushing myself harder on the rower, trying to focus on a point on the wall to bring myself back to reality.

I wish I could tell him I don't know when it happened. When she became this agonizingly, desperately integral part of my life, but that would be a lie, wouldn't it? She's consumed my every thought since the second I laid eyes on her. I've been pushing away this feeling ever since I saw Will that Christmas. He was alive for the first time after all the shit that transpired after Lily's death, not the Will I knew but not a ghost of himself either. I was relieved, initially, but when he told us about Olivia, I felt something settle inside me— this weight that I've carried every day since. I decided, that day, that this is how she would get to be a part of my life. My parents on the other hand were *not* relieved, in fact quite the opposite. Olivia was Lily's best friend and if you polled my mother and Will's dad, it was disturbing and just wouldn't do; not after all they'd done to ignore Will's "association" with "that girl."

That's what Lily was to my parents, but that's not who she was to Will. If you'd asked me who Lily was to Will that summer, I would've told you that she was everything. So putting my feelings aside for a girl I saw once at a party seemed like a no-brainer. I took the words of my therapist and ran with them. Olivia was my fixation, something I equated to a perfect life, impossible to achieve.

I knew that night in the bar, after watching Olivia, the stunning, confident, mind boggling woman become this wilted version of herself— I knew I should tell her. I needed to tell her.

Looking at my little brother, I know why I haven't. He's the reason I've kept my mouth shut. It's hard to reconcile how I see him with how the world does, this arrogant asshole who betrays the woman he apparently loves with the boy I grew up with who just wanted to have a moment of his dad's attention that didn't center around his success at throwing a ball in a basket. Still, there's this shadow looming and I think allowing Will to continue this lie has ended up hurting him more than helping him.

It's time to move on. Coach's voice wrenches me from my thoughts.

"Chapman, Cabot. Weights, now." Will moves to the machines with a clenched jaw. I feel the panic pick back up in my chest and I count the steps to the weight rack. It was inevitable, having to talk to Will today, and yet the nerves in my chest erupt. I know we need to talk. I need to convince him to tell Olivia the truth. I bite down my emotions, forcing myself to start the conversation.

"I'll take the forty-fives." Will's voice is flat as he gestures to the plates on the rack beside me. I pull them off, putting them on the machine for Will.

"Recovery day, huh?" He looks up at me, his eyes cold before diverting his gaze back to the wall. "How have you been?" I don't have to fake the emotion when I ask because I am genuinely concerned. I've heard he's been drinking a lot and sleeping around, which I sort of expected. What I didn't expect was to see Will show up to practice looking like a shell of himself, the way he did when Lily died. His jaw twitches as he begins his set.

I roll my lips together knowing the small talk isn't going to get us anywhere so I blurt it out.

"I think you should tell her."

Will freezes mid rep, his eyes moving to mine. His voice is a raspy whisper like he hasn't spoken all morning.

"Ben, stop."

I feel my own jaw clench. I have allowed him to continue this lie for years, watching as he pushed his grief over Lily to the side, trying to mask it with the dysfunctional relationship he had with Liv. Still, that hint of desperation in his voice, his eyes begging— it's enough to give me pause.

"How long are you going to keep going like this?" I keep my voice low and even.

"Why do you even care?" he asks, meeting my question with his own. I feel the look I'm giving him before I have time to conceal it and I see the shift in his gaze. "So it is true, isn't it?" His sneer is evident, his quiet tone lethal. "I should have believed Gen, but I thought it was just another ploy for her to get in my pants."

"Fuck this," escapes Grant's mouth and we hear it from across the weight room.

The heavy kettlebell slams into the gym floor with a loud thunk as his hulking form grabs a towel off the bench beside him roughly rubbing the sweat of his face. The whole gym takes on this eerie silence. I notice Will's not even glancing Grant's way. His eyes analyzing me, expression full of disappointment as he scans my face for any sign that the rumors he's been hearing about Olivia and I aren't true. He shakes his head, his posture drooping as he drops the handles of the machine and grabs his duffle. A few feet away, Grant marches out of the gym doors and the slam as they swing shut reverberates through the gym. The noise is so loud that no one notices Will slip out the opposite side of the gym, pulling the hood of his jacket over his head.

"Woah, everything good with your boys, Cabot?"

Andrew asks from his treadmill, slowing to a snail's pace. I grab my gym bag off the floor beside me, looking after where Will snuck out before ultimately deciding to follow Grant.

"Mind your business and get that speed back up, second string," I bark at him. He grumbles under his breath and I hardly make it out as I exit.

Grant's sitting on a bench across from the gym, head buried in his phone. He barely notices me as I approach.

"Can I sit?" I ask.

I've only seen Grant lose his cool once. It was at a game where a few of the guys on the opposing team were making pretty disgusting remarks about our school's cheer team members. Grant had two of their guys pinned against a wall before I could stop dribbling the ball.

Grant sighs. "Yeah… sorry about that. I just…" he trails off, rubbing his hand roughly over his face. I look at him waiting for him to finish and he finally meets my eyes, his eyes widen.

"Bro— you look like shit."

He cracks a smile and I laugh because he's right, I do look like shit. I've slept at Olivia's the past two nights and haven't gotten more than a few hours of sleep, but I'm definitely not complaining. Grant definitely looks worse off, if I'm being honest. His hair is mussed, but not in the intentional way it usually is, and he has bags under his eyes.

"You don't look too bad yourself," I say as a joke and Grant gives a sad "ha!" in response. His eyes go back to his phone. "Hey— you good man?" My tone is cautious.

"Yeah…" He pockets his phone and takes a deep breath."Just… family stuff."

I smirk, trying to bring levity to the conversation. "I can relate to you there."

"For fucks sake, please don't talk to me about Will right now." His voice takes on a loud frustrated tone and he glances at me, clenching his fists. I'm not necessarily taken aback by his comment but the tone of his voice is out of the ordinary for Grant. Seeming to realize how aggressive he's coming off, he takes a deep breath and clears his throat.

"Look—" he says, shutting his eyes like he's trying to calm himself down. "I know you see Will in a different light than the rest of us, which is good because everyone deserves to have someone think they are a good person. I just can't watch him stomp all over…." he pauses, seeming to reconsider what he's going to say. "I can't watch him treat Olivia and others the way he does. Someone needs to stop him." He's staring straight forward glaring at the gym doors like he can see my brother through them. "I need to go," he says, standing and shoving his phone into his pocket.

Then I'm there alone, thinking about Grant and everyone who's been hurt by my brother and all the ways I could've stopped the hurt from happening, if I just hadn't left. If I just stayed and protected him and made sure he was in an okay head space. I mean Jesus Christ, the love of his life just died and I left him. I couldn't deal with this place anymore, this person who everyone wanted me to be. Even if I were here, would I have been what he needed? Was anyone what he needed?

My breathing feels strained the way it used to when I would get overwhelmed. I think of Will's stoic gaze in the gym today and all the ways I continue to hurt him, betray him. My heart begins to beat in overdrive. I clench my chest as tears prick my eyes. My throat feels dry and thick and I can't get air.

That night flashes in my head. Red solo cups littered across the lawn, Grant manning the bar for the team, the head of blonde curls following my brother into the room off the kitchen, and Olivia. Chestnut hair, black leather blazer, amber eyes, Olivia, her smile that seemed to radiate through the party, a whisper between the cheer squad.

"Did you see her talking to Ian. She's only a freshman."

Olivia biting her lip looking at Will, holding her friend's hand. Olivia.

Sweat drips down my back. I want to stop thinking about this but my vision is tunneling and all I see is her face against the backdrop of that party. The freckles sprinkled across the bridge of her nose, the fanning of her dark lashes. More whispers.

"She's so pretty."

"Did you see her talking to Will?"

She's there, her eyes are searching. I know what's coming next. It's always the final stop in this memory. Lily breaking Will's heart, my fist near his face.

Olivia. And there he is. Beside her.

27

Olivia

When I get to Ben's apartment, I'm once again struck by how much has changed in just a few short months. The first time I was here I hadn't wanted to waltz right in when he texted me to; now I'm punching in the door code without even a second thought. But just like the first time I was here, Ben's out of sight and I hear his shower running down the hall.

Opening his fridge, I inspect the contents and find that since I was here two days ago, he's stocked the entire bottom shelf with Diet Coke. I gleefully smile to myself, reveling in the fact that he would purchase such a 'toxic' drink for me and me alone. I crack one open, deciding it's enough to hold me over until our secret double date with Sloane and her tinder date later tonight.

"Ben, I'm here!" I call out as I enter his room, collapsing onto his magnificent bed, but not before putting my Coke on a coaster. I've never met a man so adamant about coasters.

I hear his shower door click open, a sliver of his hair

protruding from the door frame. "Practice ran late," he says over the sluicing sound of water. "I just got in but I'll be quick."

Checking the time, I leave the luxurious comfort of Ben's bed and remind myself that we're staying at his place tonight. We mostly split time between my place and his, though it isn't anything we've officially discussed. It's just that more often than not, I don't want to end my night with Ben. I don't want to end my day with Ben, either. I don't want to end anything, and that thought truly plagues me. When I think about it too deeply, my heart swells and I feel giddy, but my mind trips itself into a spiral where I question my sanity. It feels like I've fallen so quickly for Ben, but if I'm honest with myself, I started falling for him long before I should've been.

I shake the thought away, intent on finding an outfit for him and saving us some time. Rifling through his closet, I settle on a gray cashmere sweater, noting the chill in the air, and those jeans that I love so much. I reach up, trying my best to grab the neutral pair of sneakers I spot on a top shelf, when a wrapped package just misses my face.

It's rectangular, and I'm almost certain it's a book. There's a note on the parchment, the handwriting scrawled and barely legible, but I think it says '*Wuthering Heights* special request'. I pause, wondering if my mind is so addled with thoughts of love and lust that I'm imagining that Ben got this book for me. *But why else would he have a parchment wrapped copy of Wuthering Heights? The obvious answer is usually the right one*, I think to myself, smiling once again at the thoughtfulness of this man. Not wanting him to think I spoiled his surprise, I clumsily attempt to put it back where I found it.

I look down at what I've selected for Ben tonight, pleased, but feeling like something's missing.

A watch.

While I don't think Ben would miss it, I certainly would. Ben alone is distracting, but Ben in a watch is tortuous in the best way possible. I peruse his collection, amused to find that among his watches he seems to be collecting wearable knickknacks. At this point, I know Ben *can* be sentimental, but the plethora of concert wristbands, charity bracelets, and woven things reminds me just how sentimental he is. The glint of a seashell catches my attention and I pick up a woven bracelet almost identical to the one I saw in Lily's stuff the other day.

Hi, Lil, I think to myself, a magical feeling enveloping me. For years, I thought letting Lily back into my life would be scary, disorienting, unsettling. But instead, I'm finding her everywhere, and the reassurance her little signs give me are more than I could have ever asked for.

At the sound of footsteps behind me I turn around, not at all shocked to find Ben with a teasing smile that tells me he knows how badly I want him to drop his towel. I level my gaze with the intent on not getting distracted since we're already so close on time.

"Are those for me?" His amused smirk sends lightening through me, and I reconsider if timeliness is really that important.

"Mhm," I respond, still debating my next move, when I feel the subtle weight of that bracelet in my hand. "Where's this one from?" I ask, hoping to confirm my guardian angel's presence.

"Oh… I think," he scrunches his brows, trying to recollect where it's from, nodding when he remembers. "I'm pretty sure we got them on the boardwalk in the Hamptons." He pulls his shirt over his head, but not before dropping his towel, his smug face reemerging with a tempting twinkle in his eyes.

I step toward him, arching up on my tip toes, my hand hovering just over where he's at attention, and though I intend to just tease him a little, I find myself stroking him, my lust addled brain taking over.

"Jesus, Liv," he groans, his head falling back.

"Isn't this what you wanted?" I rasp against his neck, my lips barely touching his neck. Before I can even register, he's picked me up so I'm straddling him as he walks me toward his bed. "I was hoping we would spend more time here today," I add, biting my smile.

"I'm more than happy to make that happen." Instead of laying me down, he sits on the edge, bringing me down with him. I look down at him, his eyes heavy with anticipation and mine likely not much better. I don't look away, just discreetly rise and pull my underwear to the side before sinking down on him. A hiss escapes him as I gasp, and his mouth finds mine, his tongue running against the seam of my lips begging to be let in. And when I do, it's like I'm rolling down a hill and him with me, the intensity so fast and overwhelming that all I can do is give myself over to it. Our angle gives just enough friction, and his hands are on my chest, rubbing and pinching at just the right moment, and I fall over the edge right as he does, unsure of how it's always this perfect with him.

I rest my forehead against his, our breathing slowly normalizing, and I have the urge to say those three words. But I don't.

"We're going to be late, Cabot," I tell him with a grin,

not at all irritated by our detour, reluctantly leaving his embrace and heading to the bathroom. "Sloane said the trivia starts at 7:00 on the dot." I peer at my reflection in the mirror, my post climax flush creating a blush I wish I could recreate with makeup. He appears behind me a moment later, fully dressed, his chin resting atop my head.

"I got you a present, but something tells me you already know that." He pulls the parchment covered book from behind his back, an easy smile gracing his face. "For an investigative journalist, your snooping skills leave much to be desired," he winks.

With a roll of my eyes, I delicately peel back the parchment.

"How did you know?" I hadn't told him I wanted it. In fact, I looked at dozens of books that day and this one was just one of many.

"You get this look in your eye when you really want something. I could spot it from a mile away." He regards me with sincerity, and I feel my heart sputter, those three words sitting at the top of my throat.

"Thank you," is all I say instead, turning my head and kissing him deeply. "I…" I pause, the war over whether or not to voice this blossoming feeling raging inside me, "love this. So much. You have no idea." His eyes are heated with something more than lust, and it feels like he wants to say something too. But then he blinks it away, and I do the same.

"Have you ever *played* trivia?" he changes the topic, though the question has merit.

"Yes. Once. And I won, so I think that makes me good at all trivia," I state matter of factly, because it feels objectively true.

"Isn't it *Prison Break* trivia?" His amused expression tells me he thinks I'm not up for the challenge.

"Trivia is not about knowing things. It's about knowing *people*. Alliances are half the battle. Come on, we're going to be late." I grab his hand, feeling giddy by the ease of this, urging him down the hallway and out the door, and silently hope that I will always know nights like this with him.

28

Ben

I tap my pencil against my notebook trying to focus, but I keep glancing at my phone waiting for the next text from Olivia. I can't get her out of my head and I've been with her almost every free moment we both have.

My phone begins to ring and I quickly grab it, my heart sinking when I check the caller ID.

My mom has been calling more this week than any other since I've been back at Astor, but I've been letting it roll to voicemail. I pretend it's because I've been too busy spending time with Olivia. I already know mom's head is going to explode when I tell her. She didn't even like when *Will* was dating Olivia and that was just because she knew she was Lily's friend. I can't imagine what she's going to say to me when she finds out.

I know these calls aren't about me, though. They're about Will. Otherwise, I wouldn't have received my first missed call from Dan in the past two years. So I keep letting the voicemails roll in, trying to avoid the inevitable, I guess.

I get the notification that a few minutes later that my

voicemail box is full. I decide I better at least delete a few and that I can't keep avoiding my mom, so I listen to the most recent message.

"Ben, please call us back. I know the past few years have been a lot and I know we put a lot of pressure on you, but we are worried about Will. Wilson called and he said he's thinking of leaving the team… I know he has his ups and downs, but it never conflicts with basketball."

She emphasizes the word as if it's the most important thing in the world. I feel my jaw tense. She's right to be worried. Even the year we both had mono we didn't miss a single practice.

"It's just so unusual for him. Even that girl didn't have this effect." I cringe at the way she refers to Lily. *"We tried sending Marie to his apartment for a wellness check, but she said he wasn't there. Your father is thinking of flying down."* I hear Dan say in the background, *"Tell Ben if that's necessary, he can kiss his tuition goodbye. I don't have time for their dramatics."*

I hear my mom mumble an apology to my step father and I immediately regret not playing my role as the perfect big brother. I hear my mom shuffle to what I assume is a different room of the house and shut the door quietly.

"Ben, I know this is not easy for any of us, but especially you. We love you honey. Please, if you hear from your brother at all just let us know if he's alright. Alright, talk soon, love you." The beep at the end of the line signals the voicemail is over.

Just as I go to delete it and move on to the next one there's a sharp rap at the door. My heart somersaults at the idea that it's Olivia surprising me. I chuckle at myself as I rush to stand, fully aware of how quickly my mood changed just at the thought that it could be her. The perfect band aid to the headspace my mom just put me in. I throw a shirt on, walking down the hallway that leads from my room to the front door. I peek out the peephole only to see a mass slouched against the wall, and the image of what is clearly not Olivia, makes my stomach sink. The person's silhouette is fuzzy until finally the body adjusts and I recognize who it is.

Will.

I immediately open the door. His clothes are wrinkled and his eyes look hollow as if he hasn't slept or even been home in days. No wonder Marie hadn't seen him. He's slunk against the door jam, and it's extremely clear he's drunk and not in the way he usually is. Not the one that makes him a cocky asshole or giddy like a child— no, he's drunk the way he was that first day after Lily died.

"Ben… I," his voice is hoarse. I grab him by the collar and bring him in for a rough hug. Will embraces me as if he's needed this hug for a while, a hug without any strings. I feel him let out a long shaky breath. Will sniffs, trying to regain his composure but failing as the tears continue to silently fall down his face.

"Let's sit down, bud. I'll make you some coffee." I steer him toward the kitchen, his body which usually isn't obviously smaller than mine seeming wimpy and weak in comparison. Every centimeter of him seems to sag, as if whatever is going on with him is weighing down his very aura. His hair is greasy and unbrushed, the stubble on his face hitting that middle ground between five o'clock shadow and a beard, making him look unkempt.

I flip the coffee maker on as Will sits at the kitchen table beside me, his head in his hands. My stomach turns. Is his breakup with Olivia really affecting him this much? Did I cause this? The feeling that whatever is going on with him is unequivocally my fault hits me with such force it's hard for me to form words.

"I miss her Ben." It comes so quietly I almost miss it in the shame spiral I've found myself in. Will's head is still in his hands and the words come out muffled.

The coffee finishes brewing and I fish some mugs from the upper shelf beside the fridge. I set one down in front of Will and pour one for myself before taking a seat at the table across from him. My mind is reeling with the fact that I have really crushed my brother.

"Have you tried reaching out to her?" I hear myself answer, focusing on my coffee cup, trying to school my shaky tone into one that is calm and unobtrusive. Will's face goes blank at that and I move closer placing a firm hand on his shoulder.

"This is so fucked, Ben," he says, his jaw clenched as he shakes his head as if in disbelief, his eyes fixed at the black coffee sitting before him. "She's never coming back." He says it to himself, his voice hollow and breaking. My fingers clench and I feel my own eyes begin to water. He's talking about Lily. "Have you talked to Mom?" His tone is empty now, cold and void of all emotion.

I clear my throat trying to shake the emotion from my voice. "She's called… but no, I haven't spoken to her."

Will's relationship with our mother is different from mine. Where I feel closeness with the woman who raised us, there is a distance between the two of them. After Will's birth, our mother dealt with a depression so deep it seemed to hinder her from forming a relationship with my brother, and as I've grown older it's apparent how this has affected him. She has seemed to guard herself by letting Dan take the charge in Will's upbringing. Her constant anxiety about him at one point caused her to lean on me for incessant updates on everything, from his well being to his current emotional state.

"Can you tell her I'm fine if she calls again?" Will asks, eyes unwavering and empty as he grips the side of his mug.

"Will, you're—" before I can finish Will cuts me off, his tone biting.

"Ben, I can't talk to them right now. If dad comes here, if he talks about Lily, if I have to hear him call her 'that girl'— I'll fucking lose it." He slams his fist against the table, causing coffee to slosh out of his cup. His anger reverberating through the kitchen.

I think about how my mom spoke about Lily earlier, and I don't necessarily blame either of my parents for the lack of understanding when it came to her. To them it was a summer fling, a two month romance that wasn't going anywhere. What they seemed to not realize was that Will's love of Lily could only be compared to his love of basketball. It was so all consuming, it verged on unhealthy, and when he started dating Olivia my parents wanted nothing to do with it. They couldn't wrap their heads around how a few months with Lily could cause such deep seated emotions in him. My mom thought he had gone off the deep end, finding out he was dating his dead ex-girlfriend's best friend. Dan on the other hand thought it was funny. He said Will was obviously fine based on his winning streak on the team and the Rookie of the Year award he got the year after Lily's death.

"I just don't know what to do..." Will slouches into his chair and puts his face into his hands. I haven't seen my little brother so defeated in years. Typically he guards any real emotions behind this cultivated mask he puts on for the world. Right now, he seems like a shell of himself. "Ben, I can't keep living like this. Numb, like I feel nothing. I've been hiding from what happened to Lily for so long and now that Olivia ended things…" He closes his eyes, rubbing his temples.

"Will—"

"Ben— don't." I close my mouth at his interruption, letting him speak. "I know what you're going to say so you don't need to say it. I know I have been avoiding the whole Lily thing, I know I need to tell Liv, I know that I'm fucked in the head because of this entire situation."

I sigh, trying to figure out how to find a way to phrase my words that won't escalate this conversation, because he's not exactly wrong. I turn my chair slightly to face him.

"Will, I love you. I know you have good intentions, but the lies—"

"Jesus fucking Christ, Ben— you lied, too." He pushes up out of the seat and moves toward the sink, holding his coffee cup.

I blink, a little shocked. "I only lied to Olivia because I wanted to give you a chance to figure things out yourself. I wanted to let you do the right thing."

Will shakes his head laughing slightly, setting his coffee cup carefully on the counter, turning to face me. "I'm not talking about you lying to Liv. I'm talking about you lying to me."

My stomach sinks because I know he's right. That what I did was wrong. Even if I believe that Will and Olivia weren't meant to be together, I still was the one who came in and fucked everything up.

"Ben," he rubs his hand over his face in an effort to calm down. "You always do this."

"Always do what?" I scan his face trying to understand what he's talking about.

"You come in and you take and you take and you take. I've never had anything that was mine, you know that? I have nothing left to give Ben, you took it all. My girl, my game, hell even my dad respects you more than he's ever respected me. Mom won't even look at me!"

It's surprising, how I've never really seen it this way but looking back, I know he's right. He's always been on the back burner, always in second place and I put him there. It was so drilled into us as kids to never let anyone win, even each other. So much so that I never threw him a bone. Any scrimmage we played, I never let him take an easy shot. I never let him get with a girl without letting him know how easily I could take her. Hell, I even held my relationship with my mom over his head, checking up on him because she couldn't do it herself.

My stomach churns at the memories. I breathe in a steady breath knowing that I've changed, knowing that I'm not that guy anymore. But actions speak louder than words and thus far my actions show how little I've actually evolved. He sits back down, arms crossed as he waits for me to respond.

"I'm sorry," my voice is shaky as I meet his gaze. I feel the edges of my eyes burn with tears, my face hot with shame and embarrassment. "Will, I don't want to be that guy anymore. I know how it used to be and I really worked to change, even if my actions don't reflect that." I say more to myself than him. "When I came back I didn't think about how my return would affect you and that was wrong."

"No, Ben— " his tone is serious, solemn even. "When you *left* you didn't think about how it would affect me. Didn't consider that I would be alone here with just *Dan* in my ear after Lily's death, begging me to show him that I'm just the failure he's always known I was." His eyes cloud with frustration and pain. He pushes his hand through his hair and takes a long drink of his coffee. Setting his mug down gingerly, he meets my eyes. "You left me, Ben. Just like mom. Just like Lily. Olivia never left me, she saw me and she stayed. That was, until you got here."

It feels like he just jabbed me. The revelation of how my departure hurt Will never really struck me before. My stomach immediately sinks. He's right. Everything he's saying is right and I've been too selfish to see it. Too obsessed with fixing my own issues to see the hand he's been dealt.

"I don't blame her," he continues. "It was only a matter of time. I keep thinking of that night." A sad laugh escapes him. "The night Lily died was also the night I met Liv. You were there." He shakes his head sadly as if trying to forget the memory.

"I remember," I say, my voice gentle.

"Do you remember telling me to stay away from her?"

I meet his eyes. His gaze isn't angry, but like he's searching for an answer. "I do."

His expression turns to something like understanding.

"Ben, I know you are in love with her. It's obvious. I think I knew it that night." He lets out a sad laugh. "What's weird is I'm not even mad. I think I knew it would hurt you, if I had her first. I knew it would hurt Lily, too." I move my eyes down to the floor not knowing where to look. He's sitting in one of the kitchen chairs and I finally decide to look at him. He seems to have calmed down, his emotions waning to the point that he looks exhausted.

"I'm so sorry, Will." His gaze meets mine and we stare at each other for a minute before he lets out a long sad sigh.

"Ben, I was going to destroy everything. Olivia, our parents, myself, everything. Eventually, I would have done something to make her leave. To make everyone turn their back on me. I never loved Olivia the way I did Lily. She just… I don't know… she made me feel safe?" He's looking at his hands now with a sad smile. "I think I need to leave Astor, Ben. I can't keep doing this. Living this lie, hurting the people I love." He says the last part quietly and I feel the tears well up in my own eyes as I look at my little brother. It's hard to fault a man who was never shown love for not giving it greatly. "I haven't been good to her, Ben. I do it to Gen, too and she's been our friend for as long as I can remember. I can't stop myself from pushing people away, but I want to try. I can't keep living like this." He looks at me, desperation apparent in his eyes.

I wipe the tears now streaming down my own face. "Will, I'm here for you. What do you need?"

"We need to tell her, Ben. I need to have a clean slate to come back to and I can't if Olivia doesn't know everything."

I nod and for the first time in a while, I feel something like hope.

29
Olivia

I walk into the somewhat organized chaos that is now the newspaper office. Papers are in neat stacks spread all over the office with a few rogue coffee cups perched on them. A crazed Ian sits on the Senior Editor desk, his baggie Sonic Youth hoodie chic in a grunge sort of way, but rather casual for Ian. It's clear he hasn't left this office much, and I'm curious what has him in such a state. Coming by here isn't really a requirement, as long as I'm getting my pieces in with enough time for edits before we go to print, and all I've really had going is my style column. *And the Ben story*, I remind myself.

Setting my iced americano on my no longer pristine desk, I duck my head trying to catch Ian's attention.

"Don't you have your own, much messier, desk to go all 'beautiful mind' in?" The amount of sticky notes stuck to his journal and the desk calendar he's migrated to my desk should be criminal; the notes app exists for a reason.

He looks up at me from his laptop, a sour smirk on his face. "I only ended up here because *you've* been ignoring my texts about your assignment. I figured your desk might give me the answers you couldn't."

My teeth worry my bottom lip as I step closer to his screen, my stomach doing a nervous flip as I realize he's mad about the story.

"Ian," I start with a sigh. "I wasn't ignoring you, there just isn't anything to report. He left for personal reasons and I *promise* there's nothing sexy or scandalous about it." I tilt my head in exasperation, suddenly finding myself irritated at the way he just won't let this go. His obsession with peering into the lives of wealthy socialites and their children used to not get to me, even though I am distantly one of them, but his attention on Ben grates against me. What is he so fascinated by? His eyes narrow at me like he can read my mind.

"Nothing 'sexy or scandalous'? Oh, Olivia," he grins with disdain, shaking his head. "You really *haven't* been doing your job. You've been too busy hopping between brothers' beds from what I've heard." His words feel like a slap across the face, and I open my mouth to dispel the rumor, but he juts up from the desk, standing with me face to face, and my mouth falls shut. "I thought you'd at least be doing it with an ulterior motive in mind, but I guess you really are as stupid as I thought you were."

I swallow hard, unsure what to tackle first: the notion that I'm sleeping with both Will and Ben, or that I'm an incompetent idiot who isn't capable of reporting a story.

"My instincts are sound, Ian. There is nothing here," I reiterate, feeling the hard set of my jaw as my teeth grind against each other. "And if I didn't know any better, I'd say you were just jealous I was able to bag two ball players— *from what I've heard.*" My smile is just as sour as the one he gave me when I walked in, deciding I don't actually care what he thinks, and I take immense pleasure in the look of embarrassment that flashes across his face at my jab. While not a wide spread rumor, the story of Ian with a certain closeted power forward is certainly one that made its way to my ears. I would never repeat gossip like that, completely aware of how devastating it could be for all parties involved, but that won't stop me from deploying it in this moment just to watch him squirm. I've always been able to spin his fixation on the ultra wealthy as an ethical one; if anyone deserves a spotlight on the shit we get up to, it's us. But now that I know Ben, I know this story is a dead end. But Ian's committed to finding some dirt on this family like a runaway train.

"You're wrong," he all but seethes at me. He steps back, taking a breath before fixing his attention squarely on me. "Did you spend any time pondering the lead I gave you?" He raises his eyebrows, emphasizing how obvious he thinks the answer is. My lips purse as I shrug. "You *really* are just blind to this, aren't you?"

"Quit with the evasive bullshit and cut to the point, Ian." I feel adrenaline rush through me, dread pooling in my stomach at his expression. He looks like he's sitting on a landmine, like he's about to jump off and let it obliterate me.

"The story is Lily," he says, his voice quiet. My stomach feels like it does when you drop one hundred feet on a roller coaster before it levels out, my rational brain quelling all the unease I'd felt just moments earlier, and I laugh. I laugh so hard, my eyes start to water, and from behind my amused tears I see Ian's annoyed expression. "I'm serious, Liv. And I have two separate accounts of seeing Lily with them the summer before—"

"Ian." I catch my breath, pressing my lips together. "I

am sorry about what I said, that was a low blow, no pun intended." I stifle another laugh. "But you have to know how insane that sounds, right? But let's say you're right, and Lily somehow knew the Chapmans. What then?" My smile starts to fade as I notice his earnest expression. He fully believes this tale. He believes there's some link there.

"Well that would've been your job to find out, now wouldn't it?" His arms cross, and I know this conversation has damaged something between us— on my end and on his.

"I'm not pursuing this, Ian. If you want to make yourself look like a fool, you can do that."

"Don't worry, Liv. I wouldn't *dream* of asking you to get your hands dirty," he sneers at me, and I'm taken aback. Shaking my head, I gather my bag and turn to leave.

I turn around just before I reach the door. "Don't make your weird vendetta about my journalism skills. And just know, if this story doesn't pan out the way you want it to, you'll be pissing off the very people whose asses you kissed to crawl your way in here."

It's only once I'm outside the door that I take a deep breath, truly processing what Ian dropped on me. My instincts are what guide me in my journalism, and they're never wrong. So why do I now have a pit in my stomach?

Why does it feel like there is a shoe, and it is going to drop?

I shake the thought away, silently cursing Ian for getting in my head. Because the fact remains, what he told me is crazy. *He* is the crazy one.

* * *

It's my first time at a game since my breakup with Will. My first time back watching a game since I started seeing Ben.

And while I hear the low hush of my name while I walk through the stands, none of that is what's making my heart beat a second too fast. Instead, what Ian said to me replays in my mind over and over, spliced with scenes of that boardwalk bracelet I found in Ben's closet and the receipt I found in Lily's things.

They're just coincidences, I think to myself. I've spent so much time in the Hamptons over the years, *I've* probably been to that restaurant and don't remember. It's completely nonsensical that it would mean she knew Ben. *Except that someone said they saw them*, that unwelcome thought echoes in my mind.

I take a steadying breath as I find a spot to sit in, willing myself to appear normal, and calm, and excited. Ben practically lit up when I told him I would come to his game tonight. So despite the detour my afternoon took I'm here, proudly wearing his letterman over my sweater, glaring a silent "fuck off" to anyone with anything to say about it.

I am happy. *Happy*.

If I'm being honest, happiness has been fleeting since I got to Astor. The last time I can remember feeling so hopeful was the night of that kegger, and everything went to shit after that. Yes, I'd been happy with Will for a time, but that period is so marred with the fog of grief that I can barely remember any specific moments when I was. Breaking up with him felt like the closing of an incredibly heavy chapter in my life, and I know we're both better for it. Whatever demons Will was fighting or wasn't fighting when we were together, he has the chance to now.

We may have pushed each other toward outward facing goals and ideals, but we never pushed each other to actually be better people. To cope with our shit, to foster whatever brought us joy— I don't even think we knew what that was beyond the things we were told should matter to us. Like status. Like achieving that status at all costs.

I watch the players file out, making little eye contact with the opposing team as they do, and immediately spot Ben, his towering build and sharp jaw a beacon to me. He must feel my stare because he glances up at me, that core tightening smirk gracing his face, and I feel myself relax into my seat. A head of pushed back blonde waves attempts to jog past him, and I'd know that head of hair anywhere. It's the same one I spent years running my fingers through. My eyes trail his neck, down to his shoulders, down to his jersey, and I suddenly wonder if I shouldn't be here, if this isn't beyond insensitive, until I see him give an easy smile to his captain as Ben pats him on the shoulder. He heads to the center of the court for the jump ball, Ben retreating to his position, and the game begins.

That small exchange feels monumental, and as happy as I am that Will and Ben are on good terms, I wonder when this reconciliation happened. I wonder why he hasn't told me about it.

I try to shake it off, because *fuck* Ian for making me so on edge, but I can't. The game mesmerizes me, the players running up and down the court in a deftly choreographed dance of jumps and passes, twirls and shots.

And as I track the game, my mind plays tricks on me.

I see Lily on the court side, jumping up and down, that damn bracelet on her wrist. When they call a timeout, I swear I watch Ben throw an easy smile her way. I imagine Will waving, the three of them all in on a joke that, up here in the stands, I'm not privy to. My heartbeat quickens and I feel my breathing become irregular as my mind imagines them walking on a beach. I try to remind myself that this makes no sense, that my best friend did not *know* these men, didn't know those boys, but the more I think about it the more I feel like the crazy one.

I come to, my chest heaving as I hear the game buzzer, and my attention is dragged to Ben's athletic build, sweat dripping from his brow as he dribbles, jumps, and scores the seventy third, winning point of the game with just enough time to spare.

"AND THIRTY-TWO SCORES THE GAME POINT!" the announcer shouts over the intercom.

For all its prior clamoring, my heart simply stops. Ben's joy is palpable as he gets a sweaty bear hug from Grant, Andy, and eventually the rest of the team. I watch Grant say something discreetly to him, right before Ben's gaze finds mine. My eyes lock with Ben's, his sheer excitement doing nothing to thaw how frozen I feel, and my legs make the decision to leave before my mind has time to think. I rapidly make my way down the bleachers and toward the door leading out of the gym.

Thirty-two. Thirty-two. Thirty-two. Thirty-two.

Ian was right about me because until now, I connected zero dots between the appliqué "thirty-two" patch in my Lily box, or the fact that it was part of the doodles she left on some of the notes I kept, and Ben's number.

Thirty-two. I think I'm going to be sick.

When I reach the double glass doors, I realize it's raining, water pouring from the sky.

"Olivia!" I hear Ben call from down the corridor.

I throw open the doors, running toward the parking lot as I try not to slip on the concrete.

I can't do this. Not now. Maybe not ever.

I hear my name again, his voice piercing me through what feels like my heart, because I love him. I love him so much that I was blind to the truth: that he *was* connected to

Lily. That he left shortly after Lily died because they were something to each other and the family crisis he kept mentioning was about her.

I finally reach my car, regretful tears pouring down my face, phantom-like pain lancing through my body. Just as I move to get in my car, his hand closes on my shoulder, and I melt into his touch despite myself.

I feel fragile, and now I'm drenched, cold seeping into my bones as I turn around and take him in. Water droplets fall from the tips of his eyelashes as he blinks in his best effort to clear his vision. He's out of breath, not surprisingly tired after the game he just played and chasing me through a rainstorm. Those eyes I once let myself get lost in contort in confusion.

It hurts. *He* hurts, standing there like the beautiful liar he is, looking at me like he cares about me. *But he can't, can he?* At the thought, my face crumbles.

"Liv, please talk to me," he says, my nickname the most endearing it's ever sounded. Like I'm a child who should know better. His hand slides down my arm to meet mine, and I feel a tingle that turns into a flutter when it reaches my stomach. I shiver, partially from the cold, partially from his touch, and I shake him off, my lips pressing together until they feel numb. *I wish I felt numb.*

"What's going on?" His eyes search mine for a response, his voice tinged with slight panic, and I know it's because it's true.

I try to blink away my tears, swallowing hard as I finally wade into reality.

"How did you know Lily?"

Shock briefly flickers over his face and I begin to hope I'm wrong, but his eyes shudder, and I know I'm not. I see his Adam's apple bob as he swallows, and whatever hope I had that this was all an odd coincidence flits away.

"I was going to tell you ever—"

"Please, stop," I whisper, squeezing my eyes shut. "Why did you leave, Ben?"

"It's complicated, Liv," he pleads, moving towards me, but I take a step back. "Will said—"

"Will? This is about *you*, Ben— you and Lily." The nausea from before climbs up my throat when I say their names together. "I have to go."

"Olivia, please. If you just give it some time, I promise I'll tell you everything. I just can't—" his hand caresses my shoulder as a turn away.

"Don't," I clip, my eyes once again welling with tears. "Don't speak to me, ever again."

I can see the twinge of pain in his eyes as I say it, but it's nothing compared to the agony I feel at this moment. Distantly, Will calls my name as I get in my car, letting the door fall shut.

I don't pause. I don't glance up. I don't look back. I drive home, wondering why the people I love never actually love me in return.

30

Olivia

Ben's fingers brush the skin underneath the hem of my shirt, his lips whispering—

My eyes fly open, the skin dream-Ben was touching feeling cold, and I'm reminded that he's not actually here with me and never will be. He made sure of that when he hid his past life from me.

"Olivi-uuuuuuhhhhhh," an unfortunately familiar voice repeats, and I'm suddenly aware of the late autumn sun beating on my face. I blink back into my awareness, surprised to find Genevieve Dupont staring nervously at my face. My hand flies to my eyes, my brow, my chin, my cheek, but I feel nothing.

"What?" I snap, groggily, reaching for my laptop so that I can stuff it into my bag. I came out to the quad so that I *wouldn't* fall asleep as I researched in the library, but I guess the sleep deprivation finally won over.

I've laid in bed rather than answer any of Ian's calls over the past week, but I haven't been sleeping. I either replay my time with Ben, these years with Will, or the last few months with Lily over and over again. Because of this, deep, restful sleep has eluded me as of late. This spontaneous nap on the lawn was definitely not planned, considering I can already feel a burn across the bridge of my nose due to my lack of sunscreen.

"Do you usually take naps on the lawn?" Gen quips, her delicate nose crinkled in tempered disgust. Her usual sneer is nowhere to be found, and I feel my brows furrow in confusion.

Clearing my throat I grab my bag and stand, squinting as the setting sun begins to invade my field of vision. My eyes focus on Gen, her lithe frame contorted in apprehension. Her arms are crossed across her chest, her mini skirt-clad legs crossed at the calves, cheeks sucked in— the air around us suddenly feels thick with unease.

"What do you want, Genevieve?" I ask disinterestedly, feeling my heart thud heavily in my chest. *Did Ben ask her to talk to me? Did Will?* I ask myself, willing my heart to stop clamoring. "Come to tell me something I *don't* want to know?" I ask, bitterness coating my throat.

Rolling her eyes Gen moves toward me, looping one willowy arm around mine. "No. I've come to *talk.* Let's walk," she commands, pulling me up and leading us toward the entrance of the campus gardens. I tug myself in the opposite direction, but she only continues toward the garden, me in tow. "Maybe if you didn't treat me like an invasive species, we wouldn't have to do this," she murmurs, mostly to herself, but I hear her all the same. *Maybe if she didn't act like one, the treatment wouldn't be necessary.*

Taking in her profile, I consider, for only the second time, that Genevieve Dupont is beautiful. The usual harshness of her face, accentuated by the disdainful sneer she typically wears in my presence, is nowhere to be found.

What is left is still the making of a queen, brilliant in the way a diamond might be. Fierce, deep brown curls frame her face in a way that seems to coax you into looking into her eyes, eyes that, I'm realizing, are ablaze. The soft brown twines with a melted gold when the sun hits her. There's even some deep green flecked in. Her legs are long and her golden brown skin seems to accentuate her lithe frame. I blink rapidly, attempting to shake off this new perception. She's still Gen, gorgeous or not. The girl who's wedged herself between Will and I at every turn. *Will.* The trance wears off as soon as I remember why, most likely, we're having a talk to begin with.

"Gen, I truly have no interest in speaking to you… ever. It's strange you haven't realized that yet," I taunt, shaking her arm off me. We've reached a secluded part of the gardens, directly off the Botany Department's small brick building. Ivy winds its way up the four arches that surround us. The massive magnolia trees have started to yellow, the leaves beginning to litter the floor beneath us. Gen moves to sit on a bench, shooting me a pointed look rather than responding to my barb. She takes a deep breath, looking to the sky before resting her gaze back on me.

"Olivia, please. Can we just get over whatever this is?"

"Whatever *what* is?" She gestures between us. "Oh, you mean the past few years where you've blatantly disrespected me and attempted to steal my boyfriend?" I cross my arms and Gen rolls her eyes dramatically, finally plopping down on the bench beside us.

"Well, look how well that's worked out for me." She stretches out her arms looking around as if to ask if I see Will anywhere. "Look, I know we've had our… issues, but I really am trying to turn over a new leaf. Besides I think things have worked out rather well for you," she says pointedly, eyeing me. I scrunch my brows together trying to gauge exactly how much she knows.

"Don't look so surprised Liv, *everyone* knows. It's not like you and Ben were discreet."

I finally give in, sitting next to her on the bench, leaving about a foot between us. "If this is about Will, I don't want to hear it."

"Yes, you do," she says, turning to face me fully. "Because it's also about Lily."

My stomach lurches at the mention of her name, and I feel myself contort in confusion.

"I've been selectively dishonest with you, and I'm trying to fix that," she says, almost begrudgingly.

"Why?" I squint in suspicion. I may not be a good person, but I suspect Gen is worse.

"Oh my god, Liv. Can't you just let me atone?" she snaps, irritated, before cocking her head in surrender. "I know you saw me on Halloween and yet, you didn't say anything." She purses her lips, tilting her head as if thinking something over. "I want to be someone he deserves." She looks at me and, for not the first time, I feel like I'm seeing another side of her, one I don't think many even know exists.

I roll my lips together ultimately deciding to trust her. "Alright, tell me."

"I want to tell you how I knew Lily… and Will."

I blink, confused. Because I know how they all knew each other.

"I didn't meet her at orientation. And Will didn't meet her at that party…" she trails off, clearly second guessing her decision to tell me this by the way she avoids my eye contact. "Will and I met her in June. At a party… in the Hamptons."

I shake my head, not comprehending. "We never met you guys at a party that summer." My mind instantly goes to Ben and the secret he's been keeping from me all this time. "I would've recognized you at school."

"You weren't at the party, Liv… it was just Lily," she clarifies, nervously. Her usual sneer is still nowhere to be found, and I know she's not lying.

Still, this doesn't make any sense to me. Lily and I spent the entire summer before college together, even forgoing our usual, separate, family vacations. We were inseparable, just like we always had been.

Except when we weren't.

I bat the thought away. Lily was my best friend. Maybe she had been more aloof that summer, maybe she had snuck back into my room or hers at bizarre hours of the night… but we were growing up. It was time we had a little separateness as we grew out of teenage hood and into adulthood.

"My mom thinks it's good for us to spend some time apart every now and then. We can't be attached like this at Astor… we're maturing, Livy. Don't be weird," she'd assured me when I asked her if something was wrong.

It was the third time I'd caught her tiptoeing back into my room at 3 a.m.. I didn't mention it when it happened the fourth time, or the fifth… I stopped keeping track. Because this was a normal part of growing up. We could both do our own thing every once in a while. I didn't think she would have an entire secret relationship behind my back. My mind circles back to the memory of her saying she was going to a beach bonfire to dump someone. Was that someone Ben?

I find it hard to believe that Lily would have met Will or Gen that summer and *not* told me about it. How had Will not have mentioned it at any point in the past two years? How would he have gotten away with lying to me over and over again our entire relationship? It just doesn't make sense. Like she senses my spiral, Gen interrupts my internal reflection.

"She asked me not to say anything when I met you. And then I swear, I wanted to say something when you and Will got together, but he begged me not to, so I—"

"Well, we know how you get when Will begs," I cynically retort, attempting to disguise a feeling I haven't felt since Lily passed. The feeling of being the last one to know; that feeling when you start to guess you might be the butt of the joke.

Gen flinches, clearly hurt. "Olivia, I know you can't possibly understand what it is like to pine for someone you will *never* have, what it's like to sit by while your childhood friend chooses everyone *but* you, but know this: I am actually sorry. I'm trying to be," she pauses, searching for the right word, "better."

"Well, he's fair game now, Gen."

"As if that matters," she replies almost to herself, and her sadness outpaces mine. "He doesn't want me, Olivia. He never has."

And I actually pity her right now, because I do know what it is like to pine over someone I will never have. But at least he wants me. That might be worse. Thinking of Ben reminds me that Lily probably met Ben through them that summer, or vice versa, but it makes little sense because Will and Ben aren't particularly close. I'm realizing I don't know half of what I think I do.

"So you and Ben and Will used to party together? I find that hard to believe."

"Ha!" she scoffs at my suggestion. "Yeah, no. Ben

wasn't around much that summer. I don't know if Will was trying to have his own identity at Astor or what but he really pushed Ben away that summer, and Dan definitely didn't help that."

"What do you mean?" I ask, training my gaze on the cobblestone at our feet.

"Dan had Ben in an insane conditioning program that summer. He was barely around." It's unsettling to realize how little I know, how much everyone has hidden from me.

"Then how would he have met Lily?"

Her head cocks to the side again, like she is inspecting a broken clock. "Who, Ben?"

"Obviously, who else would I be talking about?" Her face is the picture of confusion but she answers anyway.

"I'm assuming when she met the family?" She says it as if it's as obvious as water being wet.

"Family?" I ask, shaking my head to scatter the puzzle pieces that are disturbingly falling together.

"The Chapmans? Jesus Liv, follow along," she rolls her eyes before realization dawns on her. "Oh… you think Lily was dating Ben." Pity weighs heavily in her eyes. "Lily was dating Will, Olivia."

"That can't be true," I say rapidly, squeezing the tips of my fingers together in a way I haven't in a while.

She moves her mouth to the side as if I'm a child and she's trying to break some horrifying news to me. "Olivia…"

"Gen, stop— I know it was Ben. His basketball number is literally scrawled on like half the things Lily owned," I say, my frustration palpable. Gen silently raises her eyebrows.

"What?" I almost shout. I can feel tears rapidly coming to my eyes, feeling the worry seeping out of me as if I'm missing all of the details.

"I'm surprised she bought that, is all…" As if she can sense my confusion she continues, "Will and Ben… they have an interesting dynamic, as I'm sure you now know. But back then it was different. Will sort of idolized him. Like Ben was his literal hero— he wanted to basically be Ben when he grew up. That was the first summer he really tried to put space between them, tried to stand in his own spotlight. I think in an effort to impress Lily, Will… fabricated a few things." She bites her lip. "Like, he may have told her he was the captain at Astor and said Ben's number was his? I don't know, he told so many lies that summer, and I guess after that summer too…" She eyes me cautiously, her gaze innocent as if she hasn't just lit my entire world on fire.

Betrayal smashes into me like a choppy wave and the wall of grief that I've slowly been lowering the past few weeks threatens to crumble. I feel my stomach roil when I realize Lily dated my boyfriend, or no— really *I* dated *her* boyfriend.

I should've known. How could I not know?

But I didn't, because she never told me. He never told me. No one told me.

I feel my shoulders slump and I don't even care that Gen of all people is seeing me deteriorate. I feel her eyes on me, appraising me as if to try and figure out what to say, but her silence tells me she's coming up short.

Everyone's been lying to you, that voice in my head chimes in.

Everyone's been laughing at you. I squeeze my eyes shut and even though I know my anger should be directed at Will right now all I can see is Ben. I feel the parts of my heart that weren't completely shattered start to break. Ben didn't know Lily in the way I had assumed but still, he knew her. *That's what he meant by just give it time. It wasn't his story to tell.*

But he lied. He sat there and watched as every person in my life lied to me. He lied to me.

The betrayal sits heavy on my chest.

"Gen, when did they break up?" I ask detached, not really wanting to know the ins and outs of their relationship but needing to understand at least the rough timeline.

"I'm not really sure… but I know it was Lily who did it. Will was torn up for weeks until he saw her at the kegger. And then… well… you know." She gives me a sympathetic look, but doesn't elaborate. She doesn't need to. "It destroyed him when she died, Olivia. Being with you fixed him, I guess. I don't know… you're the one thing we *don't* talk deeply about." Ancient irritation hides behind her words, but I can tell she's trying.

My stomach sinks remembering that night, the way Lily tried to talk me out of my crush on Will. The way he pursued me right in front of her. Was I just a pawn in their fucked up game? I can't stop the tears as they start to fall.

Gen looks at me sympathetically. "Look, I know this is all complete shit."

I snort wiping the tears from my face. "You could say that again."

Gen hands me a tissue from her bag. "I shouldn't be defending him— trust me when I say I'm the last person who wants to do that right now. But Will really does care about you." I crack a teary smile and Gen smiles back. "Also, it's important to note that Ben is very clearly in love with you. I know you probably feel betrayed right now and rightfully so. Just, I don't know, don't write them off completely. Let them at least give you their side of things."

Gen moves to stand up and I grab her arm, stopping her.

"Gen…" She looks at me, concern flickering over her

pretty features. "Thank you." And for a second when her eyes meet mine, there seems to be some silent truce between us. She nods and I watch her leave, my mind still reeling with the truth.

I can't quite place how I'm feeling. Part of me is definitely angry, furious even. I feel betrayed, a sadness brewing inside me that feels like it could swallow me whole, but there's this nameless feeling pushing against it, this part that feels as if this curtain has lifted and I finally see the bigger picture. Not quite relief, but close.

The wall between me and that well of grief that lives inside me seems to shrink and I realize maybe it isn't a well of grief after all— maybe it's just Lily. Like all of these moments keep bringing me closer to her, to this person she always was. For so long, I buried these memories so deep inside myself she was impossible to see. Out of self preservation, it was just easier to deal with the death of a caricature and not my best friend.

I move, grabbing my bag and feeling the chilly autumn air bristle through my hair as I wipe the rest of my tears. I decide it's finally time to start remembering.

31

Ben

I have this vivid memory of that summer. I can still feel the sun burning across the bridge of my nose in the late afternoon; feel the salty sting of ocean water spray in my eyes as we searched for Will in the dark; feel the weight that slightly lifted off my shoulders when he finally showed up the next morning, darkness marring the space under his eyes.

It should have been a harbinger for what was to come. I should've taken it as a sign but instead I assumed what I always did: that a crisis had been averted, that I'd be able to stop worrying for a few months— a year, if I'm lucky. I knew he was messed up over his break up with Lily, but to be fair he'd *never* loved a girl like that. He didn't have to say it; it was obvious to anyone with sight that he was beyond gone for that girl. It was also obvious that she had one foot out the door from the second they met. I think I'd seen her with Will during normal waking hours *once*, and I'm pretty sure he had to beg her to meet the family. Maybe she had loved him back. It's not like I talked to either of them much. I was busy basking in the freedom that was not having to worry about Will for a few weeks.

When Lily walked into his life that summer, it was like a breeze blew away all the heavy debris that'd been collecting on the bridge that connected Will and I, and rather than walk back across it I went straight the other way. I don't know if that was right or wrong, in hindsight, but I do know it was self preservation. Everything I'd done was self preservation, I guess. Other than this.

Texting and calling Olivia has proved fruitless over the past week and she hasn't come to class, so I'm shocked to see her nervously biting her lip in the meeting room doorway. She looks ready to bolt, but there's something tragic and steely in her eyes as she decides to make her way to the seat next to me.

"Cabot," she says after clearing her throat, her mouth pulling into a tight smile that does nothing to distract from the tortured look in her eyes.

"How… are you?" I ask the question feeling so out of place. "I called, Liv. I've been worried out of my mind." I'm desperate for her to look at me, speak to me, give me more than a tight lipped greeting before the lecture begins.

"Yeah," is all she gives me, flipping her notebook open and reaching into her bag for a pen. My hand reaches for hers without my permission, acting on my impulses with no regard for logic or caution. I think she's going to pull away but she doesn't. Her eyes slowly wander to mine, the steeliness in them melting away. I stand, holding onto the eye contact I was yearning for, pulling her up with me, leading her to that same corridor I found her in with Will just a few months ago. To my surprise she again, doesn't resist me, only takes a visible swallow as she swipes an invisible hair out of her face.

Her arms are crossed in front of her chest now, accentuating its steady rise. Her brows are drawn together in consternation when a swift breeze blows her hair off her shoulders, leaving bare her shoulder, her collarbone, her neck. My gaze travels from there up the side of her face, cataloging every minuscule detail. The way her jaw subtly flexes in irritation, the delicate slope of her nose, the barely there freckle at the corner of her right eye. I notice the faint scar just below her hairline, the perfect arch of her brow, the otherworldly length of her eyelashes. I dare to commit to memory all of this, and so many other things, because I'm choosing to live for myself for the first time in a long, long time. And while I hate that it took this beyond fucked up circumstance to make me choose this, I don't hate that it's for Olivia. What I do hate is how long it took me to admit that I want her— that I love her, that I've *been* in love with her. What I do hate is that I knowingly kept this girl that I *love* in the dark for so long, that I let my allegiance to my brother stop me from making better choices by her.

She pulls in a shaking breath, staring past me.

"So Will and Lily," is all she says, the faintest tremble in her voice, before she fixes her gaze on me.

"I..." I start to say, suddenly unable to translate my internal dialogue into anything coherent. "I'm so sorry, Olivia," I start in earnest. I pause, giving her time to give me *anything*, but she's silent. Which... I deserve. "I didn't tell you about Will and Lily because at first, I assumed you knew. Actually, it was all I could think about when Will told me you were together... I didn't understand how you were okay with it." She glances away, and I realize she's wounded or embarrassed? I'm not sure. "When we talked that night at the bar, I realized you didn't know. And then I thought it wasn't my place to tell you, after all these years, and maybe it wasn't then. But eventually it *was* my place, Olivia. I should have told you."

Calm has taken over her face as she asks, "And why didn't you, Ben?"

"I—" She cuts me off, still eerily calm.

"I was the last one to know, Ben. No one. Fucking. Told me. Do you understand how *awful* that feels? I can just imagine Will and Gen laughing at me, this stupid girl who has no *idea* she's been fucking her dead best friend's boyfriend for *years*." I flinch at the thought of Will and Olivia together as she huffs a sad, exasperated laugh. "But you… we were supposed to be different," she says, shaking her head. "There were a million times you could've told me. Why didn't you *tell* me, Ben?" she asks again, desperation coating her question, like my answer is the key to something. All I know is that my answer is shit.

"I was afraid, Liv," I admit, taking a step toward her. She immediately shakes her head, stepping back from me.

"It's not good enough," she all but whispers. "You're supposed to be *good* Ben, you're supposed to be *better* than that. How could you look at me, be with me, and decide *for* me that I didn't deserve to know the truth?" A tear escapes the edge of her almond shaped eyes, landing on an eyelash before her cheek. I wipe it away with the pad of my thumb and cup the side of her face, desperate to shield her from this, from *me*. Because I know why I didn't tell her.

"Listen to me, Olivia. You deserve *everything*. You deserve the moon, if that's what you want. You deserved to know, and I didn't tell you because I wanted, *so badly*, to love you in this alternate reality where I wasn't living my life thinking of Will. I wanted—"

"Love me?" she interrupts, in disbelief, and I realize that I did say that. Out loud.

"Yes, Liv," I tell her, pushing her hair back as my hand moves to cup the back of her head. "I've probably loved you since I saw you at that party."

"Why doesn't this feel like love, Ben?" Her weary eyes water, and I wish I could go back in time and do it all over.

"I would give anything to go back and do it differently. But I can't. But now that you know—"

"I'm not a good person, Ben." She's shaking her head as two more tears trail her cheek. "Who would do what I have done?" I wipe the tears away, my heart sinking as I start to understand what this is doing to her.

"Olivia, you didn't know. That doesn't make you a bad person— it makes you human."

"I knew you were Will's brother," she says, somberly.

"And I knew you were his girlfriend."

We let that— that which we've managed to mostly ignore— sit in the silence.

"He doesn't care, Liv," I finally say, tilting her head up to look at me. "I love you, Olivia Beckett. I don't care how messy it looks, seems— *is*. Because I *love* you. Isn't that all that matters?"

That tortured look returns to her eyes just before she turns her head skyward, eyes closed. When she comes back to me, I already know. I already know I've lost her, and my mind is scrambling with what to do because I *can't* lose her.

"Olivia, don't– "

"Ben, I can't love you when I don't even *like* myself," she cuts me off, smiling sadly. "I've spent the past... forever, it feels like living in someone's shadow. First Lily, then Will."

"It wouldn't be like that, Liv– it won't be like that," I try to convince her, my hand traveling to her waist and pulling her toward me.

"I can't be with you like this," she whispers, painfully.

My head drops to hers, like being close to her would somehow change her assessment of our situation. "I need to figure my shit out," she adds, stepping away from me. I stay grounded where I am, willing myself not to follow her, but reach for her hands.

"We can figure it out together, Liv," I offer, softly.

"I need space from all of this. I need space from *you*." She's adamant and sad and sure and disappointed and defeated, and I know she means it. That she needs it.

"Okay, Liv," I say, because if this is what she needs I want her to have it. I want her to be happy. But I also want *her*, however long it takes. "But I'll–"

"I don't…" she starts to say, glancing away, shaking her head. "Don't wait around for me, Ben. Please."

All I can do is huff out a laugh as disbelief clouds my judgment.

"I am *in* love with you Olivia," I say for what feels like the thousandth time, each time falling on apparently deaf ears. "And you want me to do what? Just stop? It might have been better if I could but I can't. I don't *want* to anymore. You can have your space. You can take as long as you need. But until you can look me in the eye and tell me you don't feel this… force between us? I'll keep waiting."

I watch her jaw shift as she tries to stifle a tear; watch her head tilt up to stop the tear from falling; watch her throat bob as she swallows the emotion she's holding in rather than sharing it with me; watch her sigh in resignation that I hope means I've got her, until she turns and just… walks away.

32

Olivia

The past few weeks have passed by in a haze, like some sort of fog has set in over me and I'm navigating the world, unable to shake it off. Ever since Ian released his story the entire campus seems to tip-toe around me, but I still hear their whispers, feel their stares wrap around my body. Ian was able to dig up more than I could've imagined. Reading the intimate details of Lily and Will's relationship was like a knife to the heart, but even worse were the photos.

My best friend glistening next to Will on the beach; Lily standing next to Will; Ben and their parents at a home I've never been to, Will's home. The betrayal has been this ever crushing force in my life since the story dropped and I can't help but wonder: would she have told me?

I haven't seen Ben since I told him I needed space, but I'm not sure if there's enough space in the world to help me move on from this, because somehow his deception hurts the most. I allowed myself to fall so quickly with him and part of that was because I thought he was different. Like he was someone who finally saw me and would actually do whatever they could to keep me from getting hurt. The thought of him is a constant weight on my heart, so heavy that my every thought seems to have slowed down. It's hard when the person who hurt you the most also seems to be the only person who could make you feel better. I find myself craving his touch, his words, his attention and quickly have to push those feelings away. He lied to me.

My phone dings for the hundredth time with a text from Sloane. Now that the entire campus knows about this deranged love triangle, I've basically become a hermit. I've been bunkering down in my apartment, only leaving for baked goods and McDonald's Diet Coke. I plan to stay here until I can leave for Thanksgiving break next week and I definitely don't plan to see anyone.

My phone chimes again.

SLOANE

I'm at your door!

I haphazardly read the text while pouring brownie batter into a pan. I freeze upon seeing it, catching my reflection in the mirror above my kitchen table. I look like someone who just got their heartbroken. My hair is tied up in the same bun it's been in for two days and I'm wearing a ratty crewneck that I stole from Lily our sophomore year of high school.

I don't know why I'm even the slightest bit surprised— it was only a matter of time. Sloane's been threatening me with a drop-in since the story broke. I assume Grant has some involvement in this, meaning *Ben* has some involvement in this. I feel my heartbeat just a little faster at the mere thought of him wanting to keep tabs on me. I put the bowl in the sink, quickly rinsing off my hands and trying to retie my hair so it looks at least slightly better. I've found that if I think about Ben for longer than a few seconds it makes me entirely useless the rest of the day. I walk to the front door drying my hands on the gray sweats I'm wearing. I look through the peephole and, sure enough, there's Sloane.

Sloane is one of those girls you try to emulate but ultimately fall short. She's breathtaking to say the least but in that care-free, cool girl way that makes you want her to like you, while simultaneously making you want to *be* her. Her hair is also thrown up in a messy bun, but where mine looks haphazard and greasy, her's looks like the poster child of the messy bun, the one they base messy bun tutorials off of. I'm about to throw the door open when I see another person behind her. Dark curls spill over a light blue crewneck and I instantly realize it's Gen. Suddenly, I feel somewhat self conscious. This weird truce is fairly new and she's never been in my apartment, much less seen me in less than pristine condition. I chew on my lip, debating just ignoring the ongoing dinging coming from my phone and pretending I'm not here.

"I can hear your phone, O!" Sloane yells behind the door.

My face flushes. I've never hung out with Sloane one on one, so how familiar she's acting is catching me a little off guard. I glance at my kitchen counter spotting the photo of Lily and I. I grind my teeth at the thought of her, at this massive betrayal that she doesn't even know she caused. But there's something else too. Outside of all the lies my best friend left in her wake, there's this loneliness I can't explain, like a gaping wound that I've covered up a thousand times, refusing to heal. The wound that's kept me from moving on, starting new friendships, finding a route outside of the one I drew up with Lily in mind. I take a deep breath in through my nose and decide to open the door.

"Finally," Sloane gasps, as if she's been without food or water for days instead of standing outside my door for a few minutes.

She barrels past me into my disaster of a living room and kicks off her shoes, plopping down on the couch. It takes a special kind of person to be this instantly comfortable in front of new people, in new places, and I envy her. Behind me Gen subtly clears her throat. She's shrugging off her coat, trying to hold the two bottles of rosé she brought.

"Oh, um let me help you," I say, grabbing the bottles as she gives me a timid smile in thanks. I give her one back and can't help but think how different this exchange would've been just a couple weeks ago. She hangs her coat on the rack in the entryway and then meagerly moves toward the coach, sitting a few feet away from Sloane and gracefully tucking her legs under her.

I set the wine down on the coffee table then make my way to the kitchen to grab glasses. I can hear Sloane and Gen whispering in the living room.

"Stop being so awkward," Sloane whisper shouts to Gen.

"I'm not!" Gen whisper shouts back.

I come back into the living room three glasses in hand.

"So I'm assuming this is some sort of wellness check?" My tone is dry as I pour the wine into each glass.

"You could say that," Sloane responds, grabbing the first glass eagerly. "I mean you've basically been ignoring me all week." I think back to the dozens of texts from Sloane and give her an awkward smile. "It's fine," Sloane says dramatically, "I know you're heartbroken or whatever."

I sigh, handing Gen a glass, who is nervously biting the

inside of her cheek. I sit in one of the large sage tweed lounge chairs that sit facing the couch and stare into my champagne thinking of how to respond.

"Are you okay?" I'm surprised to hear the shy kindness and real concern in Gen's tone. I look at her and I can see she's being genuine.

"Honestly," I say, sipping from my glass. "Not really." Gen nods, and Sloane makes a wincing face.

"Yeah Grant's, pissed," Sloane says, swirling the wine in her glass. "Apparently, he had no clue." I can see Gen straighten a little at the mention of Grant's name which surprisingly makes me want to smile.

"Well he's not the only one," I mumble into my glass. I down the rest of the champagne.

"Are you going home?" Gen asks, looking at the open suitcases haphazardly filled with sweaters and toiletries.

"Just for the break," I say. "I'll be at my dad's in Nantucket."

Sloane's eyebrows shoot up. "Isn't Nantucket a little… cold?"

I let out a small laugh which seems to relax both Sloane and Gen's posture slightly. "A little."

I refill my glass and Sloane's with the bottle of wine on the coffee table. Gen sips hers primly and I realize I've never seen her actually finish a drink other than that night at the Gala.

"I have seltzer if you prefer that." She looks relieved.

"Yes, is it in the fridge? I'll grab it."

She shoots up moving toward the kitchen but stops when she sees the photo of Lily on the counter. It's just for a second, but I notice how she shakes it off before opening the fridge.

"Look— I would ask if you've spoken to Ben but seeing

as I'm literally living with my brother right now I basically know everything about *that* situation and I simply will *not* be discussing the nightmare that is Will Chapman with either of you." Sloane glances at me and then Gen pointedly. I raise my eyebrows not really surprised at Sloane's blunt remark. In fact it's kind of funny, and I feel myself smile before I can stop it.

"Thank you," I say, feeling more relieved than I expected. I really don't want to rehash the same details that have been running through my brain the past few weeks. Especially considering that these two probably have more details than I do. Sloane nods.

"The reason I've brought the three of us together today, or rather bombarded Olivia with our presence, is that I have literally no friends here and will likely be staying for the foreseeable future. And... not to sound insulting but, I noticed both of you are in dire need of female friends." She glances around and I snort a laugh which causes a small smile from Gen. "Great, I'm glad you all agree." Sloane tilts her glass as if to cheers clearly satisfied with herself. "On that note, I'm thinking pizza and a true crime documentary? I would normally recommend rom-coms, but that feels maybe not the vibe right now."

I laugh, feeling levity for the first time in weeks. "Yeah I definitely would prefer something centering around feminine rage." Gen lets out a true laugh at this and I smile at her while handing Sloane the TV remote.

We settle in after ordering a large cheese pizza and picking Charlize Theron's *Monster*, which ended up being the only female serial killer film available– *go figure*. We're all snuggled into the couch, Gen and Sloane rattling on about whether they would've fell into Ted Bundy's trap, and I realize just how comfortable I feel in this moment. I haven't really felt this at ease with a group of women since Lily passed.

For the longest time it felt like filling the void she left with another friend would be a betrayal to her, but seeing how much she hid from me, my guilt seems to have dissipated. As if all this heartbreak has finally made me realize what I actually deserve, and it isn't the isolation Lily left me in.

33

Ben

The air is brisk as I walk into the courtyard of Will's apartment, the cold air hitting my nose and giving me that sense of nostalgia I always get this time of year— the kind that makes me miss my mom. I shake it off as I greet Jeff, Will's doorman.

"Any Thanksgiving plans this year?"

"Just the same old, same old Mr. Cabot. Wife's turkey and a game on the TV." Jeff's eyes crinkle at the side as he grins up at me.

I give him a wistful sigh. "That honestly sounds amazing."

He laughs. "I'm sure it doesn't compare to the feast your family has in store for you and Will this year."

I give him a small smile that doesn't reach my eyes and softly clap him on the shoulder.

"Happy Thanksgiving, Jeff."

I make my way toward the elevator slinging my duffel over my shoulder. The doors open across from Will's penthouse, a stark contrast to mine. The concrete floors and white walls make the entire place feel cold and sterile. All the furniture is in different shades of gray.

"Will," I call into the void that is his sparsely decorated apartment.

"In here," he responds, his voice ringing clear which makes me hopeful his mood has stabilized a bit. Over the course of the past two weeks I have been here almost every day making sure Will's staying far away from alcohol, eating something, and at least attempting to sleep. That alone has made a huge impact on his mood, but even more so hanging out with my brother one on one, more than we have in years, has been helping us both.

We've talked a lot, especially about Lily. Will was quick to use Olivia as a bandaid and now that the band aid has been ripped off it's clear how much Lily's death has been haunting him. We found him a grief therapist and a behavioral therapist all within walking distance of Pop's house where he'll be staying for the next year. Astor agreed to let Will take classes online for the next few semesters while he gets back on his feet. All of this is amazing and exactly what Will needs. God knows Pop helped me when I needed a breather. All that said, Will insisted that the basketball chapter of his life be closed. Dan exploded when I told him. I agreed to do it on Will's behalf as myself, Pop, and Will's new therapists all agreed that it would be best for Will to put some space between himself and our parents. Similar to the advice I received when I was on hiatus. Thinking about mom though, alone with Dan—I feel nausea roil inside me.

I walk into Will's room and it's as bare as the rest of his home. Literally just a bed in the corner of the room with all white linens. He's on his knees in the closet, shoving fistfuls of t-shirts into a duffel bag that's already filled to the brim.

"You okay, man?" I ask, gingerly sitting on the edge of

the bed. He sighs, pausing and wiping at the sweat on his forehead.

"Yeah, sorry— I just overslept and was already procrastinating when it came to packing. I'm good." His eyes meet mine in the mirror in front of him and he gives me a tight lip smile and firm nod. I offer him a smile back and he goes back to packing.

"Do you think I'm going to be a burden on grandfather?" Will asks, looking worried as he stares into his bag.

"No. Pop loves you and he's going to be glad to have you there," I reassure him, trying to reassure myself.

"He loves you, Ben… Pop doesn't really know me," Will says, shaking his head. I think about how young Will was when Dan stopped prioritizing his well being and instead only had him focus on basketball. How his relationships with our family changed. I never considered that he didn't want that but now I see how crazy it was that I didn't. How lonely Will must have felt growing up as we were pitted against each other and then against every friend he made moving forward.

My brother's shoulders slump at my pause. I push off his bed and walk toward the closet, moving through the clothes he has hung up. "Listen— Pop does love you. I think it just comes with the territory of having someone like Pop as your grandfather. You need to trust that not everyone is Dan. We don't all expect something from you Will."

I see my brother swallow hard, tears pricking his eyes.

"Thanks, Ben." He sniffs, coming to his feet. "Okay, I think I have everything I need." I look down at his two suitcases and duffel, relieved he didn't pack any suits as Pop is definitely not the type to participate in "high society," as he calls it. Will was a little worried about cutting himself off from Dan and mom, especially when it came to his trust fund. Lucky for both of us and to Dan's dismay, grandfather is loaded and loves to watch Dan squirm. Our inheritance from Pop makes Dan's look like pennies.

Mom's side of the family is basically the dairy dynasty of the east. Pop's owns more than half the dairy farms on the east coast. With his farming background, he isn't a fan of the glitz and glam that money has brought to his family. For political reasons, though, he keeps a townhouse in Boston; he can participate when he feels like it while also allowing it to be a place for his grandsons to hide out whenever needed. I know Will is going to do well there. He needs someone like Pop, someone who loves him with no strings attached.

"To Boston?" I say to my brother, a huge grin taking over my face.

He smiles back sheepishly. "Can we actually make a pit stop somewhere first? There's something I need to do."

34

Olivia

Nantucket in November has always been my safe space; one I hold close. I've come here every year since I can remember to stay in the home my grandfather built my grandmother for Thanksgiving. Just my dad and me. I remember one year I tried to get Lily to come with us.

"Why would you go to Nantucket this time of year? Isn't it closed?"

"Yeah that's kind of the draw, Lily. It'll be fun, I swear."

"Rain check, Liv. I'll come with you when it's not *hermit season there."*

I drive my dad's vintage Volvo past the closed stores and restaurants that are bustling during the summer months. I finally reach the beach and pull my wool scarf and overcoat tightly around me. The temperature is only 40 degrees but the breeze coming from the ocean is frigid, making my eyes burn.

I tuck the box holding everything I have left of my best friend under my arm and head down to the beach. I lay out a thick blanket on the sand, gingerly setting down the box and then begin pulling off my Hunter boots. I dip my toes into the freezing sand, digging little burrows for them the way I would as a kid. I let the cold seep into my bones and breathe in the salty smell of the Atlantic.

Lifting the lid of the box, I instantly wonder if I can actually do this. If I can actually say goodbye. Over the past few weeks I've been allowing myself to feel Lily's absence, at first little by little but eventually head on. I knew letting go was something I needed to do. Sitting here now I realize my grief for Lily has felt, at times, all consuming, and I'm suddenly unsure I want to know who I am without it. Just like I never wanted to know who I would've been without her, though I'm beginning to realize it's a question I should've asked myself years ago.

It feels like my entire life has been made up of these memories I shared with her, these in between fleeting moments I can't unsee— her in the passenger seat of my first car, her scuffed sneakers in the bathroom stall beside mine, the face she'd make before posing for the camera or when a song came on that she couldn't wait to sing. I set the box back down beside me and lay back on the plaid throw I took from the house, inhaling the smell of my childhood home, which immediately puts me at ease.

I talked to Sloane and Gen about this last week, about finally saying goodbye. Sloane was supportive of course, but I think the gravity of what this meant to me was too much for her. Gen on the other hand really helped me navigate some of the complex things I was feeling. I didn't realize but Gen's dad died when she was a preteen, so she's dealt with the unbearable weight of grief before.

I sit in silence, letting the sea air wrap around me as I consider the different people Lily inadvertently brought into my life, people I wish I let in much sooner. For so long it was easier to avoid my emotions entirely, pretend that Lily either never existed or would be coming back soon. The idea that I had someone who meant more to me than anyone else and I lost them wasn't something I could wrap my head around. It was like my brain and heart were playing defense against this unbearable loss, pulling me in a thousand different directions so I could pretend it meant less to me than it did. Then it does.

I close my eyes, letting the sound of the waves calm me, when I hear the sand kick up behind me. Instantly, I realize I'm not alone. Turning toward the noise, I immediately lock eyes with Will. I feel frozen in place. My heart dips as I see the emotions flash through his eyes— the same emotions that are probably flashing in my own. A million questions run through my mind.

How did he find me? Why is he here? I will myself to move, slowly pushing myself up and dusting the sand off the back of my legs as he approaches.

"Hey." His green eyes are like the color of moss with the ocean reflected in them. They're tired and his entire presence feels depleted. I realize for the first time that while I'm beginning to feel the fog lift that Lily left behind, it's just setting in for Will. I still feel all the ways he hurt me. The lies he told me to keep his grief at bay, may be different than the ones I told myself, but not by much. There's this strange solidarity between us, like a magnet pulling me toward him. Before I can think about it I wrap my arms around him and let myself feel the warmth of someone I thought I knew so well.

"Liv—" his voice chokes, his body rigid under the unexpected embrace and I feel him suck in a breath as he burrows his face into the crook of my neck. We stand there for a while, holding each other steady even when it feels like the world wants us to drown, just like we always have. Finally I pull back, wiping my nose with my sleeve.

"How did you find me?" I sniff and blink the tears begging to fall away, attempting to pull myself together.

"Ben knew where you'd be," he says, clearing his throat.

Ben. How would Ben know? My mind instantly flashes back to the conversation we had at the diner and my heart picks up. Will must notice I'm spiraling because he knocks me with his elbow. "Listen, you should talk to him. He's up in the car because he knows I needed to do this next part alone, but… Liv. I think you guys need to talk."

I turn toward the ocean trying to put a little distance between us.

"I can't. Not yet, I mean, I…" I steal a glance at Will, catching him with his lips pressed firmly together, his head down. What did it take for him to come here and advocate for Ben? To stand next to me and, in so many words, tell me that what I did to him was *okay*. It wasn't okay. He needed to know that, at a minimum, I was aware of how fucked up my behavior was. "I have a lot of things to do, Will." I give him a curt smile, colder than I want it to be. I don't want to talk about this with him. About Ben, as immature as that may be, and I need to finish what I came here to do. I shouldn't have come out here today. I'm clearly not ready to let go of Lily or own up to my own shit. Almost as if on cue, Will notices the box.

"What's that?" he asks, kneeling down and I watch as his expression morphs to one of understanding. He picks up one of the polaroids of Lily and I dressed to the nines, the lower halves of our bodies completely caked in mud. We're holding our white gowns up to show the matching rain boots we are both sporting. I kneel beside Will, tapping the photo.

"That was our debutante ball," I say wistfully, my eyes clouding as I smile thinking back to the memory. "We'd been kicked out after we were found drinking out of a flask right before we were announced. Instead of going home Lily decided we should hold a strike. Naturally, it was monsooning outside." I shake my head and Will laughs sniffling a bit. I glance at him and see a few tears silently rolling down his face.

He sets the picture back down and sees the note on the receipt, the one I thought might've been from Ben but was actually from him the entire time. Will's hand grazes it, and I feel his entire body tense beside me.

"You should have that," I tell him, picking it up and holding it toward him.

He looks down at it and says so quietly I almost miss it, "I'm not sure it's something I want to remember." His gaze hasn't left the note.

I press my lips together and force myself to ask the question that has been in my head since I found out.

"Why did you lie to me Will?" I feel the tears coming again but I try to stay strong and push them down. He moves from his kneeling position and stands, shoving his hands into his pocket once again. "This must have been what you came here to tell me, so tell me." I feel myself getting insecure, feeling betrayed all over again. How could the man I loved— who I thought chose me— actually have chosen her first? "That night at the kegger, the night before she died, you said you were looking for me..." I feel my breath sputter, an errant tear escaping down my cheek. "You never let me meet your family... is this why?" I gesture to the photos of Lily.

Will's jaw tenses as he continues to look ahead at the ocean, clearly searching for a way to explain this.

"Will, please," I demand, moving to stand directly in front of him, begging now. "Just tell me why."

He breathes in a deep breath, shutting his eyes.

"I'm sorry." He exhales for what feels like awhile. "I have a lot of shit that I need to figure out Olivia, a lot. I don't know why I lied. Maybe it was out of spite, because she lied first. I mean no one, not even her parents knew that she had dated me and everyone in my life saw me fall head over heels—" he stops himself, finally meeting my eyes. "I didn't come here to explain away something that doesn't have a good explanation. I came here because I wanted to give you the closure she couldn't give me."

We let that sit between us for a long time. I move back toward the blanket and pull a thermos out of my bag and take a sip of the coffee I brewed before leaving. I offer it to Will who takes it and holds it for a while but never moves to take a drink. We both sit staring into the ocean as if we are going to see her at the end of it.

"You hurt me Will, not even just with the Lily stuff but everyday, with how you treated me. I shouldn't have let you, but you knew I was vulnerable and you treated me like shit knowing I wouldn't leave." I shake my head to myself. "That I would have no one if I left." My voice is calm but full of resentment and I hear him suck in a sharp breath before he finally speaks.

"This is going to come out like an excuse and I don't want it to be an excuse. There is no good reason for the way I treated you other than that I was selfish." He pushes his hand through his hair then drags it over his face trying to get ahold of his emotions. "You made me feel a lot better, Liv. When she died..." I note how he can't say her name as he clears the tears out of his throat. "When she died it really fucked me up, like it was proof that everyone I love eventually leaves." I swallow, tears now running down my own face, as he continues. "You were so good to me, Olivia. Too good. You helped cover up so much of this *pain* inside me." He shakes his head. "I didn't want it to hurt when you eventually left. I didn't want to be surprised."

My eyebrows scrunch together, tears fully falling down my face as I see Will for maybe the first time. This boy who's so lost and only wants someone who won't let him go.

"Will…" I start, soft, comforting.

"No Liv— let me finish." His voice is steady and I nod.

"I think deep down I knew you were never mine. That you would eventually leave just like Lily, my mom, Ben… so I pushed you. It was never fair and it was never right. Hell, none of this is." He gestures out toward the ocean.

I nod and then we sit there in silence, allowing the devastation that was our relationship, the ways in which we hurt each other and the lies it was built off of, to really seep in and even though I know I don't want the answer, I ask him the second question that's been plaguing me since I learned about him and Lily.

"Did you love her more than you loved me?"

He stills, his eyes a mess of emotions as they meet mine. "Don't ask me that, Liv." He shakes his head, his tone sharp. "Do you love him more than you love me?" He emphasizes the word me, almost desperate for me to respond and nods toward the pier where the cars are parked. I meet his eyes again seeing the pain in his gaze. The pain I caused him, too.

"I'm sorry, Will." My voice is a whisper but I know he hears me as he grabs my hand squeezing it hard.

"Yeah, Liv. Me too." The waves crash around us as we

sit there holding hands, passing the thermos back and forth. The silence is eerie but comfortable like we are at the very precipice of a mountain we both have to climb. It feels like minutes pass but the way the sun seems to lower in the sky tells me it's probably been hours. We both have gone through every item in the box, Will sharing moments about Lily that I haven't heard before and me doing the same for him. A peace washes over me.

"I need to say goodbye to her, Will," I say, my voice quiet. He nods.

"Can I stay, while you say goodbye?" he asks. His voice feels far away like maybe I made him up, like maybe this was all a dream and I'll wake up next to Lily tangled in her hair and frustrated and we'll get a coffee at our favorite cafe near campus and share a croissant. She'll tell me the truth. She'll tell me *everything*.

I get up rolling my jeans to my knees and moving the items back into the box. "I think I need to do this alone."

He stands wiping off his own pants and nods. It's awkward, this new distance between us, like we need to relearn how to navigate each other.

"Thank you, Liv," he says, rolling his lips together the emotion prominent in his features, "for everything." I blink back fresh tears and watch him walk back up the pier. Alone, I pick up the box and suck in a deep breath looking at the expanse of water in front of me. I begin to wade out into the freezing cold water. I feel my body go almost numb as I begin to lightly set the different memories into the ocean.

Mothers teach their daughters about heartbreak, to protect their hearts from boys— but they don't teach us how to shield our hearts from each other. The unencumbered invulnerable love that comes from having a best friend. The kind that hurts so much more when it ends because that person has gotten every little piece of you, every feeling, every truth and you don't know yourself without them. I wade deeper, feeling the icy water hit the hem of my rolled up jeans, and finally let the wall that's been shielding me from all of this grief, from Lily, fall.

35

Olivia

"Hope the company I sent your way was okay," my dad greets me, his familiar smile doing more to warm me than the fire he must've lit while I was gone. I release the breath I'd been holding since the beach and sink into his embrace.

"Yeah, Dad," I nod, breathing him in. Nantucket in the winter, my dad and I. Something I can always count on, regardless of what's happening elsewhere. "We needed that conversation, I think." And maybe it's the gravity of that conversation, and the tidal wave of emotions that are still washing over me, but I have to ask if she's here. Like maybe she'd have some kernel of truth to get me through this. "Caroline didn't want to come?" I try my hardest not to let that inkling of hope seep into my voice.

"You know how Mom is, sweetheart. Never not on call." He gives me a tight lipped smile before turning around to stir something on the stove. It's only now that I register the scent of cinnamon and apples and realize he's stirring the cider.

Caroline, who conceived me, nurtured me in her womb,

and birthed me, had very little to do with nurturing me beyond the age of three. She comes from a long line of doctors, each known for either inventing or fueling the discovery of something miraculous. By the time she'd conceived me, she'd "failed" to contribute to that legacy the way she thought she would. If you ask me, being *the* top surgeon in your field is a legacy making accomplishment in and of itself, but if you asked her, she'd say the long hours she spent in the OR, the lab, or conferences would one day be worth it if only she could… fill in the ever changing blank. I think I might've mourned her physical and emotional absence more if I didn't have my dad. I know she loves me, in that way mothers must viscerally love their children, but she doesn't know me. It didn't really bother me, this apparent lack in my life, until I lost Lily.

Not that Lily was a mother figure to me, but *her* mom was, in a way. Grace Newhouse shepherded the both of us, as if we were sisters. I had a dad who showered me with love and believed in me so intensely, and a faux mother who mediated every best friend tiff, smoothed every heartbreak, swooped in when I felt the blood trickle down my leg in the sixth grade, compared dresses with me for prom— I really didn't need anyone else.

When Lily left, when she died, I called Dad. He told me to come home. We'd find a therapist, I could take a gap year, and I could heal. I didn't want that, though; what I wanted was to start my freshman year at Astor with Lily. Thinking back to that time I can see now how young I was. How emotionally naive and immature I was. I hung up on my Dad, furious that he'd even suggest doing something so rash. A few days later, I called Lily's mom. When I'd seen her that awful morning, I'd known she was irrevocably changed. How couldn't you be, after something like that? I just also thought there would still be space for me in her life.

When she picked up the phone, she sounded far away. She said she couldn't bear to hear my voice, that I reminded her too much of Lily. That she knows I must be suffering too, but for her sake she needs me to leave her alone. That she'd reach out when she could.

It was only then that I realized I don't really have a mother. Maybe my own mother would've been less partial to Lily. Maybe she would've shepherded me down my own path, parallel to my best friend's but separate. Maybe my mother would have done these things if she saw me flailing in adolescence but she didn't because… I had Lily.

"Where'd you go, Liv?" my dad's voice cuts into my thoughts. I take a deep inhale of the warm aroma as he hands me a mug, steam rising from it.

"Just thinking about Lily," I tell him, deciding not to say I just released a bunch of her stuff into the ocean.

He nods slowly, his eyes squinting, carefully assessing me.

"Did I ever tell you about my friend Harold?" *Here we go*, I think to myself, amused. My dad couldn't simply give a sage piece of advice, or regale a straightforward crumb of wisdom. He had to tell you about a "friend."

I give him a knowing smile, laughing despite myself. "Nope. Never heard of Harold until this very moment, actually."

"Well, Harold was always hanging around this other guy we knew. Now, this was decades ago— we were a bunch of lowly L1s, desperate to get a good study room in the age of pen and paper sign up sheets. Ages ago, if you can even imagine it." He laughs at his own joke.

My lips press together in amusement. "Go on."

"Yes well, when I met him, he hadn't met Seth yet. Hadn't been *tainted* so to speak. He was funny, sure of himself, a real hoot to be around. At some point he latched onto Seth— Seth who was certainly not a hoot. At least not as much of a hoot as Harold. Anyway, as much as Harold and Seth together were a good time, it was obvious he was playing second fiddle to Seth. Seth who, before meeting Harold, could barely get the courage to pick up at a bar! Really it was unbelievable." He's shaking his head at the very thought. "Well, year two comes along and we're expecting the same sort of group to form, and Seth is nowhere to be found. Turns out, he transferred to a different program, didn't even tell him. I was kind of relieved. I mean, Seth was kind of a drag. Harold, though — it was like he forgot how to be himself."

"Well that's fucking sad," slips out of my mouth, and I cringe at my own profanity. To my surprise, my dad just raises his eyebrows. "I assume I'm Harold?"

He sputters, as if shocked that his parable was so transparent. "I… yes. But you didn't let me finish!"

"Please do continue to tell me about my likeness to the *pathetic* Harold," I say emphatically, crossing my arms. If I wasn't so entertained, I'd be offended.

"Sweetheart," he starts, moving toward me, his brows furrow. Hands on my shoulder, he gives me a soft shake. "Not pathetic. Human. Imperfect. You… Olivia, you loved Lily. I know you did. And if Lily was still here, I know beyond a shadow of a doubt that you two would still be thick as thieves. But I also know if she was here, neither of you would be the girls we sent off to Astor three years ago. And you *shouldn't* be." He subtly pushes me down into one of the comfy armchairs across from the roaring fire, taking up residence in the one beside it. He takes a sip of his cider, staring into his mug for a moment, as if he's reading tea leaves.

"The moment you came into this world, Olivia, you were just like your mom, maybe more aware of things outside your orbit, sure, but that same determination. I didn't know a baby could be so determined. And that determination grew into a silent confidence; you just oozed it, Liv. Solve a Rubik's cube? Little Liv thinks she could do it if you just give her enough time. Brazenly took scissors to her hair when I wasn't looking? It would certainly be stylish by the time you came home from preschool the next day. It's natural for that surety to diminish as you grow into adolescence but… I'd hoped college would be a time for you rediscover that part of yourself."

"What do you mean?" I ask him, quietly.

"I… Lily was a great friend to you, and you to her. I don't want you to think I didn't see that. But you girls had a way of *being* to each other that… I guess is what teenage girls do. That quiet confidence got so small, especially when Lily was around."

"Yeah. I'm starting to realize there were many parts of myself that got small around Lily." I feel the resentment start to rise, quickly followed by that acidic guilt. "It was just so hard not to compare myself to her; it was unconscious. She was this beautiful, idyllic, sprite of a person and I was me and I think teenage girls just… eat away at each other and call it friendship. I mean I love Lily, still. I can realize she was shitty to me and still love her, can't I?" I ask him in earnest, like his answer could save me from what I'm feeling.

"Oh, Olivia," he says, giving me his knowing smile. "Life is filled with realization after realization that the people we love the most have an immense capacity for being shitty to us."

"Okay, well, that is bleak. I don't know if I want the rest of this TED talk," I admit, rolling my eyes.

"We are human, Olivia. Tell me. Were you never a poor friend to Lily?"

"I…" I think back to that definitive decade of my life, quickly scouring my mind for any stand out memories where I could've made her feel the way she made me feel. "I don't know," I say, defeated. How could I not know? I'm sure I was, but I'm blind to it.

"Lily was just a girl, just like you were just a girl. This idea you had of her— what did you say? An idyllic sprite? That wasn't real, Olivia. That's who she was *to you*. Don't you wonder what that might've been like for her? For the girl she probably also loved most in the world to have this imaginary bar set for her to reach?"

I pause, stunned by my dad's assessment of me. It feels embarrassing. Like I've spent this semester ruminating on the worst parts of my friendship without acknowledging all the ways I'd played a role in those parts. I feel my eyes start to water and shut them hard.

I feel my dad's hand over mine. "Sweetheart, I only want you to accept what you had with Lily. I believe that, looking back, you realize that Lily did a lot to hinder you. But I also believe that, if you're honest with yourself, you might discover ways you stifled her." The observation hits me in my gut, but miraculously my tears start to dry and that acidic guilt begins to melt away. I'm breathing steadily, and while I don't feel better, I feel clearer.

I open my eyes, turning to my dad. "Did Harold ever get back to himself?"

"There was nothing to get back to. Only somewhere to go, Olivia."

36

Ben

Two years ago

"Yo get your nose out of that book, you're missing all the action." Andy playfully shoves my book out of my hands, which I don't find funny at all. I stand to my full height, a good five inches over his.

"Did you forget who the fuck I am?" I ask looking down at him.

He huffs a nervous laugh. "Chill, Cap— there's just a lot of ladies here tonight, I thought maybe I could be your wingman." He shrugs his shoulders, but I can see his body cringe away from me ever so slightly and I feel a little bad for him— I'm sure the rest of the team notices, too. I slap him hard on the shoulder.

"I'm just fuckin' with you man. Who's on the roster?" He grins and starts going on about some of the jersey chasers from last year.

Grant comes up behind me, slinging an arm over my shoulder.

"Sorry to interrupt but I gotta steal our captain for a few." Andy rolls his eyes, clearly irritated as he walks away. We move toward the kegs behind the frat's makeshift bar. I feel the familiar stickiness of the tap as I go to pour myself a beer.

"What's up man?" I ask, sipping the foam out of my beer.

I look around. The party is insane. Hundreds of people from freshman to super seniors fill the yard underneath what seems to be several hundred strands of market lights that illuminate the area, more than likely donated by whichever donor alumni wants to show off his money.

"I wanted to just casually point out that your brother seems to be trailing that girl over there that you said wants nothing to do with him?" He points to my brother and his ex-girlfriend who, against my better judgment but out of respect for her, he has kept a secret the past several months. She ultimately, unsurprisingly to me, pulverized his heart.

"Who is she by the way?" Grant asks, clearly ogling her with wide eyes.

"Don't worry about it," I say sternly, narrowing my eyes.

I'm not really sure what Will or now seemingly Grant see in my brother's ex, Lily. I mean she's definitely attractive but in a sort of typical, nothing I haven't seen before, way. She's short, blonde, et cetera, but her personality was always kind of lacking to me. Having a conversation with her is like watching paint dry. At the dinner table with my family she'd use this fake as fuck voice when talking to my parents, like she was a child, which I personally found disturbing, and I swear this girl has never had a solid opinion on anything. I also found it bizarre that she wanted to keep the relationship a secret. Not to toot my own horn but us Cabot/Chapman boys have always been considered a catch, so her not wanting to parade Will around town–kind of a red flag to me.

My brother is so similar to how I was before I came to Astor— completely naive. Dan kept us on a rigorous training schedule for years, making our social lives in high school basically non-existent. Being that Lily really is Will's first heartbreak, I know he can barely function now that she all but dumped him out of the blue.

Gen is clearly trying to follow my marching orders, which were to be a complete bitch to Lily and her crew. I figured if anyone could pull off trying to keep my brother away from his "one true love," it would be his best friend. Clearly, I was wrong. She seems more obsessed with trying to keep Will's attention away from the brunette with her back to me. In fact, Lily seems to be kind of a wallflower for once, which secretly fills me with glee, considering she made the entire summer about her.

I analyze the brunette's silhouette, trying to make out if I recognize it. I can tell right away this girl is hot— just by the way she stands. She's tall, her shoulders are back and squared like she's about to go into combat with Gen, and her hair tumbles down her back in loose waves just barely hitting above her waist. I find myself wanting to twist it around my hands and—

"Who is that?" I nod toward their group and Grant follows my gaze.

"Oh man— that girl." He makes a whoo-ee type sound while miming rubbing sweat off his forehead. I stare at him a bit irritated that he hasn't just told me who she is. He smiles, shaking his head, noticing that he's pissing me off.

"Her name is Olivia. Dude, she was in my orientation cohort and when I tell you every man in that group had his jaw on the ground looking at that girl." His eyes are basically twinkling at the memory. "She's fiery though man, she'd eat you alive." He gives me his signature booming laugh and says to himself, "That's something I'd pay to see," while sloppily topping off his own beer before wandering off in search of a napkin. I turn back and notice that she's gone. I begin scanning the party for her just as I feel fingers grip my arm.

"I'm over this, Ben. Can I be off duty now? He's clearly not going to give this up. Plus, I like her."

Gen is clearly frustrated and I have to give it to her—she's really being a good sport considering she's had a crush on my brother since birth. I never understood why Will didn't give her a go. She's a bit cold, but who wouldn't be with the mom she has. Plus, she has the whole ice princess ballerina thing going for her. I give her puppy dog eyes.

"Please, Gen, for Will's sake, won't you help rid him of the girl who broke his heart?" I put my hand over my heart solemnly and she rolls her eyes. "Besides maybe he'll finally start dating you as some sort of rebound situation," I say, shrugging and refilling the beer I just finished chugging.

Her eyes instantly fill with emotion and her face looks like I just slapped her.

"Ben, what the fuck? Not cool," Grant says lightly, suddenly reappearing, putting his hand on Gen's back in an attempt to comfort her.

"You both are fucking assholes," she whisper yells and knocks my beer on to my shirt, storming off. Grant stares after her for a second like he's pondering going after her and mindlessly hands me a wad of paper towel.

"Jesus," I sigh, sopping wet with my freshly poured beer.

"That was shitty man," Grant says clearly, still miffed with me, as if a beer poured on me isn't punishment enough. One thing I love about Grant, other than him being the most genuine guy I've ever met, is his willingness to always call me on my shit. He doesn't care about my money— he's got his own; he doesn't care about my basketball rank because basketball isn't end game to him. He honestly has no reason not to call me on my shit, which is what makes him my most genuine friend.

"I know, I know. I'll apologize to her later— I'm gonna go change my shirt," I say, tossing my cup into the trash. "Hey— don't let my brother pour those girls drinks. Lily or my future wife," I say, smiling as I walk backwards knowing what a cocky asshole I look like.

I pull a new shirt out of my backpack and over my head, when I notice a few girls checking me out. I give them a smirk and a half wave and they giggle in unison. Honestly, it kind of creeps me out. I pull my copy of *Romeo and Juliet* out of my back pocket and shove it in my backpack knowing I need to finish annotating it before Lit class tomorrow.

"I love that book," one of them calls. The girl has that freshman air about her.

"Oh yeah?" I ask. "You don't think it's kind of sad?" Her eyes go wide as if she thought I'd ignore her. She begins to stammer. "You okay...?" I ask, trying to hold in a laugh at the poor girl's expense.

"She's just nervous," her friend pipes up quickly.

"Got it. Well, nice to meet you," I nod at the group and begin to make my way back outside to the makeshift bar when I see her... Olivia? I think that's what Grant said. My pulse is racing. It's dark where they're standing so there's a shadow cast across her face ever so slightly, but I see her. The shape of her face, this pouty mouth that instantly makes my heart stammer. Her low cut shirt with this leather jacket on top. I take a step forward trying to get a better view and I can tell she's saying her goodbyes to Ian and his boyfriend and some other girl I don't recognize.

"Hey, can I ask you guys a question?" I ask, nodding back toward the group of giggling girls.

"Yes of course, anything," the louder friend says in what feels like super speed.

"You guys know her?" I say and point toward Olivia.

"Oh my god, of course. That's Olivia! She's basically like the queen of us freshmen."

So they are freshmen, I think as the louder one drunkenly cackles at her own… joke? Was it a joke? The quiet friend speaks up.

"Her name's Olivia Beckett," she squeaks. "She's best friends with Lily Newhouse who also is really popular, but um Olivia's a lot nicer and *so* smart. I heard that Will Chapman is going to ask her out…you're his brother right?" Her face is crimson now and I scrunch my eyebrows at them.

"Who told you that?" My tone comes out harsh causing the girl to turn bright red.

"Um… that you're his brother?" she stutters. I roll my eyes realizing this girl clearly came to her own conclusion.

"No— that he's asking Olivia out?" I say, my tone is a bit more annoyed than before.

"OH!" She begins nervously giggling and I realize I should probably just leave these girls alone.

"Have a good night ladies." As I step away, I hear them murmuring.

"He was totally interested."

"He's so hot."

I huff a laugh as I go back to the deck.

I stand off under an overhang no one is around needing some quiet. The air is thick with the smell of stale beer and the music is blaring. I roll my shoulders back, trying to hype myself up to be the captain of the Lions. Astor's golden boy, or whatever fucking title these people want to put on my shoulders. I feel like the past two years have been a whirlwind of me trying to be this guy that I just am not. The "most valuable player" in more ways than one, from getting laid every night to making every three pointer this team's seen this season.

Sometimes I don't recognize myself, like I'm an imposter in my own body. Seeing Will here has taken a lot more of a toll on me than I realized. I look around for him, not seeing him or Lily in the crowd. I know he's trying to keep his distance from me. He mentioned it a few times when we were packing for the semester.

"I'm not going to live under your shadow, Ben. I don't have to."

Little does he know, I don't want that anyway. Will is a *really* good ball player. He always has been. I just worry *he* isn't the one who loves the game and instead just wants to be the best to finally win Dan's approval. I know from experience he'll never get it.

The wind picks up and I feel an energy around me. When I look up I see her again— Olivia. I feel myself involuntarily swallowing. Her brown hair is whipping around her face and finally, in the privacy of the corner I've hidden myself in, I can really take her in. I stare at her, my eyes unwavering as I scan her face. She's breathtaking.

I don't think I've felt this on edge about a girl at Astor before, like an eeriness I can't place. I don't think I've seen a girl like this in general. Her posture is just so sure of herself, like she knows she's going to win even though she hasn't even entered the game. I need to talk to her. I move to my feet and see her gaze shift to mine. There's no way she can see me but it feels like she's staring into my soul.

"Yo cap!" Andy hollers. "Your little bro is freaking out in Jackson's room. Can you handle this?"

I swear under my breath. I knew this would happen. Will is hot headed; it was only a matter of time before he got in a fight here.

As I approach I can hear him begging and immediately feel my gut bottom out. This is not how he should be starting his freshman year.

"How can you say this meant nothing Lily?" He's pleading from behind the door.

"Will, I can't keep repeating the same thing! We were just hooking up and you obviously took it more seriously than I did. I'm sorry but you need to get the fuck out of my way and let me leave this room. Now." Lily's voice is more stern than I've heard it before and I'm worried Will's going to do something stupid.

"That's bullshit!" As if on cue, I hear the sound of drywall smashing. I open the door and peer at Lily, seemingly bored by all of this and my very crushed younger brother whose hand is currently in the hole he just put in the wall. She's sitting primly on the bed and uncrosses her legs, moving to stand.

"Listen— I need to leave. My head is killing me from the noise and I just don't feel like this is getting us anywhere. I'm sorry, Will, but you *need* to move on." She nods at me as she slips behind me and out the door. Will crashes down on the bed behind me and throws his arm over his eyes. I sit next to him and pointedly hand him my beer.

"Is this from my captain or my brother?" Will says, defeated, peeking out from under his arms.

"Don't be a prick and drink it," I respond and silence hangs between us. "It's from your brother," I sigh, breaking the tension and rolling my eyes.

He finally cracks a smile. "Well, that was embarrassing," he says, sitting up just enough to chug the beer.

"Happens to the best of us," I say, rubbing my hands on my legs and looking at the hole in the drywall. "Well, maybe work on the anger part." We both chuckle then sigh.

"Mom wants me to look out for you," I say mostly to myself and immediately regret it.

"Mom can fuck off," he mutters, taking another gulp of the beer and then letting his head fall back to the mattress.

"Will," I warn.

"Ben," he responds, widening his eyes as if to ask what I'm going to do. I let it go like I always do with him.

"Look I just came in here to tell you that I have your back, and there's lots of beautiful girls out there. Lily is just one of them." I do my best to sound supportive. Will pushes up off the bed to stand.

"Thanks bro, but I don't need your help." He looks in the mirror and fixes his hair. I can tell he's a little drunk which is probably why his emotions are everywhere. Because of Dan's insane training schedule Will's probably never had a proper drink, just like I hadn't before coming to Astor. "Who knows maybe I'll bone Lily's hot friend just to piss her off... I think her name's Olivia? Apparently Lily started a rumor that I'm going to ask the girl out anyway. Might as well give her what she wants." He gives me a wink and a cocky grin. He goes to shut the door and my hand reaches out almost by instinct to stop it, slamming it shut. His hands fly up defensively. "Bro, what the fuck?"

"So what, you're just going to revenge fuck this girl's best friend? Is that it?"

His eyes search mine, clearly confused by my outburst. "I don't see why you care, you don't even know this girl." He pauses, squinting at me. "Wait a minute… do you know this girl?"

"Don't fucking talk to her, don't talk about her, don't even look in her general direction," the venom drips from my words, shocking even myself as a somewhat primal instinct has taken over me.

"Stop telling me what to do, Ben. You don't own the girl," Will hisses pushing against me, trying to get me to lose my balance. I slam him back into the frame of the door.

"Dude, fuck off." He shoves harder and I finally let go.

"You need fucking help man," Will yells, slamming the door.

I sit down on the bed pushing my hands through my hair. *What was that?* I feel my heart rate picking up, fisting the sheets and feeling myself start to panic. I lost control and took it all out on Will like I always do.

I don't know what's been causing these panic attacks. I've been getting them before every game and now whenever I talk to Will. I feel my lungs constrict and slowly move to go lock the door. I don't want anyone seeing this. I lay myself on the bed and tuck my legs into my chest until I'm in the fetal position, trying to still my heart rate. I shut my eyes hard and try to think of anything to get my mind off the sensation of not getting enough air. I see that long brown hair barely touching her waist, her lips, those confident, intense eyes.

37

Olivia

I'm not the girl I was when I got to Astor. Too much has happened, sure, but that discounts the gravity of the passage of time. It discounts the natural aging and maturation process that I've been afforded. Lily never got the benefit of more time. She will forever be frozen as that eighteen year old girl, walking into the first kegger of the season, her best friend on her arm and a thousand wishes in her head. I started that year in a cloud of grief, the wishes I'd made alongside her buried deep inside me.

And that's okay, I realize. Those grief years *were* the time that passed. They *were* the years in which I aged and matured. I'm not meant to be the girl I was before my life happened to me, and while I wish beyond anything that Lily was still here with me, I don't wish to be frozen forever as the girl I was when she was here.

I park outside the diner and watch the moonlight glisten off the lake it sits by. Saying goodbye to Lily feels like ages ago, but it was only this morning that I sat on the sand, rifling through memory after memory of my best friend,

Will of all people by my side. That I waded into the ocean and released the parts of her I'd been hoarding to myself in grief.

I hadn't realized how much I needed to see Will until he showed up on the beach. I thought that what he needed from me was to disappear, to leave him alone. To let him process the last few months alone while I just silently dealt with what he did. What I didn't realize was that he was processing so much more than the shitty end of our relationship.

I feel relief knowing he knew we were doomed from the start. There'd always been this foreboding sense the other shoe was going to drop with Will; I assumed it was going to be an affair, or some public scandal a few years into his professional basketball career. That'd I'd be moments away from a definitive career moment, and some shitty mistake he made would fuck it up and veer us off course. I lived in fear of the moment that Will decided he wanted more out of his relationship, wanted something different from me. Everything about our relationship was charted out in my head because on paper we were so, so perfect.

When I saw Will on the beach I, for a split second, remembered how perfect it felt in the beginning. How I quickly collated a future for us and how quickly he cosigned. But then I remembered that even from that seemingly innocent first moment, it was all built on lies. I know Will didn't mean to hurt me. I guess maybe we're even.

A door slams to my left and I'm brought back to the parking lot of Harbor Diner. I'm bone tired after today, but there's nothing I want more than a steaming cup of Brad's shitty diner coffee and a slice of apple pie.

I drag myself out of the car and toward the door, stopping short when I notice a familiar head of tousled brown hair face down at the booth to the right. Brad jumps up when he sees me, flinging the door open with his megawatt smile.

"Livy!" he exclaims, pulling me in for a hug. "It's a little late for you, no?"

I distractedly check the time, only now realizing it's 11:15 at night.

"Lots on my mind, Brad," I say distractedly, my gaze settling on who I've now realized is Ben, fast asleep at my favorite diner.

My stomach feels like it could drop or float right out of me. The doorbell chimes behind me and I watch Ben's head groggily rise from the table, his hand rifling through his hair as he reacquaints himself with his surroundings. His book falls shut; his eyes meet mine. Even from where I'm standing, I can see the bags under his eyes, can trace the ghost of a smile on his lips as he looks at me. I feel like I'm standing on the ledge of a mountain, terrified that I could fall, shaking with anticipation, giddy fear enveloping my heart.

I realize I've been standing in the entryway, staring across the diner at this man, for entirely too long. I walk toward his booth, hyper aware of each stride, as he stands, his lips pressing into a line.

"Olivia," he says, his voice full of want and desperation, as if he's been waiting for me his whole life, not just for a few hours in this diner.

"Ben," comes out as almost a whisper as I take him in. He's so handsome, even in his miserable state. His hair is wild as if he's been running his hands through it all night, his face lined with sleep from laying it on the hard diner table, and even though it's not even midnight, he has circles under his eyes like he hasn't slept in days. He takes a step toward me and I reflexively move back. His face is wounded and I instantly feel the icy walls around my heart begin to melt.

He motions to the bench across from him.

"Can I—" he clears his throat and bites his lip nervously. "Olivia, I want to tell you everything, can you please—" He motions to the bench again, his eyes so full of desperation, waiting for me to slide in before sitting back down. He's sitting up straight, and I can tell his hands are in his pockets. I wish they were on the table so I could hold them, ground myself with them, because I feel absolutely untethered here, like I'm shooting in the dark with no plan.

"Everything?" My voice is so quiet it's hard to recognize and I see his features melt, like he's taking me in for the first time. His eyes cloud with emotions and I feel so small, so fragile. Ben could break me right now, if he wanted to, and yet here I am trusting him not to, choosing not to run away.

"Everything," he says. "It doesn't change what I did but I at least need you to know."

"Okay," I tell him, taking in a shaky breath and letting it go. I'm bracing myself, petrified by the idea of finding out something new, but I trust him. I'm choosing to trust him.

"I saw you," he starts. "That night before Lily passed, at the party at Garland House."

My breath hitches. He's told me this before but I didn't expect him to talk about that night, that this is where everything starts. But how could it not? He stares down at his coffee.

"Do you want a coffee?" His voice is unsteady.

"Ben—" I redirect, my eyes pleading. My mind is overwhelmed with the need to know whatever it is he's going to tell me, the need for his reason to be enough.

"Yeah, okay. I'm sorry," he looks past me as if he's

trying to compose himself. "When I was at Astor, I wasn't who I am now. I was this…" he pushes his hands through his hair, "I was just someone I didn't like. I let my emotions and the perception of others control me. I took advantage of my status and I was really shitty to… a lot of people."

His eyes search my face for understanding. "I was basically just a version of what Will became. Maybe worse, actually." He looks defeated, shaking his head. "I had a lot of pressure from my family and the team and I was watching Will make the same mistakes I was… it was all too much." He pauses, taking a breath before continuing. "I started having these massive panic attacks. I couldn't get them under control." His eyes fall shut, his jaw clenching, and he puts his head in his hands for a moment before meeting my eyes.

"I was trying so hard to keep it together, but the thought of that next year, the thought of being captain, of being who everyone saw me as… it was suffocating me, Liv." His voice is solemn now, the gravity of what he must've felt reflected in his gaze. "But then I went to that kegger. I saw you that night and… I know this is going to sound crazy or maybe pathetic, but something shifted in me. You were standing among all those people, like you knew exactly who you were and how you fit into this world." He cocks this half smile at me and I feel my body heat. "I had never felt like that before. The pull I felt toward you, Liv, I… I can't explain it. When I saw you, I just knew."

"Knew what?" I dare to ask, my heart racing at the idea that this is fate. That everything I've felt toward Ben until this moment was inevitable.

"That you were meant for me. That I had to try to make you mine."

I feel my blush overtake every square inch of my face, the heat on my body spreading, and it only makes him smile wider.

"You were surrounded by Lily and Will and Gen and you were just magnetic. It was like everything around you faded away and you were all I could see." He's looking at me with eyes full of wonder, like I'm the most magnificent thing he's ever seen, and I feel the tears brimming at my eyes. He reaches over the booth and brushes them away. His face gets serious again.

"That night, Will was going through a lot. Lily had broken up with him and started this rumor that you two were together." My eyes widen. I hadn't heard this rumor, but after all the secrets I've learned about Lily, I know it's probably the truth.

"Even then I knew you deserved better. Better than me, and better than Will. He got in this huge fight with Lily and he said he was going to ask you out and—" he shakes his head, pausing like he's trying to shake the feeling of the memory away. "I couldn't handle it. I completely lost it. I almost fought him, like I slammed him against the door and was ready to bash his face in just at the thought of him using you like that. I hadn't even met you yet." His face is red with embarrassment and sadness.

"I had a massive panic attack, probably the biggest one I'd had in a while, and the only thing that brought me back to reality was thinking about you. But I knew I had to leave; I couldn't keep wearing this mask, pretending to be this person I just wasn't. When Lily died, I saw something change in Will, too. I think that was what finally broke me. I saw him morph into the person I never wanted him to be. Someone I already was." He gets quiet and I see his eyes wet with tears.

"Ben—" my voice breaks as my tears start falling too.

"Please, Olivia, I know I fucked up. I should have told you that first day, I should have said everything then." He wipes his hand over his face trying to calm down and I get up to move beside him. "But the deeper it got with you… I just didn't want to lose you. I didn't want to lose the opportunity to get to know you, to love you, to just be near you."

His voice catches like he might start crying and I stand there in front of him as if in invitation. He pushes to stand, wrapping his arms around me and pulling me in. He sinks his face into my hair and I let my body melt into him. His warmth wraps around me and I feel for the first time today like I can breathe.

"I don't think you can lose me, Ben," I admit, feeling an enormous weight begin to roll off my shoulders as I let myself fully give in to this. "I love you too much."

And it's true. Maybe we were tragic, or maybe we are fated, or maybe we've clawed our way to each other against the better judgment of the gods or whoever; I can't bring myself to care. Not while knowing what I know now, and feeling how I feel despite all of it. *If my heart can so eagerly leap into his hands, like it is in this moment, who am I to keep fighting it?* I exhale at the thought, the sensation of giving in to this so blissfully right.

"I love *you*, Olivia," he says tenderly. "I think I loved you that first night I saw you because there hasn't been a day that's passed that I haven't thought about you. That I haven't tried to be the man I think you deserve. You are every thought I think, every word I read. I am so wrapped up in the thought of you, every detail that you are, it's impossible for me to unravel from it. Even if I could, I wouldn't want to."

I sink further into his chest feeling like I can't hold him tightly enough.

"I'm sorry that I didn't let you tell me sooner," I say, feeling guilty that I denied him this opportunity while I wallowed in what I'm realizing was self-pity.

"You could've taken as much time as you needed. I told you I'd wait for you, Olivia," he reminds me, earnestly.

"I thought I needed to figure this next part out alone," I say against his chest, explaining myself.

"I hate that you thought that," he tells me.

"I am fucked up, Ben." My voice catches in my throat. "And you need to know that there is a *lot* I haven't dealt with, and that the grief I've been carrying comes in waves, and that I'm not totally sure I know how to function without a very clear preconceived notion of what my life is going to look like and—" he cuts off my rambling, grabbing my hand.

"Olivia, all I want is to be in all of that, with you. To be there for you. To hold your hand while your life— *our* life— happens. I don't want some fictional, finished version of you. This version of you is my fantasy. I want you now; I want you tomorrow; I want you always, anyway that you are."

My tears cascade down my face, and he releases me slightly to look down into my eyes, his thumb swiping across my cheek bone in an effort to wipe my tears.

"Shakespeare really does have a way with words," I deflect tearfully, overwhelmed by the way he loves me.

"Christopher Marlowe," he corrects me, with a wink his eyes brimming too, "never had a muse like you." I laugh a hearty, throaty laugh, any self consciousness I'd still been harboring washing away with each tear. I embrace him tighter, not wanting this moment to end.

"Don't leave," I say quietly, but I know he hears me because he softens, like he's letting out a breath he's been holding, like he thought I might push him away.

"Never," he murmurs into my hair.

I pull back and meet his eyes. I know I'm a mess, my face streaked with tears and my hair tangled from the beach earlier, but he grins down at me with this smile only meant for me, like I'm the best thing he's ever seen. I grin back and then he kisses me.

I feel the earth stop around us. The sounds of the diner fades out as he pulls me in harder, his hand tangling in my hair while his other pulls me in at my waist, and I realize this is the type of kiss they write songs about. It's earth shattering, life changing. It's the kind of kiss people have and say, *"He kissed me, and I knew I would marry them."* My stomach is full of butterflies springing to life and whatever cloud had unwittingly colonized the space above me begins to dissipate, the lofty air of hope swirling around us. I feel different, so different from the girl at the beach. So different from the girl I was a few months ago. So, so different from the girl who came to Astor. I feel reborn, like my life is this beautiful landscape I get to explore. With him.

He pulls away and his eyes echo my thoughts. I know he feels it, too.

"I'll never leave, Liv." And then his lips press against mine, and he kisses me again.

Epilogue
Olivia

I slip on the black silk chiffon dress, trying to reach the back zipper, when I feel a large, rough hand run across my lower back. Ben lowers his mouth to my ear, his minty breath making my spine tingle.

"Let me help you with this," he murmurs, the brush of his fingers on my skin sending a rush through me.

Even after the past few weeks, I can't help the flush that spreads up my chest and I feel Ben's smile before I see it. I turn and take him in in his Tom Ford suit, tailored to fit him in exactly all the right places. My eyes soak in every inch of him. It's sometimes shocking just how dreamy he is, and that's on a normal day.

Tonight, in this suit, Ben Cabot is possessing.

I let him zip me up, giving him a demure smile.

"We can't be late Ben, Gen would be so upset." I swat him with the back of my hand, but he catches it, kissing the back of it lightly.

"I never thought I'd see the day you'd be concerned with upsetting Genevieve."

I roll my eyes, even though I know he's right. Not even a few months ago, I would have told anyone with ears that Gen was my sworn enemy. It seems unlikely that she would so rapidly become one of my closest friends, but alas here I am, in Ben's grandfather's townhome, getting ready for her performance as the Sugar Plum Fairy in *The Nutcracker*.

This is now the third time I have gone to Pop's apartment and with only a week until Christmas it's cozier than ever. There's a fire crackling in the foyer and somewhere off in the distance Pop's has a Bing Crosby Christmas record playing from a turntable.

I walk toward the full length mirror where Ben is now fidgeting with his tie. I begin straightening it for him and feel my blush creep back in under his gaze.

"I'm really happy, Liv."

I smile still staring at the tie. "Yeah?"

He tilts my chin up to look at him, his brown eyes darken like they always do when he wants me to know he means what he's saying.

"I'm *really* happy, Liv."

I bite my lip trying to disguise my smile, but he stops me, pulling me in and kissing me. He explores my lips with his, timidly at first, before pulling me closer, his hand cradling the back of my head as he seems to drink me in, like he needs me to survive, and time seems to hit a standstill. I think every kiss with Ben is earth shattering, the best kiss I've ever had, and yet he always finds a way to one up himself. I pull away and I'm met with Ben's ridiculously perfect face, his lips puffy and pink from the kiss and his eyes filled with so much intensity that I'm tempted to blow the entire night off and stay in bed with him. I pat his tie, reorienting myself, and move to the mirror, reapplying my now smeared lipstick.

There's a light knock out the door and Ben clears his throat trying to get ahold of his own hormones, apparently.

"Come in." His voice is hoarse, and I feel like I'm about to go feral with need, but I force myself to get it together. Will enters, holding one hand over his eyes.

"Everyone decent?" Ben chuckles and I roll my eyes.

If I'm being honest, the way Will and I so rapidly went from serious relationship to pretty good friends is shocking even to me. Maybe it's due to the fact that him and Ben have gotten so close or this weird trauma bond we have since dealing with Lily's death, but for whatever reason, any awkwardness we initially felt has basically disappeared.

"Um— you're not dressed yet?" I can't help but let frustration seep into my tone as I glance at my phone to check the time. "Will— we need to be there in like thirty minutes, get ready!" Will rolls his eyes.

"Last time I checked, you're his girlfriend now. If I needed someone to nag me, I'd be living with my mother," he says, gesturing to Ben.

"Will…" Ben's tone is a deep rumble, warning his brother that he's toeing the line with how he's speaking to me, and I can't help but want to rip Ben's clothes off at this exact moment. Will rolls his eyes dramatically and plops down on the bed.

"Besides," he continues, hands behind his head as he stares up at the ceiling. "I'm not going."

Ben and I share a knowing glance. Ever since the whole story with Lily came out something has shifted with Will and Gen, and no one really knows why. Well… Ben doesn't know why. I feel like I'm bursting with all of the secrets Gen and Sloane have trusted me with this past month, and after not having real girlfriends for the past two years, I really don't want to break their trust. Thus, I have been a vault.

I perch next to Will on the bed, folding my hands over my knees.

"Would you like to talk about it, William?" I ask teasingly, tilting my head, and he sighs.

"Not really, no. I just— shouldn't be there." He glances at me as if to say he knows I know and to keep my mouth shut. I give him an incredulous look but remain silent. Ben, still fixated on making sure his tie is perfect, groans into the mirror.

"Will, what'd you do?"

Will props himself on his elbows. "Why do we all assume that I was the one to do something?"

"History," I say.

"Reputation," Ben chimes in.

"Okay, okay. Chill." Will stands smoothing out his pants. "Everything is fine, I just want to be respectful and give her space. Especially on such a big night."

I stand too, moving back toward Ben. "I think that's very mature of you."

"See. I'm *mature*," Will says to Ben.

"Uh-huh," Ben says, barely paying attention.

"Dude, how are you going to play for the pros if you can't keep up with a basic conversation?"

Ben sighs, giving up on the tie and yanking it off completely, which honestly is the hotter option anyway. He moves toward me putting his arm around my waist.

"I don't actually know anything yet. The draft isn't until July, so I'd appreciate it if you'd stop jinxing it."

"Jinxing it?" I laugh. "Who knew you were so superstitious?"

"It's hard not to be when all your wishes keep coming true." Ben smiles, winking at me and my heart flips.

"Okay— barf. I'm leaving." Will moves toward the door and I can't help but laugh.

"You sure you're okay, man?" Ben's voice takes on a more serious tone.

Will turns to face us, walking backward through the door.

"I'm fine. Seriously. Have a good night you two, and *please* for the love of god use protection." With that he slips out and I sigh.

"What am I going to do when you get drafted?" I let myself melt into Ben, reveling in the way his arms are wrapped around my waist.

"Well, hopefully it will be the Celtics who pick me and then you'll be in the city just as much as I will, with your big new column and all."

"Hmm," I hum in contentment, spinning around to face him. He isn't wrong— the Boston Common, home of my brand new column due to my fall out with Ian, is pretty much walking distance from the stadium. "It would be awfully convenient. I could just crash at your place after a long, arduous day at the paper…" I say wistfully, half joking and half serious.

"I think by that point it would be *our* place, though, no?" His eyes twinkle with mischief, but there's a hint of something serious there, and I feel my heart beat in my chest.

"And how would that work?" I ask him, pretending to pick a piece of lint off his shoulder. "With me still at school and you…" I glance away, the reminder that a life of professional basketball also means one where he's frequently gone. "… on the road." I look back up at him, surprised to find him grinning.

"Well," he starts, his hands traveling down my back

until they rest, somewhat possessively, on my ass, "Astor *is* only less than an hour out from the city. So you could commute. And I—" he pauses, regarding me seriously. "I will always make coming back to you a priority, Liv."

"And once I'm done with school?" I ask him, my heart in my throat. We've talked around this before, but one of us has always veered the conversation in a different direction. Like we haven't wanted to scare each other with the implication of us, long term. And I don't know if it's the Bing Crosby, or the snow outside, or that I'm meeting his family next week, but I want to know.

"And once you're done with school… I would never ask you to stop your life for me, Liv. So if staying here, or moving to wherever, is what you want to do, then we'll figure it out. And if you want to come on the road with me, then we'll figure that out, too. Whatever it is," he tells me, brushing a strand of my hair back, "we'll figure it out. Together," he grins.

"Together," I sigh, wrapping my arms around his neck. "I love that sound of that," I whisper in his ear, my lips trailing the side of his neck before he sweeps them up in an all too brief kiss.

"We have lots of time to do lots of things together, Beckett," he smirks, that charming smile of his almost enough for me to forgive the way he redirects my advances. "But if traffic is anything like it usually is, we'll barely make it before they close the doors."

I groan, knowing he's right, but not before mentally calculating just how icy Gen would be toward me if she found out I was late. With the newness of our friendship, it's not worth the risk.

"You know…" he starts, his eyes twinkling with

mischief, "Pop's town car has a pretty good privacy screen from what I remember."

"And you're just now telling me this?" I grab his hand, leading him toward the front door. "*When* you make the first draft pick, I expect a town car with a privacy screen to be the first thing we buy."

"Oh, I already have ideas on the first thing I will buy." He kisses my hand, I swear I feel his lips brush purposefully against my ring finger.

I grin up at him and his eyes sweep over me like I'm his most prized possession. Like everything could go to hell, but as long as we are here together everything will be okay. He laces his fingers through mine as he leads me into the court-yard, the trees glistening with Christmas lights as the first snow of the year makes its way down, a flake hitting the tip of my nose. He gently uses the pad of his thumb to wipe it away.

"I love you, Olivia Beckett," he says, the tenderness of his gaze warming me despite the cold outside.

I wrap my arms around his neck and meet his gaze, unable to stop the grin from spreading across my face. The perfection of this moment isn't squandered on me, the lights twinkling around us like a universe in which only we exist as a white blanket of snow seems to envelope the world at our feet.

I stand on my tip toes, grazing his lips with mine as I whisper, just for him to hear, "I love you too, Ben Cabot."

Meanwhile, at Astor Hill...

GRANT

You sure about this?

GEN

Aww, getting cold feet?

GRANT

This was your idea.

GEN

And you said yes 😇

omw 

If you thought Ben and Olivia were the only ones up to no good, you were sorely mistaken...

Keep a look out for the second book in the *Astor Hill* series!

Acknowledgments

This book was such a labor of love for the both of us. It was born out of mindless, aspirational chatter at our favorite sushi restaurant, in the car eating ice cream cones outside of McDonald's, and well past midnight as our babies (rarely) peacefully slept. Starting this book felt like a crazy idea, but now, more than three years later, it feels like the most logical decision in the world.

We want to first thank our readers for taking a chance and picking up this book. We have poured so much of ourselves into this series and we are so excited for the opportunity to share it with you. We can't wait to see this series evolve and for you to embark on this journey with us and the rest of the characters in Astor Hill! Special shoutout to all of our focus group and ARC readers. Your feedback and initial response to our book has truly been such a high point for us; it was so exciting getting to see everyone fall in love with these characters for the first time, and we know that feeling will continue as others choose to read this story.

Next— the one, the only, Paige Rita at P.S Published. You have been a saint when it has come to all things PR and publishing, and your assistance, optimism, and endless amount of support have been such a light in navigating this madness. We truly couldn't have asked for a more creative yet business savvy person to assist in promoting and publishing our book. The way you really delve into our story and treat our characters with such care makes us feel right at home when working with you.

Bailey Sulcer, the artist that you are! We are truly stunned by your talent and the way you so graciously offered your design services for our book cover. Your talent absorbed all of our random tangents and vague feedback, resulting in the most stunning cover. You really were able to capture our world so beautifully and we couldn't have asked for a better person to do it.

Thank you to our husbands, Jered & Christian, for listening to us drone on and on not only about our book, but about all the romances we've read over the past few years. Thank you for taking care of our babies while we spent hours writing and outlining, and thank you for dealing with the incessant co-writing sessions taking up space in your respective living rooms and kitchens for the better half of the past few years.

Finally, thank you to Georgie, Ellis, June, & Gavin for being the lights of our lives and driving us to carve out a space where we truly feel the best versions of ourselves. We hope this journey influences all of you to carve your own paths and follow your dreams.

About the Author

Sydney Madison is a best-friend writing duo based in Orlando, Florida who write heartwarming love stories with a captivating edge. While they revel in the lighter side of life—like sushi dates and book chats—they dive deep into the complexities of love and relationships in their writing. Balancing heart and intrigue, they craft stories that explore the shadows of relationships not always acknowledged in the typical happily ever after.

When they're not conjuring up their next novel, you can find them plotting their literary escapades over spicy tuna rolls and plenty of caffeine!

Sign up for their newsletter on their website and follow their Instagram to be the first to glimpse a peak at Gen & Grant's story!